The Monster's Daughter

Also by Kim Antieau

Novels

The Blue Tail • *Broken Moon* • *Butch*
Church of the Old Mermaids • *Coyote Cowgirl* • *Deathmark*
The Desert Siren • *The Fish Wife* • *Her Frozen Wild*
The Gaia Websters • *Jewelweed Station*
The Jigsaw Woman • *Maternal Instincts* • *Mercy, Unbound*
Queendom: Feast of the Saints • *The Rift* • *Ruby's Imagine*
Swans in Winter • *Whackadoodle Times* • *Whackadoodle Times Two*

Nonfiction

Answering the Creative Call
*Certified: Learning to Repair Myself and the World
in the Emerald City*
Counting on Wildflowers: An Entanglement
Old Mermaids Book of Days and Nights • *The Old Mermaids Oracle*
*The Salmon Mysteries:
a Reimagining of the Eleusinian Mysteries*
*The Salmon Mysteries Workbook:
Reimagining the Eleusinian Mysteries*
Under the Tucson Moon

Collections

Entangled Realities (with Mario Milosevic)
The First Book of Old Mermaids Tales
Tales Fabulous and Fairy • *Trudging to Eden*

Chapbook

Blossoms

Blog

www.kimantieau.com

The Monster's Daughter

Kim Antieau

Green Snake PUBLISHING

To my dad,
Lloyd Antieau.
Thanks for being my papa.

Part One

Chapter One

My father was born. Not from woman alone but pieced together by some pretend god called a scientist. It was not my father's disgrace, not a blemish on his record. He can be forgiven much because of his beginnings. Can't he?

Who is the real monster?

Even before I knew of my father's genesis, I believed he could do no wrong: at least to me. He could do wrong to others. I had seen the fear in my mother's eyes long before she left us— or long before my father sent her away. Or whatever happened to her. Maybe she went on a sea voyage. Perhaps she ran off with Mr. Martin's son, or the preacher man. The stories changed over the years, depending upon who was telling the tale. After she left, my father said, "Now it is just the two of us, as it should be."

I have no true childhood recollections of my mother. I have memories of remembering her. She always seemed far from me, from my experience of life. It was my father who was ever-present. I remember getting lost in his lap when I was as tiny as can be, while he told stories or read to me. I was never afraid of him even though he was so big. He treated me with such tenderness and care.

When I think of my mother, I don't see any light. It was almost as if she were some kind of shadow who came into my father's life to give birth to me—and then she disappeared. Sometimes I missed the idea of her. Sometimes I missed the ordinary life I believed I would have had if she had remained with us.

But I was not created for ordinary life.

Neither was Mr. Em.

My father—Mr. Em—never said a bad or good word about my mother. I knew her name was Juliet Lee, and she had blond hair and blue eyes. I knew this because a small portrait of her hung on one of my bedroom walls.

Betsy Shaw was the one who told me the woman in the painting was my mother. Betsy Shaw was my father's housekeeper. She had been with me for as long as I could remember—although she did not go with us when my father and I left Oregon in search of California gold.

She told him, "Mr. Em, you shouldn't be taking that child on such a perilous journey. You done it once, and it was no good. And if I go with you this time, you'll think it is the right thing to do."

"Mrs. Shaw, we all survived the journey out here just fine," Mr. Em told her. "Emily was too young to remember anything that happened then anyway. This time she can enjoy the scenery, come to know the land. This is a big country. She should know it before she decides where she will spend her life. Besides, it is more dangerous to leave her at home, even with you here. I do not trust the world to care for my child as well as I can."

Betsy Shaw was not persuaded.

Neither was my father.

Wait. I get ahead of myself. You, dear reader, may want a more linear approach to my story. For instance, you might want to know when and where I was born. The when was 1837 give or take a year; the where was Missouri. But what does a date and a place tell you? And how do you know I'm telling you the truth? Or that I even know the truth? You cannot always rely on me to give you the facts. For one thing, I do want to protect the people who have protected us; just because our paths crossed doesn't mean they want to become public characters in this narrative. Mostly, I want to protect the land. The land—the place—shaped me more than any human hand ever did—and I am obliged to protect it, to hide it from those who would destroy it by their attention.

Besides, I have learned that facts may connote the truth, but they are not entirely the truth. Anyone's tale has an essential truth, like a pearl created from an irritated oyster—or like the priceless gem found at the heart, at the center, of a dragon's treasure. But that doesn't necessarily have anything to do with facts.

Are you surprised at my mention of dragons? You don't believe dragons exist? Perhaps no, perhaps yes. You probably don't believe in monsters either. I will tell you one thing that is absolutely good and true: Monsters do exist. And I would know because I am the monster's daughter. One can find monsters in the most unexpected places, and they are nearly always human in nature.

But I am here to convey to you the truth of my life and my father's life in the best way that I can.

What do I know of my father's life before I was born? I read the book, of course. He gave it to me when I was about 13. He said when I finished it, he would answer any questions I had. By that time in my life, I already knew his corporeal person had been pieced together from parts of deceased people. I learned this fact of my father's existence when I was quite young—or rather, I should say I somehow always knew it. He didn't hide it from me. He wasn't ashamed of it. He said, "None of us is responsible for how we came into this world. We are only responsible for what we do while we are here."

He didn't hide the fact that he was the progeny of a scientist who should not have been tinkering in God's business.

"People cannot be cooked," my father said. "There is no recipe. Take this heart and that brain and that leg, stir, add sugar and then bake. Life isn't like that. Although, in my case, it was nearly like that. I am one of a kind. He never did it again and no one else would dare do it."

Sometimes when my father talked, he reminded me of the politicians we heard at the village center or in the town hall. Other times he sounded like the preacher who occasionally stopped by to lecture my father on the proper way to raise a child—or like one of the farmers who came to my father's mill for sawdust or lumber.

My father was a self-taught man. Later, when Abraham Lincoln became president, Mr. Em said, "That man educated himself just as I did. Lincoln didn't have much schooling, and his father treated him like a slave. Have you seen photographs of him? He is rather monstrous looking, too. An ugly man as president. Who would have guessed such a thing?" He seemed to think of himself and Lincoln as some kind of kin because of their upbringing—and their looks.

When Mr. Em's creator—Dr. Ef—first saw him alive, he had run screaming from the room. I never understood that. If Dr. Ef had sewn my father together from body parts, didn't he know what he looked like? Or did he believe the spark of creation— that spark of divine life—would transform Mr. Em into a hand- some man? Creation equals beauty?

I must stop here in the narrative to make it clear that my

father was not ugly. He was a large man, to be sure. With long straight black hair that he wore like an Indian. In fact, some people mistook him for an Indian, even though his skin was preternaturally white in spots and not so white in other places. I remember when I was a child someone at the mercantile asking my father why one of his arms was white and the other arm was almost brown.

Mr. Em held out his left white arm, pulled up his shirt sleeve, and then said in his booming voice, "This arm I picked up from a king when I was traveling in Persia. The royalty there have more than two arms, and they are very generous. Never say you like anything when you're visiting Persia because whatever it is, they will give it to you. When I admired the king's arms, he gave me one. They also have the best surgeons in the world so it was quite painless. Well, except for the lopping off of my old arm. That was downright agonizing. But you can't refuse a sultan. Or king. And this arm—" He dropped his white arm to his side and then held out his right arm and pulled up the sleeve. "Now this I got from a grizzly bear I met during my travels with the Lewis and Clark expedition. It was soon after I arrived on the shores of this great country. I went West with them and was called upon to wrestle a grizzly bear to the ground. He did not go easy. In the process, he ripped off my arm. Naturally I was obliged to take his." He nodded. "Fortunately, the Indian medicine men had run into this kind of thing before and they attached my new grizzly arm." My father made a fist. "Now you know why I was such a good lumberman."

Everyone in the store listened, dumbfounded. No one asked a single question. I giggled. I liked when my father told stories. He was not a particularly gregarious man when we were in public. In fact, being around many people seemed painful for him, and I believe he only did it because he wanted me to have the benefit of society and community. I seem to remember we were only in the mercantile that day because Betsy Shaw insisted my father purchase some material so she could make me a dress.

"She's five years old and she looks like a boy," Betsy Shaw said.

"She looks like herself," Mr. Em said. "The clothes do not make the child."

My mother had been gone a year or more by then. Betsy Shaw was still cutting my hair short, just as my mother had.

"Everyone thinks she is a boy," Betsy Shaw said. "How will she ever make friends? She needs to go to school, grow out her hair, and wear a dress."

My father wanted to teach me himself, as he had done since I was a baby, but Betsy Shaw was firm about me going to school. Because my father listened to her and acquiesced to her wishes so often I believed for some years that she was really my mother. Especially since I barely remembered Juliet Lee—and because the stories about where my mother was frequently changed. The latest one was that she now lived back East with her wealthy family.

Perhaps she did live with them. Or maybe she had killed herself. Or my father killed her. That's what one of the children said when I finally started school. A boy whispered in my ear, "Your father is a monster who killed your mother. That makes you the monster's daughter. Or maybe you're a monster, too."

I hit him in the mouth with the book I was holding at the time. The blow put his lip through his bottom teeth—or it put his bottom teeth through his lip. I'm not sure which.

I may have been little, but I was uncommonly strong. That was one of the advantages of having a father who had come from the dead. He had brought with him the qualities of Heaven and Hell, I supposed, and handed them down to me.

The boy screamed, and the teacher sent me home.

I remember running home that day. All by myself. I remember the feel of the dress on my legs as I ran, as I kicked up a breeze. Above me, the sky was blue. On all other sides of me was meadow. By then, my hair was down to my shoulders and bounced as I ran. On my father's land, I was often alone, but once I left those confines, Mr. Em or Betsy Shaw was nearly always with me. Now I was alone. I laughed as I ran and held my hands up to the sky.

I felt so free.

I knew why the boy had called my father a monster, but I was surprised he called me one, too. My father had made a point of reassuring me that his sins were his alone. Maybe the boy thought I was a monster because of my hair: It was mostly white with streaks of red and brown. Someone once called me a skunk because of my hair. Betsy Shaw said my mother cut my hair down to the quick because she didn't want anyone to see that it was multicolored. They might think me a witch. And then there were my eyes. One was brown and the other was green.

"Thank goodness they don't hang witches any more," Betsy Shaw told me as she put a bow in my hair one morning.

"I'm not a witch," I said. Whatever that was.

"You do have one foot in this world," Betsy Shaw said, "and another one in the other world."

"No, Betsy Shaw, I have one eye in this world and one eye in the other worlds, " I told her.

I pulled out the bow.

I was quite precocious then. I was pleased that I was different from everyone else. I didn't care what they thought about me.

Or I believed I didn't care until I was out of sight of my father and some boy called him a monster and me the monster's daughter.

My father was very angry with the teacher for sending me home alone. If she ever did it again, he said, he would have her fired. What about the poor boy? the teacher asked. Perhaps he had learnt his lesson, my father said, and it was all right if he was allowed to come to school again.

I did not think that was what the teacher meant.

Neither did my father.

My father sat in the back of the classroom for the next couple of days so that the children could see him and know how big he was. I was almost abnormally tiny at that point in my life. My father often joked that I could live in the palm of his hand. Now everyone knew that I had a giant for a protector.

I do not believe anyone ever teased me again.

But, wait.

I was telling you about my father's life and I meandered this way. I'm not sure how that happened. Shall we go back to my father's beginnings? Dr. Ef created Mr. Em and then deserted him. My father ended up on an ice floe somewhere north—he was always vague about exactly where. He thought for certain he would die, but he was rescued by the auspiciously-named freighter *Sanctuary*. After Mr. Em put out a raging fire that threatened to take down the whole ship and crew, he and the captain became good friends and the captain helped fund his way to America. Mr. Em lived in the eastern part of the United States for a short time, but he was too conspicuous there, he said. He needed to be with the hoi polloi. The common people didn't care about his past or his looks, and the West always needed big men.

And my father was a big man in many ways.

My father lived alone, on the edges of the frontier, somewhere near or on the Missouri, lumbering and milling and making a small fortune, until he met Juliet Lee. They married. Or they didn't. In any case, I was born.

When I finished reading the book about my father's creation, I asked him if it was all true.

"No," he said.

"Did you kill Dr. Ef's brother?"

"I did," he said. "It was an accident. I meant only to kidnap him and frighten Dr. Ef, but I did not understand my strength then."

"Did you kill Dr. Ef's friend?"

My father nodded. "I did. We fought. He lost."

Was my father a murderer or someone who merely defended himself?

"And his wife, did you kill Dr. Ef's wife?"

"I am responsible for her death," he said. "I came to her on their wedding night, and I told her what I was. I told her what her husband had done: how he had created the abomination that was me."

I stared at my father. For some reason I didn't care about the death of Dr. Ef's brother or friend—perhaps I was a monster, too—but I cared about this young wife.

My father stared back at me. Finally he said, "She killed herself. She couldn't bear to be with a man who had touched me, who had created me."

My father swallowed. He hesitated, cleared his throat, and then said, "I changed, my daughter. I am not the man I was, bent on revenge because of my creator's misdeeds. I am a new man. Again. Something happened that day, when Dr. Ef's wife killed herself. It was as if a fog started to clear from my brain. I was very new then. Maybe a soul came into my body that day. All of that time, I had been soulless. I had been in such pain. Perhaps Mrs. Ef's soul came to inhabit this body. But from then on, I never caused violence to another person—unless it was in self-defense. I have done my best to be a new man, for you, Emily, my daughter. For you and for her, Dr. Ef's poor unfortunate wife. I hope you can learn from my mistakes, my daughter, and remember these mistakes if you ever think about getting revenge for what happened to you. Vengeance is a monster. Avoid it if you can."

We had this conversation after the events in the Meadow, after we had left Oregon and moved permanently to California.

"I don't think about revenge," I said. That was a lie.

We stared at each other then, my father and I. I had many thoughts running through my head, but suddenly I fixated on my name. I had always thought I was called Emily for my parents. "Em" for Mr. Em and "ly" for Juliet Lee. Now I wondered if Mrs. Ef's name had been Emily. For some reason, I didn't care that my father was not naturally born and I didn't seem to care that he had killed at least two people. I did care if I was named after a dead woman.

"Was her name really Emily?" I finally asked my father.

"What?" He frowned. He had not expected that question. "No, her name was not Emily."

"Have you lied to me about anything?"

"How do you define a lie?" he asked.

"Mr. Em, you know perfectly well what a lie is," I said.

"I have not lied to you about anything of import," he said. "I have not told you every detail about my life or yours. I have told you the truth, as I know it, and I've spared you some details."

"Are you really my flesh and blood father?" I asked.

"I am," he said. "Can you not tell that? Don't you feel that we are linked through time and space and flesh?"

I did not have to think about this to answer. I felt my father deep in my bones. I knew we were kin. When I wasn't near him, I knew how he felt. I could hear his heartbeat. I breathed with him. And for the first decade or more of my life, when we were together, I felt completely safe. I felt like myself with Mr. Em— my own true self—and I knew Mr. Em loved me more than anything on Earth or in Heaven.

This feeling gave me clarity—and comfort. I felt bound to my father and to the places where we lived together.

I remember the years of my childhood spent in Oregon and California, but I have few memories of when we lived in Missouri. After my mother left us, Mr. Em decided civilized country was not for him. My mother had not been charmed by what she called frontier life. My father had lived in Europe. He had been a sailor. He had been part of exploratory expeditions all over America. He did not think of life along the Missouri river as *frontier* life.

Mr. Em did not talk about his past much. I had heard the old men who sat in creaky wooden chairs outside the mercantile telling stories of their youth. They always sounded like they were exaggerating or lying. Mr. Em did not do that. I believed everything he said was true. When he said he wrestled a grizzly bear, I could imagine that happening. He was stronger than any man or woman I had ever known. And he could chop down a tree faster than a natural storm could bring one down—and certainly faster than any other man.

He was the best lumberman in Oregon, but after a few years, he quit doing that and took over the mill. I knew why he quit, though he never told anyone else. He said he couldn't bear to bring down one more tree that had been rooted to the land for a thousand years. All of their wisdom disappeared each time one hit the ground, he believed. When he felled a tree, my father listened for their last whispers on the wind, but he couldn't understand what he heard. This meant everything was lost each and every time a tree came down.

Mr. Em rarely spoke of his time before he came to the United States, and he didn't like to talk about the years he lived back East either. Every once in a while, he would talk about the various expeditions he had been on. He had traveled with Lewis and Clark for a short time. He left the expedition because he could not abide bondage of any kind. Mr. Em said no good work could ever be achieved if it was done in servitude: servitude to a man, country, or god. Lewis and Clark took slaves on the expedition, and Mr. Em did not think this was right. He stayed until he could no longer continue. When he decided—or realized—he was essentially condoning slavery by his mere presence on the expedition, he left.

Mr. Em was not pleased with the way the men on the expedition treated the Indian women either. In some places, the Indian men offered the women as sexual slaves to the white men, and the white men were happy to oblige.

Mr. Em was telling me all of this one day soon before we were scheduled to leave for our first trip to California. I was 11, I believe. It was 1848. Betsy Shaw was putting logs into the wood stove before going into the kitchen to make us lunch.

When Betsy Shaw heard Mr. Em talking about the Indian women, she said, "What is the difference between that and women who are married to white men? Marriage, for a woman, is another form of slavery."

Mr. Em looked over at her, blinked several times, and then said, "You are exactly correct, Mrs. Shaw. I had never thought of it in those terms."

"Was Juliet Lee a slave then?" I asked. "Is that why she left? Did you set her free?"

My father looked at me and said, "I did set her free. Perhaps that is why she left."

"And you, Betsy Shaw," I said. "Are you a slave or are you free?" My father always called her Mrs. Shaw, so I assumed she had a husband somewhere.

"My husband is long dead," Betsy Shaw said. On this day, rain was slapping the house, hard, as though someone somewhere were tossing bucket after bucket of water against the clapboard sides.

"Did you love your husband?" I asked.

Why was it that children always asked about love? As if love mattered. As if love determined everything.

"No, I did not love him," Betsy Shaw said. Her lips curled. She squeezed her eyes together. She looked as though she had eaten something putrid. "I was 15 and he was 40 and drunk most of the time, and when he was drunk, he was mean. He pretty near beat me to death half a dozen times. The last time he tried to get at me, I ran behind a door and locked it. He was a small man—in every way possible. I figured he couldn't break down the door. He shot at me, though, several times. The sound and the breaking wood knocked me to the floor—to the ground. It wasn't more than a shack we lived in. I don't even remember why or how there was a door. But he broke into the room and saw me on the ground. Figured I was dead, I guess, so he put a bullet in his head. Thank the Lord. I was saved that day. I found the bullet. It went in one of his ears and out the other. I don't know how it killed him, seeing he didn't have a brain, but it did. I saved the bullet."

Just then, Betsy Shaw reached inside her dress and pulled out a string that was hanging around her neck. I had noticed the string before and figured she had a crucifix on it. She walked toward us and leaned down slightly so I could see the spent bullet hanging from the string.

In the next second, she tucked the bullet and string back inside her frock.

"Now, how about some lunch? I've got fresh cod. Don't forget to wash up, Emily."

She left the room. Mr. Em and I looked at one another, speechless. That was the first time Betsy Shaw had ever said anything about her before-us life—and I had been pestering her about her past since I was a baby.

"That goes to show us," Mr. Em finally said, "that what we

think is the worst day of our lives can turn out to be the best day."

At lunch, Betsy Shaw and Mr. Em talked about the trip we had taken from Missouri to get to Oregon. I'm not sure why. Maybe because Betsy was worried about us leaving for California and she wanted to remind Mr. Em how treacherous that first trip had been. Maybe Mr. Em was nervous, too.

I was nearly four when we left Missouri, so I remembered little of the trip, if anything. We started out as part of a wagon train, but we did not stay with them. My father knew the country better than the master and he knew the Indians better than anyone. He didn't say so, but Betsy Shaw did. And I knew it to be true.

Sometimes when I look up at the stars on a cool summer night, I think I remember something of that trip. A whisper, perhaps. An old woman leaning over me, blocking out the stars, wanting to take me somewhere or tell me something. Me calling out to Mr. Em.

I'm not sure if I actually remember this or if I remember them telling me about the old woman no one could see but me. Later when the Peakes were showing Mr. Em and I photographs of their relatives, I recognized one of them as the old woman who kept trying to tell me something. She was Mr. Peake's mother, and she had died days before the wagon train started out.

We left the wagon train soon after that. Betsy Shaw said the others on the wagon train thought we were as good as committing suicide by leaving, but my father knew where he was going. And he was a great hunter. He didn't like to kill game and he hated skinning and butchering them, but he did it. He never came back to us empty-handed.

I vaguely remember feeling somewhat relieved—or lightened—when we were on our own. I remember standing in the woods all by myself, dwarfed by these huge old trees, listening to the world sing to me. It was the most amazing song. It wasn't like any music I had heard humans make with instruments. Maybe a bit like a human voice—or all the human voices combined with the voices of the plants and animals. Or maybe like the voice of a mother soothing her child to sleep. Only this was more of a "wake up" song. As though the trees and the ground beneath my feet and the breeze rustling through the leaves were encouraging me to wake up and take it all in.

It's only a sliver of a memory.

I remember a night sky, too. Me on my back staring up at the stars, the wagon rocking me as we traveled. Seeing a shooting star, hearing it whisper my name. And me whispering its name back.

I can't remember now what its name was.

Nevertheless, I still sometimes hear the whispers of stars.

I met Jamie and Annie Simmons and their son Henry on the wagon train. Jamie and Mr. Em had been friends for many years before and had decided to travel West together. I don't actually recall when I first met Henry and his parents, but Betsy and Mr. Em enjoyed teasing me about Henry, who was a year or more older than I was. They said it was love at first sight. We walked right up to one another, kissed each other on the lips, and then I knocked Henry to the ground.

My father had tried to convince Jamie to come with us when we left the wagon train. Someone had gotten cholera the day before we left. That was the real reason my father wanted to leave—not so much because people kept coming up to me and asking if I'd seen any of their dead relatives.

Jamie's wife did not want to come with us. She was more afraid of the wilderness than she was of the cholera. She was part Indian, but she didn't remember the life. She wanted to stay in the city and had no desire to travel West. When I was older,

I often wondered why she hadn't left Jamie and stayed in Missouri.

She didn't understand that my father had been over this ground before. He knew this world. He could have saved all of us. Jamie, Annie, and Henry stayed with the train. We learned later that Annie died of the cholera, and Jamie and Henry settled in California. Jamie and Mr. Em wrote to one another occasionally, and he was the one who told Mr. Em about the gold he had found on his land in northern California. He said my father should come before everyone else in the world found out about it. Said maybe it was already too late. But Jamie had secured permission from the Wintu people who lived in the area where he found the gold—even though legally it was his land—and one way or another, he was going to make his fortune.

Mr. Em was tired of running the mill, he told me, and he was not all that fond of the people in our town. Nothing specific. He never fought with anyone that I knew about. But he did not have many friends either, besides myself and Betsy Shaw. Maybe he missed my mother. I didn't know. I don't think I gave it much thought. The idea of traveling to California to look for gold sounded exciting to the 11-year-old me. If we found enough gold, Mr. Em told me, we could buy lots of land and do whatever we liked for the rest of our lives.

Betsy Shaw was unhappy about us leaving, especially without her. She was afraid I would start to see things (and people) who weren't there. Or maybe she was more afraid that I would start to see things (and people) who weren't there and then I'd tell others about it. Telling people wasn't very wise.

I knew that. That was why I generally kept what I saw or heard to myself. I would tell Mr. Em, even though he was typically puzzled. He would ask me to describe what I was seeing, he would have me point, and then he would squint in that direction or he would lean down low so that he was at my height. But he never saw or heard what I saw or heard. Betsy Shaw told Mr. Em that many children had imaginary companions and that was probably what was happening with me.

I didn't think that explained seeing dead Mrs. Peake or many of the other things I had seen over the years. As I grew older I heard and saw less of these "imaginary companions." Perhaps it was because no one else shared my world view. Perhaps in the end it is impossible to continue to see what others don't. Can we actually hold different views—different visions—from our contemporaries for long without going mad?

I didn't particularly miss the visions once they faded, and every once in a while they would return and I would see a ghost of something not there. I did enjoy seeing the animals that sometimes accompanied people. A skunk followed Robbie Francis everywhere he went. Each time Leo Jones came near Robbie, the skunk's tail quivered. Leo Jones didn't see the skunk. For all I know, Robbie didn't see the skunk either. But once the skunk raised her tail, Leo Jones turned and walked away. Which was a good thing since Leo Jones was not a good boy and I was sure he'd grow up to be a bad man. No animal or person followed Leo: I sometimes wondered if that was his problem.

After a while, the skunk either left Robbie Francis or else I could no longer see it. When I told Indian Mary about the animals I sometimes saw, she said they were probably spirit animals who protected and guided the people they followed. She had never heard of anyone seeing them with their eyes—only with their hearts—but she said I must be very special to have such an unusual ability.

Although I stopped seeing the spirit animals as much as I got older, I never stopped talking to the trees, animals, plants, the sky, the weather. I carried on a constant conversation with my world. Sometimes when we hadn't had enough sun, I would stand out in the rain and talk to the Weather Spirits—which was what Indian Mary called them. I would ask very politely to see the Sun for a few days. If the Rain would go away for a while, I'd promise to sing to it, dance for it, or praise it. Indian Mary said all beings wanted some kind of acknowledgement and attention. "These are our neighbors," she said. "They will not be good neighbors if we're always cursing them or ignoring them."

After I asked, the Rain would almost always subside for a few days, and we would enjoy the Sun while we could.

I cannot seem to keep on the main path of this narrative, can I? I wander off into the marshes again and again. Sometimes the memories come like a flood and I must tell you as I remember them. My father was always the more articulate one of the two of us, the one who could weave a story out of nearly nothing. I felt things, but I couldn't always describe what was happening to me.

May I say that I was not frightened about our trip to California? I had been on numerous hunting and camping trips with my father since I was too little to remember. I could use a rifle and a bow and arrow—even though the rifle was nearly bigger than I was. Mr. Em had taught me to use a revolver, too, just in case. I knew how to skin almost any dead creature. How to dry or salt almost any kind of meat. And he had Betsy Shaw teach me manners. Mr. Em was the most refined person I ever knew, but he said he was ill-equipped to teach a girl child how to conduct herself in the world of human beings.

In other words, as young as I was then, my father had taught me well. I knew how to take care of myself, and I knew how to be polite around company. Besides, I was going to be with my father on this trip: No harm could come to me with him near. In fact, I couldn't fathom any harm ever coming to me.

Before I fell asleep that night, the night before we left, Betsy Shaw came and sat in the chair next to my bed.

"I had a dream," Betsy Shaw said. "In it, you were drowned."

I watched her face in the golden lamp light. Her expression didn't waver. She had been telling me her dreams for many years. None of them had ever come true.

"Well, then, that means I have no fear of drowning," I said. "Not a single one of your dreams has ever come true. I don't know why you are so worried. We will be fine. Maybe you're afraid you'll miss us too much."

Betsy Shaw shook her head. "You think too much of your father. He is only a man. He cannot do everything. He is mortal, like everyone else."

I sat up in bed. "He is not only a man. He is made up of the parts of many men. Maybe parts of women, too. We don't really know, do we? And how do you know he is mortal? He is old now, isn't he? Yet I don't think he has changed since I was little."

Betsy Shaw smiled then. "Yes, when you were little was such a long time ago. Let me tell you this: He does not always understand the world of men. You know that. You used to see into the other world. Where you go now—to this California place—you must try to see into the other world. When men smell gold, they go crazy."

"Can you actually smell gold?" I asked. "That would be something."

"I don't know," Betsy Shaw said. "Listen to what I am telling you. Some things have a power that is all their own. We don't necessarily understand it. And gold is one of those things. Remember King Midas wanted it so badly he turned his only daughter into gold."

"But that was a mistake," I said. "He didn't mean to hurt her."

Betsy Shaw nodded. "Yes, so you do understand. Now go to sleep. Listen to your dreams."

I got back down under the covers. I didn't understand. My father would not turn me into gold, even by accident.

Chapter Two

Mr. Em and I left for California early the next morning. The mules were cantankerous at first. Miracle nearly bucked off his load. (He was called Miracle because it was a miracle he hadn't been killed before Mr. Em bought him from Mr. Johnson.) He settled down once we started and he saw that Jangles was carrying a bigger load than he was. At least, that's why I thought he settled. My horse, Holiday, was gentle and sure-footed, and she never gave me or anyone a lick of trouble. She and my father's draft horse, Mountain, were best of friends. So we were a happy group.

We traveled through familiar territory for the first part of the trip. It was warm going, and we had plenty of food. One night we stayed at a friend of my father's, Mr. Henderson. He lived alone with his teenaged daughter, Sarah. Mr. Em had warned me ahead of time not to say anything about gold to anyone—ever— and I kept my mouth shut when Mr. Henderson asked us where we were headed.

"We're visiting an old friend of the family," Mr. Em said. "He has some land he wants me to look at and maybe go in on a purchase with him."

"You'd leave this civilized land for California?" Mr. Henderson asked. He shook his head. "Nothing but desert, rattlesnakes, and Spanish down there, and what Indians aren't already killed."

I hadn't met Mr. Henderson before, so I didn't know what kind of friendship my father and he had. My father nodded and didn't argue with his friend.

"Though I seem to remember you always got on with the Injuns, no matter where we went," Henderson said. "Maybe you see them as your own kind."

"I don't have any of my own kind," Mr. Em said, "except for Emily here."

"I feel the same about my Sarah," he said, "and her momma, may her soul rest in peace."

Henderson's daughter Sarah didn't seem to belong in this dark old house with her father. She had beautiful blond hair. When she walked around the house, it seemed like a light followed her.

"I'm gonna leave this place some day," she whispered to me after dinner. "I don't want to be slopping pigs and marrying some dirt digger." She shuddered. "I can sing. I bet I can dance, too, but if Papa caught me dancing he'd whip me. Singing he allows as long as they be hymns I'm singin'. Sometimes I sing other things and Papa hears me and asks what it is and I says, 'it's only a hymn, Papa. You going deaf or something?'" She smiled. "I can see it, you know. I'm gonna marry a rich man and we're gonna live in a big house on a hill."

I wondered if she saw things the way I saw things. But I didn't ask her.

"I've been practicing my diction so that nobody in the city

will know how poor I was," she said. "Yes. I'm gonna have a beautiful child and a beautiful life with my rich husband."

"Why must he be rich?" I asked. "Wouldn't it be better if he were kind?"

"Can't he be kind and rich?" she asked. "If I have to choose, I choose rich. My daddy is kind and poor, and he is miserable. So was my momma."

"How kind can he be if he'd whip you for dancing?"

She shrugged. "It's just his way."

"Why do you need a husband?" I asked. "If you can sing and dance, can't you make your own way in the world?"

She laughed. "You so young you don't know nothing. But come visit me in my mansion some day. You be welcome. I can see by the light in your eyes that you see things, too. My momma did and so did her momma. I do, too, some. I dreamed you was coming here. I knew it. I saw your hair. I like your hair. If you come visit me years from now, I'll still know you by your hair."

"And I'll know yours," I said. "It lights up in the dark."

"I know it does," she said, keeping her voice down. "I think it scares Papa near to death. He thinks he's crazy for seeing it so he never mentions it. It didn't start until Momma died. I think it's like a lantern, lighting my way to the new world. Now don't forget to come see me in the city."

"I won't," I said, although I had no idea how I would ever find her in whatever city.

After we had left the Hendersons far behind us, I told my father what Sarah had said to me.

"I didn't understand most of it," I said. "Like why would she need a husband?"

"Because women aren't allowed to work in most places," Mr. Em said. "And you need money to get by in this world."

"Why aren't they allowed?"

"I don't really know," he said. "That's the way it's been for a long time. I hope it will be different for you when you're grown. I hope you'll have a choice about how you live in this world. Married life can be hard on women. Once they marry, their husbands are responsible for them, and they don't have much say in the course of their lives—at least not legally."

"If they don't marry, do women have a say?"

"In some respects," he said, "but that's a difficult road, too."

"So life would be easier for me if I were a boy?" I asked.

"I will try to make life as easy as possible for you," Mr. Em said.

"That doesn't answer my question," I said.

"I know."

We met few people along the way, but the few we did encounter were friendly enough. Most nights Mr. Em and I camped. Sometimes we fished. Sometimes we bought food from a nearby farmer or rancher. Mr. Em went into the woods to hunt once or twice.

Our days were comfortably routine, and it did not rain once.

Then finally, we came to the Siskiyou Mountains. The trail out of the valley and up into the mountains seemed abrupt. One minute we were looking out at the spring grasses undulating in the meadows, and then we were stepping onto the mountains. I got off Holiday to leave an offering on the land. I set a green creek stone on the brown earth.

"May we pass in peace," I whispered.

Mr. Em nodded his approval. I got back on the horse, and Mr. Em and I continued our journey.

Indian Mary had taught me to respect every place I went. It was good to sing or pray when I stepped over a threshold, she had told me. Only she didn't use the word threshold. Maybe she said "opening." She was a Coquelle Indian who had married a white man—Jefferson Bartlett—who then died. Folks wanted to run her out of town after he died because Bartlett had debts she couldn't pay. Besides that, she was an Indian woman on her own. Mr. Em paid the debts and tried to help Indian Mary find her Indian family, but they were all dead. Most of the Coquelle Indians were dead. She stayed in town and helped during salmon season, although some years she could not stop weeping. She told me she remembered the ceremonies from her childhood, when they welcomed the baby salmon into the world in the spring and then welcomed the returning salmon home in the fall. It made her heart ache that no one sang the songs any more, no one honored the salmon.

"They take," she told Emily. "The white people take. If someone don't say the prayers, the salmon will go away and find a better place. Or else they'll disappear altogether."

"The prayers didn't work in the first place," I said to her once. "Everyone you know is dead and you prayed for them. Why would you keep praying now?"

"Why do you keep breathing?" she asked. "It's what we do to stay alive."

Betsy Shaw believed Indian Mary was crazy. She did not like that Mr. Em helped her or that I was her friend.

"One day she will burn this town to the ground," Betsy Shaw said. "You wait and see."

"Did you dream it?" I asked.

"I did," she said.

"Then I am confident it will never come to pass," I said.

Sometimes it did seem like Indian Mary was crazy. She didn't remember her real name. Or so she said. When I was little, I saw animals and people all around her—the animals and people no one else saw. But after a while, they faded away, and Indian Mary seemed to lose her senses more often after that.

Anyway, Mr. Em and I traveled through the mountains. I was in awe. I lived in the Pacific Northwest, so I had lived amongst mountains most of my life. But this was different. We were now up on the mountains, and they were so different from the lone peaks of the Cascades. These mountains mashed up against one another like members of a large extended family. I felt almost breathless on them, and I gulped the air. It tasted sweet, like the flower end of a clover blossom.

When we reached the summit, my father and I got off our horses and danced a little jig together. I believe the mules and horses thought we had gone mad. We didn't care. We danced, ate a bit, then kept going.

We couldn't get over and down the mountains all in one day, but Mr. Em wanted us to get as far as we could. The Native people did not live in the mountains and seldom lingered unless they were engaged in ceremonial rites. My father did not believe in a god nor did he believe in spirits, but he also realized that the people who had lived in a particular place for generations knew more than those who had not.

So we traveled swiftly up, intending to get over and down the mountains as quickly as we could.

It grew foggy soon after we summited. Even though the trail was well-marked, my father suddenly grew apprehensive. He got off Mountain and tied my horse to his "as a precaution." I didn't know what this action was a precaution against, but I trusted my father. The horses were not skittish, but the mules dug in more often than usual as we traveled through the fog, often refusing to go any further. My father got so irritated with Miracle, he cried, "I wish I'd brought a whip!"

I had never seen my father whip an animal, and he wasn't

about to do so now. Instead he stood behind Miracle and roared and growled until Miracle bleated and jumped forward.

Eventually the fog thinned, and we could see far enough ahead to know we weren't walking over an abyss. We could not see as far as Mount Shasta, which was disappointing. I had heard stories about the White Mountain and the Big Men Who Live Under the Mountain from Indian Mary and Betsy Shaw.

"Big men?" I said. "Bigger than Mr. Em?"

"Bigger."

"Hah!" I said. "I don't believe it."

"If you see one," Indian Mary said, "turn away quickly and pretend it never happened. And never tell anyone ever. It is not a good sign to see them."

Betsy Shaw said, "Don't listen to her. She's crazy. If you see one, turn away quickly, spit into the wind, and pray for them to be gone. And run if all else fails. I think they look for little white girls to bring home as brides for their children."

I didn't see any "big men" as we traveled in the general direction of the White Mountain, but the fog made for an eerie day. I kept thinking I saw something or someone out of the corner of my eye. I hoped it wasn't a mountain lion stalking our mules or a grizzly bear hoping to steal our supplies. I was glad when the fog lifted in time for us to make camp. It was the coldest night of our trip. I kept close to my father's back as we slept. The heat he generated was better than any fire.

In the morning, the sky was clear. Mr. Em found large human-like footprints around our camp. We stood together looking over the tracks.

"Looks like some barefoot fool was walking near the fire," Mr. Em said. He frowned. "I never heard a thing. You?"

I shook my head.

He said quietly, "We've got to remember that we're not hunting for gold. Anyone gets a whiff of what we're doing, and it's all over."

"I know, Mr. Em. You already said so."

"Just emphasizing the importance of this particular discretion."

"You don't think these prints are from the Big Men Who Live Under the Mountain come looking for a white child bride, do you?" I asked.

My father looked at me. "Pardon me?"

I started to tell him, but he stopped me with a shake of his head.

"Never mind," he said. "You must learn to distinguish the difference between truth and fairy tale or myth."

"But you told me there is truth in every story," I said.

"Yes, but—" He shrugged. "There are no big men here looking for you. From what I understand, they live on the White Mountain and we are far from there."

I was relieved.

I don't remember much about the descent. And I don't remember much about finding the camp Jamie and Henry had already set up. In some ways, the land reminded me of home: a valley, lots of pine trees higher up with cottonwood trees and the like down by the river, just beginning to leaf out. We couldn't see the White Mountain from where we were, but I did get a glimpse of her on our way down into the valley. She was a beauty, slouching into the land like a queen who had found her throne.

Jamie was a small Irish man with skin burnt and then browned by the sun. His brown hair was chopped raggedy and looked like it hadn't been washed in a year or so. He clasped me in his arms and said how good it was to see me again. I didn't remember him, but his smell was familiar and vaguely comforting: a combination of unburned tobacco and earth.

Jamie's son Henry was shyer than his father, taller, and darker—his mother's Indian blood, no doubt—but he held out his hand first to Mr. Em and then to me. His black hair nearly covered his eyes, and I remember I had an urge to reach out and brush it back.

We shook hands, the two of us, and it was as if with that touch we remembered being kids together so long ago. We were instant friends again.

We kissed like we had when we met that first time. Then I pushed him down. He laughed as he stood up and brushed himself off.

"Just like old times," he said. "You wanna see everything?"

"Of course!"

"Come on then," Henry said.

I heard my father and Jamie laugh as we began running, taking off at nearly the same moment.

Henry took me first to an anthill at the edge of the woods, on the other side of the meadow. It was an impressive structure. I had never seen one so big. The red and black ants were running around the biscuit-colored dirt, going so quickly that it was difficult to watch only one and see where she was going.

"It's the sun," Henry said. "Watch this." He stood near the anthill so that part of his shadow was cast over the hill. Immediately the ants moved out of the sun and continued their work in Henry's shadow, moving a bit slower.

"They like you," I said.

"Nothing to do with me," he said. "You try."

He stepped out of the way, and the ants immediately began scurrying in the sun again. I positioned myself so that part of my shadow sheltered the hill. Once again, the ants hurried to my shadow and slowed down as they went about their business.

"We had an anthill near our school once," I said. "I was fascinated with their activity. But once the boys discovered it, they stomped on it until nothing was left of it."

"I do not approve of the violent streak so many boys have," he said. "There is a time and a place for destruction. But those ants weren't doing anything to those boys, I wager."

I remember looking at Henry as he stared down at the ants. I was often told that I acted much older than my years, but here was this boy—this Henry—who was talking more like an adult than any boy or girl I had ever known. Of course, he could have been repeating something he had heard. I didn't know. But right then and there, I figured we would be friends for life.

Next he showed me an old juniper tree growing out of a rock face, its trunk twisted as though some giant had tried to wring it right out of the rock.

"My dad says this is a holy tree," he said. "Every year we pick berries from it and he makes jam and wine from them. Keeps us safe from sickness every winter. My dad used to put me on his shoulders so we could reach the berries. I don't know what we'll do this year. I'm too big for my father's shoulders."

"I bet you've followed that path into the woods," I said, pointing. "It looks like it goes right up behind the old juniper and then deep into the forest."

He squinted and then looked back at me. "I'm not seeing what you're seeing," he said.

This time I squinted. I saw it clear as day: a kind of shiny silvery path in the slate gray rocks.

"I'll show you," I said. "Give me a leg up."

He linked his fingers and leaned over. I put my foot in his hands and used his lift to get me up onto a kind of ledge in the rocks and moss. Before I stood again, Henry reached out his hand, and I helped pull him up next to me.

"Do you see it now?" I asked.

He shook his head. "You must be able to see what the animals leave behind," he said. "Like a tracker. My father is a good tracker, and I am fair to middling."

I realized then I must be seeing that which was invisible— like when I saw the spirit animals or people like Mrs. Peake—so I didn't say anything else. I stood up and began to follow the path.

It led us right up to the Old Juniper. I could feel her breath as we neared. She breathed in Meadow and breathed out Mountain. I reached out and touched one of her twisted branches. Henry did the same. If I ever needed a hiding place, I knew I could come here. Anyone below would not be able to see me. The Old Juniper would always protect us, I was certain—although it felt peculiar to be thinking of places where I could hide to be safe. Safe from what?

We let go of the juniper and kept walking up a ways. The path curved around the rock and we were faced with a jumble of bushes. Fortunately I could still see the path. I walked between the bushes and beneath more twisted junipers and other evergreens until we were in a pine forest.

Henry stopped and looked around. "I know where we are," he said.

I followed Henry for a bit until we were on the edge of the Meadow again. We could see our fathers still standing by the tents, talking. We went back into the woods. Now I could see two new paths—not silver paths but ones made from animal or human feet; the silver path we had followed to get here was gone. I blinked, trying to make it reappear, but it didn't.

Henry pointed. "That left path goes to the privy we dug. Right is for hunting and wandering, although nowadays Papa doesn't want me wandering too far. He doesn't want me running into anyone who might wonder what we're doing here. There's a cave up there. Bats like it some, bears like it some. If you go far enough into the cave there's the prettiest swimming hole with an opening at the bottom of it. If you swim down into that you'll eventually end up in the creek. When it's warmer, I'll show it to you."

"You've been here lots," I said.

"Sure," he said. "We come every year. It's our land, but it's only this winter that changed things—I mean the gold. The creek is full of it now. Wasn't before. Or else we couldn't see if before."

We were walking up the right hand trail now. It wound through a dark woods made up mostly of Douglas firs and cedar trees. Grape holly grew near the trees, and we walked by a patch of vanilla leaf, their light green leaves waving in a breeze I couldn't feel, reminding me as they always did of small green hands waving hello or goodbye.

"I don't think I've ever seen real gold," I said.

"Nothing like it," Henry said. "At least that's what Papa says. I would imagine emeralds and rubies are pretty, too."

I laughed. "I don't think you'll find rubies and emeralds in these hills."

"There could be," he said. "You ever hear of Jack Stoddard?"

I shook my head.

"He was a pirate," he said. "Ran aground somewhere north of San Francisco. The story goes he buried his treasure someplace in these hills, somewhere near Mount Shasta."

"How'd he get his treasure from the ocean to here?" I asked.

"I didn't say here here," Henry said. "But somewhere around here. He was a big man, like your father. Maybe they're related. They say he dropped his treasure and then went to live with the Big Men Who Live Under the Mountain."

"That's not a true story," I told him.

We turned around and headed out of the forest.

Henry shrugged. "It's what I heard."

"And they couldn't be related to my father," I said. "He's one of a kind."

"We're all one of a kind," Henry said. "I guess. Except for twins."

We stepped into the sunshine and started to walk across the Meadow.

"My father was made from the pieces of many different dead people," I said. "He has no real parents. So it is a fact that no one is like him."

"That sounds like a made-up story, too," Henry said. "But it is interesting. I like your hair. I don't remember that from before. I wish mine was more than one color. Is that why you can see things I can't see?"

I shook my head. "No. It's my eyes." I stopped so he could look at my eyes.

"Wow!" he said. "Do you see different things from each eye?"

"Not that I know."

Just then I saw a mountain lion out of the corner of my eye, behind Henry. I grabbed Henry and pulled him closer to me as I cried, "Watch out!"

He turned around quickly to see what I saw. The mountain lion sat on its haunches, yawned, and then stretched out on the grass. I realized then I could see beyond him—through him—to our fathers on the other side of the Meadow.

I was seeing spirit animals again.

"You have a mountain lion," I said. "I thought it was flesh and blood, but it's not."

Henry looked around. "I want to see him," he said.

"What makes you think it's male?" I said. More often than not, if a creature was following a human being, it was the opposite sex to the human.

"Why do I have a mountain lion following me?" he asked. "Will it hurt me?"

"No, she won't hurt you," I said. "Have you ever heard of guardian angels?" He nodded. "I think it's like that."

"I have a guardian mountain lion?"

I shrugged. "Why not?"

Henry smiled. "This is going to be a fun summer."

I laughed.

Our fathers called to us, and we ran across the Meadow to join them.

Chapter Three

Before my father and I arrived, Henry and Jamie had built two cots, one for me and one for Mr. Em. It had not taken much for mine to come into existence, but they had to shore up Mr. Em's so that it was more like a bed than a cot. Mr. Em did not like sleeping on the ground—even though he often did so when he was camping.

I sometimes wondered if he didn't like sleeping on the earth because he remembered being in the cold ground after he died. Well, after the different people who were him had died.

I even asked him about it once. When I was quite young, I felt free to ask him anything. As I got older, I became more aware of him as his own person—or persons, as it were—and I realized he had feelings which could be wounded.

On that first night on our new cots in the large tent Jamie and Henry had put up for us, I asked Mr. Em, "Do you remember what it was like to be dead?"

He didn't say anything at first. In the distance, coyotes yipped as the moon rose up over the ridge.

"I remember feeling dead because I hated everything," he said, "and everyone. I hated life itself."

"How can you hate life itself?" I asked. "Did you hate flowers?"

Mr. Em chuckled. Or cleared his throat. Then he said, "Yes, I hated flowers. I especially hated anything beautiful because I was so ugly."

"You are not ugly, Mr. Em," I said. "You could have your pick of nearly any woman in Riverside."

Riverside wasn't actually the name of the place where we lived in Oregon. Or Washington. Or wherever we lived—remember, I'm not telling you the truth about everything. In any case, our town was like so many other towns along any number of rivers.

"Women don't want to be with me because I am beautiful," he said. "It is because I can provide a good life for them."

"I think you are beautiful," I said. "I don't care what anyone says. Not that anyone says anything. About you. No one ever says anything. And I wouldn't let them if they did. Is that why you didn't remarry? You wanted someone who thought you were beautiful?"

"No," he said. "I didn't remarry because I am already married. And I don't expect anyone to think me beautiful, except perhaps my daughter who is trying not to hurt an old monster's feelings."

"You're still married?" I said. "To my mother?"

"Yes, Emily," he said.

"So if something happened to you, I would be forced to live with her because you are still married to her?"

"You would most likely go live with her whether we were married or not," he said, "because she is your mother."

"She would get your fortune then," I said, "because you are married. I would be a pauper."

"I have no fortune," he said. "And her family is already rich. Perhaps you would rather live with them if you are so concerned about fortunes."

"We will find a fortune in gold here," I said. "We will be rich by the end of this."

"That is my hope," he said. "I would like to move us to California and buy land. If we have lots of land, I believe, our way in the world will be easier, and you will have a fortune when you are ready to marry."

"Marry?" I made a noise. "Why should I marry? Not unless what is mine stays mine."

"If you fall in love, you won't care about such things," Mr. Em said.

"Did you care?" I asked. "Are you saying all of this because I am a girl and not a boy?"

"I am only saying that one day you will fall in love and you will want your beloved to share in all of your riches."

"I have just realized you have completely avoided answering my original question, about what it feels like to be dead."

"Are you not tired?" he said. "We have a great deal of work to do in the morning."

"Still avoiding the question, Mr. Em," I said.

"Wouldn't you like to call me 'father' or 'papa' someday?" he asked. "I've observed that most children call their father something like that."

"But I've always called you Mr. Em," I said. "You aren't like other fathers, so why should I call you something like father or papa?"

He didn't say anything for a moment. I could hear him shifting on his cot although I could not see him in the darkness of the tent.

"I think the terms are meant to connote affection," he said.

"Not necessarily," I said. "Christine Winter hates her stepfather and she sneers every time she calls him 'Daddy,' like someone would if they were cursing."

"Don't ever call me daddy then," he said. "Unless you feel affection for the name and me."

"But, Mr. Em," I said, "I feel more affection for you than for anyone or anything in this world or the next. If you would like me to call you something besides Mr. Em, I will, of course."

"No, no," he said. "It is entirely up to you."

"All right," I said. "So many of those names feel childish to me. I am, after all, nearly 11 years old. I do like the sound of 'papa.' Maybe, someday, if I feel like I need something particular from you, or if I'm feeling—I don't know. Maybe." I was silent. "Mr. Em, you have successfully avoided answering my question."

"I told you," he said. "I felt dead when I was hateful. But that passed. I don't feel that way any longer. As for remembering anything from the lives of the puzzle pieces that make up this body: As far as I can tell, I don't remember anything."

"Wouldn't you like to?" I asked. "They're more like your parents than the man who sewed you together, aren't they? He was only the seamstress."

"That is certainly an original way of looking at it," he said. "Now go to sleep. If you keep thinking on this, you'll have nightmares."

"Why should I have nightmares?" I asked.

"Emily," he said.

"Yes, Mr. Em. I am closing my eyes and buttoning my lips this instant."

I don't remember if I dreamed anything at all that night. The next morning after a splendid breakfast of eggs, potatoes, and beans, we began panning for gold.

We started the morning out in the sun, squatting just in the water looking for pieces of gold. Mr. Em didn't do any squatting, but he was a good lookout. He would see something shiny in the stream, point at it, and I would wade into the water and see what it was. And mostly they were gold pieces. Small nuggets, big nuggets, in-between nuggets.

"You didn't need our help for this," Mr. Em said. "There must be two or three fortunes here."

"There's too much for the boy and me to pick up," Jamie said. "Rather you have it than some thief. Sooner or later, news of this will get out. Must be like this all over the region now."

"Maybe the mountains let loose Jack Stoddard's treasure," Henry said.

Mr. Em looked at Jamie. Jamie said, "You never heard of the pirate Jack Stoddard? Local folks have been looking for his treasure for decades now, I've been told. They think he ran aground and then came inland for some reason or another."

"Henry said he went to join the Big Men living under Mount Shasta," I said. I reached my hand into the icy water and grasped something cold and hard. I came up with a small nugget twisted on its side like a fat yellow worm. I tossed it into Mr. Em's stash.

"Maybe he came to find one of those brides the Big Men were always stealing," Mr. Em said. He winked at me. I rolled my eyes. I knew he didn't believe any of it.

"I don't care where the gold came from," Jaime said, "as long as no one wants it back."

Henry was a hard worker. I worked hard, too, but he seemed to have a zeal for it. The cold water made my legs ache. If I squatted for too long, my knees hurt. I liked it better later in the day when we worked in the shade and the water didn't seem quite as cold.

The days became routine, and I was happy. It was only me

and my father—whose company I enjoyed—and Jamie and Henry. Jamie was almost as good a storyteller as my father, although his tales usually involved the fairy folk and someone Irish who had drunk too much whiskey. The nights and days got warmer, and wildflowers spread across the Meadow. The cottonwoods and birch trees leafed out. And the air was filled with the songs of a million birds, it seemed. We had plenty to eat—Jamie and Mr. Em always found game when they went looking and all of us harvested greens in the Meadow and the forest. It was too early for fruit or berries, but we had some canned goodies to supplement our diets.

During the day, we panned for gold. The supply seemed endless. When I asked my father why no one had found it before, he told me that the indigenous people didn't value it the way the whites did, and no other whites knew about the gold, yet. Besides, it may have been unearthed this year.

Every morning before we started, Jamie said a kind of prayer, asking permission to take from the river that which was not ours. He promised we would not take it all, nor would we use it for any evil purposes. Then he scattered a bit of tobacco into the wind and poured a few drops of whiskey onto the ground. Every night when we finished, we said a prayer of thanks to the river, the land, and the mountains. And then Mr. Em and Jamie would go together to hide the gold. Not from us—although Henry and I did not go with them—but from the hordes of people they believed would descend upon this valley if news of the gold got out.

At lunch times and in the late afternoons, Henry and I often explored the woods or the Meadow together. We found a family of mice living in a rotten log. At first they were like tiny pink worms with tails. Gradually, they became more like mice. We never saw the parents—they must have hidden every time we peeked inside the log.

We watched bald eagles in the process of building a nest. We didn't actually see where the nest was, but we observed the giant birds flying overhead carrying twigs and sometimes sticks that looked bigger and heavier than the birds themselves.

Sometimes we lay on the meadow grass which grew taller by the day. We would stare up at the clouds passing overhead and point out figures in the clouds.

"That one resembles a genie," Henry would say. The shapes he saw often belonged to fantastical creatures.

"Has he come to protect us or grant our wishes?" I asked.

"I don't know," Henry said. "Maybe he's come to visit the Big Men Who Live Under the Mountain."

"Do you think there are any real Big Men?" I asked.

"Before you and Mr. Em came, I thought I saw one in the woods," he said. "It was almost night and I was on the way to the privy. I ran all the way back to camp."

"You were afraid?"

"Of course I was afraid," he said. "He was huge!"

"My father is huge," I said. "Are you afraid of him?"

"No," he said. "Maybe a little. But he doesn't have hair all over his body."

"He might," I said. "We don't know. Besides, does the lack of hair mean someone is harmless?"

"No!" he said. "At least I don't think so." He turned over onto his belly and looked at me. "He seemed wild, the Big Man. Like a wild animal, I suppose. And wild animals can hurt us if they are cornered. Or maybe even if they are hungry."

"You probably saw a bear," I said. "People often mistake bears for other humans."

Henry shrugged. "It could be," he said, "although I have lived in the woods for all of my life and I have seen plenty of bears and never mistook a one of them for a man or anything like a man."

Sometimes as we lay in grass, we'd turn around onto our bellies, dig our elbows into the earth, and arm wrestle. I was stronger than Henry—I was stronger than most people—so I usually won. Henry never seemed to mind; he always wanted to keep playing.

We decided we were best friends and we would be best friends forever. This meant that we had to tell each other the truth, always. And we had to tell each other our secrets. I figured I had already told Henry everything. One day he told me, "I know how to be invisible."

"Truly? That must come in handy."

"It does," he said. "Especially when I want to watch animals."

"I could never be invisible." I touched my hair.

"Sure you can be," Henry said. "Even with your hair—which I like. Be very still. Even your mind. And soon you'll blend into the surroundings. Let's practice it now. I hear my dad calling for me. He'll come looking, but he won't find us."

We lay down again and got very still. For a few moments, I heard Jamie's voice from faraway, and the sound of the grass slapping his pant legs as he walked toward us. That faded as I gazed up at the clouds, and I breathed deeply, I imagined myself sinking into the ground, I imagined rising up to the clouds. And that's what I felt like I was doing. From above, I saw all: Mr. Em, Jamie, Henry, the mountain lion, the Old Juniper, the meadow grass, the trees, the eagle. I smiled. As I rose higher, I saw the mountain. It was all quite pleasant.

And then I heard my name. It sounded like someone in the distance was calling to me. Someone on the other side of the mountain, maybe? But then I recognized the voice. Voices. Henry, Jamie. And Mr. Em. Jamie sounded panicked. Mr. Em's voice was strong, certain. He was calling me home. He had done it all of my life; every time I wandered too far afield I was always able to hear his voice.

"Emily, Emily."

Until it sounded as though it was in my ear. Then I could feel my small hand wrapped up in his huge fingers.

I opened my eyes. I smiled and sat up.

"It didn't work, Henry," I said. "I'm not invisible."

Henry looked at his father and then back at me.

"They didn't find us at first," he said. "I finally called them when you wouldn't come awake."

"I never went to sleep," I said.

"Your eyes were open, but you weren't there," Henry said. He looked at Mr. Em. "Like I said, I was teaching her to be invisible. It starts with being still."

Mr. Em nodded. "Emily is rarely still," he said. "And I do believe she wandered far afield again, only this time she left her body behind."

"I didn't know I could do that," I said. "It was quite enjoyable."

"I'm glad," Mr. Em said, "but I'm not certain you should do it again. Not until we find someone else who can do it, too, so they can teach you how to come back."

"I would have come back," I said. "Eventually."

I got up from the grass. Henry and I followed our fathers back to the creek.

"I will admit you scared me," Henry said. "So I called to your father. I figured that was the right thing to do."

"If you're in trouble," I said, "calling Mr. Em is always the right thing to do."

A couple of times, a group of Indians—including Mr. Em's friend Sitiu—came to the meadow. Jamie and Mr. Em traded with them for food and fishing line, and they invited the Indians to eat with us. I didn't understand their language, but Mr. Em did, and he seemed to enjoy their company.

Henry and I ran around the Meadow with two of Sitiu's grandsons. One time the Indian boys climbed a ridge—with us following—and showed us animal paintings on a rock we hadn't seen before. Some of the figures seemed to be human *and* animal. A couple of the figures were much larger than the others. I wondered if they were depictions of the Big Men Who Live Under the Mountain.

I liked being around the Indian boys. I liked how easy they seemed to be in the world. They weren't self-conscious. They were confident—although I don't know if I would have used that word then. Next to the two Indian boys, Henry and I seemed like country bumpkins, completely out of place in this meadow, on this land. We were interlopers. We were searching for gold in order to leave and live the good life; yet, the good life was all around us, worth far more than gold.

Mr. Em understood the real value of this place, of the Meadow. Of any place, actually. But he had had great hardship in the beginning of his strange life. Being ostracized and hunted had not been an easy life. He believed if he provided a service to the community and had an ample supply of money, he and I would be safe. He didn't use that word when he spoke to me of such things—he did not want me to be a fearful child. I think he would have been perfectly content to stay alone in the woods with me, making his living from the land. I would have been happy, too, then, because I was with him. But he never wanted me to feel strange—or estranged from the community of people. He knew what that was like. And he had told me on more than one occasion that he wished he could do more for Indian Mary. She was without her tribe, so she was alone. Mr. Em did not want me to be alone.

I was always a little sad when the Indians left us. Sometimes they helped us pan for gold, and Mr. Em and Jamie wanted them to keep whatever they found. Sitiu was not interested.

When I asked Mr. Em what Sitiu said when he refused the gold, Mr. Em told me, "He said that he could not eat yellow stones. As long as he had fish and acorns, his people were happy. He also said he didn't understand white men. He thought they were all crazy."

"'They?'" I asked. "Aren't you a white man?"

"I don't think he puts me in that category," Mr. Em said. "I've known Sitiu for many years. I've tried to explain to him who I was, but he believes I'm related to the Big Men Who Live Under the Mountain."

"Maybe you are," I said. "Maybe Dr. Ef lied to you about your origins."

"That would make a nice fairy tale, my daughter, but it is not true. I know who I am."

And so the days and nights went. I don't believe I was ever as happy as I was during those weeks living in the Meadow.

Then it all changed.

Chapter Four

Picking up gold from the creek bed was as easy as picking sallal berries from bushes that grew all through most of the woods where I grew up in Oregon. One berry after another, barely had to move—just step over the Oregon grape, or pick them, too, while you were at it.

The more gold we found, the more fun we had. At the end of each day, Jamie and Mr. Em hid what gold we'd found all over the Meadow. (The plan was to dig it up or uncover it all before we left.) We were certain we were very rich. Sometimes when I dug down deep into the creek bed, I found huge nuggets. The others said I was some kind of gold genius. The truth was that I listened to the Creek, I listened to the Gold. I asked if any of them wanted to come home with us to make us rich. I promised our intentions were honorable. Making a living for oneself and one's family is an honorable goal, after all. It wasn't that I heard the Creek say, "It is all yours. Pick it up." It was more like I heard the hint of a hint of a hint of a whisper, "Over here, over here."

I was barefoot most of the time now and as brown as an Indian. I had Mr. Em cut off all my hair after one too many sticks got tangled in it. I was sure I looked like a boy again, as I had when I was little, and I was glad for it. I felt a certain kind of freedom running around without the feel of my strange head of hair.

Henry and I were inseparable, but then the four of us were never far from one another. And a cross word was never said between us. We got along as well as any four people in the world ever got along, I'd imagine.

Then I began to dream. I was usually floating above the Meadow, as I had been the day I was trying to be invisible with Henry. I'd get higher and higher until I could see the various Indian people in the area, living, working, sitting around fires. Doing what people do. I saw other people, too. White people. They were laughing and living, too, but they did not live with the land. They were looking for something or someone, and I could tell they were mean. I wasn't sure if they knew they were mean. Maybe they were only hungry or lost or fearful. But the more I watched them, the more they looked like locusts just before they decided to give up the solitary life and swarm together to devour everything in their path.

I would wake up from these dreams drenched in sweat. I told Mr. Em about them. At first he was afraid I was sick from malaria—because of the sweats—but I didn't have a fever. It was fear that made me sweat.

My dreams had never come true before, but Mr. Em told Jamie about them. Our fathers instructed Henry and me to stay close to them for the time being, in case strangers were about. Every night, they hid the pans as well as the gold. We didn't want any evidence in camp that we were looking for gold.

Then one day we worked downstream quite a ways from

camp for most of the day. As we headed back, we heard a dog bark before we could see our tents. Mr. Em quickly hid the gold we'd found that day behind a tree, and Henry and I slung fishing poles over our shoulders. Mr. Em and Jamie held their rifles at the ready. As we stepped into the Meadow, I spotted a dog sniffing around our campfire. Then I saw three more dogs, only when I looked right at them, they changed into huge monstrous-looking creatures—like something out of a fairy tale book. I blinked and they were dogs again, dogs with red lights in their eyes.

I backed up until I was behind Mr. Em.

"What did you see?" he whispered.

"Three monster dogs," I said, "with red eyes."

He nodded. "I see three men and a dog," he said.

Jamie said. "Yep. I'll go around to the right and come up behind. Henry, you stay with Mr. Em."

"Stay close," Mr. Em said softly.

Then he strode into the Meadow, toward camp.

"Hello, neighbor," he said, his voice booming. I saw the three men now. One of them was about to open the flap on one of our tents. All three men stopped and looked toward my father. I saw fear flicker across their faces. Mr. Em waved, which made him look even bigger. "Welcome," he said.

In a couple of strides, Mr. Em was in our camp, standing by the ashes of our fire. Henry and I stood behind Mr. Em, but we did not cower. We stood our ground. It was our ground, and these men were trespassers. Interlopers.

And worse. I knew they were so much worse. But I swallowed the fear and didn't rub my stomach when the fear made it hurt.

"We went fishing and caught nothing this afternoon," Mr. Em said, "but we were about to make supper. You're welcome to stay."

The men didn't carry rifles, but they did have on holsters

with guns in them. Their horses were nearby, grazing. Our horses were across the Meadow.

"I'm Mr. Em," he said. He held out one hand. The tall skinny man, the one nearest to Mr. Em, the one with the dirtiest clothes, hesitated and then shook Mr. Em's hand. I could see Mr. Em held his hand tightly so that there'd be no mistaking how strong he was.

"I'm Jake McMahon," the man said. "This here is Danny Collins and Jimmy Kelly."

Danny Collins and Jimmy Kelly appeared to be younger than Jake McMahon and fidgety. I saw Jimmy Kelly's fingers start to wander to his gun and then slide away again. He looked like a boy, with hair so blond it was nearly white—except it was too dirty to be any true color. And Danny Collins seemed to be only a little older than Jimmy Kelly, with bright red hair and freckled skin. Neither of them looked particularly happy to be in our company.

"Sit down," Mr. Em said. "We'll make coffee."

Jimmy Kelly's hands went to his gun butt again, but then we all heard the snap and crack of a rifle being unbroken. The three men looked behind them. Jamie was walking up, rifle slightly raised. He smiled as he stopped.

"I apologize," he said, his Irish accent thicker than usual. "Didn't mean to startle ya."

He didn't come any closer.

"Son, make our guests coffee," Jamie said.

"Get the men some food, too," Mr. Em said. I knew he was talking to me even though he didn't say my name. He didn't want them to know my name. I ran to the deep cool spot in the creek where we had set the small portable larder Jamie had fashioned for us.

"This is my friend Mr. Simmons," I heard Mr. Em say. "We're

here for some vacation time with our children. What brings you onto Mr. Simmons's property?"

I grabbed some things from the larder. I can't remember what. Maybe dried meat and fruit preserves. I ran back up to the others and began handing the food around to the strange men, nearly dropping the pieces of smoked meat to keep from having any part of my fingers touch any part of their fingers. Jimmy Kelly and Danny Collins sat down near the ashy fire that Henry was attempting to start up again so he could cook the coffee. The men gnawed on the food like starved animals.

"We was looking for gold," Jimmy Kelly said, his mouth full of bread.

Jake McMahon gave him a fierce look. Would have shot him, I was certain, if he had half a chance.

"We're hunting," Jake McMahon said. "Smelled your fire last night and thought we'd come by to make sure all was well. I've heard some settlers had trouble with the Indians."

I had stepped back to be closer to Mr. Em. Jamie still held his gun at the ready, but natural-like, so it didn't look like he was pointing it at the men—even though he was.

"Haven't heard about any trouble with any Indians," Jamie said. "Everyone gets along here."

Jake McMahon bit off a piece of jerky and nodded. "I see that now. Everyone is quite friendly. We talked to the Indians nearby and asked if we could fish and hunt down by the creek, further down, off your property, and they said that was fine with them."

I doubted these men had asked the Indians anything. Maybe they had demanded "permission." Or maybe they camped where they wanted to camp and figured they'd shoot anyone who bothered them.

"While we're here," Jake McMahon said, "we might look

for gold. I heard tell there be treasure in these hills. Or gold in these streams."

Henry set the coffee pot near the now crackling fire. Then he stepped back. We instinctively wanted to be out of reach of these men.

"There's always someone talking about gold," Jamie said. "As far back as Cortez's time. Usually nothing good comes of it."

"But if someone were to find gold," Jake McMahon said, "he shouldn't keep it to himself. That wouldn't be right. Especially now that California is part of the United States of America. It belongs to all of us. And some people—not us, of course—don't put any stock in land deeds given out by the Mexican government. Wouldn't be worth nothing, as far as most people were concerned."

"Good thing my deed is from the United States of America then," Jamie said, "in case we run into those kinds of people."

Jake McMahon shrugged. "Probably most people wouldn't care. If you got gold here, they'd probably run you off, or at least squat and look for gold themselves."

Jamie shrugged, too; perhaps imitating Jake McMahon. "Wouldn't bother me none since I have no qualms about shooting trespassers."

I glanced at Mr. Em. He was watching Jake McMahon.

"That ain't very friendly," Jake McMahon said. "What happened to share and share alike?"

Jamie grinned. Mr. Em smiled.

"I have no fears about anyone running me off," Jamie said. "Cuz there ain't gold here. Wish there was. This land was for sale for many years before I took ownership. It's not big enough to farm and the game ain't that plentiful. It's a good vacation spot."

Jake McMahon swallowed the last of his food. Then he wiped his dirty hands on his dirty trousers.

"Thank you for your hospitality," he said, "but we should be getting on. Let us know if we can do anything for you. We're neighbors now."

The other two men got up, and soon all three were walking toward their horses. Jimmy Kelly's hand kept reaching for his gun, but Jake McMahon said something to him, and he ran his fingers through his hair instead.

After the men rode off, I felt relieved. My father and Jamie were not.

"They know what we're doing," Jamie said. "They could have been watching us for days."

"I don't think so," Mr. Em said. "They didn't strike me as bright enough to keep themselves hidden and quiet."

"How are we ever going to get the gold out of here?" Jamie asked.

"I'll have to think on it," Mr. Em said. "Let's do nothing for the next couple days and see what happens."

Something about the men troubled all of us. I was certain they were who I had dreamed about. Mr. Em said he had half a mind to pack up and go, to get us out of harm's way and leave the gold behind. After Henry and I were safely home, Jamie and Mr. Em would return to collect the gold.

"No!" I cried. "You can't leave us. And you can't come back here alone. They are bad men."

Mr. Em looked at me. He had never heard me talk this way, and I think it startled him.

"I know they are bad men," Mr. Em said. "That is why I want to get you away from them."

I shook my head. "Not if you're coming back. You always told me not to let people push me around. Aren't you letting these men push us around? This is Jamie's land. They don't have any right to it."

"Sometimes might is right," Mr. Em said.

"And you're the mightiest of them all," I said.

The following day, Mr. Em and Jamie instructed us to stay hidden—invisible—until they came back. They intended to spy on the men and then return to our camp before dark.

Henry and I stayed on the edge between the woods and the Meadow, where we were certain no one could see us. When we got bored with that, we hid up by the Old Juniper. That brought us to mid-morning. It was hot and still in the Meadow. I heard only the buzzing of some insect somewhere.

"I don't know if I can stay still all day," I said. "There must be somewhere we can be hidden and do something at the same time."

Henry grinned. "I know just the place. Follow me. And stay invisible."

I didn't know if I was invisible or not, but I followed Henry away from the Old Juniper. We dropped down into the woods and went south a ways, following a path deep into the woods, until Henry stopped and whispered, "Here it is."

I looked around. I saw pine and fir trees, vine maple, and Oregon grape and sallal bushes.

"Here is what?" I asked.

Henry ducked behind one of the vine maples. I followed. What I thought was a rock face behind the trees was an opening into the rock. A cave.

Henry took my hand. "Come on," he said.

We went into the dark. Henry barely hesitated. I tugged on his hand a bit so that I had time for my eyes to adjust. The cave smelled like dust and damp all at once. I thought I heard the sound of some tiny critter scurrying away or toward us.

"Keep your head down," Henry said.

I did as he instructed and held tightly to his sweaty hand.

"This is a great hiding place," Henry said. He was still whispering. "But there's more."

I could see a light ahead of us. Not light from a lamp or lantern, but daylight. A few steps more and we were standing at the edge of an opening to the outside. Above was the blue sky and surrounding us were tall Douglas firs and a waterfall feeding into a small pool below.

"The water in the pool is amazing," Henry said. "I don't know why, but I float when I'm in it. And it's warm, but not sickly warm, if you know what I mean."

I shook my head. No, I didn't know what he meant.

"How do you get to it?" I asked.

Henry looked at me and grinned.

"From here, there's only one way I know about," he said. He looked down.

"Jump?" From here the swimming hole looked too small. What if I jumped and missed?

"Come on," he said. "I've done it a dozen times, and I've never missed."

I nodded. "Okay. You first."

He shook his head. "No, we'll go together."

"Then we're sure to die," I said. "It can't be big enough for the two of us to jump into."

"It's much bigger than it looks, and it's only about a 10 foot jump."

"Truly?"

He still had a hold of my hand. "On the count of three. One, two, three and we jump on three." He kicked off his shoes.

I nodded and took off my shoes, too.

Henry said, "One, two, three."

We jumped.

Or stepped off.

We flew through the air. I felt free, just as I had the time I was expelled from school and ran home by myself. I laughed, mid-air. I could stay here all day.

And then suddenly, I hit water, feet first, and my body shot straight down.

I had forgotten to hold my breath.

I gulped water.

It tasted like mountain.

Were those the whispers of the Big Men Who Live Under the Mountain I heard? Did the Big Men have Big Women or was that why they left the mountain looking for brides?

I started to choke. Were those jewels shining in the sand at the bottom of the bottomless pool?

I felt Henry's hand on my arm. Or was it a man's hand?

Something pulled me straight up until I was partly in the sky and partly in the pool.

I coughed and coughed, choking on my own breath.

"Can't you swim?" Henry asked. He looked worried. I imagined he was trying to figure out how to rescue me if I didn't stop coughing.

Finally I sneezed several times, and then I could breathe again.

"They say we breathe water in the womb," I said, still a bit breathless. "I wonder how that is possible. And yes, I can swim. Of course. I just—I just forgot to close my mouth."

Henry started to laugh and splashed water at me. I did feel buoyant in the pond, as if something was holding me up. If I stopped moving my feet, I didn't sink immediately; after a moment, I tipped over a bit.

Henry swam to the edge of the pool and rested his arms on the rocks. I did the same. We stayed in the water and in the sun for a time, enjoying the quiet and isolation.

That was one of the many things I liked about Henry: He

could be silent. Most of the children I knew from school were always chattering—even when they weren't talking to me, which they usually weren't. Sometimes I liked to spend time in the world without hearing human voices. And around Henry, I could be still. Henry was often still. We'd be walking in the forest together and he would see something that intrigued him and he would stand still, gazing at whatever it was. Sometimes I wouldn't notice that he wasn't behind me right away. I'd turn around and he'd be gone, and I'd retrace my steps to him. He could find the amazing in nearly anything: a fallen leaf, a moth the color of tree bark, a feather floating down from the sky, a bird song. In that way, he was like Mr. Em who was similarly amazed at the ordinary.

After we'd been in the pool for a while, I said, "Didn't you say this fed into the creek somehow?"

"Yep," he said.

"Show me."

He shook his head. "You have to hold your breath for a long time," he said. "You have to be able to swim down and then swim through this hole."

"I can hold my breath for as long as you can," I said. "How did you find it?"

"Sitiu's grandson showed me last summer," he said.

"Show me," I said again.

"Hold your breath to the count of 100," he said.

I took a deep breath, and then I held it. Henry counted off.

I barely made it to 70.

"What can you get to?" I asked.

"110," he said. "It takes about 30 seconds to get to the opening because you're pushing against the water the entire time. Once in the opening, the water pushes you through, but you still need to hold your breath until you get out in the creek, so that's another 30 seconds, at least. You can practice. Then I'll show you the opening."

I considered arguing with him about it, but I knew he was right. It wouldn't be much fun if I ended up drowned. I was a practical child and so was Henry. This quality of ours partnered well with our imaginative play. Yes, there may be an invisible mountain lion following Henry everywhere he went, but we never supposed we could walk up to a visible mountain lion and shake hands with it. I could float above my body to spot danger coming or going, but I wouldn't try to jump off a precipice to see if I could fly.

I believed that made me a practical imaginative.

Maybe it only meant I wasn't brave enough to believe in the impossible.

After a while, we decided we should go back to the Meadow. Fortunately, it was a fairly easy climb back up into the cave. Someone had carved footholds into the rock at some point—or maybe the steps had come into being naturally as people climbed up from the pool over the years.

We put our shoes back on and ran shivering through the cool cave and out into the forest. Soon enough we were back in the Meadow, running around in the sun in the hopes that our clothes would dry faster. We had completely forgotten that we were supposed to be hiding—or at least we were supposed to try to stay unobserved from any passing strangers.

Late that afternoon, Mr. Em and Jamie returned with two dead rabbits. They skinned and gutted them while Henry and I got the fire going.

"There's more than three of them," Jamie told us. "There are probably three crews of three panning for gold downstream."

"Did you talk with them?" I asked.

"We did," Mr. Em said. "We told them where the boundaries of the property are. They seemed friendly enough, except for those three we met yesterday. Something not right with them. But I'm thinking it'll be all right. They'll leave us be."

I watched Mr. Em as he talked. He didn't believe what he was saying, and it wasn't like him to try and avoid the truth. My stomach fluttered. I didn't know why I felt such anxiety. It was quite unusual for me.

We didn't do any more panning for gold for a few days. Mr. Em or Jamie went to check on the other panners every day without the miners knowing they were there. It seemed that the miners had forgotten all about us.

We began panning again.

One day Sitiu came to our camp accompanied by his grandsons and a few other Indians. They didn't join us in the creek or sit around the campfire. Sitiu and the others talked with Jamie and Mr. Em for a few minutes. Then Mr. Em and Jamie got their rifles. Sitiu and his men hurried ahead, walking along the creek, heading downstream.

Henry and I ran over to our fathers.

"Mr. Em, what's happened?" I asked.

He said, "Those men who are looking for gold, they say they've had some tools stolen. They're accusing the Indians. Sitiu has asked us to speak up for them. You and Henry stay here. We shouldn't be long."

I shook my head. "No, Mr. Em. Don't leave us here alone."

I didn't know why, but I wanted to go with them.

Mr. Em looked at Jamie, who shrugged.

"Stay close to us at all times," Mr. Em said.

I nodded.

Mr. Em and Jamie hastened after Sitiu, and Henry and I ran to keep up with them.

It took longer to get to the panners than I thought it would. The terrain wasn't exactly easy. By the time we came to the first encampment, my legs and arms were scratched and bleeding from the berry bushes I had barely skirted and the saplings that had repeatedly slapped me. Henry was a little better off. I was embarrassed and hoped no one would notice and think I was some kind of city girl.

But no one was paying any attention to me. We stepped into a small clearing near the creek. Six men I didn't know stood up quickly from the campfire when Mr. Em, Jamie, and Sitiu and his men came forward.

"Greetings," Jamie called. "It is peace we bring."

Jamie and Mr. Em shook hands with the men. The three men we had met the other day were not in the clearing or around the campfire.

"We don't want any trouble," one of the men said. He looked a little older than the others, maybe Mr. Em's age—whatever that was. "But our equipment keeps going missing. It's always after one of these Injuns comes visiting. We think they've been stealing from us."

Mr. Em translated to Sitiu, even though it was pretty much what they already knew. Sitiu said something, and Mr. Em said, "He doesn't believe any of his people would steal from you. But he wants to remain friends, so he will go back to his village and see if he can find what is missing. Can you tell us what is gone?"

"My pickax," another white man said.

"My knife," the third white man said.

"One of our gold pans," First White Man said.

Mr. Em translated.

Sitiu said something, and Mr. Em said, "He'll go now and try to find the missing items."

Sitiu turned and began hurrying away.

I had seen Sitiu do this many times before. Every time he left our camp, he ran—or hurried. He joked that he was trying to stay ahead of his grandsons, but I figured it was just his way. He liked to move.

Sometimes I'll still dream of him running. Sometimes I see a figure running in my dreams and I believe it is Sitiu until he turns around and it is my own face I see.

What happened next happened so quickly that it's difficult to put it all together, even now.

I saw black spreading across the back of Sitiu's shirt before I heard the shotgun blast. The sound was so loud I was temporarily deaf. Sitiu kept running—at least I thought he did. I saw him running into the woods, but when I looked back, I saw Sitiu's grandsons and Mr. Em and Jamie running to the fallen figure on the ground: Sitiu.

I hung back. I knew he was dead. I had seen enough dead animals to know when the spirit was gone—when the life force had abandoned the body. Or whatever it was that happened when that which had been living was suddenly dead.

Everything seemed to happen in slow motion.

I turned to look in the direction of the sound of the shotgun blast.

No wonder my ears were ringing: Jake McMahon was standing right next to me, holding his gun. A puff of smoke rose from the barrel of it.

Henry put his hand on my arm.

I looked at him. He was crying.

Things sped up to normal again.

"What did you do that for?" one of the other men said to McMahon.

"I thought he was getting away," Jake McMahon said.

Mr. Em sprung from Sitiu and toward Jake McMahon. He looked grievously angry, and I was afraid he would kill McMahon then and there with his bare hands.

One of the men stepped between Mr. Em and Jake.

"You kill an Indian, they'll give you five dollars for his scalp," McMahon said. "You kill a white man, they'll hang you."

Jimmy Kelly and Danny Collins were now standing behind Jake McMahon. I wondered if they had been there all along. Jimmy Kelly looked over at me. He seemed to see me, for the first time, and I didn't like it. I moved away, toward Mr. Em.

"No one is taking any scalps," Mr. Em said, his voice choked in anger.

"Then someone owes me five dollars," Jake McMahon said.

Danny Collins and Jimmy Kelly snickered.

The other Indians were standing now, surrounding Sitiu's body.

"He was going to see if he could retrieve our equipment," First White Man said. "Why did you kill him?"

"I told you," Jake McMahon said, sounding irritated. "I thought he was getting away. I say we kill them all before they go back to their village and rile everyone up. They'll come back and kill us in our sleep."

All the white men—save Mr. Em and Jamie—turned to look at the Indians.

I could see they were considering it.

I saw the future unfolding in my mind's eye.

"Someone stop this," I wanted to scream. Mr. Em must have read my mind. He raised his gun to his shoulder.

"Anyone shoots, you're going down, McMahon," Mr. Em said.

"Not if someone gets you first," Jake McMahon said.

Jamie raised his gun. "Someone gets him, then I get you," Jamie said.

No one moved.

Mr. Em said something to the Indians.

Nothing happened for a moment. Nothing changed.

And then Sitiu's grandsons picked up his body and carried him into the woods.

Seconds later, the Indians were gone.

Invisible.

I could see the silver traces of their footsteps in the woods. I hoped no one else could see them.

I heard wailing.

I wasn't certain if it was something only I heard or not.

But now wasn't the time.

First White Man said, "Come. This was an accident. We are brothers, neighbors. Nothing more need to come of this."

"This wasn't an accident," Mr. Em said. "This was murder."

Jake McMahon laughed again. He put down his gun. "You can't murder an Injun. That's like saying someone murdered a rabbit they had for dinner."

Jamie slowly lowered his gun.

Mr. Em did the same.

"If anything happens to any of those men or their families," Mr. Em said, "you will all answer to me, no matter who is responsible."

"And if they come slit our throats in our sleep, you gonna be responsible for that?" Jake McMahon said. "Come on, boys. We got work to do."

Jake McMahon and his two friends turned away and left the clearing, heading in the opposite direction of Sitiu's people. I could see their trail, too, but anyone could. We heard them trampling away for a long time.

"Stay and eat with us," First White Man said. "We must become friends again."

"We were never friends," Mr. Em said. "All of you stay away from us. Anyone trespasses, we will shoot to kill. You cannot treat human beings like they are nothing and expect no consequences."

"We leave it in God's hands," First White Man said. "He will right any wrongs when the time comes."

One of the other men cleared his throat and then said, "The law ain't doing nothing about their thievin' so we've got to do something. It ain't right."

Suddenly, I saw three distinct silver paths, snaking through the clearing. I followed the first one. It went from the campfire down to the creek. I ran along the silver path. I climbed rocks to get to the water and there, lodged between two boulders, was a pan. I pulled it out and ran back to the campfire. All the men were watching me.

"Is this your lost pan?" I asked, holding it up. I don't know where I got the temerity to speak to these men who repulsed me, but I did. First White Man took the pan from me.

"Yes, I believe that is the pan."

I ran down another silver path. This one went into the woods. I followed it toward a stink. This must lead to the privy. One path stopped. I dug around. Under the leaves was a knife. I picked it up. I followed another path. It led right to the privy. I could see the end of the pickax sticking up from the latrine.

I turned around and ran back to the camp.

I held out the knife. The third man took it.

"And your pickax is sticking out of the shit," I said. "Perhaps you should empty your pockets and take off your belts before you use the latrine. Before you accuse others of theft."

It was as if someone else were occupying my body. I felt old and furious. How could grown men be so stupid?

And then suddenly, the silver paths I had seen disappeared and I realized I was a small girl standing in front of many large men.

Mr. Em held out his hand. I hurried over to him and took his hand in my mine.

"How'd the boy do that?" First White Man asked.

I almost laughed.

They thought I was a boy.

What would they think if they knew I was a girl?

Mr. Em didn't say anything.

The four of us turned around and walked away. Our fathers herded Henry and me in front of them. Jamie walked backward until we reached the edge of the woods. Then Mr. Em turned his head toward the men and said, "Remember what I said. I hold you all responsible if anything happens to the Indians."

Chapter Five

I can't remember much about the trek back to our camp. We said very little to one another as Mr. Em gently hurried us along. At one point, he even put me on his back, something he hadn't done for many years, as he strode quickly through the riparian woods.

At our campsite, we started a fire to make a meal. Jamie and Mr. Em talked quietly about our options. If we left straightaway, Jake McMahon and the others would think they had run us off. That wouldn't be good for us since it was Jamie's land and he wanted to be able to return. It also wouldn't be good for the local Indians. The remaining miners, led by Jake McMahon, would run roughshod over them. The sheriff wouldn't be able to do much: Indians had no rights under the law. In fact, the government of California paid a bounty for every Indian killed.

"What those men did to the Indians is our responsibility," Mr. Em said. "We brought them here."

"How do you figure?" Jamie asked. "I didn't invite them."

"We're white people," Mr. Em said. "They're part of our tribe."

"You consider yourself white?" Jamie asked. "Brother, have you looked at yourself in the mirror lately? I don't know what race you are, but you're not of them. I am not of them."

I was startled that Jamie brought up Mr. Em's appearance. Henry and I both looked over at the men but nothing had changed between them. The tone of the conversation stayed the same. Maybe Mr. Em wasn't as sensitive about his looks as I had always imagined.

"It's true," Mr. Em said. "I feel no connection to them. I felt more of a kinship to Sitiu than to any of those men. Hell, I feel more of a kinship with the Big Men Who Live Under the Mountain than I do with Jake McMahon and the other two cretins. Let us stay a few more days and then be off. We have enough gold to begin again."

Jamie nodded. "I agree."

Jamie and Mr. Em took turns on watch that night, but I slept through it all, without dreaming. In the morning, outside in the meadow under that blue, blue sky, everything looked the same: beautiful and comfortable. Jamie and Henry were joking about something as they made breakfast. Mr. Em stood peering into the distance—or into his mind. A hawk called out overhead. I wanted to believe the worst was over.

And then I saw Sitiu standing at the edge of the shadows near the creek.

My heart started racing.

"He's alive!" I screamed.

I'm sure I screamed.

I ran toward him. I had never been so happy to see anyone in my life.

He didn't move as I came toward him. But he watched me. At least I thought he watched me.

I heard Mr. Em calling my name.

Then I stood—in the sun—a few feet from Sitiu.

"Sitiu!" I said. "I am so happy to see you. We were afraid they had killed you."

Sitiu didn't move.

It was then I realized he looked like Henry's mountain lion and Mrs. Peake, the old dead woman I had seen on the wagon train.

I started to cry. I didn't cry often, but there, standing next to this image of Sitiu, I began to cry.

Henry was suddenly next to me.

"What do you see?" he asked.

"Sitiu," I said. I wiped away my tears.

Henry looked where I was looking.

"You mean his ghost?" Henry asked.

I shook my head.

Mr. Em and Jamie were soon standing beside me.

"What is it?" Mr. Em asked.

I didn't want to tell him. Sitiu watched me.

But it wasn't Sitiu. Who was it?

What was it?

"Sitiu," Henry said. "She sees Sitiu."

Jamie said. "What?" He cleared his throat. "You mean like she did on the wagon train? Like with Mrs. Peake?"

Sitiu closed his eyes and then opened them again. "When the light appears, it is time to jump," he said. "It will feel like life and death. You get to choose."

"But I would always choose life," I said.

"What's happening?" Jamie asked.

Sitiu stepped away from us. After a few moments, he disappeared into the creek. I blinked and he was gone. I blinked again and he was standing there near the water, almost invisible in the dappled sunlight that filtered down through the trees.

"Emily," Mr. Em said.

I looked at my father.

"He told me to jump when I see the light," I said. "And that it would feel like life and death and I could choose."

"I think we should leave," Jamie said. He looked downright pale. The freckles on his forehead stood out, as though someone had drawn red dots on him.

We all walked back to camp. No one said anything else about Sitiu. Every once in a while I would glance back toward the creek and see him in the shadows.

After we ate, I asked Mr. Em, "What is he?"

"What do you think he is?" Mr. Em asked.

"Henry asked if he was a ghost," I said. "I don't believe in things like ghosts, do you?"

Mr. Em smiled. "I don't think it matters what I believe. It matters what is true. We don't know what is life and what isn't, do we? Something is different when a being dies. It is without breath, true, but the difference feels greater than that. Bigger than that. Some sort of . . ." He looked around, as though searching for a word in the valley air. "Some sort of spirit inhabits our bodies, it seems. Maybe it wanders around after the body dies."

"If that is true," I said, "why do they look the same as when they are in the body? What I saw looked like Mrs. Peake. What I see looks like Sitiu. But it is not Sitiu. He is very still. Sitiu was rarely still."

"Perhaps you are seeing a personification of the land," Mr. Em said. "Maybe this place wished to convey something to you, so they used the image of Sitiu."

I considered that. "Each place is different," I said. "Each place has a different kind of spirit, doesn't it? A sense about it. Maybe it figures we can only understand another like ourselves." I looked at my father. "Could this be true?"

"I don't really know, daughter," he said. "If that is a ghost of Sitiu, I can't help but wonder what it means. I am made up of the parts of many different people. What happened to the spirit that inhabited these body parts? Are they wandering the Earth looking for that which belonged to them? Or did they all merge into this body as the spark of life brought me alive?"

I had never heard my father talk like this. I was puzzled—and a little alarmed.

"Perhaps all these years I have been haunted," he said, "or my actual existence is the result of an elaborate haunting."

I stared at him. He looked at me and seemed to suddenly realize his error.

"I am sorry, daughter," he said. "I do not know why you are seeing Sitiu or why he has given you this message. I am sure in the fullness of time it will all become clear. Or is that what worries you?" He patted my hand. "You have never been a worrier. What has happened?"

"What has happened is that I saw a man gunned down yesterday," I said. "And I know those men will return here."

"I trust your instincts," Mr. Em said. "But I will tell you that I think they are cowards and bullies. Bullies back down when they are threatened with a force mightier than they are, and I am mightier than they are. We will be safe."

Later, we all went to Sitiu's village where everyone was in mourning. Wailing came from all around me, from the people and the land, it seemed. My entire body vibrated. Suddenly I did not want to be around all of these people. In fact, I wanted to be back home in Oregon, safe on my own land, in my own house.

This was unlike me.

It was as if I had become a different person the moment I saw Sitiu gunned down.

And when I think back on it now, how could that not be the case? Henry must have been different, too, and my father, and

Jamie. Shouldn't everyone have been affected by the murder of this man?

We didn't stay long in the village, just long enough to ascertain whether the Indians would attack the gold miners. As far as Mr. Em could tell, they had no plans for revenge against the white men. Mr. Em warned them to stay on guard because Jake McMahon and the others might come to the village. The villagers didn't understand why the white men would want to harm them. The white men were the ones who had killed their Sitiu. It didn't make any sense to them.

It didn't make any sense to me either.

Mr. Em and Jamie took turns on watch again that night. I slept without dreaming.

In the morning, Mr. Em and Jamie told us we would be leaving first thing the next day. We would dig up the gold and pack it before dawn, and then we would leave.

Henry and I went up and sat next to the Old Juniper together.

"I want to try going through the swimming hole before we leave," I told Henry.

"Have you been practicing holding your breath?"

I nodded. I held my breath, and he began counting.

He got to 30 and I still had plenty of breath. By 40, I wished I had taken a bigger gulp of air. But I hung on to 60.

At 75 I let out a gasp and then breathed again.

He shrugged. "Maybe next year," he said.

I shook my head. "No, I don't believe I will ever be back here again," I said.

"Is Sitiu still here?" Henry asked.

I looked around. "Maybe," I said. "I see a kind of light in the shadows across the Meadow from us."

"Does it scare you when you see things like that?" he asked.

"Not usually," I said. "At least I don't think so. But this time, it's strange. I didn't see his grandsons in the village yesterday. You think they're all right? I kept thinking what I would do if someone killed Mr. Em."

"I don't believe anyone could kill Mr. Em," Henry said.

"Sure they could," I said. "He's not immortal. He's a man."

"A very strange man," Henry said.

He said it without malice or judgment. Everything Henry said was without malice or judgment. I laughed.

"Yes, strange but not immortal," I said. "I've seen him bruised. I've seen him bleed."

"You've seen him bleed?" Henry asked. "What color was it?"

"What do you mean what color was it?" I said. "It was green, like my own blood. What color did you think it would be?"

Henry's mouth dropped open.

"What?" I said. "You mean your blood isn't green? Now who's strange?"

Henry gently slugged me in the shoulder. I started to laugh.

"His blood is red, you ridiculous boy," I said.

Henry grinned.

"Let's go to the pool and practice," I said.

We jumped up and followed the path away from Old Juniper and into the woods. At the intersection of trails, Henry said, "I need to run to the privy."

"I'll meet you at the cave," I said.

I started to run in the opposite direction from Henry when suddenly Jimmy Kelly stepped out of the woods in front of me. I started to call out to Henry, but Jimmy Kelly clapped his filthy hand over my mouth.

"Don't say a word and you won't get hurt," Jimmy Kelly said.

I could hear a struggle behind me. Someone must have gotten Henry.

I bit Jimmy Kelly's hand. He yelled and dropped his hand.

With his other hand, he knocked me to the ground.

I saw stars.

"Don't hurt him," someone said. "We need them both alive. At least for now."

Jimmy Kelly tried to pick me up by my arm. I pulled away. He jerked me hard and pulled my arm out of my shoulder socket. I screamed. Kelly immediately stuffed cloth into my mouth. I choked and fell to the ground.

In the next moment, Jake McMahon was leaning over me.

"Try to relax," he said.

He put his foot on my dislocated shoulder and reached for my arm.

That was all I knew until I opened my eyes and saw I was inside a tent or some kind of half-tent, half-building. A lantern cast a golden glow around the enclosure. Henry sat next to me on the cold dirt floor. His hands were tied behind him, and a kerchief covered his mouth.

My shoulder didn't hurt any more. I was so relieved that it took me a moment to realize Jake McMahon and his men had kidnapped us.

Jake McMahon was sitting near us in a chair with his legs crossed and up on some kind of wooden table.

"What do you want?" I asked.

Jake smiled. "How's the shoulder, son?" he asked.

They still thought I was a boy.

"Fine," I said. "You can't keep us here. My father will not stand for it."

Jake McMahon did not seem concerned about my father. I wondered why that was. Nearly everyone—even those people who liked Mr. Em—was slightly afraid of him.

"We can't pan here any longer," McMahon said. "If we stay, the Indians will slit our throats in our sleep."

"It would serve you right," I said.

Henry nudged me. I glanced at him. He wanted me to be quiet.

"We need to move on," McMahon said, "but we don't have any gold. That's because your fathers took it all. It's only fair and right that we get our share."

"We don't have any damn gold," I said. "We came here to fish and swim."

"I'm not stupid, boy," he said, "and if you keep lying, I will beat you until you wish you only had a dislocated shoulder."

For a moment, I thought about telling him I was a girl. Men were supposed to treat girls and women gently, right? I glanced at Henry. His eyes opened wide.

Apparently he thought it was safer if I remained a boy.

Suddenly Jimmy Kelly was there again. He held a knife in one hand. He was grinning. I began to shiver.

"Cut it out, Jimmy," McMahon said. He shook his head. "I am surrounded by degenerates. He's going to take some of your hair to your fathers, to let them know we're serious. If they give us the gold, all will be well for you. If not, we may have to cut off something besides your hair."

Jimmy grabbed some strands of my very short hair and sawed them off. He handed the hair to McMahon and then cut a strand of Henry's long black hair.

McMahon took a red kerchief from his pocket and dropped the hair into it. Then he tied it up and handed it to Jimmy Kelly. A moment later, Jimmy Kelly stepped out of the tent.

McMahon got up from the chair. "What's going on with your hair anyway? I never seen nothing quite that color. You dye it with something?"

"It was part of my initiation into the guild of the Big Men

Who Live Under the Mountain," I said. "I'm one of them now, so they'll protect me with their lives, just like my father will."

McMahon stared at me for a moment, and then he started to leave the tent. He turned back and said, "I won't tie you up or put anything over your mouth, but if you scream or try to escape, I'll hurt your friend there. His father isn't quite as big as yours." He laughed.

"Why did you murder Sitiu?" I asked. "He didn't do anything to you."

"Who is Sitiu?" He said the name differently than I had. It was if he were spitting out the name: "Sit Who?"

"I hope my father doesn't give you a single nugget," I said.

Jake McMahon left the tent. I turned to Henry and untied the kerchief from his mouth.

"Thank you," he said, breathing deeply. "I know where we are. It's just up the ridge from the cave. If we could escape and get to the cave, they would never find us. It's nearly straight down from here."

I nodded. "Okay. Let's try that. Maybe when they fall asleep or something. But if we get caught, he said he'd hurt you."

Henry looked afraid, but he said, "I think it's better if we try to get away. He didn't hesitate to kill Sitiu."

"That's because he thinks of Indians as animals," I said. "I'm hoping he sees us differently."

They left us alone in that tent for hours, sitting close together on the floor, shivering. We thought we might die. I had never thought about dying before and I didn't think about it then: But I knew it was a distinct possibility. I tried to untie Henry's hands, but the knot was too tight and I couldn't get it to move.

"I'm sorry about this," Henry whispered.

"You didn't do it," I said.

"But I should have stopped it," he said. "I'm older and bigger."

"You're not much bigger than I am," I said, "and I beat you at arm wrestling all the time. If you think you should have stopped them because you are a boy and I am a girl, I'm gonna slug you. Besides, I'm the one who sees things that aren't there. I should have seen this coming."

I put my arms around Henry. He leaned against me. I imagined we were the only two people in the world. Just us, just us. No one could hurt us. No one.

"When I'm older," Henry whispered, "I want to explore the world. Or at least part of it. I want to see the creatures, the plants, the mountains, the oceans. I like drawing them. While I'm drawing them I feel as though I'm a part of them, you know. Like I belong to them, or something. You'll come, too. Right? We'll be together. We have to be together."

"Friends forever," I said. "I'd like to explore one place, one place that is mine. Where I can learn every nook and cranny. I'd know all the creatures and they would know me. I would know all the plants and they would know me."

Henry nodded. He was still shivering.

"Why am I shaking?" he said.

"It's fear," I said. "I've seen animals shiver when they're afraid."

"Aren't you afraid?" he asked.

"Yes," I said. "But you're shaking enough for both of us."

"Men aren't supposed to be afraid," he said.

I held him tighter. "Of course men get afraid. Haven't you ever seen your father afraid?"

He nodded. "When my mother died. I was afraid, too. Still seems like the world is emptier with her gone. Wouldn't you like to see your mother again?"

I shrugged. "Maybe. Some day. Sure. See if I look like her."

"You must," he said. We looked into each other's eyes. We

were so close his breath was my breath. "Because you don't look like Mr. Em, except the hair a little."

He gave out one shudder, and then his shivering began to subside. I kept my arms around him.

"I like your idea," he said. "Getting to know one place. Feeling at home there. I promise, Emmy, one day we'll ride around our home, and we'll learn every nook and cranny of it, together. Let's promise to always be together if we get out of this."

"Okay," I said. "And let's promise to always tell each other the truth."

"And to always be friends," Henry said.

"If we're always going to be together," I said, "I'd hope we'd be best friends."

Henry's lips quivered in an almost-smile.

"We'll be out of this soon," I said as I laid my head on Henry's shoulder. I hoped I was right.

When I look back at it now, it's strange what happened next. I figured Jake McMahon would return and engage us in conversation—or something. I assumed we were important to this drama, but I realized later that we were only pieces on a game board. Jake McMahon and his men had no regard for us at all. I couldn't say or do anything to get them to like us or to think twice about hurting us.

At one point, Danny Collins brought us bread and water. Jake McMahon followed him into the tent. With the two men in the tent, it seemed too small—and airless.

"It stinks in here," McMahon said. "Did one of you piss in here?"

Henry had tried to hold it in but after a couple of hours, he had relieved himself in a corner.

"No matter," Jake McMahon said. "You won't be here much longer and we won't be here at all."

McMahon sat in the chair again. Danny Collins moved back

toward the opening flap. He looked mildly uncomfortable. For a moment, I thought I could get him on our side.

"You," McMahon said to me. "Come here."

I got up and walked the few feet to stand before him.

"You're an odd one," he said, "with an odd father. I understand that. My father was odd. And he was strict. Probably a good thing because I was always getting into trouble. I kept running away, too. So one day my father put his mark on me. That's what he called it. His mark. It was a cross, to remind me of the Lord's word. I didn't give a shit about the Lord's word, or anyone else's really. He made a cross. Afterward, I took a knife and carved it out further so that it was an X." He pulled up his right sleeve and showed me the inside of his right forearm. There I saw a two-inch by two-inch X. The scar was pink and raised up from the rest of his arm. "He thought it would keep me home or keep me holy or keep me something. I don't know what he thought. For me, once I put the carving on myself, I felt like a man. I wasn't much older than you are now. I was responsible for my life. And that's what I am now: I am responsible for my life and what happens in it."

I listened and wondered why he was telling me this.

He looked at me. "We haven't heard from your fathers and Jimmy hasn't come back. I think we need to let them know that I'm not negotiating. They give me the gold and I give them you. Period. They don't give me the gold, they don't get you."

He nodded to Danny Collins who then went over to Henry and pulled him to a standing position. Then he pinned Henry's arms to his back—even though his wrists were already tied—and put his hand over his mouth.

"Don't hurt him," I said. "I'll do whatever you want."

"Good," McMahon said. He pulled out his knife. "Straddle that chair, boy, facing away from me. That way you can't get away." I did as he told me. "I'm going to put my mark on you.

Your friend here is going to see what I do and then I'm going to let him go tell your father what I've done. If you scream, I'll cut him, too."

"I don't think I'll be able to help myself," I said, "because it will hurt."

McMahon pulled a kerchief out of his pocket. "Put it in your mouth. You can bite on it or scream into it."

I took the kerchief and put it in my mouth. It tasted like alcohol and filth.

McMahon reached for a liquor bottle I hadn't seen under the table. He poured some of the liquid over the knife. Then he walked around so that he was at my back. I glanced behind me. McMahon situated himself so that Henry could see what he was doing.

"This will hurt," McMahon said, "but think of it this way: After it's over, you'll be a man, and no one will be able to hurt you like this again. Now lift up your shirt."

I did as I was told. Fortunately, I had not started to develop breasts yet, so I could continue to fool McMahon into believing I was a boy.

At first, I thought he was going to make a relatively small mark, like the one he had shown me on his arm. He made the first prick up near my left shoulder blade. I had cut myself accidentally with a knife before. I knew what it would feel like. Only this pain didn't stop right away. McMahon dragged the knife down my back to the right, stopping near my right hip bone.

Time has dulled the memory of the pain. I can't describe in detail what it was like. I remember everything got very still in the tent and silent, even though I could hear Henry struggling against his captor, even though I could hear Jake McMahon's breath as he carved up my back. The blood tickled my back, and it felt like water was dripping onto my skin. I felt temporary relief as Jake McMahon moved the knife away from me. But then he brought it down onto and into my skin near my right shoulder blade and dragged it down again. This time he seemed to go a little deeper into my flesh.

I can't remember if I screamed or cried or moved. I must not have moved because Jake McMahon didn't say a word the entire time.

Then it was over. I dropped my shirt down again.

I staggered to my feet and turned around.

Jake McMahon's knife dripped with my blood. He wiped the blade on his pant leg. Then he looked at Henry.

"Did you see that, boy?"

Danny Collins let Henry go.

"Yes, I saw it," Henry said.

"Danny will take you back to your camp," he said. "You tell them the gold better be at the rendezvous point within three hours or it'll be a finger or ear next."

"I can't leave he—I can't leave him here," Henry said. "Don't make me go."

"Henry," I said. "Please go. It's the only way."

"Cover his eyes," McMahon said. "We don't want him leading his father back here."

"Walk him back to the place where we took them," McMahon said. "Can you find your way back from there?"

Henry nodded. He looked at me, pleading with me again with his eyes. I tried to smile, but I think I grimaced.

Danny tied a kerchief over Henry's eyes.

Then they were gone. I was alone in the tent with Jake McMahon. He looked at me and grinned. "That wasn't so bad, was it?"

I didn't say anything.

"Turn around," he said. I did what he said. He lifted my shirt. "Still bleeding. What? You half pig?" He laughed. "Lean over."

He picked up the bottle of liquor again. I wasn't sure what he was going to do next, but I knew it would hurt. I heard him open the bottle. Then I heard a kind of gurgle as the liquid poured out.

When it hit my skin—my wound—I screamed.

"Shut the fuck up," he said. "I'm trying to help you."

My knees buckled.

"You want a swig?" he asked.

I didn't look at him. I shook my head. I heard him take a drink. "Don't get any ideas," he said. "I'll be right outside."

I heard him walk out of the tent.

I sat on the floor shivering for a few minutes with my eyes closed.

My back throbbed.

I looked at the lantern.

When the light appears, it is time to jump.

I looked around. There was no place to jump to here.

Suddenly I saw a silver path running from where I sat on the ground to the other side of the tent, away from the opening flap. I could hear Jake McMahon moving around outside. Was he whistling? Singing?

If he got drunk, what other injuries would he inflict on me?

My father wasn't going to find me in time.

I had to get away.

I quietly stood and followed the silver path to the other side of the tent. I crouched down and lifted the canvas. It was dark outside, but I could see the way—the silver path led down the ridge toward the cave.

When the light appears, it is time to jump.

The cave. Yes!

"If you have to piss, you tell me," Jake called. "I'll take you into the woods. I don't want you pissing in the tent again. No reason to act like animals."

"Yes, sir," I said.

In the next moment, I lifted the canvas as far as I could and I crawled underneath it. Without hesitating, I ran down the silver path, trusting that it was leading me home—leading me to some destiny I didn't comprehend yet. I tripped once and immediately sprang to my feet.

I could do this, I could do this, I could do this.

I didn't look back. Didn't look back.

I ran for my life.

I ducked into the cave, the cave I could barely see in the darkness. I kept my head down as I hurried to the opening I knew was at the back of the cave. My heart was racing. I stopped at the edge.

I heard the waterfall. But I didn't know where the pool was. I couldn't see it. What if I jumped and landed on stone?

I heard a roar.

It sounded like a lion's roar.

Or what I imagined a lion sounded like.

Then I realized it was a man's roar.

It was Jake McMahon.

He knew I was gone.

But he didn't know where. He couldn't see the silver path.

I could hear him running through the brush.

"I will kill you!" he cried.

And I knew it to be true.

"What do I do?" I said. "What do I do?"

Suddenly I saw light and looked down. The pool below me was lit green. Tiny creatures swam near the surface. My father had told me about phosphorescent fish he had observed while out to sea. Was that what I was seeing now?

When the light appears, it is time to jump.

And then what? I still couldn't hold my breath long enough to reach the hole, swim through it, and get to the creek.

Yes, I could reach it, and then the water would pull me through it.

I heard the roar again.

I took several deep breaths. Held my breath.

Then I jumped.

For a moment, I was flying again.

My body went straight down. I kept my eyes open. The creatures scattered momentarily. I saw jewels strewn all over the sandy bottom of the pool. Emeralds? Diamonds? Rubies? Jade? I wanted to laugh. Had Henry been right? Had his pirate left his treasure here?

I reached for the jewels, reached out, tried to grasp them, but then I saw the hole, the opening, and I felt the tug of water, pulling me, pulling me.

The light went out.

I was running out of breath.

Swimming out of breath.

Only I wasn't swimming any longer. The water was carrying me, sucking me through the opening in the rock and then down. I felt the earth dragging on my body, stones filling me up, the earth tearing at my back.

I breathed water.

And then I stopped moving. Maybe I dreamed. Maybe I passed out. Even now I cannot be certain what happened.

Someone pushed on my back.

I threw up.

I twitched. I felt more earthbound than I had ever been in my life.

I felt big arms lifting me.

"Papa," I cried.

Only it was not my father.

It was so dark.

I was squishy with water.

Later, many years later, I thought it must have been like being reborn.

Then the big arms laid me gently on the ground.

I heard first Henry call my name. And then my father.

I gasped and coughed. I tried to open my eyes and see into the dark. All I saw was a silver path and a big man walking away from me.

Then the path and the man were gone.

My father was lifting me into his arms, crushing me against his chest.

I began to cry.

"I am so sorry, darling daughter," he said. "I am so sorry."

I held tightly to my father as I wept, as he wept.

I was glad to be back, but I knew nothing would ever be the same again.

Chapter Six

I am still fairly confused about the events of that night and the next day or two. But I will try to relay what I think I know to be true in some kind of comprehensible order. Of course, I can no longer be certain what is true and what is another kind of truth—not a lie, not a fabrication, per se. Maybe another way of viewing reality? I don't know. Maybe because so much of it seems fabulous now so my mind rejects it as fact and instead sees it as a waking dream concocted by a rattled imagination.

From what I was able to gather, after Jimmy Kelly came into camp and said Jake McMahon had kidnapped us, Mr. Em and Jamie dug up as much of the gold as they could in a short period of time and gave it to Jimmy Kelly who then left. Soon after Henry came running into camp, yelling and crying after Danny Collins set him loose. Henry told Mr. Em and Jamie what McMahon had done to me, and they realized Kelly had never made it to the rendezvous point—or else he had run off with the gold.

My father and Jamie tracked Jimmy Kelly—in the dark—and found his lame horse and Jimmy dead. His horse must have stumbled on the ridge and Jimmy Kelly fell off and hit his head. Mr. Em and Jamie got the gold from Jimmy Kelly and took it to Danny Collins at the rendezvous place.

A few moments after Collins left, Mr. Em, Henry, and Jamie heard screaming or yelling. They were never certain who screamed or who yelled. They ran toward the sound with my father taking fewer strides than Jamie or Henry, I'm sure. Sometimes when I think of Mr. Em running to find me, I see him as a kind of awkward giant striding over trees, hills—over mountains—to get back to me.

They told me later that they didn't see a Big Man or any Big Men. They found me at the water's edge, soaked and bleeding. Then the day turned gray with dawn. They took off my clothes and wrapped me in a blanket. My father held me, next to the fire, rubbing my arms to keep me warm.

He was careful not to touch my back.

"Is he going to come here to get me?" I asked my father.

He shook his head. "He wanted the gold," he said. "He has the gold. He's long gone."

"I wish he were dead," I said.

"There's gravel in your back," Mr. Em said, "in the cuts. We need to get it out."

"Can't we leave it?" I asked. "I don't want anyone to see it. I don't want anyone to touch it. It hurts."

"I know, daughter, I know."

Jamie and Henry left to find the sheriff. After Henry was out of my sight, I started to feel panicky. Where was he? Would he be back? Would I ever see him again? I didn't understand what was happening to me. Why was I suddenly so afraid?

"Mr. Em," I said. "Where's Henry? I want Henry back."

"He'll return soon," Mr. Em said. "Come. I think the women in the village can help you."

I got dressed. Mr. Em saddled my horse. I got on, and he led me and Holiday through the woods to the Indian village.

Once at the village, Mr. Em lifted me from the horse and the village women took me away. We sat on the grass, in the sun, and they looked at my back. At first they were very quiet.

One of them burned sweetgrass or sage and blew the smoke over me. I cried. They began to sing. Or maybe they were talking. I didn't know. I lay on my stomach on the cool grass while they worked on my back.

Every time they removed a piece of gravel, I felt immense relief.

After a while, they put a soft shirt on me and brought me something to eat.

My father came to me then. He looked older than I ever thought he could be. Wrinkles ran up and down his face like newly discovered rivers. In the sunlight, I saw where his hair was turning white in areas and red in others. I guessed his hair would soon look like mine—and I was right. Within months, his hair was white except for the streaks of brown and red running through it. There was no mistaking then that we were father and daughter.

But now, the women handed me a small leather pouch.

"What is this?"

One of the women pointed to my back and said something.

My father said, "These are the stones they picked out of your back."

I held out the pouch to her. "No, thank you. I don't want them."

None of the women would take the pouch back.

"Like gold," one of them said.

I set the pouch on the ground. One of the women leaned over

and picked it up. She handed it to Mr. Em. He opened it, held out his palm, and poured the gravel onto it.

Only it was not gravel.

Unless gravel can be made from gemstones.

I stood up and gazed at the stones on my father's palm. It looked like he had a handful of emeralds, rubies, jade, diamonds, and more rocks.

My father said something to the women. They nodded.

"They got these from your back," he said.

"What?"

Mr. Em asked the women again.

I stared at the stones. Wouldn't Henry be pleased? I had somehow stumbled upon his pirate's treasure.

Or something.

Mr. Em put the stones back into the pouch. He held out the bag to me. "It's yours," he said. "You get to choose what to do with them."

"Give them to the women," I said. "I don't want them."

Mr. Em didn't hesitate. I don't believe he had a greedy bone in his body. He held out the pouch to the women and said something to them.

None of them would take the pouch. The women embraced me, one by one, and then left me and my father alone.

"You can have it," I said. "You can have it all."

"There's a fortune in this pouch," he said. "You won't have to worry about money for the rest of your life."

"And I'll have Jake McMahon's mark on me for the rest of my life, too, won't I?"

I remember saying that. I remember feeling old, as old as the mountain which suddenly felt like my kin.

Wasn't my father supposed to protect me from monsters like Jake McMahon?

Mr. Em cleared his throat.

"What?" I said.

"The women said there's more," he said. "They couldn't get all of them out. My guess is that as you heal, your body will push the rest of the jewels out."

I didn't say anything. I wanted to scream.

"Do you want to tell me what happened?" Mr. Em asked.

"No," I said. "I want to scream."

"Go ahead," he said. "Scream."

I opened my mouth and screamed. The sound was so loud, the trees shook.

The scream ended in a wail and then in sobs.

My father put his arms around me and held me.

Eventually I pushed away from him.

"You said Jimmy Kelly is dead?" I said.

My father nodded.

"I want to see him," I said.

"No, Emily, you don't need to see him."

"Yes. He's the one who took me. He put his grimy hand over my mouth. I bit him. I tasted his flesh. And now he's dead. I want to see him. I want to know he's really dead."

My father shook his head. "That is too ghoulish," he said. "I can promise you that he is dead."

"I want them all to be dead," I said.

Mr. Em pressed his lips together. I thought he might try to talk me out of my anger. Before this day, before this moment, I had never wished anything dead, let alone another human being. What he said was, "I understand, daughter."

How could he possibly understand? He was a big man. No one had ever hurt him. I wished I was big. I wished I was the size of a mountain. Then I would crush Jake McMahon and everyone like him.

"I need to go to the miners' camp and tell the other men what happened," he said. "And have them help me bury Jimmy Kelly. Are you ready to go now?"

I looked around. I preferred staying in the village to going back to camp right now. I was still worried Jake McMahon was lurking around somewhere. But I nodded, and I went with my father. I don't remember if I said goodbye to anyone. Did I thank them?

We returned to our camp, left Holiday with the mules and Mountain, and then we walked to the miners' camp. I stayed behind Mr. Em so that I would be safe from briar bushes this time.

Before long, we reached the clearing. None of the men were there, so Mr. Em called out to them. Before long, the six men gathered around my father.

"Jake McMahon, Jimmy Kelly, and Danny Collins kidnapped our children," Mr. Em said. "They wanted our gold. We gave it to them. Simmons has gone to fetch the sheriff. If any of you helped them hurt our children, if you abetted them in any way, you are to blame for what happened."

I stepped around Mr. Em. I turned away from the men and lifted my shirt to show them my back. I heard gasps. I kept my shirt up. Finally Mr. Em patted my shoulder and I dropped my shirt.

"Jake McMahon did that," Mr. Em said. "He is a sick and dangerous man. If you know where he is or where his people are, in good conscience, you must tell me now."

First White Man said, "We are all so sorry that this happened to you and your family. But none of us had anything to do with it." The other men nodded.

Mr. Em didn't say anything for a moment. He looked angry again. I wondered what he was thinking. I bet all the men wondered what he was thinking.

Wondered what he was going to do.

"Jimmy Kelly is dead," Mr. Em said. "You best help me bury him before the animals get to him."

All six men somberly walked behind us as we headed back toward our camp. My father wanted me to stay in camp and wait for him while they buried Jimmy, but I refused.

"What if Jake McMahon comes and takes me again?" I asked.

Mr. Em didn't have an answer to that, so I continued on with the rest of the men.

Jimmy Kelly was lying at the bottom of a rocky escarpment, his lame horse standing not far off. His dirty white hair was like a light in the forest. I ran to him before my father could stop me. His body was strangely askew, his legs and arms at odd angles from his body. The palm of his right hand was up and open. This was the hand he had put over my face. I leaned down and looked at this hand. It was dirty, as I had thought. I didn't see my bite marks. Was it this hand or the other that had knocked me to the ground and then jerked me back up so hard I dislocated my shoulder?

His eyes were closed.

Did that mean he died slowly? All the dead animals I had ever seen always had their eyes open. Except for our old mare Allspice, who died in her sleep.

I heard a rifle clicking closed. I got up quickly and turned toward the sound.

First White Man was aiming his gun at the lame horse.

"No!" I screamed.

Startled, First White Man dropped his rifle to his side.

"Emily." Mr. Em came to my side. "The horse is lame. It's the merciful thing to do."

"Maybe it's only bruised," I said. "Maybe the Indians could help her. Or you. You're good with animals. Did you check? Did anyone check?"

I heard the panic in my voice, and I'm certain my father heard it, too.

He walked over to the mare, knelt to the ground, and felt her front right leg. She didn't want him to touch it, but eventually he was able to palpate it.

After a moment, Mr. Em stood.

"I can feel the splinter," Mr. Em said. "It can't be mended."

"Maybe it can," I said. "Maybe the Big Men could fix her. They saved me."

"They kept you from drowning," he said, "but they didn't heal your back."

I shook my head. "So what? Maybe they could fix her broken leg. Isn't it worth a try? I would wait here with her."

I looked around to see if any silver paths showed up to lead the way for me.

Nothing.

"Em," my father said. "If we don't put her down now, wolves or mountain lions are going to tear her apart tonight. I'm surprised it hasn't happened already. Isn't it kinder if we put her down?"

"Is that what you want to do to me now?" I screamed.

I was marked. *I* was damaged. *I* was all but lame. We were the same, me and the horse.

Weren't we?

"Emily," Mr. Em said, taking a hold of my arms. "It is not the same. You will get over what has happened to you. You will heal. I promise."

I pulled away from him and ran into the woods. I didn't stop running until I reached the Meadow. I realized I was alone. My heart began to race in a panic. Then I ran toward Old Juniper. I followed the invisible silver path until I was behind the juniper. Then I curled up against her and the rocky mossy ground.

I slept.

For ages.

I dreamed the Big Men came to visit me. So did the Mountain. And Sitiu. We danced. The flowers danced with us. They told me many things. I tried to memorize every word they said for when I woke up. *If* I woke up. Sitiu had said it would be a choice between life and death, and it was. I liked being with the Mountain and Old Juniper. For a while, I had the mother I never knew I missed.

I shrunk and grew a shell like a pillbug.

Nobody was ever going to find me. Even if they came looking.

I never heard the shot that put the horse out of her misery. I didn't hear the pickaxes digging up the earth to bury poor Jimmy Kelly.

That's how I thought about him: poor Jimmy Kelly. He wasn't so much older than I was then. Now he was dead.

They told me later that Henry came to Old Juniper several times and didn't see me. Everyone was looking for me.

Then Henry stood by Old Juniper and asked her to give me up.

That was when the invisible became visible. Henry saw me by the old tree. He lifted me up and carried me in his arms as though he was one of the Big Men. Gradually I stirred, threw off my shell, and uncurled myself.

Unfurled myself?

I put my arms around Henry's neck and began to cry or moan.

Did Henry whisper, "Don't ever leave me again?"

And did I promise, "I won't?"

Later he swore this was what happened, but I didn't remember it. Not for a long time. I only knew that I came back to this world in Henry's arms.

After Henry brought me back to camp, after I could stand

on my own feet again, Mr. Em didn't ask me where I had been. I went into our tent. The clothes I had been wearing when they found me by the creek still lay in a bundle on the floor. I picked them up and carried them outside. I walked to the creek and stood at the edge. I didn't know if I wanted to hurl the clothes into the water or if I wanted to wash them.

I shook out the shirt. Sand went flying everywhere. The green fabric was stained nearly black from my blood—the same color as Sitiu's back when he was killed.

I dropped the shirt onto the ground. I picked up my pants and shook them. Sand flew again, but I heard something rattling in my pockets.

I hadn't had anything in my pockets.

I reached into the left-hand pocket.

I felt rocks.

I pulled them out.

They were jewels. Much bigger jewels than the ones they'd found in my back.

I reached into my other pocket.

More gems.

I dropped the pants and held the gemstones in my hands. I could feel them pulsing, as though they were alive. Maybe they were.

How had they gotten in my pockets? I figured when the water pushed me along the creek bed was how the little gems had gotten scraped into my wound.

But that didn't explain these.

They were beautiful.

And I didn't want them.

I moved closer to the water. I bent over with the intention of dropping them all into the creek.

Just then I saw Sitiu across the stream.

I stood again.

"Thank you," I said. "You saved me."

He shook his head. "You saved you." I could tell he was looking at the jewels in my hand.

"I'm putting them back," I said. "I don't want them. If I keep them, I'll just be another greedy bastard like Jake McMahon."

I didn't like saying his name.

"They are a gift," Sitiu said. "They will be of value to you."

"I'd rather have air," I said, "or Old Juniper. I'd rather have fish to eat, water to drink. I'd rather have a place to run, free from people like . . . like him."

I was going to cry again, and I did not want to cry.

Sitiu nodded. For a moment—only a moment—it was as if I were looking at the living breathing Sitiu again, as though he was going to start running along the stream, laughing and telling a story I couldn't understand because I didn't know his language.

"It is a gift," he said. And I knew then that I couldn't refuse it. I had to take it. So I stuffed the stones into my pockets.

When I looked up again, Sitiu was gone.

I left my old clothes creekside and went back to camp.

The sheriff and posse—which included Jamie and the other miners—caught Danny Collins with part of the gold. He swore he didn't know where McMahon was headed.

They never found any trace of Jake McMahon or the gold he stole.

The wound on my back began to heal. Every once in a while it would itch. I did everything in my power not to scratch, but every once in a while, I couldn't resist. Every time I raked my fingers across the becoming scars, another tiny gem popped out. I would look at it and then add it to the pouch my father kept for me.

Our fathers dug up the rest of the gold and split it.

One day Henry and I sat close together by the Old Juniper. We would be parting ways the next day, at least temporarily.

"I'm sorry I had to leave you," Henry said. "In the tent."

"You had to go," I said. "I wanted you to go. It was easier getting free on my own."

An eagle flew above us. We watched it for a few minutes.

"Emily, I want you to put an X on my back," he said.

"No!" I said. "Why would you say that? That's horrible."

"That's what a best friend would do," he said. "If you're hurt, I should hurt. If you're scarred, I'll be scarred. We'll become like blood brothers."

I shook my head. "Then you would be forever marked like I am. What wife would want you? No."

"Do you think having a mark on your body will change your life?" he asked.

"It already has," I said. "Look, I've got the strange hair and strange eyes. Now I have this thing on my back."

"Which no one will ever see," he said. "Besides, I'm going to be your husband, and you wouldn't care if I had a scar."

"What do you mean I'm going to be your wife?" I said. "Who says? I don't plan on being anyone's wife! I don't see how being a wife ever helped anyone."

Henry thought about that. Then he said, "When we were talking, you know, when we were captive, I figured we'd be married, in the future. If you were my wife and I was your husband, we could always be together. No one could separate us."

"No one will separate us," I said.

"We can talk about this in a few years," he said.

"Henry, I saw the light," I said, "like Sitiu said. There were fluorescent fish or bugs or something in the pool."

"Or maybe the Big Men or the mountain lit the way for you," he said.

"I thought I saw jewels at the bottom of the pool," I said.

"I tried to grab them and then the water pulled at me and I shot through the hole. But I couldn't breathe. I drowned, or close to it, and the Big Men—or a Big Man—saved me. When you go through the hole, do you get dragged along the river bottom?"

"No," he said. "Is that what happened to you?"

I nodded. I leaned forward and lifted my shirt so Henry could see my back.

"Oh man," he said.

"Is it that bad?"

"It is pretty bad," he said.

"Is it healing?" I asked. "Will it scar or will it completely heal?" I already knew the answer to that, but I was hoping I was wrong.

"It will scar," he said. "There's something underneath the cuts."

"It's gravel," I said, "from when I was dragged along the river bottom."

"I can see one right here," he said. "A piece of a stone popping out."

"Yeah," I said. "It does that. If you can get it, will you pull it out?"

"Won't that hurt?"

"No."

A moment later, I felt a great sense of relief—like when you pull out a sliver. I sighed, grinned, and dropped my shirt.

Henry held the stone out to me.

"It's a diamond," he said. "You had a diamond in your back."

I looked at the small cut diamond. "Yup. You have it now."

"What? No! It's yours."

"I don't want it," I said. "It reminds me of what he did."

"Why?" Henry asked. "He didn't do this. The river did this. Or the Big Men. Or something. Not him."

"Please keep it," I said. I reached into my pocket and pulled out a handful of the jewels I had been hiding. "Open your hand." I poured the jewels into his hand. "And these are yours, too. I figure being best friends is like being partners, so we should split everything evenly."

"Was this all in your back?"

I laughed. I don't know why. It seemed funny imagining all these big jewels coming out of my back.

"No, they were in my pockets," I said. "I don't know how they got there. Maybe I grabbed them and don't remember, but I dreamed—or remembered—that the Big Men were crying or talking or something when they found me and they stuffed the gems into my pockets, trying to make me feel better. Or maybe I made that all up. I don't know. Maybe that creek is filled with jewels and we don't know it."

"We worked on that creek for weeks," Henry said. "We only found gold. I can't keep these, you know."

"I was told the gems are a gift to me," I said, "and I get to do whatever I like with them, and I want to give them to you."

"We need to tell our fathers," Henry said.

I reluctantly agreed. At dinner that night, Henry and I emptied our pockets and showed our fathers what we had.

Jamie was speechless.

Mr. Em looked at me.

"They were in my pockets," I said. "In the pants I was wearing when I was kidnapped."

Mr. Em frowned.

"I saw more at the swimming hole, " I said, "the one by the cave."

"I've been swimming there many times," Henry said, "and I never saw anything, so I think they wanted Emily to have them."

"Who is they?" Jamie asked.

Henry didn't say anything, and I didn't feel like enlightening Jamie—mostly because I didn't know who the they was.

"I tried to put the jewels back in the creek," I said, "but Sitiu told me I shouldn't refuse a gift."

My father didn't say anything. I wonder now, looking back at all of this, what on Earth he must have thought about what I was saying. Did it seem bizarre? Did he wonder about my sanity? I didn't know.

"I gave half of the gems to Henry," I said.

Mr. Em nodded. "Good. This is what I think: We can't tell anyone about this. Maybe you found the pirate treasure. Maybe in this spot jewels bubble up from the mountain. Maybe that's nature's way here. Or perhaps the Big Men are your protectors. I don't know the truth of any of this, but if we tell people about this, the land will be overrun—even more than it will be now because of the gold."

"But won't people figure it out," Jamie said, "if we try to cash it in?"

"If we decide to cash it in, we can go to Portland or San Francisco," Mr. Em said, "where no one knows us. What do you say? I shudder to think what would happen to Sitiu's village if this got out."

"What about the women who treated my wound?" I asked. "They saw the jewels."

Mr. Em nodded. "I will speak to them and the other villagers and let them know that it would be dangerous to tell other white people. And we should probably not even talk about it to one another, in case someone overhears us. Agreed?"

"Agreed," Jamie said. Henry and I nodded.

I gave the rest of the gems to Mr. Em. "You take care of them," I said. "I don't know what to do with them."

The next day we broke camp. We tried to make it look as though we had never been there. Henry and I said goodbye to

Old Juniper, to the creek, the Meadow. To the sky and the mountain beyond. We left an offering of tobacco and alcohol.

The four of us rode together for a while, and then we parted company. I reached out my right hand to Henry as he reached his out to me. We each grasped the other's wrist and held firmly.

I never wanted to let go.

"Don't disappear on me again," he said.

"I won't," I said. "Try and visit me in my dreams. You never know."

Then, slowly, we ungrasped our fingers. I missed him immediately, even as I looked at him and he looked at me.

A few moments later, when Henry and Jamie were out of sight, Mr. Em and I headed for home.

Chapter Seven

I wish I could say that when we returned to Oregon life went on blissfully from there. But my transition to home life did not go well. I had nightmares nearly every night for weeks. During the day, my back itched and ached and occasionally bled when one of the stones pushed through my scars.

I asked the doctor if he could open up the wounds again and take out the stones. He told me that would be cruel and it would put me at risk of infection.

I had never been a particularly angry or willful child, but I became one almost overnight. When my back would start to itch, I'd pick up something fragile, and then with a great cry, I'd dash it to the ground, relishing the sound of whatever it was breaking to pieces—usually something glass or porcelain.

My father didn't know what to do with me or for me. He brought Indian Mary in to live with us. At first Betsy Shaw was annoyed, but then the two of them became friends as they tried to help me.

I didn't want their help.

I wanted to go back in time and stop what had happened to me.

If I couldn't do that, I wanted Henry.

Sometimes I let Betsy Shaw and Indian Mary near me. Indian Mary would rub healing salve onto my back while Betsy Shaw read me stories. Every once in a while, a gemstone would pop out of the X on my back while Indian Mary was putting on the salve. She'd show the gem to me, and I'd tell her to keep it. She refused. Then I'd try to give it to Betsy and she'd refuse, too.

When the itchiness got bad, I wept in frustration. Eventually Betsy Shaw got witch hazel from somewhere and Indian Mary added it to the salve, and the itchiness began to wane. I prayed to the witch hazel tree—which I had never seen—and sometimes she showed up in my dreams as a woman dressed in white—or a woman who glowed white. She sang to me while she rubbed my back. Her fingers didn't touch my skin. Instead, they went deep into my body. I asked her to say hello to Old Juniper for me—I figured all trees must know all other trees.

My father was trying to buy property in California so we could move, but my condition kept him close to home. Often I didn't want to see him. Other times, I wanted him to be closer than my own skin.

One night after I woke up screaming from another nightmare I could not remember, Mr. Em sat in a chair next to my bed and held my hand.

"Do you remember how you and Henry practiced being invisible?"

I nodded.

"And you floated away?"

I nodded again. The nightmares left me speechless.

"Why don't you try that again," he said, "only don't go too far away—just make yourself invisible to the nightmares. But we need to figure out how you can get back home first, to your body again, after you've been invisible."

That wasn't really being invisible, I wanted to tell him. That was leaving the Earth. That was becoming part of the Sky.

"I know," he said. Reading my mind again. "When I squeeze your hand that means you have to come back. How does that sound?"

I nodded.

I closed my eyes and tried to remember what Henry had taught me about being invisible. I hadn't done it for a while. I had to be still, I remembered. Breathe deeply and be still. Imagine myself as the air, the wind, the mountain, the sky. The stillness, that was the key.

I felt myself sinking into the bed.

And then I was rising up, up. Up into the night sky.

I could see our house, our land, our village.

Higher. The ocean. Ahhhh. The mountains.

I wondered where Henry was.

As soon as I thought it, I was in his bedroom, looking down on him. He was sleeping, curled up beneath his blankets. He looked bigger than the last time I had seen him, which had only been a few months. And he looked like the child he was, too.

I lay on the bed next to him and pressed my back up against his.

I heard him murmur, "Emmy."

I smiled, closed my eyes, and fell asleep.

After a time, I felt someone squeezing my hand.

I opened my eyes, and I was in my own bed.

It was morning.

"How was that?" Mr. Em asked. He looked disheveled, and I wondered if he had fallen asleep in the chair.

"No nightmares," I said. I started to tell him that I had found Henry—because I used to tell him everything. But I didn't. I felt strangely distant from him, and that made my heart ache.

Would things ever be the same again?

Eventually my wounds—physical and spiritual—healed over. I was able to sleep through the night without nightmares or itching. Plus, school began again. I made friends with two new girls: Laurel and Katie. I still missed Henry, but it was nice not to be alone at school. Laurel and Katie were more interested in indoor things than I was—clothes, cooking, sewing, hair—but they also liked my stories about fairies, Big Men Who Live Under the Mountain, and talking trees. I never told them any real life stories about me. I didn't tell anyone about what happened to me in the Meadow. Slowly, the memories of that time receded. After a while, I started to wonder if any of it had actually happened. Until I'd catch a glimpse of my back while I was dressing or undressing. Or when I'd wake up in the morning to find another gem in my bed, excreted from my back while I slept.

Once I seemed back to normal, my father left for California to look at properties there. He asked me if I had any particular requirements for our new home. I didn't say what we both knew: I didn't want to live anywhere near the Meadow.

"Lots of open spaces," I said, "where I can run forever. And a big sky. Maybe a forest where Jamie's fairies can live. And water, of course. There should be water. And no gold. No gold anywhere on the land."

Before Mr. Em left, he embraced me and lifted me off the floor as he had done many times before. He wanted to keep holding me, but I wriggled free—and he set me down as soon as I pushed away. He looked startled.

He looked hurt.

I wanted to tell him to try again. I bet I could hang on for longer. But I didn't say anything to reassure him.

He said, "You're getting too old for your old dad, aren't you?"

I made myself laugh. "Never, Mr. Em."

"Are you old enough to call me Papa yet?" he asked.

I didn't answer him. Instead I said I had to go meet Laurel and Katie.

"Have a good trip, Mr. Em!" I called as I ran away.

I knew I was being cruel to him, but I couldn't make myself act any other way. I wasn't sure then why I was angry with him or why I didn't feel the same about him any longer, but now I understand that I blamed him for what had happened to me. He was the biggest and strongest man in the world: He should have been able to protect his one and only daughter.

Some weeks later, Mr. Em returned home. He told me he had purchased a ranch alongside another ranch—one that Jamie Simmons now owned. Both ranches were thousands of acres. I didn't really know how big an acre was, but I figured thousands of acres must be huge—especially when Mr. Em told me it was a hundred times more land than we had now.

I didn't care. As soon as he told me Jamie and Henry would be living next door to us, I was ready to leave without a backward glance. Mr. Em quickly sold the mill and our house and land. Indian Mary decided to stay behind and return to her own house. Mr. Em gave her enough money to live comfortably for the rest of her life. He offered the same to Betsy Shaw, but she chose to come with us.

At school, they threw me a bon voyage party with cookies and cake. I looked around the room and felt no affection for any of them, not even for Laurel and Katie or my teacher. I ate the cake and tried to smile, but I suddenly wondered if something was terribly wrong with me. Maybe when Jake McMahon carved up my back, he had killed whatever was good in me. As far as I could tell, I didn't love anyone any more, not even Mr. Em. What if we got to our new home and I didn't love Henry any more either?

I felt crushed by this prospect. I couldn't stay in the school room any longer. I dropped my cake and began to run. I don't know if anyone called after me or tried to stop me. I opened the door and ran and ran. My heart was racing. Maybe that awful boy who had told me I was a monster and a monster's daughter had been right. Jake McMahon had seen that in me. That was why he had put his mark on me: Now everyone would know that I was a monster, too.

I ran right into our house and into Mr. Em's office. Mr. Em was sitting at his desk, writing.

"What is it?" he asked as he got up from his chair.

"I don't love anyone!" I said. "I am a monster. They were right! That's why he did this to me. He could tell he and I were alike."

Mr. Em knelt before me. He put his hands on my arms, but I shook them off. Tears streamed down my cheeks and into my mouth and down my neck.

"No," he said. "You are nothing like him and you certainly aren't a monster."

"I don't feel anything!" I cried. "I don't care that we're leaving this place. I don't care that I'll never see Indian Mary again. I don't care about Laurel or Katie. I don't care. I don't love anything or anyone any more!" I sobbed.

"I know it must feel awful," he said. "I've felt that way before."

"You mean there are times when you haven't loved me?" I asked. "Because I don't love you and it feels horrible."

"I have always loved you," Mr. Em said.

"What if I don't love Henry? Only monsters don't love, right?"

"I don't know," he said. "Maybe monsters love. Some people call me a monster, and I have loved you every moment of your life."

"I've never loved Juliet Lee," I said. "Everyone loves their mother, but I don't." I was hiccupping as I cried.

"You loved her when you knew her," Mr. Em said. "It's there, darling daughter, I promise you. I promise you that you still love me and you still love Henry. You love the sky and the trees and the land and Betsy Shaw and Indian Mary. You've had your heart broken, and while it's mending, your feelings have gone into hiding. But they will come back."

"When?"

"I don't know," he said.

"How do you know they'll come back?" I said. "You don't know everything and you can't do everything."

"I know that, daughter," he said, "but I promise you—I swear to you—that you will love again. I swear on everything that is holy."

"You don't consider anything holy," I said. My sobs had almost stopped. I wiped the tears away with my sleeve.

"The word holy comes from the German word that means whole," he said. "And I consider many things whole. You are whole."

I shook my head. "He had my blood on him, on the knife. He wiped it on his dirty pants as though it was nothing. As though what he had done was nothing! He took a part of me away with him. That means I am not whole."

Mr. Em put his hands on my arms again. "Look at me," he said.

I looked at my feet.

"Daughter, I want you to look at me."

I looked up into his green eyes. It was like looking into a beautiful forest.

"No part of you is any part of him," he said. "You are whole. You are holy. You are yourself and no one else."

"But you've always told me that we're all a part of each other," I said. "And we are all equal."

"I didn't mean that literally," he said. "It was my way of encouraging you to treat all people as equals."

"But people aren't equal," I said. "They are not the same. Or if they are the same, then I am as bad as he is."

"No part of you is any part of him," he said again. "You are whole. You are holy. You are yourself and no one else."

I nodded.

He dropped his hands from my arms—probably because he knew I didn't want to be touched.

"And I think you're right," he said, "we aren't all equal—but not because of our sex or skin color or station in life. We become unequal because of our actions. But don't let his actions take away anything from you. He is the criminal, not you."

Even though I felt reassured by my father, I was still worried I wouldn't love Henry when I saw him again. But just then, I let my father take my hand and we went into the kitchen together where Betsy Shaw made us something to eat.

I nervously helped prepare for our move. I decided I would know one way or another if I was a monster or not once I saw Henry. If I felt nothing for him, that would mean I was broken beyond repair.

Wouldn't it?

Betsy Shaw left before us, along with a wagon or more filled with our belongings.

My father and I went on horseback. For some time, we followed the same route we had taken to go to the Meadow. I kept a lookout for the Big Men Who Live Under the Mountain, but I didn't see or sense anything. I was relieved when we headed west and south of where we had been last year. I did not want to accidentally run into Jake McMahon.

As we traveled further south and west, I felt a pall begin to lift from my soul. I began to talk more and joke around with Mr. Em. Mr. Em immediately joined in, ignoring the fact that I had said little to him for a year or more. Soon enough we were on our land. I got off Holiday, said a prayer, and dropped sweet-grass from my fingers. It had been a while since I had given thanks for anything, but I gave thanks for our new home and I asked the spirits of the place to allow us safe passage.

We traveled over greens hills and down into steep canyons. We saw trees and shrubs I didn't recognize. We passed by clumps of prickly pear cacti—my father told me the name—and I jumped off Holiday so I could see my first real life cactus up close. I gently touched the thorns. I knew if I pressed a little harder, the thorn would draw blood. I'd have to remember never to get in a fight with a cactus because it would win.

We saw hawks and eagles riding the thermals above us. They reminded me of home, and I felt a momentary pang of home-sickness. We passed through a thicket of scrub oak—never my favorite tree—and we made certain the horses skirted around the accompanying poison oak, for our sake more than for theirs. I had never seen a horse catch poison oak, but I had been tortured by it several times when I was younger.

I felt welcomed by the land. I can't really articulate what that meant at the time—maybe it was because I didn't feel weighed down any longer. Maybe it was because I was laughing and talking again. I felt like I had come home. It was similar to the feeling I had had when we first arrived at the Meadow. But I didn't think about that then. I was glad to be . . . happy.

I had not seen anything "invisible" on this trip. In fact, I had not seen anything invisible since I had last seen Sitiu—unless one counted my nighttime visits to Henry when I was having nightmares. I didn't mind not seeing invisible silver paths or invisible people and animals. I knew my abilities to see what wasn't there had probably saved my life when I escaped Jake McMahon, but I wanted an ordinary life. Ordinary people did not see silver paths or spirit animals. At least, that was what I believed at the time. Of course, I had no idea what having an ordinary life entailed.

I still don't.

Finally we rode down a long drive. When the house came into view, I was shocked. It was a huge old Spanish Colonial building sheltered beneath giant sycamore trees. I looked around and saw barns and other buildings. Beyond them, green hills rolled away into the distance. Above, the sky was big and blue.

"We must be very rich," I said to Mr. Em.

"We are," he said. "And the family who owned this was eager to sell."

As we neared the house, I could see people milling around outside. I squinted. Looked like Betsy Shaw. Was that Jamie? Where was Henry?

Holiday began trotting toward the house. Maybe I had kicked her. I don't remember. I only remember I needed to go faster.

Where was Henry?

There. That tall boy. Was that Henry?

I stopped Holiday and slid off her. Henry was running toward me.

I started to laugh. Yes, that was Henry, my best friend in the world.

I ran toward him. A moment later, we were in each other's arms. He picked me up and twirled me around. I laughed and cried.

I was so glad to see him, smell him, hear him.

Love him.

I felt something break open, break apart.

Or fall into place.

"Put me down," I said, laughing.

He did as he was told. We stepped apart, both of us grinning.

Then we kissed each other on the lips, as we had when we were nearly babies. And then I pushed him, as I had all those years ago. And last year. Only this time, he didn't fall down.

"Wow," I said. "You have grown."

"You, too," he said. "You look like a girl."

"You mean these," I said, pointing to my becoming breasts. "It was bound to happen sooner or later."

"No, I meant your hair. You've grown it out."

I laughed. I couldn't help it. Henry laughed, too.

In the next moments, Betsy Shaw, Jamie, and the others were surrounding me and Mr. Em, and welcoming us to our new home.

The house was huge, but not as big as I first thought. It was a rectangular building with an outdoor courtyard at the center of it. I got my pick of any bedroom in the place, and I chose one that looked out at the rolling hills to the east.

Then Henry and I ran from room to room. He had seen it all before, and he said it was a twin to their house. The houses had been built at the same time for two brothers and their families. I told Henry we should all move in together into one house.

"They talked about it," Henry said, "but Dad is sweet on our new housekeeper, Katherine, and I think they're going to get married. She wanted her own house."

"Do you like her?"

He shrugged. "I don't think she likes me very much," he said.

"Does your dad know? That she doesn't like you?"

"Right now she can do no wrong as far as Dad is concerned," Henry said.

He wasn't telling me something.

"What's going on?" I asked.

"Nothing," he said. Clearly he didn't want to talk about it. I pressed him, but he said, "I'm here and not there, so let me be here."

"What?" I said.

He laughed. "You know what I mean."

Henry stayed the night, sleeping in the room next to mine. I woke up once in the middle of the night. I slipped out of bed, opened the door between our rooms, and tiptoed into Henry's room. I watched him sleep for a time. He looked just like he had when I used to leave my body and wander over to see him some nights.

This time, he opened his eyes.

"Emmy?" he whispered.

"Yes, it's me," I said.

"I used to dream you came to see me," he said.

"I did," I said. "I came all the time. I slept right next to you, with my back pressed up next to yours—the way I slept next to my father when I was too cold. I was having nightmares and it helped to come and see you."

He reached behind him and pulled down the covers.

"It helped me, too," he said. "I had nightmares for a long time."

I climbed in bed next to him. He turned away from me and I pressed my back against his. He sighed, and I could hear the happiness in his sigh.

"Nothing is the same any more," I whispered. I put my hands between my cheek and the pillow.

"No, it's not," Henry said. "But it's going to be better."

"Promise," I said.

"I promise."

In the morning, Henry and I awakened at the same moment. We both sat up, looked at each other, and grinned. Then we saw Betsy Shaw and Mr. Em standing in the open doorway.

"I love it here, Mr. Em," I said as I got up out of bed. "I could stay forever. What's for breakfast?"

I padded out of Henry's room, using the adjoining door. I glanced back and saw Betsy Shaw and Mr. Em watching me. I shrugged and went to my room and got dressed.

After breakfast—porridge and fruit—Henry and I went to the stables, saddled our horses, and rode out onto the land.

"It goes on and on and on," Henry said. "I can't show you every nook and cranny yet, but we can start."

"So is this it, then, home?" I asked, remembering our conversation when we were held captive by Jake McMahon—when Henry promised to show me every nook and cranny of our home.

"Maybe," he said.

And so we spent that first full day riding around my new ranch. Henry showed me Wild Creek and Big River and the forests that ran alongside them. He took me on wild animal trails going up and down the green hills—or maybe they were cattle trails, I didn't know. From afar, many of the hills looked too steep and so crowded with chaparral that we'd never get through, but once we reached them, the way became clear. Sometimes we dropped into gulches and Henry showed me tadpole ponds and tall marsh grass, so different from the nearly desert-like surrounding landscape. In other places, I could smell the ocean, and a hint of fog drifted through sycamore and alder trees. I had never seen so many different landscapes in one area—one huge area. Henry was so excited about it all. He told me he had been drawing all the plants and animals he could find. He was certain some species existed here that no one had catalogued or classified yet. He was thrilled by the prospect of being the first. I was happy he was so happy, and I remember wondering if I would ever have something like that in my life.

"Closer to the ocean are these conifers—redwoods they call them—that seem to go up forever," Henry said, "but that's a long ride away. Redwood House is near there. And the cattle are northeast of here. Dad and Mr. Em are going to get horses, too."

"That's better than cattle," I said.

"What's wrong with cattle?" Henry asked.

"They don't have much personality," I said.

Henry laughed. "And horses do?"

I patted Holiday's neck. "Sure they do." I didn't want to hurt Holiday's feelings. I looked at Henry and shook my head. "At least they're pretty," I whispered.

Henry laughed.

At lunch we sat along the stream and ate sandwiches Betsy Shaw had packed for us. The horses grazed nearby. I breathed deeply the quiet, the cool breeze coming off the creek, the sound of the horses clipping off grass and chewing it, and Henry's sighs as he ate.

"Do you like it here?" I asked Henry.

He nodded. "Especially now that you're here. I missed you. As soon as you left, I missed you."

"Me, too," I said. "I am surprised how much older you look."

"You, too," he said. "You must have grown six inches."

"Do you want to see?" I started to lift my shirt.

"Your breasts?"

I laughed. "No! My back. Why? Do you want to see my breasts? They're kind of strange looking."

"No, I don't want to see your breasts," Henry said. "At least,

I don't think I'm supposed to look at them once they start growing."

"Why? Will they wilt away if someone sees them?"

Henry shook his head. I grinned. It was fun to tease him. I turned around so that my back was toward him, and I lifted my shirt so he could see the scars on my back.

"It's healed up good," he said. "Are stones still coming out of them?"

"Yes, every once in a while," I said. "You can touch it if you want."

"It doesn't hurt?"

I shook my head. I didn't really know if it hurt. Indian Mary was the only one I ever let touch it, and that was because she had to when she was putting on the salve.

Henry didn't say anything at first. A few moments later, I felt his fingers at the beginning of the first cut, near my left shoulder. He traced first one line and then the other.

I shivered.

"Does it hurt now, when I touch it?" he asked.

I couldn't explain how it felt.

Finally I said, "It tickles."

Henry reached out and stroked the scars again.

I was sure that each time Henry touched the scars, they got smaller and smaller.

"Anything going away?" I asked.

Henry said, "Not that I can tell."

Finally I let my shirt fall down again. "I think they're smaller," I said, "even if you can't tell. I can tell, from the inside. It's smaller."

"Man, Emily, I'm—"

"No, don't feel bad every time you see me," I said. "Then it will never be done. I just want us to be Henry and Emily, best friends again."

"We are," Henry said. "I don't feel bad every time I see you. Nothing like that."

"Good," I said. "Now take me to a bird's nest or a rotting carcass or a scary ravine. Show me some of the things only you know."

That night after dinner, Mr. Em came to my room and sat with me for a time.

"How was your day?" he asked.

"It was great," I said. "Best day in a long while. There's this place down by Wild Creek where you can sit on these huge stones and it feels like you're a part of the creek. The sound of the water is all around. Henry calls them Singing Rocks. And up near Berry Ridge—that's what Henry called it—we saw the biggest bird I've ever seen. Huge! It looked like a really big vulture. Henry said it's called a condor."

"Sounds like Henry knows a lot about this place," he said.

Henry was spending the night in the room next to mine again. I glanced over at the door between our rooms. It was slightly ajar.

"Henry knows everything," I said. I got into bed.

"Henry is a good boy," he said. "You seem back to your old self. That must feel nice."

I didn't correct him. I did not feel like my old self. I just felt better.

"Mr. Em, what is it you want to say to me?" I asked. "You look like you've swallowed a porcupine or something equally troublesome."

"You and Henry are growing up," he said. "You are becoming young men and women. Or he is becoming a young man and you will soon become a young woman."

"Yes. And?"

He cleared his throat. "Men and women do not sleep in the same bed unless they are married."

I frowned. "But I've slept with you, and we are not married."

He flinched a bit. "When we are camping we often sleep close together, this is true, but I am your father and you are my daughter. Oh my. This feels really awkward."

I almost laughed at him. I had rarely seen him reticent to say what was on his mind.

"When men and women who are not related are close together like that, in bed, they often experience sexual desires."

"Like when the animals mate?" I asked. "It's not like that with us. Henry and I are best friends."

"Best friends can also be lovers," Mr. Em said. "And he is older than you are. It's a delicate age."

I had liked sleeping with Henry, but it hadn't felt any different from when I had fallen asleep with my father or with Katie and Laurel when I'd slept over at their homes.

"What would be wrong with Henry and I having sex?" I asked.

"You're 12 years old!" Mr. Em said.

My eyes widened at his exclamation.

"Animals are much younger than that when they have sex," I said.

"You are not an animal," he said.

"I am! You taught me that."

"Yes, okay, you are an animal," he said. "But you are a human child, and you are far too young to engage in sexual relations."

"I know," I said. "I don't intend to have sexual relations with Henry or anyone else. I have no intention of getting married. Henry already talked about it. When we were staying in the Meadow. I told him I wasn't getting married ever."

Mr. Em started to say something, but he stopped himself. Looking back at it now and knowing my father as I do, I suspect he was going to tell me that people could and often do have sexual relations without getting married, but then he realized telling me that particular fact would not help his cause at the moment.

"Have no worries, Mr. Em," I said. "Henry and I are the best of friends. So no sex for us."

Mr. Em cringed. Then he slapped his legs and stood.

"Glad to hear it," he said. He leaned over and kissed my forehead. "Sweet dreams."

And he left the room. I put my face in my pillow and laughed. Poor father. When I was sure he was gone, I got out of bed and went into Henry's room. He was sitting on the edge of his bed in the dark. I sat next to him.

"Did you hear all of that?" I asked.

"Yep."

We started to laugh.

"I've never heard Mr. Em at a loss for words," he said.

"The last year or so hasn't been easy on him," I said. "I was . . . not happy."

"My father has tried to talk to me about sex," he said. "He gets kind of stupid. He told me I must respect girls and women and never get naked with them until I'm married."

We laughed again, quietly.

"You know I love you," Henry said. "I still think we should be married one day."

"I know," I said. "I love you, too."

I wanted to say, "Knowing I love you saved my life," but I didn't quite know how to articulate my feelings yet.

We kissed each other in the dark. I felt butterflies in my stomach. I wanted to keep on kissing him.

And I wanted to stop.

So I stopped.

"Can we stay best friends for now?" I said. "So much has changed and happened. I want things to be normal for a while."

"What is normal?" Henry asked. I didn't answer. He nodded. "Like Mr. Em said, we're still kids."

"Just taller and with bigger breasts," I said.

Henry laughed and shook his head. "Guess you better go back to your room."

"Guess so," I said.

We looked at each other and smiled. At the same time, we slipped down under the covers, with our backs to each other.

"Make sure I leave before sunup," I whispered.

He reached over and patted my hip, as if to acknowledge what I'd said.

Then we fell asleep together.

When I woke again, Henry and I were in each other's arms. Not like lovers, but like two friends holding each other in our dreams. Even today, after so many years, the memory of this fills me with such tenderness.

If I'd known what was going to happen, if I had known our future, maybe I would have married Henry then and there. Or maybe I would have run from him and from that place. From everyone I knew and loved.

Instead, I awakened before dawn, disentangled myself from Henry, and went back to my own bed, where I fell asleep and stayed asleep until Betsy Shaw came to wake me.

Chapter Eight

For the next few weeks, I spent most of my time out of doors with Henry. I was only vaguely aware of what was happening on the ranch itself and learned the details only later. After Jake McMahon carved that X on my back, I was oblivious to most of the outside world for many years—unless it came to my doorstep.

It turned out that most of the workers on the ranch were no better than slaves. The former owners had kidnapped or coerced many Indians to the ranch and then kept them in indefinite servitude. The non-Indian workers were also nothing more than indentured servants. My father "freed" them all once he understood what had happened to them. Then he tried to help each of the Indians get back to their people. Many of them had been on the ranch for so long—more than one generation—that they didn't know where their people were and their children could not speak their native languages.

Mr. Em did what he could. He was the most egalitarian person I ever knew. He hired all kinds of people and always had—men and women, Negroes, Indians, Mexicans. If the Chinese had wanted to work on the ranch, he would have hired them, too. Mr. Em told me "our" workers were able to live well because of my generosity.

"My generosity?" I asked. "What do you mean?"

"You want them to have a living wage, correct?"

"Of course," I said. "Everyone deserves to live well." Mr. Em had taught me that.

"It is your treasure that pays them," he said. "It is what the creek gave to you, what the Big Men gave to you."

I was glad for that, I supposed, but truthfully, I didn't much care about anyone else's happiness at that point in my life.

Since I wasn't fond of cattle, my father gradually sold them off and purchased more horses. The main wrangler was a free man called Titus Jefferson. He was gentle with the horses and never let anyone lay a harsh hand on any of them. Most of the other wranglers were Indians, except for Nancy Nichols. (My father was the only one in the area who hired women as ranch hands—although I didn't know this was odd until I was an adult.)

Watching Nichols and Titus with the horses was like watching dancers on the stage. (Yes, my father made certain I had culture in my life. When we lived in Oregon he took me to the theatre. Once we were in California, he had a stage built on our land so that theater companies could work and perform there for all the people who lived nearby.) Nichols was tiny and pale, with short black hair—she was Spanish—and Titus was tall and dark with short curly hair—he was African—and together, they calmed the horses.

Titus was very solemn with the horses, but he was an animated storyteller, and he and Mr. Em competed to see who could tell the most outlandish tales. And Nichols seemed happy all the time—and affectionate. Whenever she saw Henry and me, she opened her arms and kissed and hugged us.

"Children," she'd say in her accented English, "you need as many hugs and kisses as you can get every day of your life." She'd kiss our cheeks or ask Henry to bend down so she could kiss the top of his head. "Especially motherless children. Come, I will be your mother any time you need one!"

I suppose if it had been someone else, we wouldn't have enjoyed the affection or attention, but we liked Nichols. She was silly and wise all at the same time.

"Now put on your hat," she'd say. "Too much sun will give you nightmares."

Or she'd say, "Drink this tea. It'll prevent heartache."

Or, "Remember love is the most important thing. Yes. More important than money. Even more important than horses." Then she'd laugh.

Henry and I both assumed these were the kinds of things a mother would say. We didn't really know, though, since we were motherless children, as Nichols said.

Nichols was also what they called a "curandera"—a kind of healer. She made folk remedies for nearly everything that could ail horse or human. Between her, Rose, and Betsy Shaw, most of the people and animals on the ranch rarely needed to see a doctor.

Nichols helped name the ranch, too.

One day we were all sitting around the long wooden kitchen table, and Mr. Em asked me what we should call the ranch.

"What did the Indians call it when they lived on this land?" I asked.

"Probably many things," Mr. Em said, "since it is a very big ranch. Where the house is, they called it 'refuge from the wind.'"

"I like the idea of a refuge," I said. "But Refuge Ranch sounds strange."

"Refugio," Nichols said. She was sitting across from us. She scooped up beans from her plate with a piece of cornbread. "The Spanish word for refuge is refugio."

I mouthed the word "refugio."

"Refugio Ranch," Mr. Em said.

"Yep," I said.

Jamie named his ranch Paradise.

Soon after we moved to Refugio Ranch, tens of thousands of people began flocking to California to look for gold. Most came from back East, but thousands arrived from other countries, too. They traveled by land and water. Some newspaper writers called them argonauts—like the hero Jason, they were looking for the Golden Fleece.

I didn't see anything heroic about their quest: I was afraid they were all like Jake McMahon. And many comported themselves just like Jack McMahon had. They were violent, greedy, and uncivilized. Or maybe they were actually civilized: They believed they could do whatever they wanted, commit any crime just because they were white and felt they were entitled. They trespassed, they killed Indians, they polluted the waters.

When I first learned about the gold rush, I was terrified. Mr. Em assured me that no one would bother us. He hired security to make certain no one was trespassing on our land or on Jamie's. We were far from any gold strikes, Mr. Em assured me.

I tried to forget about the gold hunters.

Mr. Em had a schoolhouse built on our land. He invited the children of the ranchers and their workers to attend. (Some of the hired help attended, too, when they could, to learn to read and write.) Mr. Em hired a teacher, Miss Irving; she lived in a little apartment at the back of the school. So many children attended that Mr. Em had them build another room and he hired another teacher—Mr. Michaels. Fortunately, Miss Irving and Mr. Michaels fell in love and eventually got married. Mr. Em built them a house on our land. They stayed for several years, until the town got big enough for a school; then Mr. Em helped finance the new school.

For many people, as time went on, Refugio Ranch became a kind of paradise. I didn't realize this for many years. I was glad for all the people we helped. I was glad we created a community—although I recognize now that it wasn't a community of equals. Whoever holds the purse strings controls nearly everything. But Mr. Em did his best. Mr. Em remembered how difficult life had been for him in his early years when he had no money and no prospects. He wanted to alleviate the suffering of others in similar circumstances.

He paid the ranch hands enough so that they could get married and buy land, and he often sold them parcels on the ranch. Our ranch quickly became more like a village than a ranch owned by a single family.

We had our own little Utopia.

Mr. Em also bought a mercantile and mill in the village closest to the ranch. He found someone he trusted to run them. I rarely visited either place and don't have many memories of them.

That first year, Mr. Em was mostly home, establishing the new ranch and making certain I was settling in. He was not interested in the day-to-day running of the ranch. After a few months, he promoted Diana George, one of his ranch hands, to manager. She could rope better, shoot better, and coax better than anyone. Period. Everyone said so. Yet the other ranchers had been hesitant to hire her, especially the Spanish ranchers. Not my father. He knew Diana had to be tough to survive life amongst the other ranch hands, and she was.

Sometimes Henry and I would ride out to wherever Diana

was working so I could watch her. She moved in the world just like Sitiu's grandsons had: She was comfortable in her body, comfortable in this world. If she saw us watching her, she'd say something like, "What are you two beautiful reprobates doing? Get off your asses and help me."

She always found us something to do. We'd help her mend a fence or a saddle or help her rope a horse or a cow. Move a rock. Feed the chickens. Anything.

Other times she told us to go away and have fun. "Enjoy the sunshine!" She knew Henry was taking an inventory of the area flora and fauna, so she'd encourage him to go count and draw. She had an office in the barn, but she didn't like being in it too much. Sometimes we'd pass by the door and she'd be growling about paperwork. Her growl sounded like a wolf's.

Henry and I visited each other nearly every day—the ride back and forth between houses wasn't too long. I liked being at my house better than his, even though they were nearly identical. Our house was always busy and noisy with ranch hands and Betsy Shaw yelling at someone or Titus and Nichols eating and talking about a new horse or Diana and my father discussing— in loud voices—what they needed to do next on the ranch. At Henry's house, their housekeeper Katherine kept things quiet and orderly.

I didn't like Katherine from the start. She was sugar sweet to me. I was suspicious of people who were too nice; I always suspected the niceness was a cover-up for nastiness. Her niceness seemed inauthentic. Katherine always smiled sweetly and asked if she could do anything for me, but once she turned away—to look at Henry, for instance—her smiled disappeared, instantly.

She didn't like Henry. I didn't understand why Jamie or Mr. Em couldn't see it. Because if Jamie saw it, he would fire her, wouldn't he? That's what I believed. Of course, she was sugar sweet to him, too. It was clear to me that she wanted to be mistress of the house, and Jamie was flattered by her attention.

Whenever Katherine came over to Refugio, everyone seemed to like her. Henry tried hard with her, too, which irritated me. He picked flowers for her, waited on her as though he was her servant—fetched her knitting needles, her embroidery, a glass of water. She never liked the flowers, and she always claimed Henry brought her the wrong needles, the wrong embroidery, or the wrong glass of water.

"She isn't nice to you," I told Henry, "so why are you nice to her?"

"She might be my new mother," he said. "I need to make her feel welcome by me."

I made a noise. "I don't see why," I said.

He shrugged. "I'm hoping she'll start to like me. I want my father to be happy."

"She's not your mother," I said. "Even if she married your father."

Henry was not convinced.

I knew something was wrong with her.

I told my father that Katherine was unkind to Henry. Mr. Em asked me for examples. I told him about her constant criticism of Henry.

He said, "Maybe she's a bad-tempered person and it doesn't have anything to do with Henry. She isn't cruel, is she?"

"Isn't it cruel to withhold your affection from a child?" I asked.

Mr. Em thought about it for a moment, and then he said, "I suppose it is."

Then one day when we were all at Refugio for a meal, I noticed Katherine looked at Rose the same way she looked at Henry. Rose worked in the house with Betsy Shaw. She was an Indian who had lived on the ranch all of her life. Mr. Em had tried to find the rest of her family—those who didn't live on the ranch—but he was unsuccessful. She was shy and kind, and she and Betsy Shaw had become great friends. She and her son, Thomas, lived in the house with us and treated us well.

I began watching how Katherine interacted with other people at the gathering. She was effusive with me, with Mr. Em and Jamie, even with Diana and Nichols—although Diana only watched Katherine and didn't say much to her. But Katherine barely said a word to Titus or Betsy Shaw, and she completely ignored Henry and Rose.

Diana saw me watching Katherine. She came over and stood next to me and looked over at Katherine.

"Something not right about that woman," Diana said.

I nodded. Katherine took a kerchief from her bag and wiped off a glass that Rose had brought her. She did it quickly, without anyone else noticing as far as I could tell.

"Rose gave her that glass," I told Diana.

Diana watched.

"And she's not nice to Henry," I said.

Diana looked over at Henry. As he got older, he was looking more and more like his half-Indian mother and less like his Irish father.

"You don't say," Diana said.

Katherine didn't like Indians or blacks?

Henry walked by Katherine, and she moved out of his way so that not even the hem of her dress touched any part of him. Her facial expression did not change, but I saw hatred on her face. It was as though she had suddenly put on a mask of red— only that isn't a very good description of what I saw. It was as if another visage was imposed over the one everyone else saw. And I knew no one else could see what I did. Or feel what I felt. Once I saw the red—the "extra" face—I felt waves of violent hatred coming from Katherine.

This meant she could or would hurt Henry.

"What's wrong, Em?" Diana asked.

"She hates Henry," I said. "And I think she will hurt him, or already has."

"You know things?" Diana asked.

I looked up at her. "Sometimes."

She nodded. "I have an aunt like that," she said. "You best go tell your papa."

"I've already told him Katherine doesn't like Henry," I said.

"That was before," she said.

"Before what?"

She clapped me on the back. "Before you saw what you just saw. Now go on."

I thought about going to Henry first and asking him about Katherine again. But as I walked across the room toward him, Mr. Em saw me and asked me what was wrong. We went into his study. I told him what I had seen and felt.

"You think she'd hurt him?" he asked.

I nodded. Or maybe she already had.

I couldn't make myself say it out loud.

Mr. Em bit his lip. "Jamie wants to marry her," he said.

"I know," I said.

I could see Mr. Em wanted to ask me more questions. Or maybe he didn't. Maybe I only imagined that he didn't believe me. What he said was, "Are you willing to tell Jamie? He trusts you. He knows you see things other people don't."

I felt like I was a hundred years old again. "Yes. I can tell him."

After most everyone had gone home, Mr. Em told me to meet him in the study. Then he got Jamie and brought him into the room where I was waiting.

"Jamie," Mr. Em said after he had shut the door, "Emily has seen some things, and we feel like she needs to tell you."

"Of course," he said. "What is it?"

I cleared my throat. Then I said, "Katherine does not like Indians."

Jamie glanced over at Mr. Em.

"Pardon me, child?"

"She hates Indians," I said. "And blacks, I think, but mostly she hates Henry. I saw it all over her face today. She loathes him. And I think she might hurt him. It's that kind of hate."

Jamie laughed. "Katherine is the kindest person I have ever met! She would never hurt anyone or be unkind to a single person."

"You've never noticed how she treats Henry?" I asked.

"Mr. Em, I know Emily has certain abilities," Jamie said, "but this is beyond the pale."

I looked from Jamie to Mr. Em. Jamie was angry, but he believed me—even though he didn't want to.

"I've noticed she is strict with him," he said, "but isn't that a mother's job?" He glanced at Mr. Em. "I'll talk to her. She can change her ways."

"I think she's already hurt him." I blurted it out. I hadn't meant to say it.

"Has he told you so?" Mr. Em asked.

I shook my head. What had I done? I didn't know for certain Katherine had hurt him. I hadn't seen anything—visible or invisible. I had only felt the intensity of her hatred.

Even Jake McMahon had not been hateful. His actions were hateful, to be sure, but I hadn't felt waves of hatred emanating from him.

Jamie went to the door and opened it. He leaned out and called to Henry. A moment later, Henry joined us in my father's study. Henry smiled at me and then looked at his father and Mr. Em.

"Henry," Jamie said, "is there anything you need to tell me about Katherine?"

Henry frowned. He glanced at me and then looked back at his father. He shook his head. "No. I mean, what do you mean?"

"Do you like her?"

Henry glanced at me again. I could feel my heart beating in my chest. As I looked at Henry, I suddenly thought I must be wrong. He was a big boy now, nearly a man. How could a small woman like Katherine hurt him?

"I—I." He stopped. "What's going on?"

"Emily has seen something," Jamie said, "the way she sees things. She thinks Katherine is hurting you."

He looked at me. "Why didn't you come to me?"

"I started to," I said, "but—"

"I told you Dad loves her," Henry said. "We were going to be a family. I want him to be happy."

"Henry," Jamie said. "You need to tell me what has happened."

"I don't always do things the way she wants me to," he said. "And so she whips me. She says it's for my own good. So that nothing bad happens again." He stood up straight. "I need it, Dad. She said if I had been stronger, wiser, more disciplined, Emily would never have been hurt."

My eyes widened.

She knew his weak spot. She had seen it.

She saw things, too.

And used her "sight" against people.

"You told her about what happened to me?" I cried, looking at Jamie.

"It happened to all of us," Jamie said. "It haunts me. I was going to marry her. Of course I told her."

"You had no right!" I said. "It happened to me and Henry! It happened to us. You had no right to tell that wicked woman anything about us!"

I was so angry I wanted to scream. I wanted to hit something. Or someone.

I tried to breath deeply.

Wait, wait, I told myself. Wait.

I looked at Henry. How could I not have known how he was suffering? Why couldn't I see that?

"I'm so sorry, Henry," I said. "I'm sorry I didn't know."

"I didn't want you to know," he said.

I wanted to say, "You promised to always tell me the truth." But I didn't.

"Henry," Jamie said, "there was nothing you could have done to save yourself or Emily. And as it turns out, you were both saved."

"Emily wasn't," he said. "You didn't see what he did to her. I had to watch it and I couldn't do anything to stop it." He swallowed. "I should have been able to do something."

"You showed me the pool," I said. "You jumped in and I jumped in with you. If you hadn't done that beforehand, I wouldn't have known where to run to. He would have caught me again. I'm sure of it. You did save me, Henry. You did."

Mr. Em said, "Henry, sometimes terrible things happen in our lives and we can't do anything about it. I wished I had done something, anything, to have protected you both from what happened."

I swallowed. My heart was pounding too hard. I could feel it in my chest. My ears. Someone should have protected us. We were children. Weren't adults supposed to protect children from harm? Mr. Em had never been a child. He didn't know. He didn't know how small one felt. How vulnerable.

"Where did she hurt you?" Jamie asked.

What a strange question. I closed my eyes. I felt like I was going to pass out.

I knew. I knew exactly where she hurt him.

I lifted up the back of Henry's shirt.

"Emily," Henry said, his voice pleading.

I pulled his shirt up further until I could see all of his back and the red lash marks that created several large Xs on his back.

I'm not entirely sure what happened next. I think I may have gone temporarily mad. I saw red, I felt myself floating up out of my body, and I screamed.

No, I roared.

Maybe Henry's mother inhabited my body for a few minutes.

Maybe the trauma of what had happened to me bubbled to the surface just then.

I ran from Mr. Em's study before anyone could stop me. I ran across the room—sprang across the room—to where Katherine stood, and I began pummeling her.

"How dare you, dare you, dare you!" I screamed as my fists struck her. I didn't even see her, once I reached her. I was so furious, I pounded away my frustration and anger on her flesh.

Or maybe I saw her as Jake McMahon.

The ferocity of my blows knocked her to the ground.

They all tried to pull me off. Whoever they were. No one knew how strong I was, except for Henry and Mr. Em. Mr. Em was the only one who was able to pick me up and carry me away.

He dropped me onto my bed and told Betsy Shaw to stay with me. He needn't have said anything. I didn't move. I curled into a ball and cried.

I learned later that Katherine acknowledged hitting Henry and was not sorry for it. "Spare the rod, spoil the child," she said. I wished someone had asked her why, if she was so proud of her actions, why she had hidden what she'd done from Jamie. Jamie sent her packing that day. He gave her a little money, and Titus drove her into town.

When I learned Henry and Jamie had left Refugio and gone back to their ranch, I began to cry. Then I began screaming for Henry. I don't remember much about this part of it. I remember I felt desperate to see Henry. I had waited nearly a year to see him again, and now, after only being with him for a few months, I felt like I had lost him again.

I wasn't very rational.

Hours later, Mr. Em sat next to my bed. He spoke to me calmly until I stopped screaming Henry's name.

"Henry is all right, daughter," Mr. Em said. "He is safe. Katherine is gone. The marks on his back will heal. It doesn't look like they ever even bled."

I stopped crying and looked at Mr. Em. "Are you trying to tell me his wound isn't very serious? Mr. Em, can't you see? His heart is broken, just as mine was. And I didn't see that until now. I didn't know it."

"None of us knew," he said.

"Then you all are to blame, too!" I said. "But I should have known!"

"Do you think perhaps you and Henry have an unnatural attachment to one another?" he asked.

He looked bereft. I knew he feared I was returning to my old ways, becoming who I had been right after I was kidnapped.

"I don't even know what that means," I said. "Who told you we had an unnatural attachment?"

"I went into town and talked to Dr. Dyer."

My eyes narrowed. "If you told Dr. Dyer what happened to me, I will never speak to you again."

"Emily, what would you have me do? No, I didn't tell him

the details. I said you and Henry had been held hostage and now you were . . . overly protective of Henry."

"Overly protective?" I said. I shook my head. "Katherine whipped Henry! She should have been beaten into the ground!"

I was roaring again.

"Emily," he said, trying to get my attention, trying to find his daughter again.

"She knew things the way I know things and she used it to hurt him! She should never never never do that!"

"And you have strength that other people don't have," he said, "and you must never use that to hurt other people."

I shook my head. "I am allowed to protect those I love!"

"If she was standing over Henry with a whip," he said, "then, yes, you could do what you needed to do to stop it. But you must learn to be judicious. You must learn to control yourself. You weren't protecting Henry in those moments when you fell upon Katherine. You were avenging his wounds. There is a difference. Do you understand that?"

Betsy Shaw and Nichols came into the room then. Betsy Shaw handed me a glass of what looked like water.

"Drink it," Nichols said. "This will help. It won't make you stop feeling, love. It will just help. It's moonlight in water." She nodded. "I promise."

I drank it.

"Emily, do you understand what I've told you?" Mr. Em asked.

I nodded. "I think so," I said. "But I want to see Henry. I need to see Henry."

I started to cry. Mr. Em looked at Betsy Shaw and Nichols.

"I don't know what to do," Mr. Em said. "The doctor suggested I keep them apart for a while."

"No," Betsy Shaw said. "She has been so much happier since we've been here."

"The doctor is wrong," Nichols said. "You must know that in your heart, Mr. Em. Henry and Emily, they are—how do you say it?—they are kindred spirits, only they are linked via their hearts."

Mr. Em didn't say anything else. He left my room. Betsy Shaw and Nichols helped me get under the covers.

"In the morning," Nichols whispered, "we'll go get Henry."

I nodded. I cried myself to sleep.

When I opened my eyes again, it was still dark. Moonlight fell across me and the bed.

Henry stood in the moonlight.

I sat up.

"Are you really here?" I asked.

"Yes," he said. "As soon as Dad fell asleep, I rode back."

"You could have been eaten by a mountain lion," I said. "Or fallen into a ravine."

"Could have," he said. "Didn't." He took off his shoes.

I opened the covers and Henry got into bed with me. We faced one another.

"If we're going to continue being best friends," I said, "we need to renew our promises to one another. You promised to always tell me the truth. You didn't."

"I know," he said. "I knew you would think what she was doing was wrong."

"It was wrong," I said.

"Parents whip their children all the time," he said.

"That does not make it right," I said. "You didn't deserve that. You weren't responsible for what happened to us."

"I'll try to remember that," he said. He lay on his back and I curled up next to him, with my head on his shoulder. "I promise to tell you the truth from this day forward. At least I'll try."

"Okay," I said. "And promise not to let anyone hurt you again, even if you think you deserve it."

He didn't say anything for a moment. I nudged him.

"All right, I promise not to let anyone hurt me again," he said, "even if I think I deserve it."

"Which you don't," I said, "and you never will. No one deserves to be hurt like that."

"Can we not talk about it any more?" he said. "I want to sleep."

"Mr. Em says the doctor thinks we have an unnatural attachment to one another," I said.

"What does that mean?"

"Nothing," I said. "Nothing at all."

"I know what it means," Henry said. He pulled me closer to him. "It means the doctor's an idiot."

I giggled. "Yup. Promise me you'll never leave me."

"I promise."

"Say it," I said.

"I promise to never leave you."

I smiled and closed my eyes. I was almost asleep when Henry whispered, "I hope I never get you pissed off at me. I had no idea you packed such a wallop."

"Let it be a lesson to you and everyone else," I said. "After you left, I was screaming your name. I can barely talk from screaming your name."

"That was a waste of energy," he said. "I couldn't hear you. I was far, far away."

I lightly punched him in the stomach.

"I think I'm driving my father crazy," I said.

"Seeing us in bed together will drive him even crazier," he said.

We started to giggle. Then we shushed each other and turned away and pressed our backs together, X to X.

I dreamed I was in paradise.

Chapter Nine

For the rest of that first summer, we all fell into a kind of routine. Mr. Em was busy directing the building of the school house and decent living quarters for the hired hands and their families. Henry and I spent most days together but not every day. Sometimes I explored the ranch on my own. I also met the children of some of the ranch hands, and we'd go off together. I remember Daniel and Victoria and Mary Ann, Julia, and Willie. I was always surprised when the Indian children had European names, but when I asked them what their true names were, they had no idea what I was talking about. "These are our true names," they'd say.

By the end of the summer, my nightmares and tantrums were over and my abduction and scarring was nearly forgotten. Mr. Em never mentioned it, and Henry and I rarely talked about it.

Henry and I sometimes sneaked off to the redwoods. I loved the redwoods. I felt as though they were whispering to me each time I saw them—whispering the secrets of everything. Even though I didn't yet understand their language, I was certain someday I would. Their whispering was music to my ears—and to my soul.

I liked the small and cozy Redwood House, too. Henry and I had ridden there several times over the six months or more that I'd been at Refugio, even though Mr. Em and Betsy Shaw told us it was too far away. We'd leave early in the morning without telling anyone where we were going. Once or twice we even climbed down the steep cliffs to the sandy beaches. There was something cleansing about standing at the edge of the continent, letting sea spray slap our faces.

"This is the end of the world," Henry said on one of the days we stood on the tidemark, staring out at the ocean. "And the beginning of a new one."

"What do you suppose goes on beneath the surface?" I asked. "It must be an entirely different world."

"My dad said his father told him stories of treasures beneath the sea, stories about women with tails instead of legs who lured men to their deaths below."

"Why would they do that?" I asked.

Henry shrugged. "They probably didn't. Maybe it was a breakdown in communication. The mermaids were saying, 'we're lonely; come on down and see us,' and the men were hearing 'if you don't jump into the sea now we'll kill you.'"

I laughed. "Neither version is very satisfying."

"We could live here, you know," Henry said, "in Redwood House and watch the sea day and night to discover what really goes on beneath the wave. We could get to the truth."

"That's all we'd do, watch the sea?" I asked. "That doesn't sound very exciting."

He looked away from the ocean and fixed his gaze on me. "Is that what you want from life? Excitement?"

"No," I said. "I don't know what I want. I don't think about it much. Do you?"

We sat on the sand. I remember the sand was so hot my feet hurt until I dug them into the dirt beneath. And I remember the feel of Henry's body so close to me. We weren't touching, but I could feel his heat. I liked that. I liked knowing that he was near to me.

"Sure, I think about it," he said. "I want to learn all about nature and draw it. And be in it, with it, a part of it. You're already like that. It's as though you're carrying on a constant conversation with everything around you, even when you're not saying a word. And of course I want to be with you. I figure we'll be together until the end of our days."

"Of course," I said.

"We could raise our children in Redwood House," he said. "If you want to stay here. I can't imagine ever living anywhere else but on this land."

"Me neither," I said. "But don't count on children."

"Why not?"

"If you can birth them, then we can have them," I said, "otherwise, I'm not so sure."

"But it's perfectly natural," he said. "Animals do it all the time. Women do, too."

"Nevertheless," I said. "I think we should hold off on this conversation for a few more years, don't you?"

"We can wait," he said. But he kept talking about it. "And Mr. Em could always live with us, you know. My dad, too, if he wants."

"Sure," I said.

"You don't sound sure," he said. "Aren't you and Mr. Em getting along?"

"I suppose," I said. "Things have been different since the kidnapping, you know. I felt like I was broken, or something.

Like there's been something wrong with me since we left the Meadow."

He nodded. "I know," he said. "I felt the same way, until I saw you when you first got home. Then I felt all right."

"I do feel all right," I said, "when it comes to you. Everything else still feels strange." I sighed. Even with Henry, it was hard to talk about this. So I said, "But I'd rather talk about Redwood House. What color do you want to paint the rooms?"

"It depends upon what the room will be used for," Henry said.

And so our conversation continued until we had redone the entire house in our image of adulthood.

Just before we started back to school, Mr. Em invited everyone over for a picnic and celebration down near the redwoods and Redwood House. We all left early on horseback or in wagons or buggies, everyone carting food and tents. Once there, we had a glorious day of eating, talking, and playing games.

Mr. Em and I competed in the parent and child relay race, along with Jamie and Henry and six other "couples." None of the mothers raced, which surprised me, but I supposed it would have been difficult to race in a dress. Nichols, Diana, and I were the only females dressed in trousers.

Mr. Em could not run very well or very fast, but I was fast, so I figured we had a chance. Before Mr. Em walked to his starting point—the children ran the first leg of the relay, the adults the second leg—he said to me, "You could substitute someone else as your parent. Someone who can run better than I can. Diana or Nichols would be glad to be your foster mother."

I patted my father on the arm. It was the first time in a long while that I had touched him.

"Go on, Mr. Em," I said. "You always told me winning isn't everything."

He shrugged and kept walking toward the other fathers.

"But it is something," I called after him. "So try."

He glanced back at me. I grinned. Because Mr. Em was so large, moving quickly was not his forte. Plus, he didn't enjoy being physical when so many people were watching. I was surprised he had agreed to compete in the race. He was probably still trying to make everything right between us.

I still wasn't sure I loved him.

"Get ready!" Nichols called.

The children stood on the starting line, waiting, each grasping a baton—small sticks we'd pilfered from the forest floor. I glanced over at Henry, who was down the line a ways. He smiled. He knew how fast I could run, but few others did. I used to beat him regularly when we raced in the Meadow. Now his legs were longer than mine, so we sometimes tied, sometimes beat one another.

"One, two, go!" Nichols cried.

I ran and ran. I could see my father up ahead. I wished he was further away, so I could keep running. As usual, I felt completely free when I ran. I wished I had undone my braid. I wanted to feel the wind in my hair. I wanted to be boundless.

I reached Mr. Em before any of the other children reached their fathers. I gave him the baton, and he was off. I could hear the shouts of the crowd. "Go, Henry! Go, Willie!"

"Go, Mr. Em!" I cried as he lumbered up the hill, the first father away. Henry came to stand beside me.

As I watched Mr. Em run, he suddenly looked vulnerable. He was good at so many things but not at this. It was strange to see him almost ineffectual.

No, that was the wrong word. I remember standing under the blue August sky, tasting the sea, and watching my father run and trying to figure out which word would best describe what I was seeing. He didn't run very well. I had seen bears run on all fours, and he almost looked like an upright bear.

I had been angry at him because of the kidnapping. I mean, I thought he could do anything and everything: Why couldn't he keep a criminal like Jake McMahon from hurting me?

Now I saw he couldn't run very well. I had known that, of course. But now I really saw it. I knew he was running for me, he was doing this for me.

I glanced at the crowd behind me, in the near distance. I hoped they were cheering for Mr. Em. I hoped they didn't notice he wasn't running well.

I heard shouts of "Go, Mr. Em!"

The other fathers had almost caught up to Mr. Em. He was trying to run faster. He must have heard them coming up behind him. The faster he ran, the more precarious his gait seemed. It looked like he would fall over any second.

I didn't want him to fall. I didn't want him to feel humiliated.

To fall while everyone watched.

"It's okay," I whispered. "You can slow down. Slow down, Papa, slow down."

And then he tripped.

He fell right on his face.

I could hear the gasp of the crowd.

The other men stopped, to go to him. He waved them off. They kept running.

"Look, he's getting up," Henry said.

Yes. My father pushed himself up. Looked for the baton he had dropped, picked it up, and then he began running again.

I laughed.

Willie's father had reached the finish line, and people were cheering.

Nearly all the fathers had reached the finish line by the time Mr. Em got there. He sank to the ground as he crossed the line. He held up his stick.

Everyone cheered.

He waved to me.

I started to cry and laugh at the same time. All of a sudden my heart was filled up. Filled up!

I ran toward my father. I didn't care if he couldn't do everything and anything. It wasn't his fault that Jake McMahon carved up my back. It was Jake McMahon's sin. It wasn't my father's fault he couldn't run well. Dr. Ef hadn't thought about how freeing it was for a soul to be able to go, go, go, when he sewed my father together.

None of it mattered.

I loved my father again.

Probably always had.

I ran to Mr. Em. When I reached him, I jumped on him, straddling him, knocking him to the ground. I put my arms around his neck and kissed his face.

"You were right," I whispered. "My heart is healed."

He laughed and put his arms around me. We embraced. I think he may have cried.

I don't know for sure.

Mr. Em got up from the ground, still holding onto me—what other father could do that?—and then he hoisted me up onto his shoulders and we began walking back to the starting line.

He patted Willie's father's shoulder and called out, "To the victor!"

Everyone cheered Willie's dad.

But they cheered us, too. I saw tears in Betsy Shaw's eyes as we approached, and Jamie reached up and squeezed my hand. Mr. Em held the baton up to me. I took it and raised it high.

And the crowd roared.

Part Two

Chapter Ten

Those years on Refugio were the happiest of my life. The more I understood about the land, the more content I became. Soon I knew the coolest spots on a hot August day or the warmest glens when winter gales were upon us. I knew the bald eagles returned about the time the swans left. And once the hummingbirds disappeared, I knew winter was coming. I knew the green hills hid a multitude of wildflowers that came into full bloom in the summer, changing some of the hills from green to purple or lavender. Then it all became golden and smelled like dust. Or corn. Mountain lions walked through the golden grass, looking as though they were swimming through a sea of gold. And I came to know all of this with Henry by my side. He knew where we could find wild things better than anyone alive—at least, that was my belief.

Some winters the elk came down low and grazed in our valleys and the lower regions of our hills. Wolves and mountain lions stalked them, but it was often to no avail. I used to think

Mr. Em was like a bear, but after watching the elk, I decided he was more like them. They kicked away predators like Mr. Em would brush dust from his shoulders.

I couldn't cross Wild Creek in the winter or spring, but come early summer, it was low enough for me to walk across it without fear of drowning. By early fall, it hadn't enough energy or water to topple anyone, including me.

Singing Rocks on Wild Creek was one of my favorite spots. Henry and I spent many an afternoon there. We especially liked coming there after picking berries. We'd sit with our feet dangling in the creek while trying not to eat everything we had picked.

One hot summer day as Henry and I stood under the alders near Heron Marsh, we were suddenly surrounded by what seemed like a million dragonflies. They were red, orange, yellow, black and white, and rust-colored, flying about us and darting around the cattails that grew amongst the unusually high marsh grass. Henry put out his arms as if in benediction to the dragonflies.

"Aren't they beautiful?" he said.

I nodded.

"My father says dragonflies are really fairies," Henry said, "who followed the Irish here to the New World."

I put out my arms, too. I reached out until my fingertips touched Henry's fingertips. He moved a couple inches closer until he could grasp my fingers. We held onto each other this way for a long time, with the dragonflies swirling around us.

Every year, every season, Henry filled up drawing books with pictures and words about nearly every plant, insect, reptile, fish, and mammal he could find. I went with him on most of his "expeditions" on Refugio Ranch and his father's land, Paradise. Although I no longer saw invisible creatures, I did often have a sense of when something was just over this hill or around that corner.

I was adept at finding bones, which thrilled Henry. Unlike other naturalists and biologists, he had no desire to dissect any fauna. He wanted to see them in their natural world, but he didn't mind finding a skeleton now and again. Sometimes I would get a feeling—as though someone I couldn't see was leading me right to the bones. I found the bones of elk, deer, coyote, wolf, raccoon, and rabbit. Once, I found a human skull. I didn't hesitate to pick it up.

"Alas, poor Yorick!" I said, holding the skull aloft.

"Oh, man," Henry said. "What if we've disturbed a burial ground of some kind?"

I shrugged. "There's nothing we can do about it now," I said. "I've already touched the skull. If there's a curse, I'm cursed. Besides, everyone who ever belonged to this place is long dead."

"Look around," Henry said. "Do you see anyone?"

I set the skull back in the ground, lodged up next to a rock, not 20 feet from a creek.

"You mean do I see ghosts?" I asked.

He nodded.

"No, that doesn't happen any more," I said.

"Why?"

I shrugged. "Probably because I don't want it to. What good did it ever do me? Nothing I saw or heard saved me from being kidnapped and mutilated."

I startled myself by saying these words out loud. Henry and I got very quiet.

Then Henry said, "I understand. I feel the same way. Nothing I ever learned from my dad or in school helped me stop what happened either."

We returned to the house and told my father we had found a human skull. He went out to the site with Diana and some of the other ranch hands. They didn't find any more human bones, so we said a prayer and buried the skull. Everyone figured the skull was Indian, and my father wanted to make certain we didn't do anything to desecrate the remains.

My father was especially sensitive to the plight of the indigenous people. He generally felt more comfortable with Indians than he did with people of European heritage. I was never certain why. Maybe because the Indians didn't turn away from him. If they thought he was odd, they'd say something. "Why is your skin yellow here and brown there?" "Why are you so tall?" Whereas white people looked or didn't look and never asked. They made up their own stories.

And Mr. Em remembered that when he first came alive, he was seen as inhuman—just as the Indians were—and he was treated badly, especially by the white European man who created him. The white men invaded Indian territory and then called the Indians inhuman and did whatever they could do to destroy them and their cultures.

During the zenith of the gold rush, Mr. Em left Refugio Ranch a few times to try to help the Indians who were being murdered or thrown off their land. He always came back from these trips dejected and heartbroken.

He invited any Indian he met to come live on our land. He understood his offer didn't change anything or fix what had been done to the indigenous people. In fact, he was one more person who seemingly had power over them. But Refugio Ranch did become a sanctuary for many Native Americans and escaped slaves. Once when a group of Chinese miners was accused of causing an outbreak of cholera, Mr. Em found them, rescued them from a mob, and brought them back to Refugio. Some of them stayed with us for a couple of years.

All of these people became part of my true education. I learned the histories of each and every person I met. They showed me little paintings of their loved ones, mostly family they had left behind in another country or another part of this country. Sometimes as I listened to their stories, I let my vision soften and I'd see that they each carried someone with them: either an ancestor or the "little" people from their country of origin.

Mr. Em told me often that I was going to get a first rate education despite the fact that this country did not sufficiently educate its women and girls. Mr. Em hired scholars from near and far (and they were nearly always from far) to come and teach us about every subject he could think of: history, biology, literature, chemistry. After the convention of women's rights in Seneca Falls, Mr. Em made certain I had a copy of their Declaration of Rights and Sentiments. He read some of it out loud to me.

"We hold these truths to be self-evident: that all men and women are created equal," he read, emphasizing "and women."

"You mean people don't believe men and women were created to be equals?" I asked.

"Under the law men and women are not equal," he said. "And most colleges and universities are closed to women, so women can't be educated like men. I've been trying to educate you better than any man. You have been educated by Nature as well as by human teachers. What do you think of that?"

"I think that is just fine." I didn't know anything different so it was difficult to imagine how else my life could have gone.

"Do you have a preference on your teachers?" Mr. Em asked.

"I suppose Nature doesn't require so much repetition," I said. "Or memorization. But Miss Irving is a great storyteller. She has tales to tell about her time in the city working in a saloon. Quite naughty. And the songs. Wow."

Mr. Em gave me a look. "I can tell you who is the storyteller here. Miss Irving most likely does not even know the word 'naughty.'"

I laughed. "Quite right, Mr. Em. I get all my naughty stories from Jamie."

"Now that I believe."

All the children benefited from Mr. Em's desire to provide me with a good education. Even after the school moved into town and I stayed on Refugio with the scholars Mr. Em hired, any of the older children were welcome to stay and learn with me. Henry took advantage of this offer; most of the other older children were glad to be out of school. I would have preferred being outside, but I did enjoy learning, and Henry was a good partner.

My father was thrilled when California entered the Union as a free state—as was I, later, when I understood better what that meant. Mr. Em continued to try and help the Indians—to stop the violence against them—but he grew more discouraged each year. He started reading anything he could on the abolitionist movement and began corresponding with abolitionists back East.

It was after we had been at Refugio for a year or more that Mr. Em gave me the book to read about his beginnings. I gave it to Henry to read, too. He wasn't shocked—I don't think Henry was ever shocked. And he didn't act differently around Mr. Em or me after he read it. I told him some of what happened in the book was true and some of it wasn't.

"He is a different man now than he was then," I said.

Henry accepted that. He accepted Mr. Em just as he accepted me.

After we had been at Refugio for two or three years, Jamie and Nichols got married. We began calling her Nancy or Mrs. Simmons. Henry called her "Mom." And she was a good mother. She loved Henry, encouraged him, and showered him with affection. She continued working with Titus, wrangling the horses, but she cut back after Henry's baby sister Alexia was born.

Henry and I stayed best friends, for the most part. When he was about 16—maybe closer to 17—and I was 14, he became a bit aloof. He seemed more like a man than a boy, and he didn't spend much time with me. It happened so gradually that it took me a while to realize what was happening. He wouldn't go swimming with me any more—at least not alone. And he always had an excuse not to come with me when I asked him to go to Redwood House.

Finally I confronted him.

"We promised to tell the truth to one another, and I expect you to tell me the truth now. Why are you avoiding me?"

"I—I am older than you are," he said. "I am a man and you are still a girl."

"So?" I said. "If I were a boy, would you say the same thing to me?"

We were sitting outside in the courtyard, after our lessons for the day.

At first Henry didn't say anything. I nudged him. "Henry. Answer me. Would you be treating me differently if I were a boy?"

"I suspect I wouldn't be having the same feelings I have if you were a boy."

"What kind of feelings?" I asked.

He looked at me.

"Oh. You mean wife and husband feelings," I said. "So?"

He shook his head. "It's not only that. I've been busy. I've been sending out letters to try and get on some expeditions."

"Aren't you too young for that?" I said.

"No," he said. "Mr. Em has a friend in San Francisco who is organizing an expedition to Central America, and he's put in a good word for me. I am the youngest person ever to get an article published in——-"

"Central America?" I said. "You aren't serious? People die on expeditions down there."

"I want to do this," he said.

"Why? I thought you were interested in this area," I said. "I thought you wanted to study this place, this nature."

He nodded. "That's true," he said, "but I have to make a way for myself in the world. I have to make a living."

"No, you don't," I said. "I gave you enough treasure to last your lifetime and beyond. Unless your father lost it somehow."

"Of course not," he said. "That money is in trust to me. You're lucky. No one expects anything from you."

"What?" I said. "You mean because I'm female! How can you say these things?" I was angry. "I paid dearly for that treasure. And I deserve a good life! I deserve a life without more suffering."

Henry put his hand over mine. I pulled away.

"We all deserve lives without suffering," he said.

"You sound like my father," I said. "Of course no one deserves to suffer. That's not true. I can think of a few people who deserve suffering."

I was up from the bench now, pacing.

"Shall I name the people who deserve suffering? Katherine, for one. Jake McMahon for two. Jimmy Kelly. Danny Collins for four."

"Jimmy Kelly is dead," Henry said.

"He should have stayed alive long enough to be punished," I said.

"Danny Collins is probably still in jail," Henry said. "I saw Katherine in town a few months ago. She works at the saloon. I think she's a prostitute. She didn't look well."

"You sound like you feel sorry for her," I said. "She's a whore and she deserves every bad thing that happens to her."

"Emily—" Mr. Em had come into the courtyard.

"I am not apologizing, Mr. Em," I said. "She deserves whatever bad befalls her. Same with the others."

"Haven't I taught you to be compassionate?" Mr. Em asked.

Henry was silent now. I looked over at him. His expression was blank.

"Not toward people who have hurt me," I said.

"Maybe those boys grew up in terrible poverty," Mr. Em said. "Maybe they didn't know better."

My eyes widened. "You are *not* excusing their behavior?"

He shook his head. "Of course not. I'm asking you to consider their lives. It does you no good to carry around this hatred."

How could he know what I carried? I never told him. I tried not to think about it or talk about it. Not until this moment. And in this moment, I was furious. I was furious and alarmed at how angry I had become so quickly. Out of the blue, it seemed.

"And what about Katherine?" I said. "What is her excuse? She was raised a racist so we should forgive her? Her parents beat her so she didn't know any better? What about you, Henry? Do you forgive her?"

Henry stood and gathered up his books. "I have forgiven her," he said. "But I don't compare what she did to me to what happened to you."

"To *us!*" I said. "It happened to *us.*"

He shook his head. "No, I did not suffer as you did."

"Henry," I said, looking into his face. I hadn't seen that expression on him for a long while. He still felt guilt for what had happened to me.

"If you'll excuse me," he said, "I better get home."

I didn't try to stop him. I sighed and looked at Mr. Em.

"I don't know where all of that came from," I said. "I got scared, I think, about Henry leaving. He said you're helping him go on an expedition to Central America. How could you do that? He could die, Mr. Em!"

"He wants to go," Mr. Em said. "It's his life's work. You can't ask him not to go."

"No, I can't," I said, "but you could tell him that your friend doesn't have any room on the expedition for him."

"Emily, that wouldn't be right."

"I don't care," I said. "I don't want him to go."

"You don't have any say about this, Emily," he said.

Then Mr. Em left me standing alone in the courtyard. I wanted to scream. I wanted to rage. I told myself I was too old for this. I had to accept that Henry was leaving.

That night I dreamed Henry died in Central America. The image was as clear as if I were awake and watching it happen. He lay in a hut, racked with fever, sweating, and he drew his last breath. I watched while they carried him out of the hut and threw him into a trench in the swamp.

That was when I screamed myself awake.

At breakfast, I told my father he had to do something to stop Henry.

"This is between you and Henry," Mr. Em said.

"He's only going because he has sexual feelings for me," I said.

Mr. Em looked up from his newspaper. "Pardon me?"

"He thinks I'm too young and he's too old," I said. "It's ridiculous. If he wants to have sex, I'll have sex."

"You are still too young for any of that. Henry is right."

"Then we'll wait," I said. "And he can wait. Why does he have to leave because of it?"

"Perhaps his feelings make him uncomfortable," Mr. Em said. "You have said that you have no intention of marrying him. He probably believes you don't have the same kind of feelings for him. It's always difficult to love someone who doesn't love you back."

"Of course I love him," I said. "That's ridiculous. No, I don't want to have sex with him. I don't want to have sex with any-one."

Mr. Em looked immensely relieved.

"But I would," I said, "if it would keep him here."

Mr. Em put down his paper and looked at me. "You must never have sex with someone unless you want to—unless you feel the desire to do so. And you must never let anyone force you or coerce you in any way."

"Henry would never do that," I said.

"I understand that," he said. "But you're talking about having sex with him to prevent him from leaving. That's not a good reason to have sex. It will change you. It will change your relationship with Henry. It's very intimate."

"I can't imagine it's more intimate than him watching some crazy man carve up my back with a knife," I said. "And over the years he's pulled a gem or more out of the scars. And I tell him everything. Isn't that intimate?"

"This would be different," Mr. Em said. "And hopefully much more pleasurable. Daughter, I know you want to try and control your life, but it is impossible. And you can't control Henry."

I had the same dream for several more nights. Every night, I woke up the entire household with my screams. Diana finally suggested I tell Henry what I had been dreaming and let him decide.

I wanted to tell him. I wanted to demand he stay home with me. Yet I wasn't sure the dream was true. I had known it was true that Katherine hated Henry. I had known that the distorted creatures I saw in my dreams were Jake McMahon and his men.

I had known the silver paths were important. I didn't know if these current dreams were true or were a result of my fears.

I decided to tell Henry anyway. We sat together on Singing Rocks. I had talked him into meeting me there.

As we sat with our feet dangling in the water, I told him the dream.

"I've had it every night since you said you might be leaving," I said.

"Do you believe it's going to happen?" he asked.

I had promised to always tell him the truth.

"I'm afraid it's going to happen," I said, "but I don't know if it's a prediction of the future or not."

He looked at me. "You don't want me to go, do you?"

"No," I said, "but I'm not going to ask you to put your desires on hold because of me. I'm just telling you what I dreamed." I wanted to scream, "Don't go, don't go, don't go!"

He nodded. "I trust you. I trust your instincts. I won't go."

I was so relieved I nearly stood up and cheered.

"There's another expedition in six months to the ancient forests in Maine. I think I'd rather go there anyway. Have you had any dreams about Maine?"

"No, just about the jungle," I said.

After that I had no more nightmares about Henry.

Before Henry left on the Maine expedition, we stood together on the land as best friends again. He was the Henry I had known for so many years, warm and loving instead of afraid and aloof. We held hands and looked into each other's eyes. Neither of us said a word. Then we embraced one another.

I hung on for dear life.

For the first week after Henry left, I kept expecting him to show up in my room in the middle of the night, but he didn't. Gradually, I had to stop thinking about him. If I kept missing him, I was certain I would go mad.

I didn't see Henry for another year. He wrote often, and I looked forward to his letters. But I rarely wrote him back. In the meantime I continued my studies, and my father hired Miss Allison to come train me in the Invisible Arts.

I had no idea what he was talking about when he first proposed this idea to me. He came out to one of the pastures where I was wandering in the footsteps of a herd of wild horses Titus and Nichols had just let loose.

"Now that Henry is gone you've got some extra time on your hands," Mr. Em said, walking alongside me.

"Henry and I had not spent much time together right before he left," I said. "I don't think I am fond of this separation of the sexes he seems to believe is necessary. We've never been separated here."

Mr. Em shrugged. "Refugio is not like the rest of the world," he said.

"I don't ever want to leave it," I said.

"I understand," he said. "I love it here, too. I only leave when others are in trouble."

"Someone is always in trouble," I said. "We can't save everyone."

"Wouldn't it be a kinder world if we were all on the same footing, though?" Mr. Em asked.

"Of course," I said. "But I am glad we are fortunate enough to have the means to help others instead of taking help ourselves. It feels powerless to need someone's assistance."

"Everyone needs help now and again," Mr. Em said.

"I don't need anything," I said. "I am happy as a clam here on Refugio with you."

"Daughter, you have always had some extraordinary abilities," he said. "Ever since you were a child. For the most part, I've ignored these abilities, educationally-speaking. And I think that's been to your detriment. You've worried that you were odd or weird and you've suppressed these tendencies of yours as best you can."

"That's not true," I said. We walked toward a lone oak tree. From one of the outside branches, a magpie watched as we approached.

"Maybe you haven't suppressed them," he said, "but you certainly haven't cultivated these . . . gifts."

"Gifts?" I leaned up against the trunk of the tree. "I don't think of them as gifts. They're too odd. They come and go. In any case, what are you getting at, Mr. Em?"

"I've done some research," he said, "and I found a woman in San Francisco who has experience in this sort of thing. I think she is called a spiritualist. Her name is Miss Allison."

"Isn't a spiritualist someone who talks to dead people?" I asked. "You can't talk to corpses, you know."

"Haven't you talked to dead people?"

"No," I said. "I don't know what Mrs. Peake was or what that being was who looked like Sitiu, but it wasn't them. It wasn't a dead person. They were like afterthoughts the land or the place had. Or something."

"In any case," Mr. Em said, "she comes highly recommended."

"By whom?"

"By many of my friends in the area," he said. Mr. Em had friends everywhere. "And if you're amenable, she's willing to come here and talk with you and see if she can teach you anything."

"Like what?" I asked. "What could she teach me?"

"How to tell the difference between a premonition and the fear that something might happen," he said, "like with those dreams you had of Henry in Central America."

"If she could do that," I said, "I'd be willing to see her."

That was how Miss Allison came into our lives.

Chapter Eleven

Even though Miss Allison was small, she was larger than life. She held her hand out to my father as she stepped through our open front door. He took her hand and kissed it. This action on his part surprised me so much I was speechless. She wore a purple hat with a huge feather sticking out of the front of it. She filled out her lilac-colored dress just as she seemed to fill up the entire house. Her eyes were so dark they looked black, and her hair was black as pitch. She was older than I thought she'd be, probably closer to Betsy Shaw's age than Diana's.

"That was the longest ride I have ever had in my life," she said. "And I first came across this great country in a wagon train."

Betsy Shaw, Mr. Em, Rose, and I stood watching Miss Allison. Rose's son, Thomas, brought in Miss Allison's suitcases.

"I may never leave if it means I have to go back the same way I came," she said. "I could use a glass of water or a bottle of wine. Or whiskey. I am not fussy. Oh, you must be Emily."

She came over to me and wrapped me up in her lilac arms. She smelled like flowers. I couldn't help it: I laughed and returned the embrace. I felt myself relax in her arms.

"Oh my," she said. "I needed that."

"Me, too," I heard myself saying.

I introduced her to Rose and Betsy Shaw.

"Oh, you beautiful women," Miss Allison said. "You have been so good to this child—who is now almost a woman, I understand. And someone else, another woman helped you. Your mother? No. Mary, I think her name was."

"Indian Mary," I said. "When I lived in Oregon she helped out. She knew a great deal about nature. Most people thought she was crazy."

"She was," Betsy Shaw said. "But it was a good crazy."

"And Rose," Miss Allison said. "Aw, I am sorry. But your ancestors are here with you, on this land." She turned to Mr. Em. "Of course I know you from our correspondence, and your friends have described you well."

"They told you I was a giant of a man?" he said. He sounded almost shy.

"Yes, they did," she said. "In all ways. A good man. I can tell straightaway they were right."

"Shall I show you to your room?" Mr. Em asked.

"Of course," she said. "We won't start working until midnight. The better to bewitch you by." She laughed and took Mr. Em's arm. "I am joking, of course. I am not a witch or a sorcerer, although I have many friends who are."

She continued talking as she walked with my father down the corridor.

I loved her right away.

After dinner her first day, Miss Allison wanted to talk to me and Mr. Em privately. The three of us went into his study and she began asking us questions.

"I understand you had an unusual birth," she said to Mr. Em.

"If you could call it a birth," he said. "A scientist took pieces of dead people and stitched them together, added a few chemicals and a spark of electricity—or who knows what—and then I was born, in a sense. I came alive."

She tilted her head a bit, as though trying to make certain she had heard him right.

"Certainly unusual," she said. "And do you have any unusual abilities?"

"Not that I know about," he said. "I am very strong. And big."

"He's a good father," I said.

"Do you consider that an unusual ability?" Miss Allison asked, looking at me.

"Yes."

Miss Allison smiled.

"How about your wife?" she asked.

"My *ex*-wife," Mr. Em said.

"When did that happen?" I asked. "Last time we talked about it you were still married."

"That was a while ago," he said. "You were the one who reminded me that it would be to your benefit if I was divorced." He looked at Miss Allison. "In case I died she was afraid she'd have to share my fortune with her mother."

He emphasized the word "fortune." I frowned. Was my father trying to charm Miss Allison?

"Mr. Em, that makes me sound quite greedy," I said.

"It makes you sound practical," Miss Allison said.

"And no, my ex-wife had no unusual abilities that I know about," he said.

"When did Emily start manifesting her abilities?" she asked.

"I noticed it first on the wagon train out here," he said. "Before that, I can't remember anything in particular. She sometimes got very quiet, which I understood was unusual for a newborn. And sometimes she got very agitated and we couldn't get her to stop crying. Well, her mother couldn't. Emily always calmed when I held her. I'm afraid this hurt her mother's feelings. Emily and I bonded from the moment she was born."

"You were there when she was born?" Miss Allison asked.

This was news to me.

"Yes," he said. "I was in the next room while Juliet Lee was in labor, and then I heard something in the midwife's voice. She sounded distressed. So I burst into the room. They were all aghast, of course, but Juliet Lee said, 'She won't come!' And I could see her crowning—I could see her head. And then she started to come out and I bent over and she slid into my hands in a gush of blood and water. Her tiny fingers tried to grasp my finger, but it was too big. She didn't even cry. She breathed in my arms and then they took her from me and gave her to her mother."

"You never told me that, Mr. Em," I said.

"Your mother was embarrassed about it," he said. "She had never heard of a husband being present at a birth. And I had seen her . . . vulnerable."

"I'd say," Miss Allison said. "If my first husband had seen me bare naked like that when I gave birth to Clyde we probably would never have had intimate relations again." She laughed. "Probably would have been a good thing. All right. What happened on the wagon train?"

And so Mr. Em and I told her about the dead woman I saw on the wagon train, about the animals I saw following people, about the silver paths, Sitiu—although not about being kidnapped and scarred—about me sensing when danger was near, about floating up above everything. None of it seemed to surprise her. She told us she would sleep on it and the next day she and I would start to work.

In the morning, she put on trousers and a shirt—so that she was dressed like me—and she asked me to take her to one of my favorite places on Refugio. Since it was late spring, I took her to a field covered in wildflowers not far from Singing Rocks.

"Now take off your shoes," she told me once we were standing in the middle of the field in the morning sun. The sky was blue, but clouds gathered in the west over the unseen ocean.

I did as I was told.

"Feel the earth on your feet," she said.

"I often go barefoot," I said. "I always feel better when I do."

She nodded. "That is because you have made a connection with the land and your body. You are one and the same, just as you are one and the same with that tree, with the creek, with the ocean. But we separate ourselves from Nature and we lose the connection—or we lose the ability to establish that connection. It's actually always there. Now what does the ground feel like on your feet? The air on your face and arms? Become aware of your feet again. What does the space between your feet and the ground feel like?"

I closed my eyes. I lifted first one foot and put it down and then did the same with the other.

"It feels like my foot and the earth are two magnets destined to always come together," I said. Like me and Henry. I opened my eyes.

"Is that right?"

"There is no right and wrong, my dear," she said. "There is just how you feel."

I nodded.

"Now," she said, "can you feel that magnet-like quality—

that destiny—as a kind of connection between you and the ground?"

"Yes," I said.

"Are you aware of the vitality of the earth coming up from the ground?" she asked.

I closed my eyes. "Yes, I think so. Or I'm imagining it."

"Good," Miss Allison said. "You're always on this planet, so you've always got that, even when you're wandering around in the sky like you sometimes do; you can think of that connection you have with the ground, with the earth, and you'll come back into your body."

"Okay."

At first, we walked rather than rode around Refugio. She wanted me to feel the earth and remember my connection to it. She wanted me barefoot as much as possible even though Mr. Em was concerned about poisonous snakes and insects.

She had me practice using all of my senses. She had me close my eyes and listen. Close my eyes and ears and sniff the air. Sometimes she would whirl me around with my eyes closed and then tell me to walk to the closest living thing. I was much better at it with my shoes off. But sometimes, I ended up walking in circles. When I couldn't find anything living, I'd bend over and touch the grass or the ground.

When I look back at my time with Miss Allison now, I can't think of many specific practices she gave me to improve my strange skills. Instead she encouraged me to be comfortable with myself. If I sensed, saw, or heard someone or something no one else did, that was perfectly acceptable. It was normal. Some people could see farther than other people and that did not make them strange. Some people could hear better than other people, some people were stronger than other people, etc. You get the idea.

Miss Allison did teach me to imagine a kind of light enveloping me like a giant egg. She said this would help prevent me from feeling overwhelmed, the way I often did around strangers.

"How did you know about that?" I asked. We were standing beside Wild Creek, down near the marshy corner where the egrets liked to gather.

"Sweetheart, you and I are very similar under the skin," she said. "I often know what people are thinking and feeling before they do. I know when trouble is around the corner."

"But I'm not always right," I said. "And I don't always know the difference between the times when I'm right and when I'm wrong."

"It's very frustrating," she said. "I once thought my brother was cheating on his wife. I kept seeing it in my mind's eye. He wasn't. My husband was cheating on me and I had no idea." She shook her head. "I suppose it's like a man who is nearsighted seeing an animal running in the distance, but when the animal gets closer, the man realizes it's not an animal but a person. It's all perspective."

"I kept dreaming my friend Henry was going to die," I told her. "I thought it was real and true, but I couldn't be certain."

"Sometimes we can tell it's true because we're very calm," she said. "The information comes to us and we don't feel afraid. It's like reading a fact in a book."

"I was very upset by those dreams," I said. "It was too horrible to imagine Henry dying. He and I are like my feet and the earth."

She looked at me, puzzled.

"We are destined to be drawn together."

She smiled. "It's harder to figure out what's true when it comes to our families and those we love."

My father and Miss Allison spent a lot of time together, too, when she wasn't working with me, and she ate every meal with us. Everyone noticed Mr. Em was sweet on her. He lived in a house full of women, so of course, we noticed. I didn't mind: I loved Miss Allison, but I didn't know if she shared his feelings and I was afraid he would get hurt. I didn't try to do anything about it, however. It was his business. I was learning I could not control everything.

During this time, I missed Henry. I ached for him. Even though he had been basically ignoring me for months before he left, I had still seen him nearly every day. Now I had only his letters to look forward to, and they were rather impersonal. It seemed like he was writing to someone he barely knew.

One day when Allison and Mr. Em were going to town, I stayed behind and rode down to Redwood House. I nearly started crying when I reached it. I felt Henry everywhere. I curled up on the porch and stared off at the ocean.

"Henry," I whispered. "Where are you?"

I closed my eyes and relaxed and imagined myself becoming invisible like Henry had taught me. I rose up out of my body and went higher and higher. I could look down on myself and then the house and the ocean, then all of California.

"Henry," I whispered.

As soon as I said his name, I was beside him. He was curled up on a small bed even though I could see it was still light outside. Was he weeping? Maybe resting. He looked healthy, so it wasn't that he was ill.

I knew I could drop down onto the bed like I used to, and I could sleep next to him, our backs pressed up against one another.

I watched him.

He had left to be away from me.

He had promised never to leave me. But he had.

I could see he was crying. Maybe he was homesick. Or maybe he had met a girl, and she had broken his heart.

Then I would go break hers.

I wanted to slip down next to him now.

I sighed.

But I had no right to interfere with his decision by coming to him now, unbidden.

"I love you, Henry," I whispered.

"Emily?" Henry turned slightly.

I thought of my connection, my bond, to the earth, and I went immediately back to California, to the Redwood House porch, where I belonged.

After Miss Allison had been with us for a few weeks, I took her to the swimming hole up near Coyote Crossing, where Wild Creek and Crescent River intersected. It was late in the summer, so the creek and river weren't running strong, revealing the swimming hole beneath the cottonwood trees, cradled by several large rocks. The water was cool and warm all at the same time, and minnows or tadpoles tickled our legs as they swam around us.

"The water is always a safe place to return to," Miss Allison said, "especially when you are feeling overwhelmed. I believe we are mostly made of water, so it's natural to be comforted by it. It's kin to us."

"The water saved my life once," I said, "and it nearly killed me."

I hadn't told her about Jake McMahon or what had happened to me and Henry. Mr. Em may have told her; if he had, she never mentioned it.

"A few years ago, Mr. Em and I met Henry and Jamie on their land in northern California," I said. "We were panning for gold."

"You must have been successful," Miss Allison said, "judging from the amount of land your father owns."

I shrugged. "We found lots of gold," I said, "but then a man decided he wanted to steal it from us. This man kidnapped us—Henry and me. When he didn't get the gold right away, he carved up my back, as a warning to my father. He sent Henry to tell Mr. Em. After Henry left, I escaped. I jumped into a swimming hole—it was very different from this one—and then I almost drowned when the creek sucked me out of hole. The Big Men Who Live Under the Mountain saved me. The kidnappers got some of the gold, but one of them died. Ultimately, the law caught one of them but not the man who carved me up."

"Is that how you think about it?" Miss Allison asked. "As though he carved you up like a Christmas turkey?"

"I don't know," I said. "I guess he didn't actually carve me. He pricked me. No, he scarred me. Here, you can see it." I turned my back to her. "Lift my shirt."

Miss Allison carefully pulled my wet shirt up until my back was exposed.

"This explains a great deal," she said. "This wound is not healed."

"What?" I hadn't looked at it in years, but I sometimes mistakenly felt it when I was getting dressed—or when it itched. Every once in a while my scars would itch; I'd scratch; another jewel would pop out.

"Of course it's healed." I was immediately sorry I had shown her. I pulled my shirt back down.

"Darlin', I'm not trying to alarm you," she said. "I can see there are still things under the skin. It's not smooth. But that's not what I mean. You are not healed from this experience."

I turned around to face her. "What happened to me, what he did to me, is long past. It will not be the defining moment of my life. It is *not* the defining moment of my life."

"It is why you and Henry are estranged," she said, "and it is why your father is so desperate to find people to help."

"Henry and I are not estranged," I said. "And my father has always wanted to help those in need. One doesn't have to be wounded to see inequity and want to alleviate suffering."

"Of course not," Miss Allison said. "But I believe it is why Henry left."

My heart started racing. I felt a familiar fury building inside of me.

I suddenly felt desperate to see Henry.

"You think he left because of my scars?" My voice sounded very high. "Because I'm ugly? Because I'm a monster?"

"Oh, no, of course not," she said.

At least I thought she said that. Sound was echoing in my head.

I couldn't see very well. Or was everything moving? Spinning.

I couldn't catch my breath.

I started shivering.

"Feel the water," Miss Allison said.

No, no, if I felt the water I would drown.

"Feel the ground beneath your feet," she said.

There was no ground. I was treading water.

"May I touch you?"

No, no, no.

Was I screaming or was that a bird overhead?

"Then move," she demanded. "Emily Ann! Move! Swim to shallower water." She was shouting.

I did as she ordered. Or else she dragged me toward shore. Wherever shore was.

I felt the ground beneath my feet.

I breathed. No water in my mouth or lungs. I was not part-fish. I was human. A breathing air human.

"Henry!" I screamed. *Henry, Henry, Henry.*

I began sobbing and shivering. Miss Allison grabbed my

arms and pulled me out of the swimming hole. Then I was in the sun and she was rubbing me with a towel.

"He left me!" I said. "He left me! He promised he would never leave me!"

"He left you a few months ago," Miss Allison said, "or he left you after being alone in that tent with that man?"

"Both," I said. "Both!" I suddenly felt angry. "He left me! And my father was never there. He said he'd always protect me. Where was he?"

"And because Henry left you alone in that tent, he can never leave you again?"

"Yes!" I said.

"But you told him to leave," Miss Allison said.

"No," I said. "No, I wanted him to stay. I told him about the dreams and he changed where he was going. Switched from Central America to Maine."

"When you were in the tent together."

I shook my head. "None of that matters. None of it. I survived. Other people have gone through much worse things than I have. Look at the Indians. Most of them have lost their entire families, for generations. Henry lost his mother."

"They weren't lost," Miss Allison said. "They died."

"What? Yes. They *died.*"

"Did you feel lost when you were in that tent?" she asked.

"Of course, yes," I said. "I didn't know where I was. I thought I was going to die. I thought he was going to kill us. And what good did any of my so-called gifts do then? The morning Sitiu was killed, the day before I was kidnapped, I was so happy. I was with my father and Henry in the most beautiful place in the world. If I have gifts or abilities, shouldn't I have known Sitiu was going to be murdered?"

"I don't know," Miss Allison said. "Why do we remember today information we needed yesterday? Why do we hear someone say something and not understand right away and then moments later, we understand? It's like any of our other senses: Things aren't always clear."

"And then the next day, or was it the next? I can't remember." I shook my head. "When Henry and I went into the woods—before we were kidnapped—shouldn't I have known what was coming? Shouldn't I have sensed *something?*"

"You didn't? Are you certain?"

"Yes, I'm certain! Sitiu appeared to me after he died. Or someone who looked like him. He told me when I saw the light it was time to jump. But he didn't tell me that someone was going to kidnap me. Wouldn't that have been a better warning?"

Miss Allison smiled wanly. "Honey, I can't tell you why this is the way things happen. It is absolutely imperfect. I understand your frustration."

"I'm so angry at Henry for leaving me," I said.

"But you told him to," she said.

I made a noise. "Not then. Now. He shouldn't have left now."

"But it was okay that he left you then?"

"Like you said, I told him to leave."

"Why?" she asked. "Why did you tell him to leave."

"Because I had seen that man kill Sitiu," I said, "and I knew he might kill us, too, and I couldn't stand the idea of watching Henry die." I shook my head. "That would have been too much. I knew I could take whatever else he did to me. To me. But not to Henry."

"And how did you know?"

I shrugged. "I just did."

"We can't avoid every bad thing that happens in our lives," Miss Allison said, "but sometimes our intuition—our knowingness—helps us get through it. Mr. Em, Jamie, and Henry didn't have that. They didn't know that you could get through whatever happened. Can you imagine what it was like for Henry to have to leave you in that tent with that mad man?"

I hadn't thought of that before.

"But why would any of this matter now?" I asked. "Why would he leave now?"

"Maybe it doesn't have anything to do with anything," Miss Allison said. "You might want to consider it sometime, some day, if something like this comes up between you and Henry again. Have you ever considered that it is the kidnapping that binds you and Henry together? Would you have continued being friends if this hadn't happened?"

"We were great friends from the moment we met," I said, "even when we were babies, before I can ever remember. And then we were friends again, before the kidnapping. Yes, we would have stayed friends, no matter what. And we have not let this separate us. In fact, I got through it because of Henry." I put my head in my hands. "I don't want to think about this any longer. This doesn't have anything to do with anything. Can you tell me what to do when I . . . when I get so scared and angry when something reminds me of the kidnapping? Sometimes I'll just get so angry I'm nearly blinded by it."

"Tell yourself, 'this is now,'" she said. "'That was then. This is now. That was then.' And remember your connection to the ground."

"This is now," I repeated. "That was then. This is now. That was then. Can't I remember my connection to Henry? It always helps to think of him."

"People come and go," Miss Allison said, "but the ground beneath our feet, the land, it is always there."

A few weeks later, we had a going away party for Miss Allison. Everyone from far and near was invited to the celebration, and most of them came. Miss Allison had endeared herself to everyone she met while she stayed with us, and she had met a lot of people. We ate, we danced, we told stories.

Afterward, I wrote to Henry and told him all about it. I had thought about what Miss Allison said, about how difficult it must have been for Henry to leave me in the tent that night, so I forgave him for leaving me this time. I figured by the time he returned, I would be grown up enough.

Enough for what?

I ended the letter with, "Miss Allison has taught me that all of my *abilities* are really just another kind of sense, like hearing, seeing, feeling. These abilities don't make me strange, they don't make me monstrous. Sometimes, the abilities may help me or those I love, but I can't blame myself because I didn't know ahead of time that we were going to be kidnapped. I feel a sense of relief when I consider this. I hope you, too, feel no responsibility for what happened. It was all his doing—of course, I won't write his name. I think of you often and hope you are well. With affection, your friend Emily."

The morning Miss Allison was leaving us, the women in the house—me, Rose, Betsy Shaw, Diana, and Miss Allison—tried to cheer up a morose Mr. Em with food and jokes—and songs. Diana knew lots of little ditties and she sang most of them that morning. Despite my father's best efforts, he could not hide the fact that he was smitten with Miss Allison, and he didn't want her to leave.

Finally, Miss Allison said, "That carriage ride up here was excruciating. Why don't you take me down to San Francisco yourself, Mr. Em? Emily can come, too, if you like."

"What a great idea," I said. "But you two go yourselves. I'm not interested."

"It would be all right?" Mr. Em asked. He was smiling now. "The ranch will be fine without me. But what about you, Emily? How will you be?"

I laughed. It was nice to see my father happy.

"I will run wild, as usual," I said.

And so began a strange kind of friendship or courtship between Mr. Em and Miss Allison. I never asked my father or Miss Allison about their relationship. Over the next several years, Mr. Em would travel to San Francisco for a few weeks once or twice a year and Miss Allison would travel to Refugio. Mr. Em always asked me along on his sojourns to San Francisco, but it took awhile before I agreed to accompany him. For many years, I didn't travel but a few miles from Refugio. It had become my refuge: or my gilded cage.

Chapter Twelve

The day Henry returned, I was out on the land looking for a lost mare and foal. Actually, the horses probably weren't lost. They most likely knew right where they were. This particular mare, Franny, was known to be a loner. Once she dropped a foal, she stayed away from the rest of the herd for months at a time. This could be particularly dangerous in a land filled with predators who would love nothing more than eating foal for dinner.

Nichols and Titus normally let the animals go where they wanted, but Franny was a valuable mare: She was so black she was nearly blue, and she was the fastest horse in the county. Not the fastest *mare* but the fastest *horse*. Her foal had been sired by Alfred, Ronnie Hoffman's prize stallion, who was the fastest horse in his county. Everyone was anxious to see how their offspring would run. (Horse racing was one of those spring and summer activities that I never cared for. I was the exception. Most everyone near and far looked forward to the yearly races.)

In any case, Titus and Nichols wanted the mare and foal found. They only knew she had given birth because one of the ranch hands spotted her and her foal in Strange Canyon when he was rounding up calves. He didn't have time to go after her, so Mr. Em sent me, and I did whatever chore they asked me to do.

In the year or so that Henry had been gone, I had taken on more and more responsibilities on the ranch. If I didn't know how to do what Mr. Em asked of me, he found someone to teach me if he couldn't.

Diana taught me how to shoot. I already knew how to hunt, but she taught me how to use small arms. Titus taught me how to use a knife. I knew how to kill an animal with a knife, but Titus taught me how to use a knife in self-defense. Plus he showed me where to kick a man if I couldn't get to a gun or a knife.

"Balls, eyes, knees," he said. "Kick, gouge, kick. Remember that and you'll do well."

"What if someone grabs me from behind?" I asked. "When it happened to me, I bit his hand, but then he punched me and dislocated my shoulder."

"Was he a man and you a child?" Titus asked.

"Yep."

"Brute force is difficult to overcome," he said. "If they get you from behind, you can try to kick their knees. But you could also reach behind and grab their testicles and squeeze as hard as you can. It'll knock them right off their feet."

"Truly?" I said. "I had no idea. Isn't that a flaw in the design of men?"

Titus laughed. "You bet it is."

Most days—once school was out—I was running after something lost or missing. This day I was looking for Franny and her foal. I tracked them from Strange Canyon up to Big Hill not far from Redwood House. It was hot out that day, and the breeze off the Pacific Ocean was enticing. I decided I could afford a detour for lunch to Redwood House.

I let Holiday loose to graze while I sat on the porch overlooking the water. I breathed deeply the ocean air as I ate cold shepherd's pie.

"I figured they must have gotten it wrong."

I turned around.

Henry was walking toward me, grinning. He had grown taller, again, and there was no mistaking he was no longer a boy. His face was too pale, and his black hair was shoulder length—and in his face, as usual.

I couldn't help it. I jumped up and ran to him. We practically knocked each other over as we embraced. He held me up off the ground and twirled me around. When he set me down, we kissed. And then I pushed him. He laughed.

We stood looking at one another. I reached over and moved a strand of black hair out of his eyes.

"Am I old enough now?" I asked.

"You do look all grown up," he said. He grinned. "And I didn't mind that kiss one bit."

"Don't all best friends kiss like that?" I asked.

"I'm pretty certain not," he said.

We kissed again.

"I know you left because you thought I was too young and you had sexual feelings for me," I said. "Or maybe other things were going on, too. But I can tell you right now I am old enough and I feel the same way about you. We've got this whole house. We could have sexual relations right here."

Henry laughed. "I had forgotten."

"What?" I asked.

"So much."

He took my hand, and we went to sit on the wooden bench on the porch.

"I have been surrounded by polite people for a year," he said.

"Are you saying I'm not polite?"

"I'm saying people don't often say what's on their minds," he said. "You always have."

"The whole truth," I said.

"Does this mean you'll marry me?" he asked.

"We're too young," I said. "They won't let us marry."

"But will you?"

"Henry, why are you asking this?" I said. "We're too young. We can be together. Why does it matter if we marry? It is no advantage to me as a female to marry. I would become someone's property."

"I would be that someone," he said, "and you would never be my property."

"Under the law I would be little better than," I said. "I can't even vote—married or not!"

Henry leaned forward and kissed me again. "It would be easier for us to travel together if we were married."

"I don't want to go anywhere," I said. "I'm happy here, at Refugio."

"We don't have to talk about any of this now," he said. "I'm only here for the summer, you know. I am going back to attend college in Boston."

"You're going to school?" I asked. "Why can't you continue studying with me? Mr. Em's scholars must be better than anything you can get back East."

"I want to make a name for myself in my profession," he said. "Education is important. Expeditions will be important."

"If that's what you want," I said. "I don't understand, but I want you to be happy."

"What do you want?" he asked. "What would you like to do?"

"This," I said. "I love being here on this land."

"You don't want to be a teacher, doctor, wife?" he asked.

"No! None of those. I want to take care of this land," I said. "You could spend a lifetime learning all about this place—as a naturalist, I mean. Is it so important to go other places?"

"Emily, you gave us all of this," he said, "my father's ranch and our fortune. I feel like I need to do something. I need to work. I need to be worthwhile. I need to be worthy of you."

I looked at him.

"What does that even mean, Henry? Of course you are worthy of me. You are worth more than everyone in the world put together."

He flinched. Then he said, "Did you find the foal and mare? That's what they told me you were doing, and I didn't believe it."

"Why not?" I asked. "I can work as hard as anyone."

"Yes, but I'd bet you'd prefer that the mare and foal run free."

I nodded. "This is true," I said. "You want to help me?"

"Sure," he said.

"Unless you'd rather stay here and have sexual relations," I said. "Because I'm willing."

Henry laughed.

We hadn't traveled far before I saw a silver path leading into a copse of trees. I hadn't seen any silver paths for years—not since the Meadow. I hesitated for only a moment before heading down the path, with Henry following.

Soon I heard a whinny. Holiday answered, and we trotted into the shade. I saw Franny standing next to a lone oak tree, favoring her right rear leg. I suddenly remembered Jimmy Kelly's lame horse, standing near his dead body. The sound of gunshot ricocheted in my head: I hadn't heard it when it happened, but now it echoed in my head. I felt slightly dizzy.

"Emily?" Henry said.

"I'm all right," I said. "This is now," I whispered. "That was then. This is now."

The foal walked from around the mother so we could see her. She was silver. I had never seen a silver horse before.

"Aren't you a beauty," I said gently.

Henry and I both dismounted, tied our horses, and then went to look at Franny's leg. As far as I could tell, it wasn't broken, just swollen. I looked around for some plantain, which I found easily enough. I said a prayer and asked the plantain for their help before I carefully tore several leaves off. I chewed on the leaves and then pressed them against the swelling. Henry used his kerchief to gently tie the plantain in place.

Suddenly, my hands seemed to be pulsing. I looked down and saw a silver spiral on each palm.

"What?" Henry said. "What do you see?"

I showed him my palms. "Do you see anything?"

He shook his head.

Without thinking about it, I put my hands on either side of Franny's leg, near the injury. She nickered and started to move away from me, but then she stopped. I felt the heat of her wound between my hands. I thought of cold ocean water. Then I moved my hands away.

"What was that?" Henry asked.

I shrugged. "Just felt the urge," I said.

After an hour or so, we checked the dressing again. The swelling had gone down substantially.

"It's going to get cold tonight," I said. "I'd prefer to be in a warm house with them in a barn where mountain lions and wolves can't get to them. It's not far to Redwood House. If we go slow, she will probably be all right, don't you think?"

"Sure," he said.

I put a halter on Franny and led her slowly up the hill and

down again toward Redwood House. She barely limped and seemed eager to go. I had to keep slowing her down. The silver foal followed happily, curious about Holiday and Henry's horse Brownie.

By the time we got the horses in the barn and fed, it was dark. I hoped my father would figure out where I was and wouldn't worry. Henry and I went inside the house and made a fire. Although the barn had plenty of hay for the horses, we didn't find much food in the house for us besides some fruit preserves in the pantry. We opened two jars of preserves and added the rest of my lunch. We sat in front of a huge fire, cross-legged, while we ate. Henry told me about his expedition in Maine—I loved his descriptions of the old forests filled with huge old apple trees. I told him about Miss Allison and our time together.

We fell asleep in front of the fire, our bedrolls next to one another, our backs together, until we woke up at the same time and we turned to one another and we embraced—with arms and legs—and we kissed. It was Henry who pulled away. Henry wanted to stop when I was ready to press myself, naked, against him. We lay on our sides looking at one another for a long while, the firelight flickering on our faces.

"Do you want to see?" I asked.

"Your breasts?" he asked, repeating what he had said to me years earlier.

"No," I said, "my back."

He swallowed. "If you want me to see it. I remember it."

"Does it repulse you?" I asked.

"Of course not," he said. He sat up, I turned onto my belly, and Henry gently lifted my shirt until my back was exposed.

"You can hardly see it in the fire light," he said.

"Liar," I said.

He ran his fingers down one scar and then the other. I shuddered.

"Does that hurt?" he asked.

"No," I whispered.

He did it again. Then he leaned over and kissed my back, his lips following the route of the scars. When he finished, I pulled off my shirt and turned over. He kissed first one breast and then the other. Then he put his hand between them, where my heart beat.

"I love you, Emily," he said.

"I love you, too," I said.

I lifted his shirt and then pulled him close to me. I don't think I had ever felt anything as exquisite as Henry's skin next to mine.

We held each other for a few more moments, and then Henry pulled away and handed me my shirt. I put it on. Henry slipped down beside me, and I rested my head on his shoulder. He put his arms around me. Soon enough, I fell asleep.

In the morning, Franny's leg appeared to be completely healed. This was good news because Henry and I were hungry and eager to get home.

Hours later, we turned the horses over to Titus and went into the house where everyone awaited us: Mr. Em, Betsy Shaw, Rose, Jamie, and Nichols. I could hear Henry's little sister, Alexia, singing somewhere in the house, but I didn't see her right away.

The adults were quiet when we came into the kitchen. They all sat around the long wooden table, apparently waiting for us.

"Something smells great," I said. "We are famished. There was hardly anything at Redwood House to eat."

"You spent the night at Redwood House?" Mr. Em asked.

I looked at Henry and winked. He gave me a look that I knew meant, "Don't torture them for too long."

I sat at the table. Henry sat next to me.

"It was cold," I said, "so we built a huge roaring fire."

"We ate supper in front of the fire," Henry said, "and that's where we slept."

"It's quite cozy," I said.

"Good, good," Jamie said. "It's good to see you two as friends again."

"We weren't ever not friends," I said. "It got a little warm with that fire, though. We were forced to strip naked to keep from roasting."

Mr. Em rolled his eyes. "Now I can tell you're pulling our legs. I'm glad to see you both home safe and sound."

"I will get you something to eat," Betsy Shaw said.

"Please!" I said. "Having sexual relations really whets the appetite."

Nichols smiled and shook her head. Betsy Shaw said, "Well, did you or didn't you?"

I looked at Henry. He shrugged. I said, "We are still virtuous, although I don't understand why having sex would mean one wasn't moral or virtuous. It is perfectly natural. Isn't it like breathing? Or sweating?"

"You can breathe on your own," Betsy Shaw said. "And you sweat on your own." She wasn't arguing against me. She was only stating a fact. And she said it as she walked into the kitchen.

"Are animals immoral?" I asked.

"Christian people would say that animals don't have a soul," Jamie said. "Since we human have souls, we can refrain from acting as animals act."

"As far as I know, animals don't murder one another," I said.

"Actually, animals do kill one another," Henry said. "And some male animals kill the young of a female so that they can mate with her."

I looked at Henry. "Truly?"

He nodded.

"That's beside our point," I said. "I understand that we should refrain from murder, kidnapping, assault, and the like. But sex is not a crime. It is supposed to be pleasurable."

"The girl has a point," Diana said.

"She does indeed," Mr. Em said. "Yes, having intimate relations with another human being is quite pleasurable, but it is not appropriate for children."

"I am hardly a child any longer," I said. "Women my age have married."

"Girls your age have married," Mr. Em said. "And I thought you didn't want to get married."

I glanced at Henry, and then I looked at Mr. Em. "I don't. But I don't intend to deprive myself of a lifetime of intimate relations because I am not legally married."

Betsy Shaw returned, carrying two plates piled with food. She set the plates in front of Henry and me.

"Even if you are not a child," Mr. Em said, "you are too young for sex and the responsibility that act entails. If you got pregnant, are you prepared to give birth and care for an infant?"

"I wouldn't get pregnant," I said. "Betsy Shaw and Indian Mary taught me how not to get pregnant long ago."

Mr. Em looked at Betsy Shaw as she sat at the table with us. She shrugged. "You told me to teach her the ways of women and that's what I've done. Of course, I also told her it doesn't always work."

"And they told me about plants that will end a pregnancy, too," I said. "We are creators and we are destroyers."

I wasn't certain if Mr. Em was aghast or glad.

"That's a better view than we are victims or children who need to be coddled," Diana said. "As women, I mean."

She was the one who had told me on numerous occasions

that I should never think of myself as "less than" even if the law and society did. She thumped my chest lightly with her fist the first time she told me that and then she added, "You are everything. Everything comes from you, as the woman. Don't forget that. Don't let any of them crush your heart—your heart is your greatest asset. The rest is brute force and any fucker can be a brute."

I didn't tell her Mr. Em hadn't come from a woman. He was not birthed the conventional way. It wouldn't matter to her, I supposed. She probably would have said, "But his parts were once people who were all birthed by women."

Now Henry cleared his throat and everyone looked at him. "Emily and I did not have sexual intercourse. But our relationship is our relationship. It is no one's business what happens from here on. Emily is a sovereign person, isn't she, Mr. Em?"

I looked at my father. He couldn't deny my sovereignty now, after years of telling me that I was my own person.

"Of course she is," Mr. Em said.

Even if the law did say I was his responsibility.

"Trust us to do what is right for us," Henry said.

And then he picked up his fork and began to eat. I did the same.

That was the end of the conversation. I was grateful for it, though. I was glad that I felt like I could talk to my father—and the rest of the household—about nearly anything. And I was glad to see Henry standing up for himself—and for us.

Later Titus asked me which leg Franny had injured. When I showed him, neither of us could find any sign of swelling or tenderness.

"What did you do?" he asked.

"I made a poultice from plantain," I said.

"She went from lame to this in less than a day?" Titus said. "I need to know where that patch of plantain is."

"Actually, it started getting better almost immediately," I said.

Titus looked at me. "What else did you do, girl? You don't need to hide from me."

"I put my hands on the poultice while it was on her leg," I said.

Titus nodded. "I'd say it was your hands done the healing, then."

I looked down at my palms. No silver spirals there today.

"Don't tell anyone," I said, "because I don't know if I could do it again."

I did try it a few times. Henry had a bruise on his forearm and I put my hands on it. When I removed my hands, the bruise appeared unchanged. Plus, I didn't see the silver spirals in my palm. Alexia fell and bumped her lip and I tried to put my hands on her face, but this distressed her. Instead, I held her while she cried, and I wished her all better. Once Henry and I were walking along Wild Creek when I saw a crow on the ground with one wing outstretched. She called out once and tried to back away from us.

I whispered, "It is just us. Henry and Emily. We are wild, too, and we don't eat crow. We intend you no malice."

Henry smiled at me. "You can speak bird again?"

"Is that what I did?" I whispered.

The crow stopped backing away. My hands began to itch. Or maybe they got hot. Pulsing. I looked down and saw a silver spiral on each palm. I knelt on the damp ground. I liked feeling the shock of the cold—of the natural. I put my hands on the ground, palms open, and the crow waddled over to me, dragging her injured wing. She let me put one hand gently on her back and then another on her wing. I closed my eyes. I didn't think about what I was doing. I didn't think. I felt my heart open. "Awww,

I'm so sorry," I whispered. In my mind, I saw her healthy, leaping into the air.

A moment later, that was exactly what happened. The crow stepped back from me, tucked her wing next to her body, and leaped up and away.

Henry knelt next to me.

"How'd you do that?" he asked.

"I have no idea," I said. "And I don't understand why I was able to do it now and couldn't do it earlier on you or Alexia."

"Maybe you can only do it on animals," Henry said.

"That wouldn't make sense, would it?" I said.

"I don't really know," he said.

"Neither do I."

After the crow flew away, Henry and I returned to the house and I told my father about me helping to heal the horse and the crow. I told him I had tried it several other times and nothing had happened. Wounds hadn't been mended and bruises hadn't disappeared.

Henry held out his arm. "It's gone now."

"But no quicker than it would have otherwise," I said.

"Not much," he said.

"Miss Allison said these abilities of mine are gifts," I said, "but they seem to come and go. I can't rely on them. Shouldn't I be able to control them?"

"I don't know, daughter," Mr. Em said. "I wish I could help. I wish I could find someone else to mentor you, to train you in this, but you are the first of your kind. You are the only one of your kind."

"As are you," I said. "Why don't you have any of these . . . abilities? I mean, I must have inherited them from you or Juliet Lee. And you said she didn't have anything like I do."

"It's not a disease, darling daughter," Mr. Em said. "I was hoping Miss Allison would help you see that."

"She did," I said, "but sometimes it feels like I don't have control over my own body."

"Have you thought about taking field notes?" Henry asked. "Like I do. I note the time and place that I spot an animal or where I find a flower. I note the weather, the day, the atmosphere, things like that. Maybe you'll notice a pattern—like why one day something happens and another day it doesn't. Write down how you're feeling, what you see, hear, smell. You can become a naturalist who specializes in her own self."

"I'll try it," I said.

I assumed I'd have time to observe myself—even though I wasn't thrilled at the prospect—and spend most of the summer with Henry, but subsequent events derailed that prospect. Henry and I had spent years together, basically alone, and now someone always wanted to accompany us. Sometimes it was an adult, sometimes Nichols and Jamie wanted us to watch Alexia, and sometimes it was one of the children of the ranch hands—although I was certain Betsy Shaw, Rose, or Mr. Em had put them up to it.

I was about to call a halt to this ridiculous interference when the fires began.

It had been a dry year and a particularly dry spring and early summer. The locals warned us that we might be in for a tough summer. We had seen small summer blazes before, usually caused by lightning, but always before, they had died out quickly.

This summer was different. The first fire began on Paradise, not far from Jamie's house, on Small Hill, after a dry thunderstorm. Fortunately the wind blew the fire down to Wild Creek, and the water put it out. Lightning storms continued for a few days; each day another fire began.

I wasn't alarmed. None of us were. I had no disturbing dreams. Once again something cataclysmic happened in our lives and I had no idea it was coming—not an inkling. I did wake up the night of the first fire coughing—but this had happened before, so I thought nothing of it. I got a glass of water and went back to sleep.

We tried to put out each fire on Jamie's land and on Refugio, but there wasn't much we could do. The few fire wagons we had quickly ran out of water, and Wild Creek and Crescent River were so low it took a long time to fill up the wagons again.

I tried to help on the fire lines for the first couple of days, but Mr. Em sent me and the other children back home. I was furious. I knew I couldn't do anything, but Henry was allowed to stay. He was considered an adult and I was still the child.

After a few days, the fires merged into one inferno. Fire fighting efforts were suspended, for the most part. The men had dug ditches at various places to try and stop the fire, but it had leaped each fire break. It seemed to love the chaparral and it spent time consuming each and every bush. Everyone hoped it would die down once it reached Big Hill since it had little fuel besides grass.

We couldn't see the fire from the hacienda, but we began to smell it.

Diana moved the livestock to places on the land that were not in danger from the fire—we hoped—so humans and our horses were the only ones remaining at the hacienda.

I was frustrated. I felt like I was stuck in the house while the world—the part of the world I loved—burned down around me.

Henry and Jamie returned to Paradise to take care of their land and animals when the fire shifted so that it was primarily on Refugio. Mr. Em finally returned home with Diana and Titus, saying there wasn't anything more they could do. We had to hope it rained or the fire burned itself out—which it would eventually once it reached the Pacific Ocean. Since we could now smell smoke, Mr. Em decided it was time to pack up and head for safe ground—wherever that was. We planned on leaving the next morning.

That night, before I went to sleep, I closed my eyes and let myself float above my body and the house and wander until I saw the fire.

It wasn't difficult to find: I had never seen anything this big before—except the ocean or the land itself. I could feel heat rolling up from it.

And it was moving quickly, like some kind of giant creature running downhill and eating everything in its way. I thought about calling out to it, as I watched from above, but decided I was vulnerable up here without my body. I went ahead of it to see where it was going. It was moving away from the hacienda, but it was headed right for Redwood House.

An instant later I was back in my bed. I sat up. I knew I had to do something.

I'm not certain what happened next—or why I did it. It was like so many things in my life. I just acted. Miss Allison had encouraged me to follow my intuition, so I suppose that was what I did. As soon as the black of night turned to the gray of predawn, I went out to the barn and saddled Holiday.

"Trust me," I whispered to her. "I won't let you get hurt."

I couldn't gallop her the entire way or I'd break her, but we went as quickly as we could. For a short time, I had to travel with a kerchief over my nose and mouth. Fortunately the wind shifted and took away the smoke. Soon the fire was on our right. Horses are terrified of fire and Holiday was no exception. I tried to keep her out of view of the fire for as long as possible.

And then we were at Redwood House. I jumped off Holiday and set her free. Then I ran away from the house and partially up Big Hill. The fire was racing down the hill toward me.

It was roaring. It was like the roar in my ears when I was

angry. Or maybe it was like the roar of a million lions. Or it was the sound I'd heard in the fireplace when a log was being devoured—only now it was amplified.

A massive wall of flames rolled over gold grass. This fire should have been low to the ground, with only grass as fuel, but it wasn't. It was as tall as a redwood. I wondered how this was possible as I stood waiting for it. It was too late to outrun it. When it came, it would roll right over me.

As it got closer, I felt something from it. Was that anger? Fury? Hunger?

It was like a thing alive. A being. Its own self.

I planted my feet in the ground, like an old tree. I could feel myself going deep, my roots reaching for the roots of all the planted beings from all around.

The fire was dancing toward me.

Dancing.

And it was screaming. Whistling? Roaring, roaring, roaring toward me.

I raised my hands into the air.

I felt old.

Ancient.

I was the land.

I opened my mouth.

Did I scream? Did I say words? Did I sing?

The flames stopped a few feet from me.

I know it was impossible. It was all impossible.

But in those moments I realized I was impossible, too.

I felt the heat of the flames on my face and chest. I knew my hair could burst into flames any second.

A tendril from the wall of fire flicked out at me and then quickly went back into the wall.

I knew then this fire was not natural.

I wasn't natural, either.

We were sisters under the skin, this fire and I.

Someone had set this fire, someone had started this conflagration.

Someone looking for treasure.

For the treasure of revenge.

This fire would devour Redwood Ranch and all of Refugio if I didn't stop it. It would go into the ocean and then turn around and come back.

All that was old and new in me cried out, "I know who you are! I see you!"

And I did see it. I saw the beauty of it. Even though it had started in revenge, it had been fueled by nature—created by the nourishment it got from the land and the air.

The fire was beautiful.

It was so beautiful my knees nearly buckled.

I felt longing from the fire. Not for me. For itself maybe. And for the ocean. For the cool ocean.

My heart opened.

Tears streamed down my face.

I imagined the fire and ocean meeting. Ahhh, what a time that would be.

The fire shivered.

I opened my mouth again and laughed.

And then the fire parted slightly and roared past me—around me, sparing me.

I turned to watch as it rolled down the hill, away from Redwood House, even away from the barns. It went straight into the ocean.

A hiss rose from the water.

A meeting of minds.

Of bodies.

Of souls?

I laughed and danced, alone, on the charred ground.

Chapter Thirteen

Holiday eagerly took me home where it seemed as though every person I had ever met was waiting for me.

"What did you do?" Mr. Em asked as everyone gathered around me.

"I saw it," I said. "I really saw it. And it was beautiful."

"Your shirt is singed," Henry said. "I feel heat coming off your back."

Betsy Shaw grabbed my arm and pulled me into the house and into my room. Diana, Nichols, and Rose followed. Henry tried to come after us, but they pushed him out of the room.

"Let us at least pretend you've never seen her naked," Nichols said as she closed my bedroom door with Henry on the other side.

"I haven't," he called.

All of these women had seen my back, so I didn't feel like I had to hide anything.

I pulled off my shirt. My back did feel a little warm.

The women were quiet as they gazed at my back. I looked over my shoulder and tried to look down, but I couldn't see anything.

"I'm not sure," Betsy Shaw said. "It looks like you were burned."

"It doesn't hurt," I said.

Diana leaned forward. "No, it's not burned. It's melted."

"Touch it and see," I said.

"No, I might hurt you," she said.

I reached back. The scars felt warm—and not as pronounced.

"Henry," I called. "Come in here."

I held my shirt up to my breasts so the women wouldn't get apoplectic.

The door opened and Henry stepped inside.

"They say there's something strange about my back," I said.

"The scars are all different colors," Henry said. "It looks like all the remaining gems beneath the scars melted. The X is now rainbow-colored." He touched the scars, running his finger down one and then the other. "It's smoother, too. Not as raised."

I heard someone coming down the hall.

"Is she well?"

My father.

"Might as well come in, Mr. Em," I said. "Everyone else is here." I looked over my shoulder. Jamie came in after my father and tugged on Henry's arm until he left.

Mr. Em stared at my back. He hadn't seen it since soon after the kidnapping.

"It looks different," he said. "It's quite . . . beautiful."

Betsy Shaw picked up the hand mirror from my dresser.

"Tell me where to put it," she said.

I looked over my shoulder at the mirror and told her to go to the left or the right and tilt it this way or that until I could see the scars. I had not looked at them in years.

Henry was right. They were nearly rainbow-colored yet the colors were richer than a rainbow, deeper: gem-colored.

They *were* beautiful, I supposed.

But they were still scars.

I knew it wasn't over. The spirit of revenge that caused the fire might not come in the shape of fire again, but it would come.

When I went with Mr. Em, Jamie, and Henry to the site of the first fire, I immediately saw a silver path. I followed it until I found a partially buried oil-soaked rag. We found something similar at two more fires. I didn't understand why the rags didn't burn, and Mr. Em couldn't explain it either. Mr. Em went to the sheriff and told him we believed the fires were arson.

Not long after, I dreamed a deer was in my room. Her tongue was hanging out. I reached for her, but she disappeared. That day, Diana discovered one of our watering holes had been poisoned. A dead deer, raccoon, and a cow lay bloated on the banks of the hole.

Mr. Em brought in security guards again, just as he had during the madness of the gold rush. He told the guards to protect the water sources. But no one could secure an entire creek or river.

This was worse than the fires.

After Mr. Em and the others removed the dead animals from the contaminated watering hole, I went to see it. No one knew how the hole was poisoned, or with what, so we didn't know how to clean it up. My father thought about filling it in. He didn't know what else to do.

I stood at the edge of the hole. The water looked clear and deep. Still. I tried to see the poison as I had seen the fire.

I saw a watering hole.

A breeze rocked the nearby alders. A magpie flew down to stand at the edge of the water.

"No," I said, and I waved at it. Reluctantly it flew away.

I closed my eyes. "I speak to the invisibles," I whispered. "Can you tell me how to heal this water hole?"

The day was quiet. The breeze brought the smell of charred wood to me. It was a common scent these days. I wondered how long it would take for the burned ground to return to normal.

"Arsenic."

I heard the word on the wind.

I looked down at the water. Someone had put arsenic in the water? That meant the hole would have to be filled in, if that was possible. Maybe some time in the future it would gurgle back to life?

Wait.

I saw a silver line. Tiny. I followed it to a spot near the edge of the watering hole.

I crouched and looked at the black earth.

I saw grain stomped into the ground. Millet?

It wasn't the water. Someone had dumped poison grain on the ground, probably figuring animals would congregate here. And they wanted us to believe the hole was contaminated.

What loathsome people.

I hurried back to the house and told Mr. Em what I had found. They dug up the area where the grain had been and buried it. Then we watched to see if wild animals came to drink—and they did—and none of them dropped dead. At least not on the spot.

I started to worry that Jake McMahon had somehow tracked us down. I asked Henry if he thought it was possible. He said no, but something was worrying him, too.

We had no idea who had set the fires or poisoned the animals, and we weren't sure how to find out who it was. It was torture waiting for the next terrible thing to happen. Finally I asked Mr. Em to go with me into town. Maybe I would see a silver path pointing to the guilty party.

I didn't go into town often, and I was surprised that each time I went, the town was bigger than it had been the time before. The gold rush had changed the entire state, including our town. Some of the miners had gone back home, but many had stayed on to become farmers, merchants, millers. Many people had made fortunes by selling merchandise to the miners. Miss Allison had cooked for the argonauts, for instance, and run a boarding house. She did quite well those first couple of years. Our town was far from the mining fields; still, many new people now populated the area.

Mr. Em drove the wagon through town slowly. I looked at each person walking, talking, riding. I knew some of the people and I waved to them. Mr. Em knew practically everyone.

We drove past the saloon. I glanced up at a second story window: Someone was looking down at us. I couldn't tell who it was, but I suddenly knew who was trying to hurt us.

"It was Katherine," I said. "It was Katherine and some man who is in the saloon, a friend of hers—maybe a customer of hers. He's bragging about it, or he has bragged about it."

I had no idea how I knew this to be true—or even if it was true. But I said it out loud. Mr. Em nodded. Then he slapped the reins across the back of the horses and drove me home. He left again, on horseback, to tell the sheriff.

As soon as Katherine was confronted, she confessed, as did her compatriot. I don't remember his name and I don't care to remember it. Why should criminals be remembered when their victims are not?

"Will she be put in jail?" I asked Mr. Em when he returned home.

"I presume so," Mr. Em said. "I'm not certain that is the best thing for her."

"Who cares about her?" I said. Jamie and Henry were at the house, too. "I want her locked away so she can't ever hurt us again."

"She's had a difficult life," Mr. Em said.

I laughed. "You are joking, aren't you? Only a crazy person sets fire to someone's land and poisons their water."

"Her boyfriend was angry about my abolition work," Mr. Em said. "He wanted to frighten me into stopping. He doesn't like that I hire freed slaves."

"That makes it worse," I said. "I wish she were dead. Him too."

"Emily," Mr. Em said.

I shook my head. "I'm serious. I'm tired of being afraid. Jake McMahon is still loose in the world and now you think it would be all right if this woman didn't go to jail. Let her go to jail! Let her rot in jail. I don't care. Henry, what do you think?"

He shrugged. "I think we should let the law take care of them," he said. "They'll get what they deserve."

I stared at the three men. I couldn't understand why they weren't enraged.

I was. It was the familiar fury that had come into my life after the kidnapping.

I breathed deeply. I tried to imagine a soothing light enveloping me.

Soon my breathing returned to normal, but I was still angry.

I put my hands on my hips. People said women were sentimental fools. That certainly wasn't true in my household. These men had a lack of appropriate outrage. My father called it compassion. I believed it was foolishness.

"Mr. Em, promise me you won't do anything to set her free."

The three men looked at one another. Finally, Mr. Em said, "I promise."

With Katherine and her man in jail, we started to relax. Once again I was hoping for time with Henry. But something had changed between us. I wasn't certain what. I had been invigorated by my interaction with the fire. I had felt alive and powerful. But what happened with Katherine reminded me too much of the kidnapping. I could feel myself pulling away from everyone, including Henry, and I couldn't seem to stop myself.

It got worse after my father called me into his study one day. He held a letter in his hand as he asked me to sit down.

I sat.

"What is it, Mr. Em?"

"I have had word about one of the men who kidnapped you," he said.

My heart started racing.

Please let Jake McMahon be dead.

Please.

"It's the one in prison," he said. He knew I didn't like to hear their names, so he didn't say it. "Do you want to know the news?"

I looked at him. I wasn't sure. Did I want to know the news?

"Is he dead?" I asked.

"Yes," he said.

"Thank goodness," I said.

"There's more," he said.

"More? How can there be more?"

My father was watching me. I could tell he wasn't certain if he should say anything else.

"I can't imagine what," I said. "There's nothing about the other one, is there? The one they never caught."

"No," he said.

"All right," I said. "Then there's nothing else I need to know, is there?"

He shook his head. "No. You're right. He's dead and you don't have to think about him."

He put the letter down.

"Thank you, Mr. Em," I said.

I left the room.

All day I kept wondering what else could be in the letter.

Then I couldn't sleep.

I got out of bed and walked through the house—in the dark. Moonlight flooded the courtyard, almost like daylight, only silver daylight, mysterious and beautiful. I lit a lamp in my father's study and looked for the letter he had been holding.

It was in the same spot where he had set it earlier in the day.

I picked it up. My hand was shaking.

"Stop that," I said.

My hand steadied.

I pulled out the letter and unfolded it.

"Dear Mr. Em," it began. It was from the sheriff who had helped catch Danny Collins. "I thought you would want to know that Danny Collins has died in jail, murdered by another prisoner. Also, the coroner notified me that they found old scars on Collins's body. Apparently he had been mutilated as a child."

I dropped the paper.

My heart started racing.

I looked up. Mr. Em was standing in the doorway.

"Do you want me to tell you the rest?" he asked.

"Yes," I said. "Tell me quickly and get it over with."

"He had old scars on his back," Mr. Em said. "There was a large X on his back."

I sank into my father's chair. "Was that the same with Jimmy Kelly?"

"I don't know," he said. "We buried him with his clothes on."

I looked at my father. "So do you think he kidnapped these boys and then mutilated them, too?"

"I don't know, Emily," he said.

"He didn't plan on ever letting me go, did he?" I asked.

Mr. Em came and knelt near me, like he used to when I was small.

"I hated the three of them so much," I said. "I wanted them all dead. And now it turns out they were probably just boys, hurt and intimidated by him. They didn't seem like victims then."

"You've got to let go of this, if you can," Mr. Em said. "It's in the past."

"This is the present," I said, repeating what Miss Allison had taught me. "That was in the past."

"Yes," he said.

"All right, Mr. Em," I said. "I will do my best."

Soon the summer was over, and Henry had to leave for school. We had started the summer closer than ever, but something had happened along the way, and now we were distant with one another again. I never did quite figure it all out.

When I said goodbye to him this time, I didn't cry. We were alone, sitting on the porch at Redwood House.

"You'll write?" I asked.

"Of course," he said. "Will you write back?"

"I will try," I said. "And you'll be back next summer."

He swallowed. I cocked my head. "What? You're not coming back next summer?"

"I'm going on an expedition," he said, "up in Canada."

"You didn't tell me," I said.

"When will I see you again?"

"It's a four year program," he said.

I felt like someone had hit me. "Are you telling me you're leaving for four years? I won't see you for four years?"

"I need to get away," he said. "I need to find my way in the world."

"Without me," I said.

"You said you won't marry me," he said.

"But I love you," I said.

"And we've hardly seen each other for weeks," he said. "We've become strangers."

I didn't have an answer. "I know. The fires and the poisoning upset me. And then when that man died and they found an X on his back. I just felt far away. I can't explain it."

"Emily, this thing—the kidnapping—is always going to be between us," he said. "You won't marry me. I think it's because you don't trust me. A husband has to be able to take care of his wife and protect her. You don't believe I can do that."

"Of course I trust you!" I said. "I told you why I won't marry you—or anyone! I don't need protection. I don't need someone to take care of me. I need someone to love me and be by my side and share my hopes and dreams."

"I don't know your hopes and dreams," he said.

I was speechless for a moment. Then I said, "That's because I don't have any! They went away when he carved an X into my back!" I shook my head. "No. That's wrong. That's wrong. That was in the past. This is now. And now I love you and want to be with you. I don't understand why that isn't enough."

"I love you, Emily," he said. "I will always love you." Then he said almost brightly. "Who knows what will happen in four years?"

We rode home together, silently. Then he rode off, headed in the direction of Paradise. I watched him go. He looked back at me once and waved. I almost went after him to tell him I'd do anything he wanted as long as he wouldn't leave me.

But I didn't.

Henry was gone. I had to figure out what to do until he came back.

If he ever came back.

I started school again. I was eager to learn whatever they could teach me. I still thought it odd that none of the teachers mentioned that which was beneath everything: a kind of invisible vitality or animation hardly anyone ever noticed—besides me. But Miss Allison had told me people didn't notice because they didn't have the skills to notice. Teachers were no exception to this.

Now that I didn't feel odd about my particular abilities, they began to come back. I regularly saw spirit animals again. And when I needed to find something or go somewhere, the silver paths often showed up, as clear as my hand in front of my face. I was always astonished that no one else could see them. I could sometimes help heal a wound or an illness. This was a miraculous skill, and I put my hands on everything and everyone who had a need.

I began to feel stronger, more like myself again.

Mr. Em became more involved in the abolitionist movement. Even though most of the abolitionist activities took place back East—and thus, far from us—Mr. Em felt he was in a good position to rescue slaves in slave states or buy slaves and bring them to California and free them. I never knew the details about how he did this. Occasionally, he went to San Francisco on the pretext of visiting Miss Allison, and then he'd returned to Refugio with men, women, and children who had been slaves and who were now free.

He didn't bring many home at once because what he was doing was against the law—at least some of it was. And the trips were traumatic for the slaves and the person who rescued them. The former slaves were usually close to collapse by the time they reached our place. They needed tender care, and we gave it to them while we kept them secret from the rest of the people on the ranch. Because of the Fugitive Slave Act of 1850, the slaves could be taken back to their former owners if they were discovered, so the less people who knew, the better.

When the former slaves were stronger, we taught those who couldn't to read and write—and most of them couldn't because it was against the law to teach a slave to read and write. I helped with this, but I wasn't especially good at teaching. Rose and her son Thomas excelled at it. Soon mother and son were the primary teachers of the former slaves.

As I'm writing this, I want to call them something besides "former slaves." They were individual people who had gone through harrowing experiences. I watched each of them and felt admiration. The ones who came to Refugio seemed to heal quickly, and all were eager to begin a life of freedom. Mr. Em hired those who wanted to stay on the ranch, if he had the need. He helped others find jobs off the ranch, or he sold or rented them a piece of land where they could farm or run livestock.

One former slave, Bernard Smith, was good with horses, so he took over for Nichols who was pregnant with another child. Bernard ended up marrying one of the rescued slave women, Beth Williams.

Eventually I asked Mr. Em if I could accompany him on one of his rescue missions.

"It's too dangerous," he said.

"Even when you pick them up in San Francisco?" I asked.

"It's a city filled with criminals and debauchery," he said. "I don't want you near that place."

"Miss Allison lives there," I said. "How bad can it be?"

"Parts of it are very bad," he said.

"It's time I see what's out in the world," I said. "If I can help, I want to help."

"I'm glad you're taking an interest in others," he said.

"At least let me go down and see Miss Allison," I said.

He conceded and took me with him on one of his trips to San Francisco. I had never been to a place with that many people, and I was overwhelmed at first. I told myself to breathe—although it stank in some places so much I didn't want to breathe. As we drove our wagon through the streets, I watched people with my eyes half-closed—better to see what was truly going on with them. That man was limping from an injury he had sustained in a fight not long ago. That woman had been beaten the night before. That man was running from the law. . . .

Miss Allison lived in a nice part of town with wide streets and huge houses. I was glad to see her, and I spent a great deal of time with her, but I slowly came to realize that I had really traveled to San Francisco to look for Jake McMahon. My father still had investigators searching for him, but they had not found anything since he disappeared after kidnapping me and Henry. Maybe *I* could find him. Perhaps a silver pathway would show up to lead me to him. I wanted him brought to justice. I wanted him tried and put in jail. I didn't actually care if he was tried because I knew he was guilty. I just wanted him in jail.

We went to Sydney-Town to pick up Dorothy Jefferson, a runaway slave who had escaped her master when he came to San Francisco on business. A friend of Mr. Em's had been hiding her for weeks.

I will admit that I was uneasy in Sydney-Town, a rather unsavory part of San Francisco. It was as if the very air I breathed was polluted with criminals. The men we passed in the street leered at me. This had never happened to me before. When I asked the men what they were looking at, my father encouraged me to be quiet. I pulled out my pistol and grinned at the men. They slunk away.

"We're bigger than they are, Mr. Em," I said. "They won't hurt us."

"Bigger does not always mean better," he said. "And besides, *you* are not bigger than they are."

"But I am stronger and I bet I can shoot better than they can," I said.

We did pick up Dorothy, and we smuggled her out of Sydney-Town and eventually out of San Francisco. As we left the city, my father reminded me, "Being tough isn't always going to save you. Sometimes it is good not to be seen. Learn to cultivate that ability."

At home, I continued studying and helping Mr. Em with the rescued slaves. I enjoyed spending time with Mr. Em. He had never talked down to me or treated me like I was stupid when I was a child. Now that I was nearly an adult, our relationship seemed to flourish. On our long trips together, we talked about literature, the ranch, plays we'd seen, philosophy, the abolitionist movement. Sometimes I asked him about his past, and he'd answer any questions I had. It always sounded like a strange fairy tale, his life, and it was difficult to imagine my father acting in the ways he had when he was younger. On these trips—and at home—he still told the best stories. I could listen to him for hours talking about giants, mermaids, sea captains, wizards, and magicians.

After a while, Mr. Em determined it was too dangerous for the former slaves to bring them into California. Mr. Em continued to send funds to abolitionists back East, but he stopped bringing slaves to Refugio. He seemed a bit adrift until Miss Allison introduced him to Miss Donna Blue who ran a brothel in Sydney-Town.

I was with him on that trip—both of us staying with Miss Allison—when Miss Allison brought Donna Blue into the parlor. Mr. Em stood when she entered and shook her hand. She had dark hair pulled away from her face into curls that swung this way and that when she moved her head. Her eyes were nearly black and her skin was whiter than any person I had ever seen before. Her lips were bright red, and her purple dress revealed the upper curves of her bosom, hugged her hips, and then snugly fit her legs to flow out a bit near her feet—reminding me of a mermaid's tail.

She was the most beautiful person I had ever seen.

Miss Allison directed her to sit with us, and then Miss Allison's housekeeper, Mrs. Wren, brought in tea. While we sipped and ate, Donna Blue told us why she was there.

"I own a respectable brothel in Sydney-Town," she said, speaking with an accent. "Our women are clean and refined. And our customers are decent men. We don't allow violence, and the women keep a fair amount of what they make. They are free to leave at any time. Unlike most of the other whorehouses—excuse me—unlike most of the other bordellos, we are not interested in exploiting children or in keeping our whores as slaves."

Mr. Em glanced over at me.

"I'm so sorry," Donna Blue said, looking at me. She flipped open a fan she held in her left hand and fanned herself. "Does Emily have an indelicate temperament? She looks as though she can take care of herself. Do you know what a whore is?"

"I do," I said. "Men pay to have sex with them. You could say they are enterprising women making a living by selling their assets."

Donna Blue laughed. "Yes! I like that! You may have seen my place, although I doubt you've been in Sydney-Town much."

"The Treasure Chest," I said.

"How did you know?" she asked. "Are you some kind of bruja? That's good. I have some bruja blood myself."

"You look like a mermaid," I said, "and I remember the sign over your establishment." It was an open wooden chest with gold coins and half-naked women spilling out of it—half-naked except for their colorful tails.

"Donna," Miss Allison said, "please tell Mr. Em why you wanted to speak to him."

"Yes, of course. Some of the women who have been held against their will and some of the girls who have been kidnapped or abused come to my place for help. I give them haven and a little money, but most of the time they end up back in one of the brothels being abused all over again. I heard you helped smuggle slaves out of the south. I wondered if you would be interested in taking some of these girls away from their dangerous situations. You wouldn't even have to come to Sydney-Town. In fact, that wouldn't be a good idea. If I could get the women up to Miss Allison—she has agreed to take them—then you could come and get them from her."

"And what would I do with them?" Mr. Em asked.

"Whatever you did with the slaves," Donna Blue said.

And so began our rescue of the whores of Sydney-Town. Every few months, we would go to San Francisco and bring back with us several young women. Some of them were younger than I was. Some had run away from home, looking for a better life, only to be seduced by a stranger who then brought them into the brothel to be sold to other men as sex slaves.

At first we didn't know what to do with the women on Refugio. I could see Mr. Em was overwhelmed by having even more women in his household, especially since they had forgotten how to behave in polite company—if they had ever known. Betsy Shaw, Nichols, and I (and sometimes Miss Allison if she was there) taught the girls manners and how to dress. This was a source of great amusement to everyone who knew me since I didn't dress like most other girls or women. However, I knew enough to tell them it wasn't a good idea to wander around someone else's house half-naked—which was something they were prone to do.

If the women didn't know how to read or they hadn't much education, Rose and Thomas taught them, just as they had the slaves. When the women were ready, Mr. Em gave them passage back home or tried to find them respectable jobs away from San Francisco.

I liked having the women in the house. They had lived lives completely alien to mine, so their stories fascinated me. Some of them went out on the land with me, but most of them were afraid of what they called the wilderness. I encouraged them to be out of doors as much as possible—especially barefoot. Some of the women thought I was crazy, but I watched them as they came outside and stood on the ground. To a one, they settled into their bodies and into their new lives much better afterward.

No one in the outer community tried to burn down the ranch, the way they had when we were helping the slaves. The minister in town did come out to make certain we hadn't started our own brothel at Refugio. When he was convinced we hadn't, he offered his assistance.

"I guess former prostitutes need God's help more than former slaves," Mr. Em said when the minister left.

Sometimes just before the women were ready to rejoin society, we'd throw a fandango at Refugio and invite the townspeople and area ranchers. Some of the women found their future husbands at these dances—and then we'd get to attend their weddings. Even though I didn't want to get married, I enjoyed weddings—I enjoyed celebrations of every kind when I was surrounded by friends and family.

Thomas ended up by marrying one of the women. He and Susannah Johnson met while he was teaching her to read. They fell in love, sitting next to one another in the school house, with Thomas pointing out each word in a book while Susannah sounded them out.

When I wasn't in school or with Mr. Em or our guests at the hacienda, I spent as much time on the land as I could, learning every nook and cranny. I began writing about and drawing the plants or animals I encountered on the ranch. I put these drawings and descriptions in a notebook I labeled simply "For Henry." I felt close to Henry each time I opened it and made a notation or drawing.

I did spend more time with my classmates than I probably had before, especially when the rescued prostitutes were gone from the hacienda. Now that I was older and more certain of myself—or less afraid of my sometimes strange abilities—I was more comfortable around people my own age. I was particularly happy when Cynthia and Peter Stevens started joining me for classes with the scholars Mr. Em had hired. Cynthia and Peter moved to Refugio with their parents who were working for Mr. Em and saving up to buy their own land.

I liked Cynthia and Peter. They both had sharp wits. And they enjoyed talking about the news of the day. We spent many hours talking about abolition—and attempting to ascertain a way we could end slavery in our time.

I could tell Peter had a particular affection for me, and I thought he was handsome. He didn't know as much about nature as Henry did—no one did—but I liked scrambling over hill and dale with him. Cynthia wasn't much of an explorer, so she usually stayed behind.

One day Peter and I ended up in a gully, lying on a comfortable patch of grass amongst the scree, looking up at the clouds. It felt good to be with another human being—another human being who really knew nothing about me. I leaned on my elbows and looked at him.

"May I kiss you?" I asked.

He looked surprised, but he smiled. "Please," he said. Before I could, he said, "But you can't tell your father."

"You are nearly a grown up man," I said, "and you're afraid of my father?"

He laughed. "Yes! My parents did not raise any stupid children."

I leaned over him, and we kissed. Then he put his arms around me and we kissed longer. When we pulled away from one another, I said, "That was nice."

"You sound surprised," he said.

"I am."

"Thank you?"

I laughed. "No, not because of you. You're nice enough. I've only ever kissed Henry."

"Henry?"

"That's right," I said. "You haven't met him. He's Jamie's son and my best friend. We aren't that close right now because he's away at school."

"So you need someone else to kiss while he is away?" Peter asked. He grinned. There was something easy about him. He didn't seem shocked that I kissed him or that I wanted to kiss him. He didn't seem to care that I had kissed Henry.

I liked him.

"Do you and Henry have an understanding?" Peter asked.

I frowned. "An understanding?"

"You'll get married one day?"

I shook my head. "No. I have no plans on marrying. I don't see the advantage in it, at least for a women."

"I understand," he said. "If I were a woman I wouldn't get married either. It's a contract to be a drudge."

"Exactly," I said. "I can't seem to get Henry to understand. I told him we could still have sexual relations. I just didn't want to be married."

"Sounds like paradise," Peter said.

"I agree." I looked over at Peter. I wanted to kiss him again. Maybe I would even have sex with him. I imagined it would be pleasant enough. As soon as I thought about, I saw it happening, like a memory of a real event, only it was more real than that. I could feel it. I could hear the fabric of our clothes as we removed them. I could feel Peter's skin against mine. I heard and felt his breath on me. I saw us fumbling at first as we tried to figure out how to get his male parts into my female parts; then it all worked—I could feel him inside of me—and it was exquisitely pleasurable. But afterward, as we lay next to one another, I wished it had been Henry instead of Peter. Because it would have been different, more meaningful, part of the grand design of my life.

I opened my eyes and shook myself. "I just saw it," I said. "The whole thing. It would be quite fun. But it wouldn't be the same as it would be with Henry."

"No, it wouldn't be the same," he said. "But I imagined it, too, and it was mighty pleasant."

I laughed. I didn't explain to him that I hadn't exactly imagined it—it was more like I had lived it and then decided not to live it.

I couldn't explain it to myself, let alone someone else.

Soon enough, Peter and I got up and raced out of the gully, both of us stumbling several times before we made it to the top of the hill where other hills rolled away from us. Then we ran. I was smaller than he was, but I could run faster—which always amazed him. As I ran ahead of him, I opened my arms wide. I felt free. As free as the clouds. As free as the hawk flying over Big Hill. Free from all worry and the past. I hoped Henry was feeling free, too.

Peter and I didn't kiss again, except once when he was leaving to go off to San Francisco where he planned to apprentice with his uncle who was a printer. He wanted to write for a newspaper and figured a job with a printer would help him. I didn't know if that were true or not, but I wished him well. When he came to say goodbye, we briefly kissed.

"You're not like other people," he said, "and I like that. You're certainly not like any other girl I've met. I expect you're one of a kind."

"We're all one of a kind," I said, but I knew he was right. I was Mr. Em's child, after all. No one else in the world like him or me.

"I enjoyed your company, too," I said.

"If you ever change your mind about what we talked about," he said, "you know where to find me."

We wrote to each other now and again. I enjoyed hearing about his life in San Francisco. Whenever Mr. Em and I went to the city, we visited him. His parents bought land from Mr. Em and started a farm. Cynthia married a local Spanish rancher. She was young and he was old, but they seemed to genuinely like one another. Peter came back for the wedding, and we danced at her reception.

And so three years went by.

One day Jamie came over to the house and asked to speak with me. I had known Jamie since I was a little girl and we were never formal with one another. Yet he asked me to sit with him in the living room, which I did. We sat side by side on the sofa.

"Henry is coming home," Jamie said.

"How wonderful!" I said. "He didn't write and tell me. Of course, he hasn't written much this year. Has he finished his studies early?"

Jamie shook his head. "No, he is coming home because he is engaged, Emily, and he's bringing his fiancé here."

I blinked. "He is engaged? To be married?"

"Yes."

I felt like someone had punched me in the face.

"Why—why are they coming here?" I asked. "Are they going to be married on your ranch?"

"No, she wants to meet me and see the place," he said. "She wants to know his family before they get married. She's the daughter of one of his professors."

I breathed deeply. I didn't know what I felt, but I knew what to say. I was 18 years old and all grown up.

"That's wonderful," I said. "I'm so glad for Henry. When will he and his beloved arrive?"

"Any day now," Jamie said.

Damn. Mr. Em was in San Francisco. If I'd only gone with him, I could have missed Henry and his soon-to-be bride.

"They want to see you," Jamie said, as if reading my mind.

"I'll be here," I said. "Where else would I be? Would you like me to get you some tea?"

I couldn't sleep that night. I had a long conversation with myself. What had I expected? Henry wanted one kind of life and I wanted another. Most people got married and had a family. It was the way of the world.

I would have to come to terms with it, one way or another. Only I hoped they weren't planning to live on Jamie's ranch. Then I'd have to see them. But if they didn't live there, I wouldn't see them. I wouldn't see Henry.

I had always expected him to come home and we would figure out our differences and be together. As the darkness throbbed around me, I realized I had been waiting for him to come home. My life was richer with Henry in it. I tolerated his absences because I didn't have a choice and because I wanted him to be happy. School was supposed to bring him happiness—not a wife!

Maybe when I saw him, I would feel nothing but friendship for him. Maybe not even that. We had been apart from one another for three long years. We had both changed.

Obviously Henry had changed. He was marrying another woman.

Because I wouldn't marry him.

I didn't understand why marriage was so important to him. Apparently he had found someone who agreed with him about the place of marriage in a relationship. Some evil little . . .

No, I couldn't start thinking like that. I couldn't hate her. That wouldn't be right. She hadn't done anything wrong. She had fallen in love with Henry. I understood that.

A few days later, we got word from Paradise Ranch that Henry and his betrothed had arrived. Mr. Em was still not home. Betsy Shaw said, "I could tell Henry you went with Mr. Em."

I shook my head. "Then I'd have to hide here until he left. I'll see him eventually."

"I always thought you two would end up together," she said.

I shrugged. "I guess not."

I went about my business as usual, which at that time was balancing the books for Diana. She was a capable accountant, but I was better. Something about getting columns of numbers to balance was soothing to me. If they didn't balance, the offending line would usually highlight itself—like my silver pathways— which I supposed was an unfair advantage.

After I balanced the books—which took a day—I helped in the garden. It had taken years of trial and error, but we finally had a thriving vegetable garden. When I finished working in the garden, I went around to see if any of the ranch hands or their families needed any healing, extra cash, food. Fortunately, everyone was thriving.

I took a walk, glad to be on the land rather than inside a building or in the garden. As I walked, I listened with all of my senses so that I could be the voice for the invisibles if the need arrived—if the land needed my help.

I heard a blue jay call out just before I turned the corner and saw Singing Rocks and Wild Creek. Henry was sitting on one of the rocks. He looked older. He was wearing a kind of suit, which was puzzling, but his pant legs were pulled up so he could dangle his feet in the water. He was talking. I couldn't hear what he was saying, but I watched his lips move. He was smiling. He looked happy.

He was so beautiful. *My Henry.* I wanted to run to him and wrap my arms around him.

Only he wasn't alone.

Part Three

Chapter Fourteen

I didn't see her right away. The dappled sunlight through the trees momentarily hid her. But then she came into view. Her curly brown hair was pulled away from her face, and she wore a simple blue frock. I had assumed since she was from Boston that she would be fancier. Henry was actually dressed fancier than she was. She was smiling, too, as she listened to Henry with her hands in her lap. She was so still she could have been a deer.

My stomach hurt. I didn't want to see this now. *Or ever.* I would have to face it, but not yet. Not yet. I started to step away quietly, to disappear back into the curve in the trail. Henry turned my way and saw me. He looked startled and then he grinned. I couldn't help but smile back at him. I was suddenly—and unnaturally—aware of how I was dressed: muddy jeans, an old shirt, boots that looked older than I was. I could wear a dress, and I did so every once in a while—something simple—but for the most part, I was more comfortable in trousers than in anything else.

It was too late to run away.

Henry got down from the stone, unrolled his trousers, and slipped on his shoes. Then he reached his hand out to help the woman down. She smiled and took his hand easily. Too easily. As though they had done this a million times before.

They walked toward me. I couldn't seem to move.

"Hello, Emily," Henry said, as though we were old school chums rather than old . . . whatever we were.

"This is Ellen," he said. "Ellen, this is Emily."

Ellen held out her hand to me. "It's so nice to finally meet you," she said. "Henry has told me so much about you."

I quickly recalled my bond with the earth—to keep myself grounded—and then I shook her hand.

"It is nice to meet you," I said. I glanced at Henry. He didn't look the least bit uncomfortable.

"Henry tells me you and he practically grew up in this place," she said. "This Singing Rocks. It is so beautiful. I hope you don't mind that he brought me here. He's spoken of it so often that I had to see it. Henry has missed home."

"I didn't realize he still considered this home," I said. "He's been away for a good long while."

"I have so many questions," Ellen said. She put her arm through mine and gently turned me away from the creek so that we were walking in the direction of the house. "What was Henry like when he was a boy?"

"Pretty much like he is now, I expect," I said.

Ellen laughed quietly. "I want stories, Emily. You were closer to him than anyone, and I want to hear all of your stories."

As we walked, I tried to think of stories about Henry that weren't personal. I wasn't going to tell her about the kidnapping or the scar on my back, or about Katherine beating him, or about the times we slept together or the times he rubbed my scar or kissed me. I wasn't going to tell her about all the time we spent at Redwood House, imagining our future together.

"He always knew where to find animals," I said, "and the best plants."

"Is that all?" Ellen asked.

"That's a great deal," I said.

I glanced at Henry. He smiled.

By the time we got back to the house, I was exhausted. Jamie and Nichols were there with their children, Alexia and Allan, along with Diana and Betsy Shaw, and two people I didn't recognize who turned out to be Ellen's parents. Diana and Betsy Shaw looked relieved when they saw Ellen's arm through mine. I tried to keep my expression as neutral as possible.

Betsy Shaw had prepared lunch for us, and I couldn't think of an excuse not to eat with them. Ellen's parents kept trying to engage me in conversation by asking me about Refugio and my father. I can't remember their names now or what they looked like—probably because I couldn't concentrate on what they were saying. I tried to remember what Miss Allison had taught me, too, but nothing seemed to be working. I wanted to be alone with Henry and find out how he was doing, yet I couldn't look at him. I could look at Ellen, and I found myself staring at her, wondering if Henry had ever kissed her—most likely—or if he had touched her bare skin—her bare back. The thought made me close my eyes. Of course if he hadn't yet touched her bare back, he would one day soon. They were to be married, after all. He would be intimate with her in way he had never been intimate with me—if he hadn't been already.

I had to stop this. I was an adult. I tapped my feet on the ground, reminding myself I was connected to this good earth. I breathed deeply.

"There must not be much opportunity for society out here," Ellen's mother said. "It must get lonely for a person such as yourself."

"I am surrounded by people most of the time," I said. "I am glad when I can get off by myself."

They laughed. Or someone did. I started to feel like myself again. I was even able to glance over at Henry who was not looking at me.

"Where can you meet other people your own age?" Ellen's mother asked. "Do you have dances?"

"We have dances here on the ranch," I told her. "And picnics and all kinds of parties. They have dances in town, too, although I rarely attend."

Diana said, "We all keep quite busy. Emily helps run the ranch, plus she does volunteer work with her father. And she's had a first rate education. Mr. Em has hired the best teachers to come and school Emily."

I smiled at Diana. She was bragging about me—feeling defensive for me. I looked around the table. Emily and her parents—and Henry—did appear different from us. We were all weatherworn, even the children. Wilder. I supposed we looked to them the way Sitiu and his grandchildren looked to me. Only I had admired the way they moved in their bodies, their confidence in this world.

I wondered if any of them were still alive.

"I'm sure," Ellen's father said, "one must miss music and theater out here. One must miss the wonders of the city."

"We have theater out here," Henry said. "And music. Mr. Em made sure of that."

"The only thing we lack out here are the criminals and noise," Jamie said. "We're all quite content. And if someone has a longing to leave—like Henry—then we happily send them on their way. We are not cosmopolitan, but we are not backward."

"I meant no offense," Ellen's father said.

"None was taken," Jamie said. "It is a different life here even from Missouri, where we lived before."

Missouri. I had nearly forgotten that I had lived there once with my father and mother. Not that I remembered any part of it. I didn't feel as though I came from Missouri. I felt like I came from this land, this part of the country.

"When's the wedding?" I asked.

"In the fall," Ellen said, "when we return to Boston. First I wanted to see some of the country and understand what it is that Henry does when he goes on his expeditions. Not that he or my father are working this trip. I have lived a provincial life. Unlike many of you: living here and there and everywhere. I have lived in the same house my entire life."

"When we travel it isn't in the kind of luxury we've had coming out here," Ellen's father said, "you can be sure of that."

"Luxury!" Ellen's mother said. "I would not label our travel accommodations as anything close to luxurious."

Everyone laughed again.

I wanted to hang myself. This was the dullest conversation I had ever been a part of.

This was the kind of life Henry wanted?

None of them had said a single word that came from the heart. Diana had when she stuck up for me. Jamie had when he talked about life out here. But the rest of it was just words filling up emptiness.

I stared at the three newcomers. Perhaps I was prejudiced. I didn't want to like them. They were likable enough if dullness were likable. Of course, perhaps they were only being polite. Betsy Shaw had told me when I was a child that people who didn't know each other well often talked about the weather or the price of corn until they knew one another better. It was a sort of kindness, I realized, this small talk, to give everyone an opportunity to relax a bit. To give me time to relax. They must realize this meeting was difficult for me.

I looked at Ellen's mother and smiled. She smiled back at me. Her eyes were blue. *Genevieve.* That was her name.

"Tell me about your trip, Genevieve," I said, reaching for her hand. "I wager you have some good stories. I'd love to hear them."

She squeezed my hand and said, "Our driver for the last leg of the trip was quite a character . . ."

I glanced over at Henry as Genevieve began her story of the hard-drinking coach driver who never meet a person he didn't swear at. Henry smiled at me, and I saw my Henry in that smile. I wanted him to be happy, so I would make his bride and future in-laws as comfortable as possible.

For two weeks, I was with Ellen and Henry frequently, despite my best efforts. I didn't try to talk to Henry alone. Each time I saw the couple together, they seemed genuinely happy. I had no wish to interfere with that.

I wrote to Miss Allison and asked her to send Mr. Em home as soon as his business was finished. With him gone, I was mistress of the house, and I didn't relish my role as hostess for the visitors. Nichols had quickly run out of things for them to do.

Fortunately it was summer, so each Sunday we had a big dinner at Refugio or Redwood House for everyone who worked on Refugio or Paradise—and anyone else from the village who wanted to attend. Although Ellen and her parents looked a little out of place at the first picnic, everyone did their best to make them feel at home, and soon they were playing along at horseshoe pitching or tag.

At one of the picnics, Nichols and Diana took me aside to ask me how I was doing.

"I'm fine," I said.

"Betsy says you're not sleeping," Nichols said. "What can I do for you, sweetheart?" She put her arm around my waist and hugged me to her.

"You could go back in time and change some things," I said. "Although I'm not sure what."

It was true that I hadn't been sleeping well, but I wasn't sure how Betsy Shaw knew that.

Nichols said, "He only took up with her because you wouldn't marry him."

"He asked me to marry him three years ago," I said. "I could have changed my mind since then."

"Have you?" Diana asked.

"No," I said, "but that's not the point. No offense, Nichols, but I don't understand why women get married."

"Because our society looks down on unmarried women," Nichols said. "Diana can get away with it because she doesn't have children."

"It was no easy road for me," Diana said. "I had to fight every step of the way until I got to Refugio. But I never had marriage in mind. I don't find men that interesting, except as occasional bed partners. For good conversation and good bed partners, I'd pick a woman every time."

"Don't you want children?" Nichols asked me.

"I don't know," I said. "But getting married essentially makes me a man's property. I'm supposed to obey him like I'm a child and he's my parent. How can you have a true equal partnership if that's the reality? Until recently, a married woman couldn't even own property. It is a disgusting institution."

"Of course it is," Nichols said, "but the laws are changing."

"I want to be myself," I said. "I want Henry to be himself. I don't understand why we have to get married to do that."

"You're being stubborn," Nichols said.

"Maybe," I said. "If Henry truly loved me, he would have understood my hesitation, my concerns. And apparently he didn't."

Nichols said, "And maybe he thought if you loved him

enough, you would have married him no matter what your concerns because you would know he was Henry and of course he would see you as an equal."

I looked at her. "Did he say that to you?"

"Not exactly," she said.

"It doesn't matter," I said. "He's made his choice. I have to learn to live with it."

I looked across the field to where Henry stood talking with Ellen. She touched his arm lightly, for only a moment, and I felt like I was going to be sick.

How was I ever going to get through this?

Finally, Mr. Em returned to Refugio. I was never so glad to see him as I was then—except maybe by the creek after the kidnapping.

"Tell me how you are," he said as we sat in his study soon after he returned.

"I felt like my world had ended at first," I said.

"Truly?" he said. "It didn't seem like the two of you were close any more. I remember when you were young I couldn't keep you apart. We thought you'd end up pregnant and married before you were 15."

"It's good to know you had confidence in me," I said.

"I should say I was afraid that might happen," he said. "I had no experience raising a daughter. I couldn't really know what was normal and what wasn't."

"Were you ever tempted to write to my mother for advice?" I asked.

He looked surprised by the question. I rarely mentioned my mother. I was a bit surprised myself.

"No, not really," he said. "I often asked Betsy Shaw and Rose, Diana, and Nichols for advice."

I smiled. "And did you follow their advice?"

"Sometimes," he said. "But you were not like any other child, and you won't be like any other woman. You are your own person with your own ways. Have you had a chance to talk with Henry?"

I shook my head. "No. And I don't want to talk to him. What would we say to one another? He's getting married. Have you ever been in love with someone who didn't love you back?"

"Yes," he said. "It is a horrible feeling."

I sighed. "His fiancé seems to like it here. What if they live here? I'd see them all the time. I don't think I could do it. And if they don't live here, that feels even worse. I don't know what to do. So I've been doing nothing. Just waiting for it to be over."

He reached out and squeezed my hand. "I'm so sorry," he said. "I know this doesn't help, but one day you will fall in love with someone else."

"Who did you love who didn't love you back?" I asked.

"It was Dr. Ef, the man who created me," he said. "I loved him because he was like a father to me. I viewed him that way. But he never cared for me or about me."

"I'm sorry, Mr. Em," I said.

"That was what drove my anger," he said. "That's why I did so many terrible things. I'm not justifying what I did. I'm only trying to convey to you that I was heartbroken. One could say I lost my mind. But that wasn't it. It was heartbreak. Fortunately, that all changed the moment you came into the world."

"I don't feel angry, Mr. Em," I said. "I'm glad for that. But it is painful. I just want to get away from the pain."

"Maybe you want to visit Miss Allison for a time," he said, "until Henry and Ellen leave."

"Maybe," I said.

Ellen wanted to visit all of our childhood haunts. I did not want to go with her and Henry, but she insisted. In my desire to be polite, I agreed to go riding with them. Henry found her a docile pony to ride since she had no experience riding. She wanted to ride sidesaddle, but no one had a sidesaddle for her. (Strictly speaking, we probably could have gotten her one from one of the Spanish ranchers not far from Refugio. I had seen some of their women out on sidesaddles). Finally Ellen put on a pair of trousers—she called them riding pants—and got on the pony.

Fortunately I missed all of this travail, although she and Henry felt the need to regale me with the details once we met up.

"She thought she would be ugly in trousers," Henry said.

"Yes, and indeed I was right. I am a sight."

We were riding slowly down One Little Hill toward Heron Marsh.

"A beautiful sight," Henry said.

I kept myself from groaning. I looked at Henry. It was the first time since he'd been home that I actually gave him a look—and this look told him to shut up.

He cleared his throat. "To her credit, Ellen didn't fall off the pony."

"Indeed, I did not!" Ellen agreed.

"A two-year-old could stay on that pony," I murmured.

"Pardon me?" Ellen asked. "The wind keeps snatching your words away."

I looked at her and smiled. "Nothing, Ellen. How are you enjoying your ride?" No reason to be contrary to her. She hadn't done anything wrong.

"It's quite liberating," Ellen said. "I should continue to wear trousers like you. I don't feel like a girl at all! That must be what it's like for you."

Suddenly I understood why Ellen wanted to spend so much time with me. She didn't consider me a woman. Apparently she didn't know how close Henry and I had been.

I took a deep breath. That was fine. That was better than fine. That was perfect. Made things more comfortable all around.

"Do you feel that way, Emily?"

"Um, liberated? I'm not sure what you mean."

"Unconstricted," she said. "You seem so unconstricted. I love the idea of it."

"You can be unconstricted, too," I said. "Get rid of your corset."

I'm not sure if Emily gasped or I only supposed she did. I was sure saying the word "corset" would be too much for her Boston sensibilities—that was why I said it. Henry took that opportunity to point out a group of egrets over by the marsh.

"Is this where the dragonflies were?" Ellen asked.

He had told her about the dragonflies?

Of course he had told her, I thought to myself. He *loves* her. He's going to tell her everything.

"Yes," Henry said. "We were standing over there." He pointed to the copse of cottonwood trees. "They must have all hatched at once for some reason. They were everywhere."

"I thought they had followed your father from Ireland," I said. "Didn't you say they were fairies?"

"They may have been, who knows?" he said. He looked over at me and smiled. "Emily and I stood right there, with our arms outstretched, while the dragonflies flew all around us."

"It was like we were praying to the dragonflies," I said. "Praying to their beauty."

"What a lovely image," Ellen said. "Do you think they'll come today? Wouldn't that be a nice coincidence?"

"I'm sure we'd see some dragonflies if we stopped," Henry said.

"No, let's go where you saw the deer give birth," she said.

I suddenly felt uncomfortable. Did Ellen want to go to each and every place Henry and I had been together?

Why? Because she didn't want them to be our places any longer? She wanted them to be hers and Henry's places.

"I'm hungry," I said. "Let's go to Singing Rocks."

Once we got to the creek, Ellen insisted on spreading out the blanket she had brought. Henry and I usually just sat on the rocks and ate. But she put the blanket down, got the picnic basket, and began distributing the food. She had potato salad, sandwiches, and boiled eggs. She sat opposite Henry and me. Somehow Henry and I ended up sitting next to one another.

"Nothing fancy," she said. "But I made them all myself."

She seemed proud of the fact that she could make a sandwich and potato salad. I looked at Henry. This time he gave me the look.

"We have a cook at home," Ellen said, "just like you do, so I'm not used to cooking. I'll learn! But I hope to have a cook, too. That would be better once we start having children. Then I can spend more time with them."

"Betsy Shaw and Rose aren't our cooks," I said.

"They do the cooking, don't they?" Henry said. "So they're cooks." He sounded irritated.

"Mr. Em and I know how to cook," I said.

"What do you cook?" Henry asked.

I bit the inside of my cheek. What did I cook? I looked at Henry and started to laugh. He grinned.

"You got me there, Henry," I said. "It's been a while since I cooked anything. Wait! I made porridge last week. Or last month. But Betsy Shaw did teach me to cook. She says every adult person should know how to take care of themselves whether they are male or female, young or old, rich or poor. She's got a point. So be proud of your potato salad, Ellen!"

Ellen smiled. "This ride has livened you up, Emily. I've never seen you quite so . . . vivid."

"Oh, Emily can talk a blue streak," Henry said. "She has

more opinions about more things than anyone else alive. And they are good opinions. She can learn a little bit about a subject and suddenly she understands it all. And she really does understand it. She cuts right to the heart of things."

"Just like you out in the wild," I said. "Henry can find a nest of mice or a wolves' den. That was great those weeks we watched the pups grow up, wasn't it? And he taught me so much about being with wild things. They are wild and we need to keep them wild."

"Speaking of food," he said. "Do you remember when we were camping in the Meadow and we caught a couple of fish and decided not to gut them?"

I laughed. "We knew how to gut them, Ellen. But we didn't want to. For one thing, it's disgusting."

"I would think so," she said.

"And we were lazy that day," Henry said. "We wanted to see how it would turn out."

We were both laughing now.

"It did not turn out," I said. "It was inedible. Our fathers were none to pleased with us. We got no supper that night."

"Served us right," Henry said.

"Where's the Meadow?" Ellen asked.

Henry and I stopped laughing and looked at her.

So he hadn't told her about the Meadow. I was glad. I looked over at him. A strand of hair was hanging in his eyes, just like it had most of his life. Without thinking about it, I reached over and brushed the strand off his forehead, just as I had a hundred times before. My fingers touched his skin as I moved his hair and I felt a shiver clear down to my toes. He looked at me, for only an instant, and then he moved back and away from me.

Ellen was watching us.

I laughed again, pretending we were still talking about bad

fish. "Yes, that was quite a night. I went to bed hungry." I bit into my sandwich and smiled at Ellen.

When we finished lunch, I told them I had work to do back at the house.

"You two keep going and have fun," I said. "I'll see you at the party on Sunday." Jamie and Nichols were throwing an engagement party for the couple on the weekend.

I waved to them as they left.

I didn't go back to the house. I took off my shoes and went to sit on Singing Rocks. Sometime later I heard someone ride up. I glanced over and saw Henry striding toward me. He looked angry.

I stood, prepared to jump from the rock, but Henry stopped a few feet from me and I couldn't get down without knocking into him. So I stayed where I was, towering over him.

"What was that?" Henry asked.

"What?" I asked. "We had a pleasant lunch together."

"You—you were trying to embarrass Ellen about her cooking," he said, "and about her riding the pony."

"I wasn't," I said. "I was trying very hard to be nice to her. I like her. She's a nice person. It's just very hard." I put my hands on my hips. "Get out of my way so I can get down from here." He didn't move. "Remember I'm just as strong as you are."

He rolled his eyes.

"Okay," I said. I jumped down and bumped right into him. To keep his balance, he reached out to grab me which caused us both to tumble into the mud together. And then we were embracing one another, holding on for dear life, it seemed, until I came to my senses and pulled away from him—or tried. He kept his arms around me. I could have gotten away. I was at least as strong as he was, but he whispered, "Wait."

I relaxed my weight against him, my face in his chest. Despite the layers of clothes between me and his skin, I could smell him, and I breathed in his scent as though it was the finest perfume—only it was better. It was Henry.

My body began shuddering with sobs.

No! This was not happening.

I pushed up off him and angrily wiped away my tears. I stood up and looked down at him again.

"You're not angry because you think I treated Ellen poorly," I said, "because you know I haven't. I have gone out of my way to make certain she and her parents have felt welcomed. You're angry because I touched you and you realized what you have with Ellen is nothing compared to what we feel for one another."

Henry stood, and we faced each other.

"What we felt for each other when we were kids," Henry said.

I pushed him away from me. "Don't you dare try to trivialize what we feel for each other! We have been connected to one another since we were children."

"And now we are adults," he said, "and we put away childish things."

"So now I'm a childish thing?" My eyes widened and then narrowed. I was so angry I wanted to hit something.

"You don't feel about me the same way I feel about you," he said. "It's always been that way. Lopsided. I—I had to move on. I had to—" He looked around as though searching for the right words. "I had to stop feeling so awful."

"What? You feel awful around me? I don't understand. I thought we loved one another. I thought we were most happy when we were together. I have never felt bad when I was with you. Even when we were in that tent together, I was saved because you were there. Saved!"

"And I feel such guilt over what happened to you," he said. "I should have been able to help you, save you in a real way."

"You did save me in a real way," I said. "And what happened then was then. This is now." I stepped back from him, suddenly realizing the full scope of what he was saying. "You see me as this scarred wounded thing. You think of *him* when you look at me?"

Henry shook his head. I could barely stand.

"No, that's not it," he said. "I see you, Emily. I see you. When Ellen and I first arrived and I saw you, my knees almost buckled. I had thought I was over you. I thought I could get over you. But then I saw you. You're so vibrant, alive. Yourself. I wanted to run to you right then and greet you just like we always do."

"With a kiss and a shove," I said.

He nodded. "I don't see you as wounded. I love you."

"I don't understand then," I said. "Tell Ellen you can't marry her. We can be together, just as we always planned."

"I can't do that," he said. "I made a promise to her. And nothing has changed, really. You still won't marry me, you still can't commit yourself to me."

"Of course I can commit myself to you!" I said. "I have. I have already done. And every day of my life that I spent with you, I was committing myself to you. And if you didn't understand that three years ago, understand it now. For me, nothing has changed. I love you with my whole heart. I want to spend the rest of my life with you. Isn't that a greater commitment than marriage which is only a legal ritual that says we're bound to one another? I only want to be bound to you by love. Nothing else matters."

Henry watched me, his eyes watering. For a moment, he almost looked convinced. Then he shook his head.

"I can't live with that kind of uncertainty," he said. "I'd always worry you were going to leave me."

I was astonished. "Why? Why would you think that?"

"Because you are so much better than I am," he said.

"Why would you think that?" I reached my hand out to him, but he stepped back.

He cleared his throat. "Ellen has decided she wants to get married here—at Paradise. So my family can be at our wedding. We'll have a church wedding when we return to Boston."

"Do you love her?" I asked.

"Of course I love her." He looked away from me.

"How could you expect me to show her all the places where you and I had been?" I said. "How could you take her to Singing Rocks, to the Heron Marsh? Couldn't you tell it was breaking my heart?"

He shook his head. "No, I couldn't tell, Emily. Last time we saw one another, you had completely withdrawn from me. I couldn't tell if you cared if I stayed or left. If you had asked me to stay, I would have. I never wanted to leave you."

"I thought you wanted to leave!" I said. "If going to school in Boston was your life's dream, I certainly wasn't going to spoil that for you. Just as I wasn't going to spoil your relationship with Ellen if she was the love of your life."

He looked at me and wiped the tears spilling onto his cheek. "You are the love of my life," he said, "and you have been since the moment I saw you on that wagon train. You don't remember it, but I do. You were laughing and there was a kind of glow around you and then you looked right at me. And I knew you saw me, clear to my soul, and I loved you instantly."

"Then you can't marry Ellen," I said. "You can't do that to her."

He looked at the ground. The world pulsated in silence. All I could hear was my own heart beating. Until I heard Henry's heart. I could see a silver line running from me to him. Even though we were separated by mere inches, it felt like an abyss. I crossed it. I put my arms around him. For a few brief moments, as I pressed myself against him, our hearts beat together, as one.

But Henry stepped away, and I dropped my arms. I looked into his eyes.

"I must marry her," he said. "Someday you'll find someone who deserves you. The wedding is Monday. The Sunday engagement party will now be a rehearsal dinner."

That was in three days.

"I won't come to your wedding," I said.

"Please."

I shook my head. "I would do almost anything for you. I would give my life to save you. But I won't watch you marry another woman."

He hung his head. Then he turned and walked away.

Chapter Fifteen

I staggered home to Mr. Em and told him everything that had happened between me and Henry. Diana and Betsy Shaw were there, too. By the end of it, Betsy Shaw was crying.

"I don't understand him at all," Betsy Shaw said.

"He sounds haunted," Diana said. "Why would he think he wasn't good enough for you?"

"I don't know," I said. "But if he's determined to marry Ellen, I won't try to stop them. I poured my heart out to him. He's destroying three lives with this decision."

"No," Mr. Em said. "You will be all right. And maybe this is the best thing. If Henry isn't willing to fight for you, then maybe he isn't worth it."

I looked at my father. He usually wasn't judgmental about other people—especially about Henry. He had never understood our relationship, hadn't since we were children, but he honored it by not asking me about it.

"You should tell her," Diana said. "Tell Ellen that Henry still loves you."

I shook my head. "No. Haven't you all been trying to teach me since I was a child that I can't control everyone and everything? Henry has made his decision. I have made mine. He doesn't respect or understand my decision not to marry. I will do him the courtesy of trying to respect and understand his decision."

"Will you go to the wedding?" Mr. Em asked.

"No," I said. "I couldn't do that. I'm afraid it would permanently break my heart. He said they're returning to Boston, so I'm hoping I won't have to see him before he goes. I will go on with my life here on Refugio. I am perfectly happy."

Later, after Diana and Betsy Shaw had retired to their respective rooms, I went into my father's study where he was sitting in his big stuffed chair reading. He looked up at me and smiled. I slid onto his lap, as I had so many times when I was a girl. I rested my head against his chest and listened to his heart. He put his arms around me, and we sat, silently, breathing together.

"You have been the best father," I whispered. "Thank you."

"You're glad you've lived with me and not your mother then?"

"I never think about her," I said, "but yes, I am glad to be with you here on Refugio. I couldn't ask for a better life." I closed my eyes. "Mr. Em, do you really think I will recover from this heartbreak?"

"I know you will," he said.

"What do you think happened to the Big Men?" I asked. "And Sitiu's grandsons and the others? Do you think they are alive and well?"

"I don't know about the Big Men," he said, "but nearly all of Sitiu's people are dead, either murdered or killed by disease. Those years of the gold rush were not kind to the Indians."

"You tried to help," I said.

"I failed."

"I hope our gold taking didn't hurt anyone," I said. Besides me and Henry. I slid out of my father's lap and onto the floor. I rested my head against his leg.

"I don't think we hurt anyone," he said. He stroked my hair. "Except you. I wish we'd never gone there."

"Not me," I said. "If we hadn't gone there, I wouldn't have reconnected with Henry, and we wouldn't have found the gems. I wish that man had never been born or that he had died before he killed Sitiu or scarred my back. The rest was magic."

"That's a good perspective," Mr. Em said.

"I learned perspective from you," I said. "You've let your past go. So have I. Except I still hate him. I still wish I knew what had happened to him. I want to know that he did poorly and that he suffered."

"Or that he changed?"

I thought about it. "All right, Mr. Em. If he changed and renounced his ways, that would satisfy me. But not as much as a bad end."

I heard him chuckle.

"Try to go to sleep," Mr. Em said.

"Maybe Henry will ride in the night to find me again," I said. "Maybe I'll wake up in the dark and there he'll be. And all will be well."

"Yes, those were the good old days," Mr. Em said.

I looked up at him and laughed. "I suppose for a father they might have been a bit troubling." I reached for his hand and he pulled me to a standing position.

"To find my 12-year-old daughter in bed with a boy?" he said. "Troubling is not the right word. Shocking is perhaps a better one. I almost shipped you back East to your mother."

"But then you decided I was an autonomous being who had to make her own decisions."

"Something like that." My father stood. I heard his knees creak. Lately it seemed that he moved a little slower than was his custom.

"You all right?" I asked.

"Just getting old," he said. "It happens to the best and worst of us if we are lucky."

I put my arm around his waist and we left his study. Together we walked down the corridor toward our rooms.

"I was shocked when I saw him in your bed," Mr. Em said. "Or were you in his? But I wasn't surprised. There was always something about the two of you."

"Like two magnets," I said, remembering what I had once told Miss Allison. "Destined to be together."

"And that broke your father's heart a little," he said, "since I thought I was your greatest love."

I smiled. "That's a given, Mr. Em."

My father squeezed my shoulders and kissed the top of my head.

"Sweet dreams, daughter."

"Sweet dreams."

I kept waking up all night, believing Henry was in the room. I'd sit up and whisper his name. No one or nothing whispered back. I did think I saw his mountain lion for a moment—the mountain lion I hadn't seen in some years. But later I wasn't sure if that had been real or part of my dreams. The next night the same thing happened. I'd awaken, believing Henry was there. When he wasn't, the ache was almost too much to bear.

I hadn't planned on going to the engagement party cum rehearsal dinner. But then just before Mr. Em and the others were leaving for Paradise, I saw a silver path leading from me to my desk. I had never seen a silver path inside our house before. I followed it to the desk. I looked through my papers and didn't find anything of import.

Then I glanced up. In one of the compartments, I spotted the notebook I had been keeping for Henry during the three years he had been away, the one with notes and sketches of the flora and fauna on the two ranches. I pulled it out and flipped through it. Nearly every page was filled. I opened to one page that had a drawing of a flower on it. "Dearest Henry," I wrote, "look what I found. It's like the wild sweet peas we've seen before, but this one is more lilac-colored than the bright pink ones. My drawing and coloring doesn't do it justice. I swear it was speaking to me, Henry. It said 'pick me, pick me.'"

I turned to another page. "My dear Henry. I know we've seen poppies before, but this entire hill was covered with them. It's the smaller hill north of Big Hill. I'll call it 'Poppy Hill.' I was walking some distance away—barefoot, mind you, and I felt a wave of love. I had been feeling down and lonely, missing you and our times together, and then I felt love! I hurried toward the feeling—who wouldn't—and I came upon this field of poppies. The entire hill was orange with them. I lay down in the midst of them, surrounded by them, enveloped by them, and I was certain that somewhere on the other side of the country you were thinking of me and sending me love."

I had drawn poppy after poppy on the opposite page. I remembered it had taken me much of the day. In the end I couldn't actually tell one poppy from another.

Other pages had drawings of flowers and plants whose names I didn't know. "This one wanted to tell me the secrets of the universe. I said I was ready but it might be more fun to wait and tell us both." "This one wanted to open my heart and fill it with love. It felt old and very wise. Later I realized I was feeling closed-hearted. That happens to me too often since the kidnapping. That's why I was distant to you before you left: I was worried that man was somewhere near, preparing to hurt me again. I know that is ridiculous, but sometimes I am still afraid. I went back to this bush and lay next to it and asked it to open my heart. Afterward I was much kinder to everyone at home. Later I found out it is called ephedra and it's also called Mormon tea. Maybe when the Mormons got here, their hearts closed up and this helped them. I love you, Henry."

I closed the book. I didn't remember writing half of what I read. When I had written to Henry in Boston while he was gone, I had never written such tender or intimate letters. I had been as aloof as he had been. Or maybe it had been the other way around: He was as aloof as I had been.

I sighed.

Why do we do the things we do?

I loved Henry more than anyone in the world—except Mr. Em, I supposed. I loved them the same. No, not the same. Equally. I shook my head. This was a child's argument. If I loved Henry so much, why had I withdrawn from him? Why couldn't I have let him know before that even if I didn't want to marry anyone, I loved him deeply?

I had been more open before. I had been more vulnerable before.

Before the kidnapping.

I hugged the book to my chest. I would take it to Henry. He deserved to see it, read it, know that I thought about him while he was away.

My father was surprised I wanted to go to the party and startled to see me in a dress. Betsy Shaw and Diana looked equally astonished.

"You've all seen me in a dress before," I said. "Now close your mouths before some insect flies in."

There was food aplenty and toasts to the future bride and groom—and dances. I felt sick the entire meal, but I was determined to give Henry the book and then ride or walk or run home. He avoided my gaze all afternoon. Finally he walked across the room to where I was sitting alone in one of the chairs against the wall.

"Would you like to dance?" he asked.

"No," I said, "but thank you." I stood and picked up the notebook and handed it to him.

"'For Henry,'" he read. "What's this?"

"I kept it while you were away," I said. "It was supposed to emulate your own notebooks."

He began flipping through it.

"Don't look at it now," I said. "Consider it a going away present."

As he looked down at it, a strand of his hair fell across his forehead. I started to reach for it and stopped myself.

"You should really cut that," I said.

He reached up and pushed the hair off his forehead.

"I don't think so," he said. "It reminds me of you."

"Get me the scissors then," I said. "I'll cut it off. You'll be a married man soon and won't be able to think about old . . . friends." I held out my hand to him. "Good luck, Henry. I wish you and Ellen all the best."

He hesitated and then he took my hand in his. I felt a spark— or a flash of heat. I wondered if he felt it, too, but I didn't ask. He shook my hand firmly. Then I pulled my hand away and walked out of the house and out of Henry's life.

When I got back to Refugio, the house seemed unusually empty. My father had asked me if I wanted him to come home early, too, but I said no. I wanted to be alone. But now the house seemed lonely and I didn't want to be there. In fact, I wanted to be hundreds of miles away. Or in some other world, so I wouldn't have to tick off the hours until Henry got married.

I packed some food, and then I saddled Holiday and set off for Redwood House. I always felt better there. It was only after I had arrived and put Holiday away in the barn that I realized I felt better here because every inch of it reminded me of Henry. By that time it was dark. Too late to head home or anywhere else. I started a fire in the main fireplace, put my bedroll in front of it, and fell asleep.

I slept until day break. Then I ate and spent most of the morning down by the beach. I watched the gray waves rolling to shore. Sanderlings kept running along the tideline, sinking their beaks into the wet sand as soon as the water receded.

I watched the sun and wondered if the wedding was over. I wondered if I should create my own ceremony, one to prevent heartbreak. I lay on the sand and whispered to it, "Don't let me break, please." I looked up at the sky, "Don't let me break. Let me be strong." I looked out at the ocean. "Let Henry be well. Let him be happy. Let him love well."

Later I fed Holiday, then fed myself. I fell asleep before it was dark. I dreamed about my mother, Juliet Lee. I didn't remember ever dreaming about her before. But there she was, walking with me down a street in San Francisco. My hair was short again, and I wore a tight-fitting dress and a hat with a feather in it. Ahead of us walked Jake McMahon.

I awoke with a start. I looked quickly around me. I was alone. It was deep night. I got up and stirred the fire into flames. Then I lay back on my bed roll.

It was Henry's wedding night. Were he and Ellen together in bed? Naked? Making love? Was he thinking of me? I hoped not. How dreadful that would be for both of them.

I closed my eyes.

I smelled Henry again and thought he was in the room. I didn't want to open my eyes and be heartbroken again.

"Henry," I whispered.

"I'm here," I heard.

I opened my eyes. In the dying firelight, I saw Henry's shadow.

"Are you really here?"

"Yes."

I sat up, jumped up, moved, did something so that I was in his lap, with my arms and legs around him. And we were kissing, kissing, kissing.

I don't know if I had ever felt such joy.

I pulled away. "Isn't this your wedding night?"

"I didn't get married," he said.

Thank goodness.

I held onto him, whispered into his ear, "You called it off?"

He shook his head. I looked at him.

"She called it off?" I moved a bit away from him. He'd only come to me after *she* had called it off. "You mean you would have gone through with it?"

"I—I don't know," he said.

I moved further away from him. "You're saying if it wasn't for her, you might be making love to her right now."

"What do you want me to say?"

"I want you to tell me why you keep breaking my heart!" I cried. "I thought you came here, to me, because you realized you couldn't marry Ellen. You couldn't do it because you loved me. But now you're saying you're here because she threw you over. How do you think that makes me feel?"

He rubbed his face. "I don't know!" He was yelling now, too. Both of us were standing.

"After the party, I found her reading the notebook you gave me," he said.

"What? That was private. That was only for you!"

"I know! Let me talk, will you? She read it, started crying, and said it was clear that you still loved me and that I must still love you. She had seen it in the way we were together, she said. She saw us talking at the party. The way you reached for my hair and then stopped yourself. She saw us shake hands. She said if we were over one another, we would have embraced, as old friends would do. We only came out here because she wanted to see if we were over one another."

"She knew? She knew I loved you?"

"She knew you had at one point," he said, "and that I loved you, too. I said I was over you, but she wanted to see for herself. So last night, she told me she couldn't marry me because of us. I didn't argue with her. I told her I was sorry. She and her parents left today."

I sank back onto my bedroll. I looked up at Henry.

"What were you thinking?" I asked. "What has happened to you? Why did you get involved with her? Why did you say you weren't good enough for me?"

I reached for his hand and pulled him down next to me.

"I forget how strong you are," he said. "I missed that. I missed so much." He reached up and touched my hair. "I missed the colors of your hair. I missed your eyes. I missed being with someone who had one foot in this world and another foot in who knows how many other worlds."

"Henry, tell me why it's so important for me to marry you."

We sat across from one another, holding hands. The firelight barely lit the room. We were mostly in shadow.

"I never told her about this place, you know," he said. "I couldn't."

"You never told her about the other things," I said. "Did you? You didn't tell her about the kidnapping and me being carved up?"

"I didn't," he said. "But you know, it's my right to talk about it, too. It didn't only happen to you. It happened to me and to our fathers. I have a right to tell people what happened to me."

"Yes," I said. "I know."

He squeezed my hands. "Remember when Katherine beat me? She used to say all kinds of things to me. About how I was a loser. How if I'd been good enough and strong enough I would have saved you and protected you. I would have stopped him and saved the gold, too. She said now no one would ever trust me or marry me. No woman would trust me because it is the man's job to protect his wife. And I believed her. I believed her because I had already thought about all of those things. It wasn't that you were a girl. It was that you were younger, smaller, and I knew the land better than you did. I should have been able to help."

"You did help! If you hadn't told me where to run to, I would have never escaped. He could have killed me—or worse. He could have made me one of his little slaves like he did with those other two boys."

"I need to get this out, Emily," he said.

"I'm sorry," I said. "Go ahead."

"So I thought if you agreed to marry me, then the sin would have been washed away. You would have forgiven me. By you saying you'd marry me, it meant you trusted me with your life. You knew I was capable of protecting you and our children, should we have any. You would have forgiven me for standing by while he carved your back. You would have forgiven me for leaving you alone in that tent with him." He began to cry. His shoulders shuddered and his head dropped to his chest. Then he looked up again. "When you said you wouldn't marry me, I figured you didn't really love me like I loved you. You didn't trust me."

"Can I speak?"

He nodded.

"I've said before that I don't blame you for anything," I said. "I won't have this man take away my happiness. He did something to us that lasted a few hours. Why should that ruin our lives? That's like carrying him around with us all of these years. I won't do it. I love you. You, Henry. You were a child, bound up just as I was. You couldn't save me. Mr. Em couldn't save me!"

"But you don't know the worst of it," he said. He shook his head, losing his voice. He coughed. "I've never told you. I've never said it out loud. It is the shame of my life, and I don't know how to make amends."

"What is it, Henry? What? I can't imagine that you've done anything shameful."

"Remember when he told me I had to leave and tell Mr. Em what I had witnessed? And you told me to go. I didn't want to leave you, but you said it was all right, so I left. After he took the blindfold off me, I ran like hell, Emily. I don't know that I ever ran so fast in my life."

"Good!" I said. "I'm glad. I was so relieved that you were out of there."

"And here's the thing, Emily," he said. "This is what I can't forgive, this is what I can't understand. I was so relieved to leave. Like a coward, I ran like hell because I was glad to be out of there. I was glad he had chosen me to leave. I was glad that I got to leave. For a few seconds I wasn't thinking about anything except my safety."

"Why is that unforgivable?" I said. "It's human! You don't think I would have been relieved if he had sent me home? Of course I would have been."

He shook his head. "I don't believe it. You're the bravest person I've ever known."

"Hah!" I said. "Henry." I took his face between my hands. "I would have been relieved, too. Anyone would have been. That is not being a coward. That is being a human being."

I wrapped him in my arms, and he sobbed.

"That bastard is responsible for so much," I said. "I swear if I found him I would kill him with my bare hands. But I don't want to waste another minute on him. Not another minute."

We lay down together in front of the fire, holding one another. Before long, we fell asleep. When I awakened, it was almost dawn. I could just barely see the ocean in the distance. Henry was asleep next to me. I stirred the fire. Then I began taking off my clothes. Henry's eyes opened. He watched me first discard my shirt, then my undershirt, my trousers, my undergarments, until I was lying naked next to him. Then I began unbuttoning his shirt. He helped by kissing me. I laughed and pulled off his trousers. Soon we were both naked. When we finally pressed ourselves against one another, skin to skin, I felt like this was what I had been heading toward for my entire life. As we made love to one another, as we whispered our love to one another, all was healed. We were healed. The world was healed. No sin had ever been committed. All was beginning once again.

Chapter Sixteen

It was full daylight when Henry and I finally fell away from one another. I lay on my stomach on my bedroll, still naked. Henry stroked my back.

"Does it ever trouble you?" Henry asked.

"No, not since the fire," I said.

"I probably shouldn't say this, but it's beautiful," he said.

"It's better than saying it's ugly," I said.

I sat up and began putting my clothes on.

"Really?" he said. He started reluctantly getting dressed too.

"We better eat something," I said. "To fortify us for later."

"That was a much better wedding night than I had anticipated," Henry said.

I looked at him. "Really, Henry?"

"I apologize. I guess that will never be amusing."

"I wouldn't say never."

"What's next?" Henry said. "Do we need to worry about you getting pregnant?"

"A little late to be discussing that now," I said.

"That's true," he said.

"But I know when I can and can't get pregnant," I said. "We don't need to worry. I don't want to talk about the future, do you, Henry? I mean, less than 24 hours ago, I thought I had lost you forever. Now I just want to be joyful that we're together."

He wrapped me in his arms.

"And you're certain you've forgiven me?" he asked.

I frowned. "There is nothing to forgive, Henry." I kissed him. "Nothing."

We had a marvelous day. We hiked down to the beach and lay on the sand together. We looked in tide pools for hours. Later we walked partway up Big Hill to the point where I had confronted the fire.

"It must be wonderful to feel so powerful," Henry said as we stood on the line of fire.

I laughed. "I didn't feel powerful. I felt old. It was almost like it wasn't me. It was a kind of instinctual thing. Probably like how you feel when you're out in the woods and you know where to go and what to do."

He gazed up the hill. His eyes looked haunted.

"Henry?"

"I've made such a mess of things," he said.

"But it's fixed now," I said. "We're together and we love each other."

"Love isn't everything," he said.

"But it is," I said. "Love is everything."

He kissed me. "Love is everything then," he said.

It didn't sound like he believed it.

We went back to the house and made love for hours. I couldn't believe I had waited so long to be with him. If I had agreed to marry him years earlier, we probably would have gotten naked a lot sooner. That would have been one advantage of saying I would marry: glorious sex with Henry.

Henry didn't bring up marriage. I was surprised and gratified. I still didn't want to marry, but if I had to choose between being married and having Henry in my life or not being married and not having Henry, I would choose Henry.

That night we fell asleep in each other's arms.

When I woke up, Henry was gone. For some reason, I wasn't surprised.

I lit a lamp and read a note he had left me.

"I think I know a way to make it right," he said. "I'll return in a few weeks if all goes as I hope. I love you. Henry."

I looked up from the note and saw a silver path running from me to the front door. I walked to the door and opened it. The silver pathway snaked out into the darkness to an end I could not see.

I stood on the porch and called out into the darkness, "Henry!"

No answer. Just the distant sound of waves crashing onto the beach.

I screamed, "Henry!"

Nothing.

I felt a cold fury rising in me.

"It didn't matter that you left me in that tent," I screamed. "It certainly doesn't matter to me that you were glad to be out of the tent. It didn't even matter that you left me to go on your first expedition or that you left to go to college—despite your promises never to leave me! It doesn't even matter that you threatened to leave me by getting married. But this, this right here and now does matter. You've left me again, Henry Simmons, and I will not forgive you for it! This is the end, Henry! I am done!"

I stepped back into the house and slammed the door shut. It

was the first time that I hadn't followed a silver pathway to its end.

In the morning when I woke up, the silver pathway was gone.

I had no idea what to do with my life next.

I took my time leaving Redwood House that first day after Henry left. I wasn't certain what waited for me at home. Eventually, I had to leave. I was out of food. I mounted Holiday and reluctantly headed home. I saw the hoof prints Henry's horse had left and I was tempted to follow. But in the end, I yelled some swear words into the wind and headed back to the hacienda.

Mr. Em stood outside the front door scanning the horizon for me. From a distance, he looked like a colorful wooden sentry. As I got closer I saw his white, red, and brown hair blowing in the wind.

Titus came out and took a hold of Holiday as I dismounted.

"We've all heard," Titus said. "He'll be back, Emily."

I patted Titus's arm. "I don't think I care any more," I said.

Mr. Em opened his arms to me and I pressed my face against his chest—well, closer to his belly since he was so tall—and we embraced one another.

I looked up at him, and he looked down at me.

"Henry stopped to get supplies at Jamie's," Mr. Em said. "He didn't tell us where he was going."

"He didn't tell me either," I said. I let my father go. "And I don't care. He said he had to make something right. Everything was already all right. He's still troubled by the kidnapping. He still thinks he could have done something." I shook my head. "He's left me too many times, Mr. Em. I have to go on with my life. I won't spend the rest of my days waiting for him and then waiting to be left. It's absurd."

The house was filled, it seemed, with nearly everyone I knew. Betsy Shaw hugged me too tightly.

"Betsy Shaw," I said, "you're going to smother me."

She let me go and wiped her tears away. She was not a demonstrative person so this display of affection surprised me.

"How are you?" she asked.

I looked at the people gathered around me. Mr. Em smiled grimly. Diana came and put her arm around my waist.

"I am fine," I said. "I have all of you. How could I be grander? Yes, Henry has left me again. But that is how it is. He's been gone for three years. What does it matter? We go on."

I awakened in the middle of the night because my back itched. I recognized the itch. This wasn't from a bug bite or an annoying rash. This was from my scars. When I reached to scratch it, I discovered the scars on my back were raised up again. I was puzzled. What did this mean? I didn't know if we had any witch hazel, and I wasn't going to wake up Betsy Shaw to find out. Instead, I closed my eyes and tried to summon the glowing white woman who used to come and help me when my back itched—the spirit of witch hazel.

Nothing happened. I sat alone in the darkness. After a few minutes, the itching subsided and I went back to sleep.

It was summertime at Refugio, so work was plentiful. I had something to do every day, all day. If I wasn't healing, I was looking for calves or foals or mending this fence or that barn door. I was everywhere doing everything. One day Mr. Em took me aside and cautioned me against overwork, but I told him I wanted to keep busy.

The nights became strange for me. I often awakened because of the itching. I asked Betsy Shaw to look at my back and she confirmed that the scars were still colorful but now raised up and bumpy, the way they had been in the beginning.

I tried not to think of Henry. I tried not to wonder what he was doing. Then one day, my father brought me a letter from Henry. As I held it in my hand, my fingers shook. I recognized his handwriting, so I knew it was from him, I knew he was safe. That was all I needed to know. I handed the letter back to my father.

"Is it possible to return to sender?" I asked. "If it is, I'd like to do that."

"Do you want me to read it?" he asked.

I hesitated. Then I said, "No. And if any more come, please ask them to return them."

"Are you sure, daughter?" he asked.

"I am."

After Henry had been gone a month or more, Jamie came to Refugio and found me at Redwood House doing repairs on the warped doors to the stalls. When I first heard Jamie's horse, my stomach lurched. I thought maybe it was Henry. I looked up and saw Jamie and wasn't certain if I was relieved or disappointed.

Once he was off his horse and next to me, Jamie didn't waste any time getting to the point.

"Henry is concerned that he hasn't heard from you," he said.

I laughed. "He won't hear from me. He left me. We made love all night—his wedding night—and then he left me. So first he almost marries another woman even though I am supposed to be the love his life. Whatever that means! And then he comes to me after she drops him, after *she* breaks off their engagement, and we make love. It was glorious, Jamie. It was the best night of my life. Then he leaves. He doesn't say goodbye. He doesn't tell me what the hell he is doing. He runs away."

"He wasn't running away," Jamie said.

I put my hand on the wooden pasture fence to steady myself. I was so angry I was shaking.

"Then what was he doing?"

"I don't really know," Jamie said. "He didn't tell me. He wouldn't tell us anything. He felt like he had to fix things."

"There was nothing to fix!" I knew it was Henry I was angry at, but Jamie was standing there, so he got the brunt of my anger. "It was perfect. We were perfect. Everything was as it should be! Apparently he can't stand to be with me for any length of time. He thinks about the kidnapping. He thinks about my scars. I don't want to be around someone who only sees monsters when he looks at me. I don't want to be the thing that reminds him of the worst moments in his life."

"I'm sure that's not the case," Jamie said.

"Then where is he?" I asked.

"He sent me a letter to give to you," Jamie said. "Will you take it."

I shook my head. "No. I've had one too many letters from him. Now, if you'll excuse me, I've got work to do." I turned away from him.

"Please, Emily. It's not like you to be so unforgiving."

I turned around and faced him. "Henry and I made promises to one another. He keeps breaking those promises again and again. That makes them meaningless. He wanted us to get married so that he would really know I was committed to him, that I trusted and believed in him. If he can't keep the simple promises we made to one another—not to lie, not to leave—if he can't be a good friend, how could he ever be a good husband?"

After Jamie left, I threw up. I was still shaking. I felt like I was coming down with some illness. I dug around my saddlebags for something that would quell the nausea, but I found only a sandwich Betsy Shaw had made—and looking at it made me feel even worse.

Like the itching, the nausea didn't last long. Soon I was able to finish my work and then head home.

For about a week, I didn't get worse and I didn't get better. I finally told Betsy Shaw. I sat on my bed, too woozy to get up.

"When was the last time you menstruated?" she asked.

I frowned. "What's that got to do with it?"

She raised an eyebrow. I groaned as it dawned on me. That would explain my tender breasts, too.

She sat on the bed next to me. "Do you want me to contact Henry?"

"No! Absolutely not," I said. "And I will tell Mr. Em when I'm ready."

"Do you want to have the baby?" she asked. "It's early enough. I can get you some herbs."

"I don't know," I said. "I—I don't know what to do yet."

That day I went down to Singing Rocks and watched Wild Creek flowing away from me. I had been sick most of the morning, but now I felt strangely rested and relaxed. I put my hand on my belly and wondered how tiny the baby was. Was it a girl or a boy? As soon as I wondered, I knew it was a girl. I closed my eyes. I could see her in my arms. I could see her laughing and running in the poppy field. Strangely enough, her hair was blond and her eyes blue.

When I opened my eyes again, I knew I wouldn't ask Betsy Shaw for the herbs. And I wouldn't tell Henry. Not yet.

I hurried back to the hacienda and found my father in his office. I went in, closed the door, and sat in the chair opposite his desk.

"Mr. Em, I have to tell you something," I said.

He nodded and gave me his full attention.

"I am pregnant," I said. The expression on my father's face didn't change. "It's a girl. I'm calling her Emma. I'm not telling Henry. He doesn't deserve to know after what he's done. I'm very excited about it, actually. And Mr. Em, you're going to be a granddad."

"I'm not sure what to say," he said. He got up and came around the desk and kissed my forehead. "Congratulations?"

"Yes, congratulations is good," I said.

"I will admit I was afraid of this when you told me you hadn't been feeling well," he said.

"By the way, I don't want Jamie or Nichols to know. I don't want anyone telling Henry."

Mr. Em sat on the edge of his desk and looked down at me.

"Don't you want him to come back?"

I took a deep breath. Did I want Henry back?

"I'm still so angry at him," I said. "But yes, of course, I want him back. If he can get over whatever is troubling him. If he can be with me. I want him back, but he has to come on his own accord. I want to know that we're still connected. If we are, he'll know I need him here. He'll return. I don't want him to come back because he hears I'm pregnant."

"I think that's a lot to expect from him, or anyone."

"I don't want to think about him now," I said. "I want to enjoy this time."

And I did enjoy it. The nausea and the itching stopped almost as soon as I realized I was pregnant. I'm sure one didn't have anything to do with the other, but that's what happened. The swelling didn't go down on my scars, however, which was odd.

Soon enough my trousers were too tight for me. Betsy Shaw altered some of them, but I had to admit that a frock was more comfortable than most of the trousers, although not as convenient when I went riding. Betsy Shaw warned me off horses. I told her being pregnant was the most natural thing in the world, so I couldn't imagine anything I did would harm the baby. Nevertheless, once the baby started showing in my belly, I didn't ride as much.

I spent much of my time wandering around the ranch, walking from one favorite place to another, talking to the baby the entire time.

"Emma, this is where the dragonflies surrounded us," I said. "They hatch every year. We'll show you." Or, "This is Redwood House, your home to be. This is where you were conceived before your father ran off to do who knows what." Or, "See those eagles? They'll head south soon. They leave about the same time the swans return. It's all a part of the cycle of this place and time."

Every day I expected to see Henry coming down a path, over a hill, around a corner. Every day I was mildly surprised that he hadn't yet returned.

I slept surprisingly well. I often dreamed of my life with Emma. Sometimes Henry was there. Sometimes he wasn't. Always, Emma was the most beautiful, loving child who had ever been born. I often woke in the morning with a smile on my face. Motherhood would be no challenge with Emma as my daughter.

Sometimes I sat with my hands on my belly, sending Emma waves of love. I was certain she sent waves back to me. I wondered if my mother had loved me as much as I loved Emma. If she had, how could she have ever left me?

I had a healthy appetite. Betsy Shaw seemed to love the challenge of cooking me whatever I craved. Diana, Titus, Rose, and Thomas were in on the secret, and they often came to visit— even Rose and Thomas who were now farming their own place when they weren't teaching former whores how to read.

One night when I was nearly five months along, I dreamed Henry had died. I awakened to a pounding heart and darkness.

"It's okay, okay," I told myself. I put my hand on my belly. "Your papa is fine, Emma. Irritating as hell, but he is well. Somewhere he is well and fine."

I lay back down in my bed and cradled my belly—and Emma. "Shhh," I said. "Everything is all right."

Then I did what I hadn't done in years. I closed my eyes, relaxed, and let myself float up above my body.

"Henry," I whispered, and I was instantly beside him. He was sleeping on a tiny bed. I watched his chest rise and fall, rise and fall. My heart instantly softened. I didn't know where he was, but he was alive. "Henry, come home to me. I want you to meet our daughter."

"Emily," he whispered.

I heard a child crying, and I immediately went back to my bed in Refugio. I was still cradling my belly.

"See, Emma," I said. "He's well. He's safe. Now let us get some sleep."

I fell asleep again. This time in the dream, Emma and I were walking through a field somewhere. I wasn't certain of the location. I only knew we were on Refugio. Emma began running. I laughed as I watched her. She turned around and ran toward me, her arms outstretched. When she reached me, I wrapped her in my arms and lifted her. I couldn't imagine that I had been alive before I came to love her. Then my hands felt something on her back. My heart started racing. I put her down. Then I lifted her shirt and looked at her back. She had two giant scars in the shape of an X across her tiny back.

My heart was racing when I awakened. I felt like I was going to be sick. I lay in bed and held my stomach again. "It's all right, it's all right. Everything is all right."

But I had a feeling something awful was about to happen.

Two days later I was standing in the kitchen with Betsy Shaw, and I began to cramp.

"Betsy!" I cried, bending over, reaching out for her.

I felt something trickling down my legs. "What's happening?"

Mr. Em heard my scream. He ran into the kitchen.

"What's wrong?" he said. "Where's the blood coming from?"

"Blood?" I looked down. Blood was streaming down my legs.

Mr. Em picked me up and carried me into my room and lay me on the bed. "I'll get help," he said. Then he ran out of the room again.

I screamed in pain. I put my hands on my belly. "No, Emma, please, Emma. You've got to stay. Stay. Please."

I felt a pulsing—or something—in my uterus. I knew then I had lost the baby. I knew she had let go, she was leaving this world. I tried everything in my power to keep her within me.

But she was gone.

Betsy Shaw ran out of the room to get towels.

I found Emma in my sheets. So tiny it was difficult at first to tell what was blood and tissue and what was Emma, but there she was. I gently picked her up and held her in the palm of my hand.

Betsy Shaw ran back into the room. "Look," I said, holding out my bloody hand to her. "She is so precious."

"Oh my god," Betsy Shaw said. "Are you still bleeding? There is blood everywhere. Has it stopped?"

I wiped the tears off my face with one hand while holding Emma in the other. What did it matter? Blood and guts: Wasn't that what life was all about?

"Emily!" Betsy Shaw yelled. "We've got to make certain you've stopped bleeding."

"And if I haven't, what are we going to do?" I said. "I'm either going to bleed to death or I'm not."

"Let me clean you up," Betsy Shaw said. "Let me take her."

I shook my head. "Not yet."

I stared down at the fetus. She barely looked human. Yet I had spent what seemed like a lifetime with her.

"Peace, Emma," I whispered to her. "Peace."

Betsy Shaw brought a small clean white cloth to me. "Let me wrap her in this," she said. "We will bury her later."

I nodded. I gently put her on the cloth. Betsy Shaw wrapped it around her, and then she started to walk away.

"Betsy Shaw," I said. "Can you check her back? Can you make certain she doesn't have a scar on her back. I didn't see one, but I want to make certain."

"Honey, she wouldn't have a scar on her back," Betsy Shaw said. "It doesn't work like that."

"How do we know?" I said. "I'm one of a kind. We don't know how it works. Maybe that's why she couldn't stay, maybe that's why she left. The scar was too much for her."

"No," Betsy Shaw said, holding the covered fetus in her hands. "You're young. First pregnancies are often very tenuous. That's all."

"That's all? That's enough. Please check, for me."

Betsy Shaw nodded. "I will. I promise."

Then she left the room.

I could feel my uterus contracting, expelling whatever was left of Emma's home. When it stopped, I wiped myself and got out of bed. I took off my bloody clothes and dropped them into the middle of the bloody sheets and blankets. I started to pull them off the bed just as Betsy Shaw returned with Diana.

I looked at them. "Did she? Was she scarred?"

"No, child," Betsy Shaw said. "She had no mark on her."

"Good," I said. "No coffin. How could there be any coffin." I laughed or smirked. "Too tiny. I will put her into the ground. She will become more a part of this place than we are."

Diana came up to me and embraced my naked self. "Darlin," she said. "Let us take care of you."

I sank into her arms and began to cry. "I was a poor mother," I said. "I must have been. I must have been! And what would I know? What? She left me. She left me!"

I'm not very clear about what happened after that. The women bathed me, dressed me, cleaned my room of the bloody mess. Mr. Em brought the midwife, but by then, there was nothing she could do. Nothing she could have done. I slept like the dead. The next morning, I insisted on going out into the cold damp autumn day and burying that part of me that had been Emma.

I gently put Emma in the ground near an oak tree at the top of Big Hill. The wind whipped around us as I covered her with dirt. I sang prayers Indian Mary had taught me. I looked around, waiting to see silver pathways or perhaps the spirit that had been Emma, but I saw only the ocean and Redwood House in the distance. Above, the sky was gray. When a seagull flew overhead, I decided the ceremony was over.

"Peace be with you," I whispered.

Then I turned away. I felt battered by loss. I didn't know where to go or what to do. Mr. Em put his arm across my shoulders, and together, we headed home.

Chapter Seventeen

The next day, Miss Allison arrived. Maybe it wasn't actually the following day, but it was soon after the miscarriage. I had gone strangely mute. I didn't want to talk, but I didn't mind company, and I enjoyed hearing their voices. It was like listening to ocean waves coming ashore: The sound was soothing but incomprehensible. Mr. Em stayed near me. He told me stories. He read the newspaper to me. He told me all would be well in the fullness of time, just as he had after I'd been kidnapped. This was worse than the kidnapping. I had lost a daughter and the man I loved. I was bereft. And my back itched.

When Miss Allison arrived, I was out walking down by Wild Creek. It was too cold and rainy, but I didn't want to be indoors. I felt restless. "Emma," I whispered as I walked along the muddy banks of the overflowing creek. "Where did you go? I saw our life together. And now it's gone. Was any of it real? Why did you leave?"

My vision was blurred from tears and rain. I didn't see the

hole in the ground because it was filled with water. I stepped right into it with one foot. And then I went down hard on one knee and then over into the mud. I quickly pushed myself up and moved away from the river bank to the grass. I had to sit back down because of the pain in my right foot. I pulled my shoe and sock off. The rain started coming down harder. My ankle was beginning to swell.

"Damn it," I said.

I put my hands around my ankle, hoping I could heal it. I closed my eyes. I didn't feel anything—except pain.

"This doesn't look like it's as much fun as it probably is."

I looked up. Peter Stevens was holding his coat over me to shield me from the rain.

"Oh, thank goodness," I said. "Put your coat back on before you catch cold. I fell and hurt my ankle. Did you ride or walk?"

"I rode," Peter said. "It didn't look like a good day for a walk."

"That's an understatement," I said. "Help me up, will you?"

"Better than that," he said. He put his arms under my legs, and I put my arms around his neck, and he picked me up and carried me away from the river to his horse. Between the two of us, I got on the horse, and then he got up behind me. He put one arm around my waist and grasped the reins with the other.

"You ready?"

"Yes," I said. "You are now officially my hero."

"That's what all the damsels in distress say."

By the time Peter got me back to the house, my ankle was throbbing and swelling a fair amount. Betsy Shaw helped me change out of my wet clothes. Then I sat cross-legged on the bed with my hands around my ankle. I imagined the silver spirals on my palms, imagined my bruises healing, my muscles mending, imagined going back in time and never stepping in the puddle.

It was not a miraculous cure, but the swelling did go down. I was able to walk on my own into the living room where Peter sat with Miss Allison and Mr. Em. The men stood when I came into the room. I went over to Peter and shook his hand and then embraced him.

"Thank you, old friend," I said. "You have perfect timing."

"If I had perfect timing I would have gotten there before you fell," he said.

"You all right, daughter?" Mr. Em asked.

I nodded. Miss Allison got up from the sofa and wrapped me in her arms and kissed my face. "We will talk soon," she said, "but I need to finish a private conversation with your father first."

Then she and Mr. Em went to the study.

"What brings you back to this corner of the world?" I asked Peter.

"I arrived with Miss Allison," he said. "My sister just had a baby, so I came up to see my new niece."

"You came here first?" I asked.

"I thought it only polite to make certain Miss Allison got to her destination safely," he said. "Besides, I wanted an excuse to see you."

"You never need an excuse," I said. "You know that."

"I heard Henry came back," he said.

I raised an eyebrow. "I suppose you heard he brought with him a bride-to-be," I said.

He nodded.

"So much for true love," I said. "Eh?"

He shrugged. "Things are often more complicated than they seem."

"Henry and I have always been connected," I said. "At least I thought we were. Maybe it's only a story we told ourselves. When I was 11, I was kidnapped, along with Henry. The kidnapper was trying to extort gold from our fathers. The man was mad, I believe, and he took a knife and cut a giant X into my back. Henry had to watch this and he wasn't able to do anything to stop it. Later I escaped and life went on. But we were bound together by that harrowing experience, I suppose. I don't think Henry has never gotten over it."

"Have you?" Peter asked.

"I still have the physical scars," I said. "Beyond that, I'm not sure. You don't look shocked by this revelation. You are the first I've ever told it to. I mean, other people know, but I've never said it all at once."

"You'll find most everyone is scarred by something in their lives," he said.

"Truly?" I said. "What are you scarred by, Peter Stevens?"

"My absolutely dull ordinariness."

I laughed. "It must be quite divine to be ordinary," I said, "if that is the case. I can tell you that being deemed extraordinary one's whole life can be a burden."

"I will trade you," he said.

I heard Mr. Em and Miss Allison raised their voices. I glanced at Peter. He shrugged.

"Do you know why she is here?" I asked. "I don't think we expected her."

He shook his head. "So, Henry didn't get married. Where is he?"

"I don't know," I said. "He left. I haven't seen him in nearly five months. He said he'd be gone for a few weeks. Maybe he's left for good this time."

"How do you feel about that?"

I looked at Peter. Then I said, "Since I miscarried our child a day or two ago, I'm not feeling very fond of him right this second. He should have been here."

"That is a heavy burden to bear alone," he said.

"I wasn't alone," I said. "I had the child with me, until she wasn't. And of course, everyone here. But I take your meaning."

Just then Mr. Em and Miss Allison emerged from the study. Mr. Em looked uncharacteristically red-faced.

"I'll go to my room," Miss Allison said.

Peter stood. "And I'll go see my folks," he said. He kissed Miss Allison on the cheek. Then he looked at me. "I'll call on you in a couple of days?"

"That would be nice," I said.

Then they were both gone, and my father and I were alone. He looked uncomfortable.

"What is it, Mr. Em?"

"Come," he said. "I have something to tell you."

We went into his study. He motioned for me to sit down. Then he closed the door. I watched him until he sat in the chair opposite mine.

"Your mother is in San Francisco," he said. "Miss Allison was at a dinner party and met her. They live down the street from one another. They became friends and realized they both knew me."

"Small world," I said.

"Your mother is used to a certain kind of society," he said. "I suppose Miss Allison is, too, so it was inevitable that they'd find one another."

"That's what you and Miss Allison were fighting about?" I asked.

He shook his head. "Your mother wants you to come down and visit her. Or she wants to come here and visit. She's with her father."

"Her father?" I said. "That would be my grandfather? I didn't realize I had such a creature."

"Your mother gave Miss Allison a letter for you," he said. He picked up an envelope from his desk and handed it to me. I took it, opened it, and pulled out the letter.

"Dear Emily," I read. "I have received the good news that you do not live so far from me. Would you care to visit? We would love to have you. Miss Allison can tell you where to find us. Come any time. You will be welcome. I hope my letters to you over the years have meant something to you. Sincerely, Juliet Lee."

I looked up at my father.

"What letters?"

He didn't say anything. He pulled open a drawer in his desk, reached in, and pulled out a small stack of letters. He handed them to me.

"Do you wish me to stay or leave?" he asked.

I didn't answer. I looked at the envelope of the first letter. It was addressed to our home in Oregon. I flipped through the rest of them. They were all addressed to the house in Oregon.

"You kept them from me all these years?"

"I did," he said.

"Why? I don't understand. Why would you do something so cruel? Were you afraid I'd want to live with her? Were you afraid she'd tell lies about you?"

"No, I was afraid she'd tell you the truth about me."

I stared at my father. I kept the bundle of letters in my lap.

"Then you'd better tell me now," I said. "It's bad enough that you kept these letters from me, what else is there? I read the book. I know you've killed people. I know you've done terrible things in your life. But you changed. You've lived an exemplary life since. What could she have said that caused you to keep her from me all of these years?"

"Let me start from the beginning," he said. "You know I haven't told you everything about my life. It was so big, what happened."

"Yes, I read the story," I said. "Please, don't make excuses. That's not like you."

"First, you remember Dr. Ef," he said. "The man who created me. I told you how betrayed I felt by him when he didn't want anything to do with me. I went crazy. I was crazy. I think now I was like an infant trying to get the attention of his parent so he can be nourished. Dr. Ef didn't want anything to do with me. He ran from me. But we were together on that ship. He didn't die, just as I didn't die. We lived. I saved the ship from fire, and the captain was so grateful he got us both passage to America. Dr. Ef wanted to escape his past, as I did. We made a kind of peace between us. He became more interested in me. I was, after all, his experiment, his creation. He wanted to see how I was turning out—now that I was no longer running around the countryside murdering people. His words, not mine.

"We came to the states together," Mr. Em said. "He made his home in Boston. I stayed a little while, but I was too noticeable. People started asking questions about me. Dr. Ef fit right into the society there. And he was a doctor, so he had a skill and he was instantly respected. We parted company and I roamed the country, exploring the West. Some 20 years or so later, Dr. Ef contacted me and asked me to return to Boston. By that time, he had remarried and had a daughter: Juliet Lee."

I must have gasped because Mr. Em stopped his narrative.

"My mother is Dr. Ef's daughter?" I asked.

"Yes," he said. "I was there for a few days, actually staying with them, which was strange, I thought, when he took me into his office and asked me to court his daughter. When I was first came alive, I asked him to create me a mate and he refused. Now, all these years later, he said, 'You wanted a wife. I have made you a wife the old-fashioned way.'"

"That is hideous," I said.

"Yes, I was shocked," he said. "I had changed from my old

ways. I was no longer filled with rage, but I still wanted some kind of recognition from this man. I wanted to be more than a monstrous experiment. In actual age, I wasn't much more than 20 years old myself. I suppose I wanted a kind of father's approval. He told me he wanted to see if I could father a child of my own. If it didn't work out with Juliet Lee, he said, he could find someone else, and he would raise the child—should one be born—watch it, see how it progressed. I was appalled, but I didn't say no. Your mother was interested in me. This was rare. Even though I was settling into my own skin, so to speak, most women were repulsed by me. She was a kind woman, but I wasn't particularly attracted to her. She thought I was. She fell in love with me. I don't know why. Her mother was against it, but Dr. Ef gave us his approval. We had a small wedding. Then the wedding night."

I held up a hand. "Please."

"I only want to say that Dr. Ef wanted details the next day," he said. "I couldn't believe what I had done. But your mother got pregnant. I was thrilled. It didn't matter if the marriage had started out as a lie, I could make it work. Then you were born. Dr. Ef was ecstatic. He fully intended to take you and keep you, but I fell in love with you instantly, and you with me. Everything changed when you were born. Juliet Lee and I left Boston with you. Dr. Ef sent people after us, I believe, but I was able to evade them. I saved you from him."

I said, "You had a terrible beginning because this man was experimenting and created you, but you decided it was acceptable to create *me* as another experiment for him? How could you do that to my mother?"

He looked down at his hands and didn't answer.

"What happened? Why did she leave us?"

"She realized I didn't love her," he said. "She asked me for the truth. I told her everything. She was devastated. She wanted to leave, but I couldn't let her take you. Dr. Ef would have had access to you. He would have treated you like his experiment rather than his grandchild. So she left without you."

"I can't believe this," I said. "My entire life has been a lie. You used my mother and then you took me away from her! That is monstrous. What her father asked you to do is monstrous, too. I can't even imagine what kind of father would do that. But you, how could *you* do it?"

"I told you I was a different person before you were born," he said. "I wasn't fully formed. I've spent my life trying to make up for it. I raised you well. I gave you a good life."

"And my mother? What about her life? She went back to that man."

"It was her choice," he said. "She could have stayed with us."

"With a man who didn't love her?" she said. "With a man who had sex with her in order to produce an experimental child? And then you lied to me my entire life. I thought my mother didn't want me."

"I never told you that," he said. "I said she left."

"But a child assumes if her parent leaves, then that parent didn't want her!" I said. "Besides, how could she want me once she knew how I had come into being?"

I stood. "I can't look at you, Mr. Em," I said. "I don't know if I will ever want to see you again. No wonder I never called you papa. You are no kind of father. Those children were right all those years ago. You are a monster."

I ran to my own room and shut the door and locked it. Suddenly everything in my world was upside down. Henry was gone, my baby was dead, and now my father was a stranger. A monster. I didn't know what I was going to do.

Mr. Em left the house within the hour. He gave a note to Betsy Shaw saying that he would go to Paradise until I was ready to see him.

"If I'm *ever* ready to see him," I said, when I read the note.

I read my mother's letters. They were filled with passages about ordinary life: about her garden, her friends, the weather. She never told me the awful truth of my genesis. She never said an unkind word about Mr. Em. She did mention her parents—my grandparents—and I was sad to learn her mother had died a few years earlier. In all of the letters, she hoped I was healthy and well and told me I was welcome to visit her any time. They moved to San Francisco after her mother died. Dr. Ef was getting on in years, but he wanted to see what adventures awaited them in the West. She hoped since she was geographically closer we could see one another.

When I finished reading the letters, I looked around my room and out the window. It all felt unfamiliar. Or wrong. Suddenly I felt as though I was homeless.

The next day when Peter visited, I told him the entire story.

This time he looked surprised.

"What are you going to do?" he asked.

"I'm leaving," I said. "I have to. It doesn't feel right here."

"Come with me," he said. "Come to San Francisco. You've got money. You can do anything you want there. You could see your mother."

"I do want to see her," I said. "But I don't really want to see my grandfather." I shuddered. "Wouldn't that be awful?"

"What would be awful?" Miss Allison came into the room. It was the first I had seen her since yesterday.

"Meeting my grandfather."

"I've met him," she said. "He's quite charming. He's in his nineties, I believe, and he doesn't look a day over 60."

"I'd like to see my mother," I said. "May I come back with

you to San Francisco, Miss Allison. Perhaps you could arrange a visit."

"Certainly," she said. "What about your father?"

"What about him?" I said.

"Well—"

"Don't defend him," I said. "I don't want to hear any defense of him, Henry, or my grandfather. I just want to go. How soon can we leave?"

"I'll make the arrangements," Peter said.

"You're coming?" I said. "You've just gotten here."

"I've seen my niece," he said. "She's quite adorable but our conversation was rather dull. I'll be ready to go back in a day or two."

My plan was to be on my way to San Francisco within the week. I didn't tell anyone besides Diana and Betsy Shaw. Both of them cried. I had never seen Diana cry, and I told her to stop it.

I went out on the land to Emma's grave and said a prayer the day before I left. Then I kissed the ground and said goodbye.

I was fairly certain I would never return.

Chapter Eighteen

At first, Betsy Shaw didn't want me to go. She said the trip would be too dangerous for someone who had just miscarried. I pointed out that women gave birth on the trail coming out here, and we didn't stop. (I didn't remember this, of course, but I had heard stories.)

The midwife examined me and said, "It's as if you were never pregnant. It's perfectly safe for you to travel."

I wanted to argue with her. I wanted to say, "What do you mean it's as if I were never pregnant? Of course I was pregnant! I talked to my baby. I planned my life with her. I dreamed about her. Can't you see the scars on my heart?"

But I didn't say anything like that. I thanked her and said to Betsy Shaw, "Now will you agree that it is all right if I leave?"

Betsy Shaw nodded. "Maybe it's a good idea for you to go away."

Before I left, Betsy Shaw gave me a bottle of witch hazel ointment she had made for my scars. They had continued to itch and swell slightly even after the miscarriage. Since they had started to bother me when I first got pregnant, I assumed they would go back to normal once the baby was gone. Of course, it had only been a few days since the miscarriage when we left.

"Have your mother rub it on your back if the itchiness gets bad," Betsy Shaw said as she put the bottle in one of the open bags on my bed.

"My mother?" I said. "That's difficult to imagine. She's a stranger to me."

"She is your mother," Betsy Shaw said.

"Did you know about the letters?" I asked.

Betsy Shaw kept her eyes on the bag and didn't say anything.

"And you kept it from me?"

"Didn't see what good it would do," she said. "She had left. She was gone."

"It seems like a lot of people are deciding what is good and bad for me," I said, "and have been for a long while."

"You were a child," she said. "Someone had to decide. Mr. Em was completely comfortable with you. But your mother— she was always ill at ease. She didn't know how to take care of you."

"You mean because I was a monster's daughter?" I asked. "I shouldn't wonder."

"I knew how to take care of you," Betsy Shaw said. "And so did Mr. Em."

"I don't know how many more betrayals I can take," I said.

"Something isn't a betrayal just because you don't agree with it," Betsy Shaw said. She looked at me. "Your father didn't betray you. He was protecting you."

"You don't know the whole truth," I said.

She shook her head. "I don't need to know nothing that happened in the past. Mr. Em never hurt you. He never hurt your mother."

"He did," I said. "He hurt her, and he hurt me by keeping me from her. How might my life have been different if she had been with me?"

"You've never cared a whit about her," Betsy Shaw said.

"Because I didn't know the truth!" I said. "And I was a child." I shook my hands. "Betsy Shaw, I thank you for what you've done for me, but now I need you to leave. I won't have you defending him or yourself for the lies that have been told to me."

Betsy Shaw nodded and left me alone.

Soon enough Miss Allison, Peter, and I were on our way to San Francisco, traveling in Mr. Em's private carriage. I didn't see Mr. Em before I left, and I didn't look back as we pulled away.

I endured the trip. Although I was physically well, I didn't feel much like company. Fortunately, neither Miss Allison or Peter required my attention. I spent much of the journey looking out at the wet world or sleeping on Peter's or Miss Allison's shoulder.

We arrived at Miss Allison's house after traveling through a fog for hours. I couldn't imagine how the driver ever found his way to her house.

In the morning, Peter was gone, and the sun was shining, the sky blue. I could see the bay in the distance, looking like a slice of twilight sky come down to lay with the earth.

Miss Allison's housekeeper, Mrs. Wren, served us an exquisite breakfast of croissants, scones, and fruit. I always looked forward to visiting Miss Allison for a chance to partake in Mrs. Wren's baked goods, and I told her so.

"I wish you could come up to Refugio and teach Betsy Shaw how to do this," I said.

"I could teach you," Mrs. Wren said, "and you could teach her."

"I'm not very good in the kitchen," I said.

"Everyone should be good in the kitchen," she said.

"I know," I said. "That's what Betsy Shaw says."

"My mother taught me and her mother taught her. Didn't your mother teach you to cook?"

I shook my head. "No. I don't even know if she cooks."

She had never mentioned cooking in her letters. I knew so little about her, and she knew absolutely nothing about me. Not yet, at least.

No time like the present to get started.

I asked Miss Allison to contact my mother and invite her over that very day.

We soon got a reply that Juliet Lee would be pleased to have tea with us.

Before she arrived, my back itched like hell. I tried to rub the ointment on myself. Then I looked through my clothes for something to wear. What kind of impression did I want to make on her?

No impression. I only wanted to be myself.

I sat down in front of the mirror on my dressing table. When my mother saw me, would she think about how Mr. Em had tricked her into marrying him—into having sex with her—just for the purposes of producing me? Would she cringe when she saw my hair? They had told me how she had cut it again and again when I was a toddling child—probably because my hair was three different colors.

And now, since the pregnancy, my hair was kinky. Even when I braided it, it stuck out this way and that. I could put on a pretense of being tame, but my hair remained wild.

I suddenly remembered that in all of my visions and dreams about Emma, she had always had blond hair. Where had that come from? Henry had black hair. And I had white, red, and brown hair. Maybe my mother had blond hair.

I stared at my hair. It was hideous. Who else looked like this? It was abnormal. I was abnormal. That was why my mother had left me, it was why Emma and Henry left me. Maybe it was even why Jake McMahon had mutilated me.

I picked up a pair of scissors on the desk. I hesitated for only an instant, and then I began cutting my hair until all that remained was a few inches here and there. I stared at myself. It didn't look better. But having short hair was less strange than having tricolored hair.

Perhaps.

Miss Allison came into the room and gasped.

"What have you done?"

"It was bothering me," I said. "The last time my mother saw me I didn't have any hair. Maybe she'll recognize me better."

"Emily," she said softly.

I put my hands in my head. "I don't know what to do," I murmured. "I don't know who I am any more. Henry is gone. Mr. Em is gone. I feel . . . left. Deserted. Not myself. They were anchors for me, Miss Allison. They were the reason for my existence."

"Oh darlin'," she said, hugging me from behind as we both looked into the mirror. "You've had a rough time, I know. But it's part of the grand adventure of your life."

I laughed. "I don't think I like that word if that's what I'm having."

"I think it means something grand is about to happen," she said. "And who knows what it will be?"

"Sometimes I know," I said. "And sometimes you know. I don't know anything now. Do you? Do you know what's about to happen?"

She shook her head. "I have no idea. Oh wait, yes, I know your mother will be here in about 10 minutes. Now get dressed."

I brushed my hair this way and that, but it still looked like I had hacked it off myself and done a poor job of it—although the longer I looked at it, the more I liked it. Diana and Nichols both wore their hair short. Maybe I would start wearing mine short permanently. I did look vaguely like a boy. I didn't mind.

I decided a dress would make me look even more incongruous, so I put on a pair of nice black trousers and a blue shirt.

I sat in the parlor, waiting nervously. Before too long, I heard someone at the front door. I glanced at Miss Allison. She smiled. Then Mrs. Wren opened the parlor door.

"Miss Juliet Lee," Mrs. Wren announced.

Then she stepped away. A small woman dressed in a dark blue coat, with her hands in a muff, stood on the threshold, smiling. A blue bonnet covered her head and most of her brown hair.

I stood. Miss Allison went to Juliet Lee, and the women briefly embraced.

"Juliet Lee," Miss Allison said, "this is your daughter Emily."

She walked toward me and held out a gloved hand. I took it.

"I am so pleased to see you," she said.

I held onto her hand. I wasn't certain if I should shake her hand or embrace her. Her blue eyes were watering.

"Sit," Miss Allison said. "I will pour tea."

We sat in silence while Miss Allison prepared the tea.

"Did you just arrive?" Juliet Lee asked.

"I did," I said. "Last night. We came with Peter Stevens. Do you know him? He works for one of the papers here. *The Bulletin* I think."

"Ah yes," she said, taking a cup from Miss Allison. "I think I've heard his name."

"He's an old family friend," I said. Miss Allison handed me a cup. Tea was not my favorite beverage, but I took a sip.

We sat in awkward silence. What does one say to a mother one hasn't seen in 14 or 15 years?

"I want you to know I never got your letters," I said, "until last week."

"I was afraid of that," she said. "I was sorry as soon as I left you and your father. But truthfully, I was relieved to be away. Not away from you, but I did not like Missouri and I had no desire to go on a wagon train. I was accustomed to a more comfortable lifestyle. I still am. I couldn't believe I left you behind. My only excuse was that I was young and homesick."

"I know what he did to you," I said. "He told me."

Juliet Lee glanced at Miss Allison. Miss Allison said, "Would you like me to leave? I don't mind."

"No," Juliet Lee said. "It's all right. Mr. Em didn't love me when we married. I loved him, desperately. But he wanted a wife and a child. He claimed my father was behind it all, but I knew that couldn't be true, and my father told me it wasn't true. Mr. Em got his child, and then he had no need for me, I suppose."

"I thought you left him," I said.

"I did," she said. "I was too hurt to stay. He said we could try to make it work, but he treated me more like a stranger than a wife."

"I know many wives who feel like strangers to their husbands," Miss Allison said.

I watched this woman who was my mother and tried to feel some kind of connection with her, but I didn't. When I listened to her speak about my father, I felt defensive for him. I kept biting my tongue so that I wouldn't say anything nice about him.

"Don't get me wrong," Juliet Lee said. "Your father was always kind to me. It only felt unkind because he didn't love me. But he tried. He did, Emily."

"Did you remarry?" I asked. "You never mentioned in your letters."

"I didn't," she said. "I've helped my father with his work. He continued working as a doctor for many years, until we came to San Francisco. Now he's invested in a company here. They do trade up and down the coast. He's got several ships. Actually, his partner, Joseph Tyler, has several ships. Papa doesn't have much to do with the day to day running of the company. Now, what about you? I know nothing of your life."

I began telling her about my life in Oregon with Mr. Em, Betsy Shaw, and Indian Mary—about all those creations visible and invisible that I interacted with every day. How the Wind and Rain and Water were my companions, along with the crows, coyotes, and spirit animals. I told her about Mr. Em sitting in the back of the classroom after the boy bullied me. I told her about Mr. Em carrying me on his shoulders so that I could feel like I was taller than anyone in the world. I told her about the stories he read to me every night before I went to bed.

As I talked, I felt my love for my father gurgling to the surface again. I had forgotten what a blessed childhood I had had.

Miss Allison and Juliet Lee listened without a word as I talked about our spring in the Meadow, about Henry, about the silver pathways, about Sitiu's murder. I hesitated for a moment—stopping my narrative mid-sentence—before plunging on, talking about Jake McMahon kidnapping us. I didn't mention the carving on my back, but I did tell her about escaping and diving into the pool.

I soon tired of talking. "And then we moved to Refugio, near Henry and his father. And we've had many happy years there. I had intended to spend the rest of my life there, but I'm not sure what will happen now. That's too long a story for our first meeting."

"I am so sorry about the kidnapping," Juliet Lee said. "That must have been very frightening. It sounds like you had a happy life before and after."

"Yes," I said. "I won't let a few hours of terror change my life forever." Even though it had changed my life. Even though Henry still hadn't shaken off the experience.

Even though I still dreamed about it.

Even though the stupid scars itched, now, again, as I sat with Miss Allison and my mother.

My mother.

How strange.

"I thank you so much for sharing this with me," Juliet Lee said. "I understand that I am a stranger to you, and I am grateful that you honored me with your story. Every few years, Mr. Em did send me updates about you. I was grateful for those."

He hadn't told me that.

"This was a good beginning," Miss Allison said.

"I would love it if you could come to our house," Juliet Lee said.

"I—I don't know," I said. "I am very angry with Mr. Em for what he did and I am equally as angry with Dr. Ef for his part in it. What they did to you was unconscionable."

"As I said, Dr. Ef has denied any part in that particular scheme," my mother said. "He did admit to creating Mr. Em, but that was all. And I'm not certain how hard you should be on your father. He loves you. He gave you a good life."

"You are very forgiving," I said.

"Think about visiting," she said. "If you don't want to meet my father, you don't need to. He is anxious to meet you! He has no other children besides me, and you are his only grandchild. I'll take leave of you both now. Thank you for your hospitality."

We stood and shook hands again. Then Miss Allison and

Juliet Lee left the room together. I sat down again and leaned against the back of the sofa.

"Well?" Miss Allison asked when she came back into the room.

"She seems nice enough," I said. "I thought I'd feel more connected to her. Because, you know, that's what I do. I feel deeply." I hadn't realized that was true until that moment. "I love people. I'm deeply in love and deeply hurt. I'm deeply joyful and I'm deeply sorrowful. When I was miscarrying Emma—Emma whom I loved more than anyone—I thought of my mother and I felt grief over her leaving me. But just now, when I was talking about my childhood, I missed Mr. Em. I missed home. I missed Henry. I don't know what I'm doing here."

"Why are you so angry with Mr. Em?" Miss Allison asked. "You always knew he did terrible things when he was younger. My god, he killed people."

"I know," I said, "but he had never done anything to me."

"He still hasn't—besides keeping the letters from you. It was your mother he deceived."

"I suppose," I said. "Right now, I want to go home."

"You can leave any time, of course," she said. "But I believe there is a reason you're here now."

"She never mentioned my hair," I said. "Is that strange?" I always thought mothers were obsessed with their daughter's hair."

"My mother certainly was," Miss Allison said. She laughed and kissed the top of my head. "Maybe she'll mention it next time."

For the next couple of weeks, I spent many days with my mother. She would come to Miss Allison's or we would meet her for lunch or tea somewhere in town. I enjoyed my mother's company, but I was startled by how much we did not have in common. Miss Allison said this was to be expected. Once we knew one another better, we would have more intimacy.

I noticed when I talked about Henry or Mr. Em, Juliet Lee was often uncomfortable. Sometimes she would actually cringe. I tried to figure out on my own what was happening, but it wasn't in my nature not to be straightforward. So I asked her.

"No, I'm not uncomfortable," she said. "It's just that you are so passionate, if that's the right word. You are so emotional about them."

"I love Henry and Mr. Em," I said. "Of course I'm passionate about them."

"You are emotional about everyone," she said. "About Betsy Shaw. Isn't she a servant? I remember her. She worked in our household. And this Diana person. Titus. Doesn't he train your horses?"

I laughed. "Those are their jobs," I said. "We all have work we do. That's not who we are. They are my friends. They helped raise me. Don't you have friends? Aren't you close to people?"

She thought about it and then said, "I help raise money for the orphans. I enjoy working with the other women on the committee. I enjoy working with my father. Or I used to. Now I run his household. I enjoy many things. Like my garden. But I suppose I'm not so heartfelt as you are."

"And you think this is not a good trait of mine?"

She smiled and patted my arm. "Of course not! I admire it. I wish I were more expressive. You are very vital."

When I wasn't with my mother and Miss Allison, I was with Peter. I enjoyed our renewed friendship. It was good to have someone to talk to about books and politics. Some nights Peter and I went to plays together.

After one play—I forget what it was because it was forgettable—we were walking away from the theater when I saw a silver path going from me to a tavern down the street.

"Peter," I asked, pointing, "do you know that place?"

"Sure," he said. "In fact, I know it well. Do you want to go in for a late supper?"

I nodded. I stepped on the silver path, slipped my arm through Peter's arm, and we walked to the tavern. Inside, I saw no silver pathways, just people—most of them men.

Peter seemed to know everyone in the place, and they shouted out to him. He waved.

"Who's the looker?" one of the men shouted.

"Someone who could break your neck if you're rude," Peter said.

"I like me a strong woman," the man yelled.

Peter and I found an empty table and ordered steak and beans.

While we ate, Peter asked, "So what's next for you? What are you going to do with your life?"

I laughed. "I have no idea," I said. "I've met my mother. I'm glad, but I don't feel like this is home or anything. I thought my destiny was here. I know that sounds odd, but as soon as Mr. Em gave me the letters and told me what had happened, I knew I had to come here. But now what?"

Peter laughed. "You have a complex inner life."

I smiled. "I've been thinking about Mr. Em and Henry. I've been so angry with them. Now, I don't know. Henry has been gone almost six months. That seems too long. He had promised he'd be back in a few weeks. Where is he?"

"Have you thought anymore about staying here?" Peter asked. "I would love it if you did. In fact, you could stay with me."

I put my hand over his. "You mean as friends?"

He smiled. "I would ask you to marry me, but I remember how angry you got with Henry about marriage."

I laughed. "Peter, I still love Henry, although I do have fond memories of *our* sexual experience."

"What sexual experience?" he said. "I missed it!"

I laughed again. This was one of the reasons I enjoyed Peter. We laughed a lot.

I leaned closer to him. "Don't you remember when we were in the gully? I experienced the whole thing—in my memory or in another time, another place—I don't always understand what's happening with me. In fact, I rarely understand. It was very real."

"Now that is an ability I would like to have," he said.

Just then a man walked up to our table. He and Peter shook hands.

"This is John Williamson, Emily," Peter said. "He's the lout who was shouting at you."

"Hello, Mr. Williamson," I said. "Would you like to sit with us?"

"So how strong is she?" he said, winking at Peter as he pulled up a chair.

"You can speak to me," I said. "In fact, if you don't, you can leave us. I'm strong enough to break your arm if I wanted to."

He looked me up and down. He wasn't leering. He was assessing.

"You don't look like nothing I couldn't handle," he said. He put his elbow on the table and held his hand open. "Show me."

"Rules?" I asked. "Can we hold onto the table or not?"

Williamson looked at Peter. Peter shrugged.

"Hands on, if you please," he said.

I put my elbow on the table, my hand open.

Suddenly the tavern seemed to come alive with sound and movement. "Wagers! Wagers!"

I looked at Peter.

"Do you know what you're doing?" he asked quietly.

I laughed. "Of course not."

Peter moved away from the table. "I've got 20 on my friend."

I heard people shouting, "I'll take that! I'll take that bet!"

"Are you sure you can handle being bested by a woman?" I asked John Williamson.

"Been bested by a woman every day of my marriage," he said, "and proud of it. You ready, sister?"

"I am ready," I said. "Oh wait, I'm left-handed." I shrugged. "Doesn't matter. This will do."

We clasped hands.

Peter said, "On three. One, two, three!"

I felt the full force of Williamson's brute strength immediately. I was prepared, and I gave back as good as I got. As we stared at one another, I could tell he was surprised my arm hadn't gone down immediately.

We stayed even for a few moments. Then I sensed his bone was beginning to twist.

I whispered to him above the noise—above the cheers. "I don't want to break your arm."

Suddenly Williamson knew I could do it, was about to do it, so he let me fold his arm down to the table.

I couldn't believe the roar. I didn't know if they were rooting for me or Williamson.

"Let's check and see if she's really a woman," one man said.

Williamson reached out and pushed the man away. "Anyone touches her," he said, "you'll have to deal with me." He looked at me. "And her!"

I laughed. The crowd roared again.

Others wanted to arm wrestle me, but I declined. Instead we bought Williamson a beer. He sipped his drink while looking at my hair. It was growing out fairly quickly, but it was still short.

"I like it," he said. "Looks like it's three different colors."

"Yes, sir," I said.

"That reminds me," he said, "there was a young man in here, oh, maybe five months ago. We was arm wrestling, too. He told me he used to wrestle a girl with white, red, and brown hair. He was drunk. He shouldn't have been wrestling anyone. But he was missing home and his girl. You know anyone else with hair like yours?"

I leaned forward. "What was his name?"

Williamson frowned and shook his head. "I can't remember. He was a good looking boy. Hadn't had the hard life of living in this place, that's for certain. Black hair. Maybe 20. He was looking for someone. He thought I'd know where to find him. Don't know why."

"Come on, John," Peter said. "You do know this city more than most. If I were looking for a dead or live body, I'd come to you."

"As you have many times," Williamson said.

"Was his name Henry?" I asked.

He nodded slowly. "I think it was," he said. "He was looking for someone called Jack Manning."

"Jake McMahon?" I asked.

"Yep, that's it."

My heart was beating so loudly I could hardly hear. Of course! Henry figured if he found Jake McMahon and brought him to justice he could lay to rest his memories and insecurities from the kidnapping. He could prove himself.

Mr. Em had been looking for Jake McMahon for six years. Why would Henry think he could find him now?

"Do you remember what you told him?" I asked.

"He didn't have much of a description of the man he was looking for," Williamson said. "Just that he had a cross carved into his right arm."

"An 'X,'" I said. I had nearly forgotten about that.

"I suggested he go down to Sydney-Town," Williamson said. "That's where all the scum end up sooner or later."

"You sent him to Sydney-Town?" I asked. My mouth went dry. I had never been to Sydney-Town without Mr. Em, and I couldn't imagine going alone.

"Did you see him again?" I asked.

He shook his head. "No. Only thought of it now because of your hair. Was he talking about you?"

"Yes," I said.

"He said you beat him every single time," Williamson said.

"I did," I said, "and he never seemed to mind."

Williamson shrugged. "Why should he? He got to hold your hand the whole time."

I smiled.

"Now, I have the missus to go home to and satisfy."

He got up and left us.

I looked at Peter. "If Henry was here five months ago," I said, "where is he now?"

Chapter Nineteen

I could hardly wait to get back to Miss Allison's place. I said good night to Peter, thanked him for everything, and then ran inside to my room and shut the door. I lay down, tried to relax, and then I let myself float out of my body.

"Henry," I whispered.

I was immediately next to him. He was curled up on his bedroll. Was he outside? I tried to look around, but I only saw darkness. And Henry. I watched him. He was breathing. He was alive.

"Henry," I whispered. "Where are you? Come back to me."

"Emily," he whispered but did not stir.

I tried to get closer to him, but I couldn't.

Then I snapped back into my body and into my room.

I sat up in bed. If what I had just done was real, then Henry was alive. But where was he? Williamson had said Henry had been drunk when he met him. Maybe Henry had gotten discouraged that he couldn't find McMahon, and he was too embarrassed to come home. Or maybe he had ended up in a brothel or a gambling house. An opium den? I shuddered. No, that wasn't Henry.

"Henry," I said out loud. "Wherever you are: It is time to come home."

The next day, Miss Allison and I got an invitation to dine with Dr. Ef and Juliet Lee at their home. I decided it was time to meet my famous grandfather.

For this first meeting with Dr. Ef, I dressed in my most unconventional clothes: men's trousers and a man's shirt with a vest over it. And work boots. I shined them up nicely, but they were leather boots. I ran my fingers through my curly colorful hair and laughed at my reflection.

I wondered what Dr. Ef would think of his experiment's offspring.

They lived in a Victorian house not far from Miss Allison's. I was surprised at how small it was. I had imagined they lived in a big mansion where Dr. Ef had plenty of room for his laboratories.

Dr. Ef answered the door. He smiled when he saw me, and I recognized the smile: I had seen it in the mirror when I gazed at my own reflection.

"My dear!" he said, grabbing a hold of my hand for a moment before embracing me. When he let go of me, he said, "Come in, come in, both of you."

We went into the house. My mother came out of the parlor and put her hand on her father's arm.

"He's been so excited all day," she said.

I looked at Dr. Ef and then at my mother. I didn't see much of a family resemblance between them. His hair was white—like mine—and his eyes milky blue. But he stood tall and he had grasped my hand tightly.

We all went into the parlor.

"Let me look at you," Dr. Ef said. He gripped my arms and looked into my eyes. "Your eyes are two different colors. Juliet had told me of this, but it is quite odd to see. And lovely, too. They weren't like that when you were born. And your hair. Your father's hair was not like this."

"It is now," I said.

"How does one account for that, I wonder?" he asked.

"Father," Juliet Lee said, "you are examining her as a scientist would examine a specimen, and I've been trying to convince her that you aren't the evil man Mr. Em told her you were."

"Mr. Em never told me you were evil," I said. "He said that you wanted him to seduce my mother and produce a child."

"That is direct," he said. "Here, sit next to me." He smiled, and we sat on the sofa next to one another.

"Your father was always very black and white about things," he said. "And his reactions were extreme. When I initially rejected him, he went on a murderous rampage."

"He was essentially a child," I said.

"A murderous child," he said.

"Father!" Juliet Lee said.

"The truth is the truth," he said, "and I can tell that her father has been very frank with her. So I am treating her with the same courtesy. Your father and I didn't see eye to eye on many things. He believed if I had a scientific interest in something, then I was inhumane. Your mother told me about your friend Henry. He is a naturalist, isn't he? I imagine he keeps notebooks filled with drawings and details about his subjects."

"That is true," I said.

"And you don't think he is monstrous, do you?"

"Of course not," I said. "But plants and insects are not people. Why did you create my father?"

"I wanted to understand life and death," he said. "Death

seems like an obscenity to me. I wanted to stop it. End it. To do that, I had to understand creation."

"Women create all the time," I said. "Why didn't you just study birth."

He laughed. "That would have been smart. I had no idea what I was doing. I was young and ignorant. I wouldn't do it today. But I still care about my own creation, just as I care for my daughter. I'm glad to know Mr. Em is well and has had a happy life. I am glad that you have been happy, too, although your mother has told me you have had some travail along the way."

"Haven't we all?" I said.

At dinner, Dr. Ef asked me detailed questions about my upbringing. For some reason, I didn't mind answering him. I told him about seeing spirit animals, about the silver pathways and my sometimes healing abilities.

"This is fascinating," he said.

"Will you write this all down in one of your notebooks?" I asked.

He laughed. "Of course I will," he said. "A notebook dedicated just to you. I have one on Miss Allison, too. I find her psychic abilities fascinating. And now to discover you have them, too. That must be something you inherited from Mr. Em because Juliet Lee has nothing like that."

"Neither does Mr. Em," I said.

"Perhaps someone else did," Dr. Ef said. "Someone who— well, let's not discuss that. It's not something we should talk about in polite company. Or at all. Mr. Em is my greatest achievement and my biggest shame. I can't tell anyone about him. I'm sure I'd be run out of town—out of the country!"

By the end of the meal, I quite understood my father's desire to please Dr. Ef. To borrow one of Betsy Shaw's colloquialisms, Dr. Ef could charm the scales off a fish.

"I would enjoy seeing your father again," Dr. Ef said. "Where is he?"

"Home, I imagine," I said. "When I found out he had hidden my mother's letters from me and tricked her into marrying him, I left home."

"Yes, it was cruel to marry a woman he didn't love," Dr. Ef said, "but look what he got. You! Probably worth it in his eyes."

I frowned. That seemed a bit unfeeling.

"You two have talked nonstop for hours," Juliet Lee said. "Miss Allison and I have sat here like ignored lumps of clay."

"I'm so sorry, dears," Dr. Ef said. "I am just overwhelmed by the presence of my beautiful granddaughter."

Afterward, I returned to Miss Allison's house and gazed at myself in the mirror. I tried to see where I resembled Mr. Em, Juliet Lee, and Dr. Ef. Dr. Ef was in my smile. My hair was like Mr. Em's. Where was my mother in my face? I didn't see her. I rubbed my face and sighed. Who the hell was I?

I shook my head. I was just me, Emily. Emily. I was still myself.

Wasn't I?

I went to my mother's house frequently. I enjoyed spending time with Juliet Lee and my grandfather—maybe because they were family. Maybe because they were odd and ordinary at the same time. My grandfather could ask an exhausting amount of questions, and sometimes I had to hold up my hand and say, "Enough, Dr. Ef."

"Please call me grandfather," he said. "Or grandpa. Dr. Ef makes me sound like some kind of crazy scientist who sewed together pieces of dead bodies to create a new human."

"But that is who you are," I said.

"That's not precisely what happened," he said.

"Do you sometimes wonder if you were crazy?" I asked. "To do such a thing?"

"Of course," he said, "and I think I still am crazy. Insanity does have its virtues."

One day when I came to the house, I found my mother in the parlor with a little girl who was playing on the floor with her back to me. She turned to look at me, and I nearly fell down.

She looked just like my Emma, the Emma of my dreams.

"Emma," I whispered.

"Yes," my mother said. "How did you know? This is Emma Tyler. Emma, this is my daughter Emily."

Emma stood, and we gazed at one another. I knew her completely, down to her precious little soul.

I knew her.

She was why I had come to San Francisco.

She smiled at me. "I know you."

"I know you, too," I said.

She walked over to me. I dropped to my knees. She put her arms around my neck. I wrapped my arms around her and held her tightly.

"I've been waiting for you," she whispered.

"I know," I said. "I'm here now."

Through the thin cloth of her dress, I felt something on her back. Raised skin. I gasped.

"Emma." I heard a voice behind me.

Startled, I let Emma go and turned around. A stern looking woman stood on the threshold of the parlor holding her hand out to Emma. "It's time to go," the woman said. "Your father will be back soon."

"My name is Emily," I told Emma. I resisted grabbing her arm to prevent her from leaving. "I'm staying with Miss Allison."

The little girl nodded. Then she took the woman's hand and

they left the room. I wanted to run after them. I wanted to snatch up Emma and carry her away. I bit the inside of my lip and waited. A few moments later, I heard the front door open and close.

I dropped into the nearest chair, my legs shaking. I swallowed. I knew my mother was watching me.

"Who was that?" I asked.

"She's Joseph Tyler's daughter," she said. "I've mentioned him. He's your grandfather's business partner."

"Where's her mother?"

"Her mother is dead," she said. "She committed suicide last year, poor thing. She was such a sweet girl, and she doted on Emma. But she came from Sydney-Town, you know. Mr. Tyler took her in. She'd once worked in a saloon. Can you imagine? Back home we would never have let a woman like that into our home, but here, things are different. Sometimes when Mr. Tyler's housekeeper has errands to run and he's not at home, she leaves Emma here. He and my father have a meeting with investors today and they probably won't be back until late tonight. I don't mind Emma's company, and I try to stay on Mr. Tyler's good side since he's Father's partner." She smiled. "Mr. Tyler loves his little girl very much. I think they are very close."

"How old is she?" I asked.

"About five, I think. Why?"

"I dreamed about her," I said. "Before I came here, I dreamed of a girl just like her."

I hadn't told Juliet Lee about my pregnancy yet.

"Why do you suppose?" she asked.

I shook my head. "I don't really understand what's happening," I said. "I think I need to go now. Give Grandpa my love." I got up and kissed my mother on the cheek.

She took one of my hands in hers. "Are you all right?"

"I am," I said. "I—I need to go."

I left the house and head toward Miss Allison's house. My heart was racing.

As I neared Miss Allison's place, I saw someone going up her walk.

It was a man. His shoulders were hunched, but I recognized the gait. I recognized the clothes.

"Henry!" I screamed. "Henry!"

The man turned, and I saw his face. He looked haggard, but he smiled when he saw me. I ran up the walk. I could hear him sobbing. Or maybe it was me.

In another moment, we were in each other's arms.

"Oh my god," Henry said. "I've imagined this moment for months."

We kissed. Then I pushed him away from me.

"Where the hell have you been?" I asked.

"It's a long story," he said. "Can we go inside? This is Miss Allison's place, isn't it?"

Mrs. Wren let us in. I asked her to bring us tea and some food for Henry. He took off his coat. He did look tired but strong and healthy.

I wiped the tears from his face and led him to the sofa.

"Tell me," I said. "What happened to you? Where have you been?"

He held my hand tightly in his.

"When I was in San Francisco with Ellen and her family, I thought I saw Jake McMahon. He was older and he was better dressed, but it still looked like him. At the time, I figured I must be wrong. But then, I dreamed about him that night you and I spent together, and I suddenly felt like if I could find him and bring him to justice then we could go on with our lives."

"We were already going on with our lives," I said.

He shook his head. "I know. In any case, I came down here looking for him. It didn't take long before I found him. I went to

Sydney-Town and asked around. No one admitted to knowing him, but it was clear they didn't like me asking questions. Then I found him. I followed him for several days. Saw where he worked and lived. I was going to turn him over to the police, but I didn't know what they'd do. It happened so long ago. I thought about killing him. Then one night as I was trying to sleep in my crummy little room, I was thinking about you and how much I loved you and suddenly everything you said made sense. I was a child when it happened. I couldn't have saved you. I had found Jake McMahon, but I realized we should decide the next course of action together—the four of us, you, me, Mr. Em, and my father. It happened to our families. I was being stupid trying to do it on my own. I planned on leaving for home the next day, but I was shanghaied before I could go. I was walking down the street, and the next thing I knew I woke up on a ship out to sea."

"That's terrible. I thought they shanghaied sailors. You're no sailor."

"Someone on the ship told me I had been kidnapped specifically because I had been asking questions about Jake Mc-Mahon," Henry said. "I was determined to escape, but I had to survive first. I learned fast. I made friends. I did a good job. They didn't let me off the ship for months. Finally we stopped in Portland. I convinced them to let me go into town. I said I had to visit a whore house. Once I got to the brothel, I ran like the devil himself. I went to your old town and found Indian Mary. I didn't have any money, so I had to get help from someone. She gave me money and other people gave me a horse and food and clothes. They all remembered you and Mr. Em."

"How did you get over the pass this time of year?" I asked.

"I talked to the weather," he said, "like you used to. I talked to the mountains. I talked to the spirits of everything and everywhere and begged them to let me pass. I begged them to let me get home." He held my hand between his hands and looked into my eyes. "Nothing mattered except to get home to you. You were right, Emily. Love is everything. I've been so stupid."

"So then what happened?"

"I got over the pass and went to Refugio," he said. "Mr. Em was there and you were gone. He told me what had happened—about him hiding your mother's letters from you. I told him I had found Jake McMahon. So he and my dad and I came here to tell you and the law about McMahon."

"Mr. Em and your father are here?"

"We're staying in a boarding house," Henry said. "I wanted to see you alone first. Besides, your father didn't think you'd want to see him."

"I've been so angry with you," I said. "I have so much to tell you. But first, where is McMahon. Do you know?"

"I don't know where he is right this minute," he said, "but I know where his office is and where his home is."

"By any chance is his new name Joseph Tyler?" I asked.

"Yes! How did you know?"

"He's my grandfather's business partner," I said. "I haven't met him, but I met his daughter today. It's another long story."

"He has a daughter?"

"Yes," I said. "And we need to rescue her."

"What do you mean?" he asked.

"We've got to take his daughter away from him."

"You want us to kidnap his daughter?" Henry asked. He cleared his throat. "I believe that would be a crime. You're not trying to get back at him by taking his daughter, are you?"

"No," I said. "I saw her today, the little girl. I held her in my arms and I think she had a scar on her back, like mine. I dreamed it, too. Henry, I'm afraid he did to her what he did to me. He's away from home today. We could take her and hide her until we talk to him. Maybe we can convince him to turn himself in.

We'll tell him we have his daughter and we won't give her back until he confesses and surrenders to the police."

"Who would we give her back to if he's in jail?"

"That's not the point," I said. "I don't know. I've got to get her away."

"All right," he said. He kissed me. "I'm so glad to see you. We might both end up in jail or at the end of a rope, but at least we're together."

I laughed. "Now you understand."

Before we left the house, I wrote on a piece of paper: "We have your daughter. You kidnapped us and stole from us and you murdered our friend. If you contact the authorities, you will be sorry."

I showed it to Henry.

"Shouldn't we go get our fathers?" Henry asked. "I brought them here so we could do this as a family."

"I am worried about the girl," I said. "If we confront Jake McMahon or if we send the police after him, he might run and take Emma with him. I can't let that happen."

"I hope you know what you're doing."

I shook my head. "I really don't."

We took Henry's carriage to Tyler's home—Jake McMahon's home. I didn't know what to call him. I kept telling myself to breathe, breathe, breathe deeply. I wondered what I'd do if I saw him. But he wasn't there. We stopped the carriage down the road a bit. I saw a silver path leading away from me to the back of the house.

"You should stay here," I said. "There's more a chance of two of us getting caught than one of us. I'll be invisible—like how you taught me."

"I don't like you going in there by yourself," he said. "McMahon is dangerous."

"He is, but he's not there," I said. "I will get Emma and bring her back here."

"How?"

"I don't know yet," I said. "But I see a silver path."

He nodded. I knew he didn't understand completely. I knew he was terrified. But he let me go.

I took the small bag I'd brought with me, and then I hurried down the path no one else could see. It went around to the door at the back of the house. I opened the door quietly and went inside. I could just see into the kitchen and I heard someone inside whistling.

"Where's that old woman?" someone in the kitchen said.

"She's asleep," someone else said. "Shouldn't have someone that old taking care of a child. At least the little girl is good at taking care of herself. I wouldn't mind a nap for myself."

The women laughed. I tiptoed past the kitchen, out of sight from them. I hurried across the foyer and went up the stairs. If this was Jake McMahon's house, he had made a good life for himself—using the gold we had found and he had stolen from us, no doubt. I saw only closed doors on the second floor and heard no noise, so I ran up to the third floor. I followed the silver path to the nursery where Emma sat playing quietly with a doll.

"Hello, love," I said quietly as I came into the room.

"Hello, Emily," she said. "Have you come to play with me?"

"I've come to rescue you," I said, "if you'd like. But first I need to ask you a question."

She smiled and nodded. I wanted to take her in my arms and run.

"Emma, I have a big X on my back," I said. "Do you know what an X is?"

She nodded. She crossed her index fingers in front of her.

"That's right, sweetheart. Do you have an X on your back?"

She shrugged.

"May I look?"

"Okay."

I unbuttoned the back of her dress and then carefully pulled down her undershirt. The pink scars were unmistakable.

"How did that happen?" I asked.

"Daddy got mad one day," she said. "And he hurt me. Momma was screaming. But it got better, like Daddy said it would, and now I can just feel it with my fingers. Momma told me you would come for me. She said that before she died. She'd had a dream about you. I did, too."

I looked around the room. "Is there a photo of your mother here?"

Emma pointed. I got up and went across the room. On the bookshelf was a framed photograph of Emma, her mother, and her father. I recognized Jake McMahon immediately. The sight of him sent shivers down my spine. He was older and he didn't look as crazy, but I knew he was still crazy. The scars on his daughter's back testify to that. I looked at Emma's mother and I knew her instantly, too. It was Sarah Henderson, the young woman I'd met on the way to California the first time, the young woman who swore she'd marry rich and live on a hill in a huge mansion. The young woman I had promised to visit one day.

I took the photograph, dropped it into the bag, and went back to Emma.

"What do you want to take with you?" I asked.

"Am I coming back?"

"Not if you don't want to," I said.

Emma put the doll in the bag. I found some of her clothes in the wardrobe, and I stuffed them into the bag. Then I dropped the note I'd written onto the floor.

"We're going to have to be invisible now," I said to Emma. "Do you know how to do that?"

She shook her head.

"We'll walk very quietly," I said, "and if you hold my hand, you should be invisible."

"Okay," she said. I held onto Emma with one hand and the bag with the other. I closed my eyes briefly and imagined myself still, still, still. And then we slowly walked down two flights of stairs. At each creak, we stopped and I listened.

But no one came. The women didn't even stop talking when we went by the kitchen. Once we got out the door, I picked up Emma and carried her to the carriage.

"Thank god," Henry said as I put Emma in the carriage next to Henry. I got in next to her and shut the door behind me.

"Henry, this is Emma. Emma, this is Henry."

"Where to?" he asked

"Peter Stevens's place. No one will think of looking for Emma there."

Chapter Twenty

Soon the three of us were running up the outside steps to Peter's tiny apartment on the second floor of a boarding house.

I knocked once on Peter's door and he opened it.

"I'm so glad you're home," I said. "May we come in?"

"Sure," he said, moving out of our way.

The three of us went inside, and Peter closed the door behind us.

Emma bounced into the room, her doll hanging from her right hand. She seemed completely unfazed by us taking her away from her home—presumably the only home she had ever known. She looked around the one room apartment curiously but not impolitely—she didn't open a single drawer, cupboard, or door.

"This is Emma," I said to Peter. "Emma, this is Peter Stevens. Emma could you and your doll—what's her name?"

"Sarah," she said.

"Like your mother?"

She nodded.

"Could you and Sarah play by the window seat while we talk to Mr. Stevens?"

"Yes, she wanted to see the view anyway," Emma said. She ran to the window seat and plopped down on it.

The three of us moved to the other side of the room, away from Emma.

"Peter, this is Henry."

Peter's eyes widened slightly and then narrowed. Henry held out his hand to him.

"Henry, this is Peter."

The men shook hands.

"So you are the famous Henry," Peter said. "Come home at last. Where have you been?"

Henry looked startled. "Do I know you?"

"I know you," Peter said. He sounded vaguely hostile. "I've asked her to live with me, you know."

"Peter," I said. "We don't have time for this."

"He's asked you to live with him?" Henry asked, looking at me. "What did you say?"

"Note I didn't ask her to marry me," Peter said, "because I respect her views on marriage. I don't need a woman to prove her love to me by shackling her with an out of date institution like marriage."

"Her *love?*" Henry said. "You love him?"

"Oh course, I love him," I said. "He's my friend." I turned to Peter. "This isn't like you."

"It makes me angry what he's put you through," Peter said.

"That's my business, isn't it?"

"What did you say when he asked you to live with him?" Henry said.

"I said I loved you."

"But she didn't say no," Peter said.

I gave him a look.

"You didn't say no?" Henry said.

"No! I didn't say no. I didn't know where you were, Henry. You had left me! On the best night of my life, you left me! As far as I knew, you deserted me. And you almost married another woman. What did you expect?"

"I didn't expect anything," Henry said. "I'm sorry. And I apologize to you, too, Mr. Stevens. I'm glad she had a friend in you during this time."

"I would never have left a woman to—"

"Peter!" I said harshly. He looked at me. "I have not had a chance to speak to Henry about everything."

Henry looked at me. "What? Did something happen while I was away?"

"Yes, the world was born and ended while you were away," I said, "but we've got other things to discuss. Peter, can you look after Emma for a couple of days?"

He looked over at Emma who was gazing out of the window and talking softly to her doll.

"Um, no," he said. "I have a deadline, plus I wouldn't know the first thing about looking after a child."

"What about your aunt and uncle?" I said. "Could they care for her? Are they good people?"

"Yes, they're good people," he said. "They have a daughter a little older than Emma. I suppose I could take her there. Why? What's going on?"

"We've found the man who kidnapped us," I said. "My father and Henry's father are here. We're going to bring the kidnapper to justice one way or another, but we wanted to make certain his daughter was safe before we did anything."

"His daughter? You kidnapped his daughter?"

"We *rescued* her," I said. "She has a scar on her back just like mine."

Henry glanced at me. He knew I rarely told anyone about the kidnapping or the scar. He looked at Peter, trying to assess our relationship, no doubt.

"He mutilated his own daughter?" Peter asked.

I nodded. "If you help us, you could get into trouble. So could your aunt and uncle. It's a lot to ask."

"We better get going then," Peter said.

"By the way, he's changed his name," I said. "The man who kidnapped us. I wonder if you came across him while doing any news stories. He now calls himself Joseph Tyler."

Peter's eyes widened again. He grabbed my arm and took me even closer to the far wall, further away from Emma.

"You kidnapped Joseph Tyler's daughter?" he asked.

"Yes. What is it?"

"Joseph Tyler is one of the most powerful men in this city," he said.

"I've never heard of him," I said. "He's not an elected official."

"No, he is not," he said, "but he's got every elected official in his pocket. And the police. You've heard of the Shanghai King of San Francisco?"

I glanced at Henry. He grimaced.

"I may have heard the name before," I said. My mouth felt dry. "Are you sure they're one and the same?"

"Yes," Peter said. "He's a dangerous criminal, Emily. You've got to take Emma back before he finds out and kills you."

"I can't take her back," I said. "I know what she went through."

"He is her father," Peter said.

"That makes it even worse!" I said. "I can't imagine how horrific it would have been if Mr. Em had done anything like that to me." I shuddered. "No, I won't return her. But I don't want to put you and your family in danger."

Where could I take her? Where would Jake McMahon never look?

And who would help me? Who did I know here? Dr. Ef was McMahon's partner. I couldn't tell him, and I wouldn't put Miss Allison in danger, especially since she lived so close to Dr. Ef.

"We need to take her to Sydney-Town," I said. "To Donna Blue. You've met her, Peter."

"Sure," he said.

"Who is she?" Henry asked.

"I wrote to you about her," I said. "She has a brothel. She helped get some of the girls out."

He nodded.

"She's got a secret room in the place," I said. "Emma could stay there."

"We can't just drive down to Sydney-Town and drop her off," Peter said. "For one thing, people will remember you because of your hair and your clothes. And they'd remember a little girl going into a brothel."

"Do you have a duffel bag?" I asked.

Peter nodded. He went to the other side of the room, got the bag, and brought it over to us.

"We could put Emma in here," I said. "Stuff some clothes around her, and you could carry her in as though she was a sack of clothes or you were a sailor visiting the brothel. In fact, let me do it. I'll dress up as a man. I won't have to change much. Give me your cap and coat, Peter."

Peter handed me his hat and coat. Henry looked stunned.

"You up for this?" I asked him.

"I trust you," Henry said. "You want to protect Emma, then I do too."

"Emma," I said, looking over at her. "We've got a game we want to play with you."

I had Emma get into and out of the bag several times to make certain she felt safe. Once inside the bag, I carefully lifted her over my shoulder. She giggled each time but she stayed still. I was once again grateful for my extraordinary strength.

Peter insisted on going with us to Sydney-Town. He and Henry stayed in the carriage as I put Emma over my shoulder like a sack of clothes and then I sauntered down the street and into the brothel.

Donna Blue was standing by the door when I entered— thankfully.

"It's *me,* Emily," I told her quietly.

She looked at me for a moment. Her eyes narrowed and then widened in recognition.

"Please take me to the secret room," I said.

Donna Blue didn't hesitate.

I followed her as she made her way to the back of the house. She unlocked a door, and we went inside. Donna Blue closed the door behind us and then lit a lamp. I gently lay the duffel bag with Emma in it on the bed.

"Emma, you can come out," I said.

Emma squirmed out of the bag and then jumped onto the floor with her arms outstretched.

"Did I fool you?" Emma asked.

"Absolutely," Donna Blue said. "You are Emma? I am Donna Blue. Welcome to my establishment."

"Thank you," Emma said.

While Emma played, I quietly I told Donna Blue the story: about my kidnapping and the scars on my back, about finding Jake McMahon and learning he had a daughter with scars on her back.

"So I took her," I said. "And I need a place to keep her safe while I work out what we're going to do with Jake McMahon. Can you keep her here for a while? I'd want you to take care of her, no one else. And she'd need to stay here, out of sight."

"Of course," Donna Blue said. "You know I would do anything for you and your father!"

"I need to tell you something first," I said. "Her father is Joseph Tyler."

"Joseph Tyler?" She bit the inside of her lip. "He is a tough man. I know him by reputation. He does not come here, so that is fortunate for us. I will keep Emma here, of course."

I embraced her. "Thank you!"

I explained to Emma that I had to leave. I assured her I would be back soon. She could trust Donna Blue. She was safe here.

"This place is called the Treasure Chest," I told Emma. "Do you know what that is?"

She shook her head.

"It's a place filled with treasure—the best kind of treasure. People who will protect you. And mermaids. You know what mermaids are, right? Miss Donna Blue here is really a mermaid. I bet she has lots of stories to tell you about when she lived in the sea."

"Of course I do," Donna Blue said. "And I've got cake and cookies. You wouldn't mind some of those, would you? After dinner, of course. I have the best cook in Sydney-Town, which, granted, isn't saying a great deal."

"I like the way she talks," Emma said.

"Me, too," I said. "You all right here?"

"Yes," Emma said. "Will Daddy find me here?"

"No," I said. "He will not."

We hugged each other. I whispered in her ear, "I'll be back soon. Everything will be all right."

"Daddy will be angry that I've left," she said. "He might hurt me again."

"He won't," I said. "I promise he will never hurt you again."

I hoped that was a promise I could keep.

"I'll be back soon," I said again.

Then we let each other go.

"I'm staying with Miss Allison," I told Donna Blue. "I'll let you know soon."

"Be careful," Donna Blue said.

Henry, Peter, and I didn't say anything on the way back to Peter's house. He made us tea, and we sat together at his tiny table, not saying anything for a long while.

"We should go talk to Dad and Mr. Em," Henry said. "They've been waiting all day for us."

I shook my head. "I can't have that conversation yet," I said. "It's nearly dark. I should go back and tell Miss Allison what has happened." I sighed. "I don't really know what to do next. We could take Emma back to Refugio with us. Leave Jake McMahon behind. He would never know where Emma was."

"He would figure it out," Peter said. "Someday. He is a notorious cutthroat. He's had people killed who shorted him on a liquor sale. Can you imagine what he'd do to someone who stole his daughter?"

"What have I done?" I whispered.

"We could get the police involved," Henry said. "Not those from here but back home—the sheriff who investigated when it first happened. Maybe he would come arrest Tyler."

Peter shrugged. "That might work. But then they'd get you on kidnapping."

"Maybe we could kill him," I said. "That would solve all of our problems."

"That's called murder," Peter said, "and that would bring on a whole host of new problems."

"He has been a blight on our lives since the day we met him," Henry said. "I could challenge him to a duel."

"He'd find a way to cheat," Peter said. "You'd be dead and he'd have his daughter back."

"Maybe we could blackmail him," I said.

"With what?" Henry said. "'If you don't turn yourself in, we'll steal your daughter?' We've already done that."

I put my head in my hands. I didn't have any answers. Why didn't I see a silver pathway? Why didn't I have a hunch or a feeling? A vision or a dream? What good were all these bizarre abilities of mine if a useful one didn't show up when I needed it?

"Maybe you should give her back," Peter said, "and pretend none of this happened."

"He might be right," Henry said.

"I don't think we can pretend it never happened!" I said. "And I couldn't live with myself if we turned her over to him."

"She's not your responsibility," Peter said. "It's not like she's your daughter."

"Of course she's my daughter," I said. "Every child is my child. Every brother is my brother, every sister is my sister. That is what my father has taught me. We aren't free until everyone is free. And if we can prevent harm from happening to someone, then we should."

Peter shook his head. "I understand. I empathize. But I care about what happens to you. She is not your Emma."

"You're wrong, Peter."

"'Your Emma'?" Henry shook his head. "I don't understand. Do you know another Emma?"

I gazed at Henry. He had creases on his forehead now. His eyes were sad. Or had they always been sad? A lock of hair hung down in his eyes. I reached up and moved the hair off his face.

"Do you want me to leave?" Peter asked quietly, sensing what was to come next. I shook my head.

Henry glanced at Peter and then looked back at me.

"Henry, I was pregnant," I said. "It was a girl. Her name was Emma. I loved her more than I've ever loved anyone—even you. Even Mr. Em. I dreamed our whole life together. She was a beautiful soul. And she looked just like Emma Tyler. I don't know what that means. I don't care. I carried our daughter in my womb for more than five months. And then she let go, and I lost her."

"We had a daughter?" Henry whispered.

"Just before I miscarried, I dreamed of Emma," I said. "She had an X on her back. That dream must have been about this Emma. I believe so much of what has happened over the past several months—maybe even years—has brought me here to rescue this child. Can you imagine if I hadn't escaped Jake Mc-Mahon? What would my life have been like? This little girl can't escape him, at least not alone. But I can help. I can save her. I'm not sure how yet. But I will. She is my daughter, Henry, as sure as the child in my womb was."

Henry put his arms around me and then pulled me up onto his lap. We held one another for a long while. Then Peter cleared his throat, and we moved apart.

"I'm sorry," I said. "You have been such a good friend, Peter. I better get back to Miss Allison."

"Are you sure you don't want to see your father tonight?" Henry asked.

I shook my head. "I was so angry when I left," I said. "I told him I never wanted to see him again. So I have to mend that fence plus tell him I've kidnapped a child and put us all in mortal danger. It's not going to be an easy conversation."

We all stood. I hugged Peter and kissed him on the cheek.

Then I held both of his arms and looked up at him. "It would have been great," I said, "but the answer is no."

He nodded. "I figured that out."

I kissed him on the lips.

Then Henry and I left. We walked down the steps in the dark, our arms around each other's waist.

"I don't know what we're going to do," I said. "I really don't."

"We'll figure out something tomorrow," he said. "At least we'll be together."

"I don't think they'll let us share jail cells," I said.

Henry and I parted reluctantly. I wanted him to go back to Jamie and Mr. Em and tell them what had happened. It was cowardly of me. But by then, I knew I had put all of us in grave danger.

I went back to Miss Allison's house and told her everything. Her shock frightened me.

"Do you have any advice on how I should proceed?" I asked.

"Go back and undo it!" she said. "Although it's too late now. You should tell your mother tomorrow. She and her father are in danger."

"They must know what kind of person he is," I said.

"Maybe not," she said. "They certainly don't know about him carving up your back. Blood is thicker than water."

"He did it to his own daughter," I said, "even though he resented his father doing it to him."

"His father did it to him?" Miss Allison asked.

I nodded. "He's got a small X carved into his arm. Ugly thing."

"History repeating itself," she said. "Maybe your mother and grandfather can give you insights into this man."

"Insights? I need to know how to get him to go to jail and

give me his daughter, freely and clearly. Do you think they'd know how to do that?"

That night in bed, my back itched. I left my body and went to find Emma. Donna Blue slept nearby. "Sleep well, Emma," I whispered.

Relieved, I fell asleep, hoping to dream the answers.

If I dreamed, I didn't remember any when I awakened.

I got dressed and looked outside. A thick fog had settled around the city. I couldn't see but a few feet out the window. I went to the front door and opened it.

A silver path led away from the house.

Finally.

I grabbed my coat and stepped onto the path. I thought I heard someone call my name. It was probably Henry and our fathers. I didn't answer. I'd be right back.

The path led me in the direction of my mother's house. Maybe Miss Allison had been right: I needed to talk to her.

The silver path went up the steps to the front door of my grandfather and mother's house. My mother had told me I didn't need to knock. I was welcome any time.

So I opened the door and stepped over the threshold.

And I came face to face with Jake McMahon.

Time seemed to stand still. We looked at one another. I was instantly terrified. I wanted to scream or run, but my feet wouldn't move. All I could do was stare at him. I saw nothing but him. At first he looked startled and annoyed. Then recognition widened his eyes. That was soon replaced by a look of fury.

"You," he said. "All grown up." He smiled. It was a sickening expression, and I remembered it well. "And a girl. So sad I didn't know it back then. Not that I've ever been particular."

I wanted to hit him. I wanted to say something, but I was frozen.

"He said it wasn't him," he said. "He swore he didn't know

anything about my daughter." He laughed. "I guess I tortured the wrong person all night."

"Who? What?" I felt panicky. Had he found Henry? Had he hurt Henry?

I started to reach for McMahon, but he grabbed my arm to stop me. I wrenched away, easily.

"Grew up strong, eh?"

"If you hurt him, I'll kill you."

He laughed. "I almost killed him. Glad I didn't. Leverage. I want my daughter returned to me now. You have no idea who you have crossed."

"I crossed you, right?" I said. "You, the lowest, meanest, most vile person on the planet. And if you think I'm going to return that girl to you under any circumstances, you're crazier than I thought you were. How could you mutilate your own daughter?"

He looked startled again, but just for a moment.

"What goes on between me and my own is my business," he said. "What did you think you'd gain by taking her?"

"I want you to turn yourself over to the sheriff," I said, "and confess to your crimes. Maybe you'll get out of prison in time to still have a life. You can see your daughter then."

He laughed. My vision was beginning to clear. My mother was standing a few feet from us.

"I have built an empire using the gold your father so generously gave me," he said.

"The gold you stole from him," I said.

"Trifles," he said. "Listen to me. You are going to return my daughter and you are going to give me all the money you have in this world. And you're going to do this by tomorrow at this time or I am going to kill your father."

"My father?" I said.

He smiled. "Yes. Your father. He came to my place of business yesterday and said he was going to take me in to the authorities. I told him I owned the police. Your father did not go down easily. And then my housekeeper came running into my office, saying my daughter had been kidnapped. I figured your papa had done it. It had to be one of you four, and he's the one who showed up on my doorstep. I guess I was wrong." He shrugged. "But it all works out for me."

He walked past me and started down the steps. Then he stopped and looked up at me. "He doesn't handle pain well," he said. "I hope I don't get impatient waiting for you." He reached into his coat pocket, pulled out a card, and then handed it to me. "That's where I'll be tomorrow morning."

"I can't get all my money in 24 hours," I said.

"Then you better find treasure somewhere," he said. "You've given me a golden opportunity that I do not intend to squander. This city is beginning to be tiresome. I've got too many people gunning for me. It would be nice to start all over again, somewhere new. My money is tied up in my ships right now. Last time around, you and your daddy funded me. I figure second time's the charm."

He continued down the steps. Then he turned around again and looked at me.

"What are you doing here anyway?"

So he didn't know I was Juliet's daughter or Dr. Ef's granddaughter.

"I was following you," I said.

"I should be more careful," he said. "I hope you have been well. As you can see, the years have been kind to me, and I suspect that trend will continue."

Then he disappeared into the fog.

Chapter Twenty-one

My mother was suddenly next to me.

"What was that all about?" she asked.

"I can't explain now," I said. "I'll be back."

And then I ran out of the house. I nearly ran the whole way back to Miss Allison's house. Mrs. Wren was setting up breakfast for five. Henry, Jamie, me, Miss Allison, and Mr. Em.

Jake McMahon must have lied. Mr. Em was here.

"Where are they?" I asked.

"The parlor," Mrs. Wren said.

I ran to the closed parlor doors and swung them open. I looked around the room. Henry rose from the sofa and came toward me. I took his hand.

"Where is Mr. Em?" I asked.

"He never came back," Henry said. "Dad said he went out yesterday midday and said he'd be back soon."

"Oh god," I said. "I was hoping it wasn't true."

Miss Allison and Jamie both got up and came toward me.

"What is it?" Miss Allison asked.

"I saw Jake McMahon," I said. "He says he has Mr. Em. He says if I don't return his daughter and give him all of our money, he'll kill Mr. Em. He said he spent the whole night torturing Mr. Em for information about Emma. What have I done? What have I done?"

Henry put his arm around me, and we sat on the sofa together.

"I could go to my bank here," Jamie said. "Most of what I have is tied up in investments, but I could get something. Your father does his banking here, too. We could get together a fair amount."

"Not enough, I'll wager," I said. "McMahon wants to leave here and start somewhere new again. Even if we got the money, what would we do about Emma?"

"You might have no choice," Miss Allison said. "She is his daughter."

"But she's not his property!" I said. "He can't carve her up like she's nothing. He can't keep taking what doesn't belong to him!"

"I don't know if you can fix this, Emily," Miss Allison said. "Perhaps we need to trust whatever is divine in this world to take care of him."

"I am divine!" I said. "And so are you and you! We are walking, talking, incarnations of the divine and we have to stop him. I have to stop him. He can't have Emma and he can't kill Mr. Em." I looked at Miss Allison. "There must be a reason for all of this. There must be! I lost my child. I lost Henry for a time. I lost my father. My back is scarred and mutilated. And now we're here. Now. This is now." I shook my head. I had to calm myself.

What could I do?

After all these years, I had finally met my grandfather. Maybe he showed up in my life now—or I showed up in his—for a reason. Maybe he could help me save my father and Emma.

I grabbed Henry's hand and said to the others. "I won't be long."

Henry and I hurried out of the house and out into the fog and headed for Dr. Ef's house.

"Were you afraid?" he asked. "To see McMahon again."

"I was terrified," I said.

He nodded. "Me, too. The first time I saw him and really knew it was him, I almost threw up." He squeezed my hand. "We'll figure something out."

At Dr. Ef's house, we went into the parlor with my mother and grandfather, and I told them about the kidnapping. Only this time, I told them about Jake McMahon carving up my back.

"He did the same thing to one of his men," I said. "And I found the same kind of scar on Emma's back."

"You mean Jake McMahon somehow found and hurt Emma?" Dr. Ef asked.

"No, I mean that her father did it to her," I said. "Jake Mc-Mahon and Joseph Tyler are the same man. When I found this out yesterday, I took Emma and I've hidden her from him."

"What?" my mother said. "Emily! How could you? They will hang you for this!"

"Grandpa, did you know that Tyler is a criminal? He has taken Mr. Em prisoner and he says he will kill him if I don't return Emma and give him all the money I have in the world. Unfortunately, I didn't bring any money with me, and I don't know how to get access to Mr. Em's."

"I didn't know what kind of man Tyler was when I first invested in the company," Dr. Ef said. "By the time I understood what he was, it was too late to get out."

"Father," my mother said. "I had no idea Tyler was danger-ous."

"Why did you ever go into business with him in the first place?" I asked.

"We had to leave Boston in a hurry. I was . . . I was doing some work which made me unpopular with the authorities. With my friends. With everyone."

I looked at my mother. She shook her head. She knew what he had done, but she didn't want to say it out loud.

"You were trying to reanimate corpses again?" I asked.

"You might say that," he said. "And a friend told me about an entrepreneur out here looking for investors. It was a good chance to begin again."

"Again," I said.

"Yes, again."

"Father," my mother said.

"I'm sorry," he said.

"Did you give Tyler all of our money?" she asked.

"Just about," he said. "Not that we had a great deal. Mr. Em sent us some when he found gold."

"Mr. Em sent us money?" Juliet Lee asked. "You never told me."

"Do you know anything about Tyler that I can use to bargain with him?" I asked. "I have to figure out how to save Mr. Em and Emma."

"Oh child," he said. "I wish I did. I thought he loved his daughter. I'm shocked he hurt her. I wouldn't be shocked at anything else he'd do. Your father is a tough man, Emily. He will survive. He can take care of himself, you know. He's risen from the dead before."

I looked at my grandfather.

"I meant that metaphorically, in this case," he said.

Henry and I returned to Miss Allison's place. Even though Henry, Jamie, and Miss Allison were with me, I had never felt so alone. Peter arrived. I had asked him yesterday to check on Emma today. He reported that she was in good spirits.

"She said you visited her in her sleep last night," Peter said. "She was very happy about that."

I smiled ruefully. "I did."

My back started itching again.

My back was itching.

"Henry, my scars are itching," I said.

"Is there anything I can do?"

"Remember the gems that used to come out of the scars?"

"Of course. Do you want me to check now?"

I nodded. I asked Peter for his coat, which he took off, and I held it up to my front while Henry lifted the back of my shirt.

"I don't see any coming out now," he said, "but your skin isn't smooth there anymore."

"It changed when I got pregnant," I said.

"Pregnant?" Jamie said.

"I'll tell you later, Dad," Henry said. "There's definitely something under the skin."

"I've got an idea," I said. "What's under my skin could be the treasure that will satisfy McMahon and save Mr. Em's life."

"Emily," Henry said. "I can't get the gems out. Your skin is over them."

"Scratch them," I said. "Scratch as hard as you want."

"No," he said. "I'm not going to hurt you. I'm not going to injure you to get them."

"It doesn't seem like that would be a very safe thing to do," Miss Allison agreed. "Maybe if one of us was a surgeon."

"My grandfather is a doctor," I said.

The fog had nearly lifted when I ran back to my mother's house. Henry and Peter ran beside me. I figured Jamie and Miss Allison were right behind us.

I ran into the house. My mother and grandfather were still in the parlor.

"I need your help, Grandpa," I said. "I need you to cut my back." I turned around and Henry lifted my shirt again.

"These scars, these are what Joseph Tyler did to you?" Dr. Ef asked. He came over to me.

"Yes," I said, "but there are jewels beneath the scars. I need the jewels now, to save my father's life. Can you cut them out?"

I felt his fingers press on my skin. He did this several times.

"I think I can do it," he said.

A few minutes later, I was sitting on his laboratory table. I looked around, wondering if the lab where my father had come to life looked the same.

"My hands shake a bit these days, dear," Dr. Ef said, "but I will do my best. Now, I will put you under."

I shook my head. "No. Just sterilize the area and cut. Henry, you can take out the jewels as he cuts."

Henry shook his head. "I'm not going to watch this twice. I'll hold your hands. Peter can get the gems."

"Granddaughter, it is going to hurt."

"I know," I said. "I've been through it before."

And so it began. Blissfully, gratefully, I don't remember very much. I know I screamed. Or maybe I didn't. Maybe I screamed in my head. I nearly broke Henry's hands. We both cried. I heard one stone after another drop into a metal pan.

Until it was over.

I wept. I laughed.

"I'm going to need to stitch you up," Dr. Ef said. "You may scar again."

"I've seen your handiwork on Mr. Em's body," I said. "I trust you."

Peter walked around to the front of me. He held a metal bowl that was filled to the top with gems.

I gasped.

"They're so beautiful," I said. He handed me the bowl. I picked through the gems: emeralds, rubies, diamonds, pieces of jade.

"This all came out of me?" I asked.

"It did," Peter said.

"I need to take them to McMahon now," I said.

"I want to go with you," Dr. Ef said.

"Why, Grandpa? You don't have anything to do with this."

"I want to support you and your father," he said. "And maybe I will have some influence on my partner, Mr. Tyler."

"All right," I said.

Miss Allison, Jamie, and Peter insisted on coming along with Henry, me, and Dr. Ef. We had to go in two separate carriages.

"Let me come in with you," Dr. Ef said.

"Why?"

"I want to be between the two of you," he said. "So I can protect you. You could let me actually give him the jewels when it's time."

"Grandfather, I am extraordinarily strong," I said. "I'll be fine. But you can come in, of course, and give him the jewels. Peter, you and Grandfather stay here for now. When we're ready to turn over the jewels, I'll have Miss Allison come get you."

Henry, Miss Allison, and I went into Jake McMahon's office. He was sitting at his desk, writing. He looked up at us.

"You've come early," he said. "Oh, is this the other one? You've grown up, too. I wouldn't have known you. Aren't you the one who was asking around town about me?" He nodded at Henry. "All those questions got you shanghaied. Lucky you weren't killed—"

"I have what you want," I said, interrupting him. "More treasure than you can imagine."

He leaned back in his chair. "Well?"

"First, tell your men to leave the building," I said. "You can keep one for your personal protection. And I want to see my father before I give you anything."

McMahon rolled his eyes. I knew he thought this was all pointless. He was going to get what he wanted, and we would all be dead.

He left the office. A few minutes later, we saw several men leave the building. Then he came back. With a nod of his head, he told us to follow him. He took us down a long corridor and then out to a large empty storage area. One side of it was open to the elements and the dull winter light shone into the storehouse.

Sitting on a chair in the middle of the huge storage area, with his hands tied in chains behind his back, was my father. His head hung down to his chest. His feet were tied with chains, too.

Was he breathing?

Was he dead?

Papa, Papa, Papa!

"This is far enough," Jake McMahon said. "You can see him."

Mr. Em slowly raised his head. His face was bruised and swollen. And bloody. He blinked, hard.

"Who's there?" he said, his voice hoarse.

My heart was in my throat.

I motioned to Miss Allison. She left us. Just then I noticed a man standing in the shadows, near a table with chairs around it. He started to follow Miss Allison.

"He goes after her, it's off," I said.

Jake McMahon went over and sat at the table. The man

stayed where he was. I wanted to run to my father, but I watched McMahon.

"So how's life been treating you, boy?" McMahon said to Henry.

"Shut up," Henry said.

"Not scared of me anymore? Shame. Because I'm a lot more dangerous than I was then."

We waited quietly. My heart was beating so hard I was sure McMahon could hear. Dr. Ef came into the room, followed by Peter and Miss Allison.

"What's he doing here?" McMahon asked.

"He wanted to help," I said.

Dr. Ef slowly and carefully emptied the bag of gems onto the table.

McMahon actually gasped.

"You can have all of these," I said, "when you let my father go. In exchange, you'll sign a piece of paper which gives me custody of your daughter."

"I knew you had a fortune somewhere," he said. "I learned that when I persuaded your father to talk. I had no idea it would be this much." He smiled and looked up at me. "But I'm afraid I can't agree to your deal. I'm just going to take it all."

Several armed men came from outside and into the open storage area.

In an instant, I was next to Jake McMahon with my hands around his throat. I had been prepared for him to betray us. He struggled to his feet as I choked him. The man in the shadows lunged for me, but Henry and Peter tackled him and took his gun.

"If any of the other men come any closer, I will crush your larynx," I yelled. McMahon was gasping. He would pass out soon. "Tell them, or you are done."

He motioned to the men. They started stepping back.

"Tell them to drop their weapons," I said.

McMahon was still trying to get away from me. "Stop it," I said. "I am stronger than you are. You will fail. Now, shall I take your life or will you tell them?" I released him enough so that he had a voice.

"Drop your weapons," he croaked.

The guns rattled as they hit the floor of the storage area. Miss Allison, Peter, and Henry ran down and collected the weapons.

"Tell them to go."

"Go," he whispered. "Go!" he croaked louder.

The men backed out until I could no longer see them.

Miss Allison went to Mr. Em's side. She tried to take off the chains.

"There's a lock on them," Miss Allison called.

"Where are the keys?" I asked.

"My pocket," McMahon said.

"Get them."

He reached into his pocket and pulled out keys. I took them from him and tossed them to Peter who ran them down to Miss Allison.

Suddenly Dr. Ef took something from his coat pocket. Before I realized it was a hypodermic needle, he plunged it into Jake McMahon's back.

"That's for what you did to my granddaughter," Dr. Ef said.

McMahon cried out. I let go of him, and he fell to the floor.

"What did you do?" I asked.

"Poison," Dr. Ef. "He'll be dead in a minute or so. Now you won't have to worry about him."

"You can't kill him!" I said.

"Why not?" he said. "He's a monster. It's a way out for all of us."

"It's murder," I said. "You have no right!"

I glanced toward the man in the shadows, but he was gone.

Jake McMahon was gasping. "I'm sorry," he said. "Please, help me. I'm so sorry."

I could hear my father moaning.

"He's not doing well," Miss Allison called.

My hands started tingling. I looked down. A shiny silver spiral pulsed on each of my palms.

Jake McMahon's eyes were opened wide as he gasped for breath. He looked so frightened. Had he been that frightened when his own father carved a cross on his arm? Had he ever been this frightened before?

"Emily!" Miss Allison was calling to me.

"Hang on, Papa," I whispered. "Hang on."

I knelt down and put my hands on Jake McMahon. I closed my eyes and breathed deeply.

"Come on, Jake McMahon," I whispered.

He gasped one more time and closed his eyes.

My hands throbbed.

The whole world looked silver. Henry stood near me, watching me, encouraging me. Silver. All. Something shifted. In McMahon. In me.

Jake McMahon gasped once and then began breathing, shallowly at first, and then more deeply.

He opened his eyes. He put his hand over my hands.

"What happened?" he asked.

"I poisoned your corrupt body," Dr. Ef said, "and Emily saved you."

Slowly, Jake McMahon sat up.

"Emily!" Miss Allison's voice was sharp.

Henry helped me up. I ran toward my father. Peter was just getting off his chains.

"Papa!" I called as I reached him. "I'm here. Papa!"

I put my hands on his chest.

"Oh daughter," Mr. Em said. "At last, I am your father."

My father survived. So did Jake McMahon.

After we got Mr. Em back to Miss Allison's place, after Mr. Em was washed up and his wounds mending, I talked to Jake McMahon, who was still stunned after coming back from the dead. He had waited outside Miss Allison's place until I let him in. We sat in the parlor together. Henry sat next to me.

"I don't taste my poison any more," McMahon said.

"You mean you don't feel the urge to cut into people?" I asked.

"I don't," he said. "Maybe you fixed that, too?"

I handed him a piece of paper that said he relinquished custody of his child to me.

"Is this legal?" he asked.

"Bindingly legal," I said. I didn't know if it was legal or not.

He read the paper and signed it.

He looked up at me. It was the first time he had really looked at me—first time he had actually seen me.

"I always thought you were something special," he said, "and you have proven me correct."

"No, you saw me as a victim," I said, "and that was all. Someone you could exploit."

"You're probably right about that," he said. "I am sorry. To you both."

He took out the bag of gems and put it on the table between us.

"These are yours," he said.

"How are you going to start a new life without any money?" I asked.

"Oh, I took a handful," he said. "Poison might be gone but my common sense is intact. Can I say goodbye to her?"

Peter had gone to get Emma at Donna Blue's place while we were tending to Mr. Em. Now he brought her into the parlor. She took my hand and kept back from her father.

"Listen, Emma," Jake McMahon said. "I am so sorry I hurt you. That was wrong of me. I'm gonna try never to hurt anyone again. But if you want to, you can live with Emily here. I think your momma would have liked that. At least until I'm sure the cure is permanent. Is that okay with you?"

"Okay," Emma said.

"Shake hands on it?" McMahon asked.

I could see tears in his eyes. Was he human finally? Or had he been all along until he lost his way?

I didn't have the answers.

Emma nodded and held out her hand to her father. McMahon got on his knees and took his daughter's hand in his. He gently shook her hand.

Then Emma put her arms around her father's neck and hugged him.

"I'm so sorry, baby," he said as he embraced her. "I hope one day you can forgive me."

And then they let each other go.

"Be happy, daughter," Jake McMahon said. He nodded to me and Henry.

Jake McMahon left the house.

Henry and I looked at each other and sighed. Then we happily embraced, each of us keeping one hand on Emma so that she was part of the hug.

Mr. Em limped into the room with Miss Allison on one side of him and Jamie on the other.

"I think it's time to go back to Refugio," Mr. Em said. "Anyone want to come with me?"

Henry and I each raised a hand. Emma looked at us and then she raised her hand.

"It's settled then," I said. "We're going home."

Chapter Twenty-two

Dr. Ef never understood why I saved Jake McMahon's life, but he was interested in how I did it. I didn't have an answer for him.

"I suppose you won't let me dissect you to find the answer?" he said.

"No, I suppose I won't."

He giggled.

Maybe he was a bit mad.

Or more than a bit . . .

He and my father had a good chat before we left. So did Mr. Em and Juliet. I promised my mother and grandfather that I would come to visit them again, and we invited them to Refugio.

I said goodbye to Peter and Miss Allison for now. Peter and Henry were becoming reluctant friends, and I was glad for that.

Once the five of us returned to Refugio, we hosted one celebration after another to welcome Emma into our community.

In late spring, after Emma had settled in at Refugio and was comfortable with Betsy Shaw, Henry and I and our fathers traveled on horseback to the Meadow. We hadn't been there since the kidnapping and figured it was time.

It looked much the same at first, but then we found holes here and there where the gold diggers had been. The Old Juniper still clung to the rock. I didn't see any silver pathways, and Sitiu wasn't wandering the creek bed. We camped for several days. Mostly we fished and talked. Henry and I explored the land again.

After we had been there for a few days, the Meadow felt almost the same as it had all of those years ago: like home.

One day the four of us went to the cave and then out on the ledge. We looked down at the pool.

"You jumped into that?" Mr. Em asked.

"Yes, Papa," I said. "Would you like to try?"

"Not unless you'd like to see me break my neck."

I held out the bag filled with the bulk of the jewels Peter had taken out of my back.

"We're all happy with this decision?" I asked.

The three men nodded.

"And so we give back to the land," I said. "We thank the Land, the Air, the Sun, the Men Who Live Under the Mountain. We return to you what was given to us."

I held Henry's hand, and then I turned the bag upside down and poured the gems into the pool.

Some of them flew away as dragonflies.

Some became birds.

One or two transfigured into butterflies.

Many became someone else's dreams.

Some dropped into the pool, one by one, and I heard laughter, felt joy, was enveloped by love.

"I am so grateful for my life," I said.

My father kissed the top of my head.

"I am grateful for your life, too," he said.

That night, Henry and I lay on our bedrolls staring up at the night sky. Jamie and Mr. Em had already gone into their tents. I heard a noise and looked over at the fire. It appeared that several very large people were dancing around our fire.

"Do you see that?" I whispered to Henry.

"What?"

I pointed to the fire. He squinted. "Almost looks like someone is dancing."

"Yes. I think they are."

"Should we join them?"

"No, let's let them be," I said.

Henry and I faced one another.

"Emily, I want to ask you something," he said.

"All right, Henry," I said. "I'm listening."

"Will you not marry me and spend the rest of our lives together?"

I laughed. "Of course I will."

We kissed.

The Men Who Live Under the Mountain kicked up sparks from the fire. They rose into the night sky, these bits of flame, and became new stars.

"Go to sleep, daughter," Mr. Em called.

"But I am so awake, Papa."

About the Author

Kim Antieau has written many novels, short stories, poems, and essays. Her work has appeared in numerous publications, both in print and online, including *The Magazine of Fantasy and Science Fiction, Asimov's SF, The Clinton Street Quarterly, The Journal of Mythic Arts, EarthFirst!, Alternet, Sage Woman,* and *Alfred Hitchcock's Mystery Magazine.* She was the founder, editor, and publisher of *Daughters of Nyx: A Magazine of Goddess Stories, Mythmaking, and Fairy Tales.* Her work has twice been short-listed for the James Tiptree Award and has appeared in many best-of-the-year anthologies. Critics have admired her "literary fearlessness" and her vivid language and imagination. Her first novel *The Jigsaw Woman* is a modern classic of feminist literature. She is also the author of a science fiction novel, *The Gaia Websters* and a contemporary tale set in the desert Southwest, *Church of the Old Mermaids. Broken Moon,* a novel for young adults, was a selection of the Junior Library Guild. She has also written other YA novels, including *Deathmark, Mercy, Unbound, Ruby's Imagine,* and *The Blue Tail.* Kim lives in the Pacific Northwest with her husband, writer Mario Milosevic. Learn more about Kim and her writing at www.kimantieau.com.